The Long Way Home

Kate Sherwood

Chapter One

Paul Gill pinched the bridge of his nose and tried to pretend his head was throbbing because of the sunlight glaring off the snow outside the office window.

"You're sure you can't duck out a bit early?" Bobby asked. For the third time.

Paul resisted the urge to pull the phone away from his ear to make faces at it. Bobby wanted to spend time with him: that was a *good* thing. They'd been together for almost four years and they weren't tired of each other. They still enjoyed each other's company, and Bobby wanted to spend more time with Paul. All good. Except…

"I've already told you 'no'. I've got a patient."

"You've got that racist asshole. He'd *love it* if someone else took over for you. You think he'd make a white guy wear *gloves* before touching him?"

"I shouldn't have told you about that." Breach of patient confidentiality? Yeah, technically, although Paul hadn't used any names, and it wasn't like "racist" was a rare enough quality to count as an identifying detail. But really, Paul should have kept his mouth shut because any time he bitched about work it was another opportunity for Bobby to tell him how he was wasting his talents and his family connections on an emotionally draining job that paid peanuts.

"He thinks you're *unclean*, Paul. He thinks he's going to catch something if you touch him with your bare brown skin, and you're putting your life on hold for him?"

"Putting my life on hold? That's a bit dramatic, isn't it? I mean, as much as I love elementary school Christmas concerts, I think I'll be okay if I miss this one."

"It's a *holiday* concert, not Christmas. Very cross-cultural. Saachi's singing a song about snowmen—there are costumes and a little dance, too. It's going to be adorable, but you're too busy helping some racist asshole to see her. How's she going to feel about that?"

"How's she going to feel if she only has fifteen or twenty family members in the audience? If her uncle's boyfriend doesn't show up? I'm pretty sure she'll survive. Honestly, the sooner that kid starts to realize she's not the absolute center of the universe, the easier things will be on all of us."

"She's the first grandkid on both sides. We all knew she was going to be spoiled." And then, obviously realizing that he wasn't getting anywhere, Bobby moved on. "You'll come for dinner afterward, though? My mom's samosas, hot and fresh… you know you can't resist."

"I'll be there for dinner. Absolutely."

"I'll see if I can hitch a ride up with someone, and then we can drive back together."

"Sounds good."

"Have fun with your racist."

It wasn't about fun, of course, but Paul didn't bother mentioning that as he ended the call. Paul was a physiotherapist; the racist needed physiotherapy. Well, he needed therapy of all kinds, but physio was the sort Paul was qualified to provide. It didn't matter that Sean Gage was an asshole; it mattered that he'd lost his legs and needed professional help to regain as much mobility as possible.

So Paul reached under the counter and found a pair of bright blue surgical gloves, then forced his face into a smile and headed out of the office into the gym. Gage hadn't arrived yet, which was typical. They'd already had five sessions, and the guy had been late for all of them. At the first, he'd taken one look at Paul and asked for another PT; when told no one else was available, he'd almost left. But the older woman who had brought him—his mother, Paul had assumed—had cried and there'd been a big emotional scene and finally Paul had offered to wear the gloves.

He'd *offered*. It had been his own damn idea to debase himself like that, and he honestly wasn't sure whether that made the whole situation better or worse.

"You think he's going to bail?" Anna asked. She was the physio assistant Paul worked with most often, and she'd witnessed all the previous visits. "I'm shocked every time he shows up. I mean, nobody *likes* doing physio—it's hard work. And lots of people feel sorry for themselves when they come here. But he takes self-pity to whole new levels. Do you ever wonder why he keeps coming back?"

Paul shrugged. He supposed part of the appeal was the opportunity to humiliate a highly trained professional who happened to have brown skin, and obviously there was some pretty serious pressure coming from Mrs. Gage. But there was something else, too. Something that could be useful, if Paul could figure out how to harness it.

Sean Gage was stubborn. Pig-headed, even, but Paul would try to think of it in terms of the man being strong-willed. It was buried deep, under all the anger and self-pity, but it was there. Paul had seen it as he'd worked Gage through his initial assessment, figuring out how much strength was left in his battered body, how much flexibility and balance had been lost after months of limited activity. If Paul was gentle and kind, Gage would shrink in on himself and act totally helpless. But if Paul spoke dismissively and acted as if Gage was pathetic? That was when the strength flared up.

Gage was an asshole and his pride was probably as fragile as his mother's smile, but it was there, and if the only way to protect it was to prove that he could do something Paul suggested was beyond him? Then whatever the exercise was, it would be *done*.

It was hardly the first time Paul had taken advantage of a similar dynamic. Well, he usually didn't have the charming overlay of aggressive racism to deal with, but even that was a tool Paul could use. Gage might have allowed himself to seem weak in front of someone he liked or trusted, but in front of a brown man? Hell, no.

Useful.

As long as Paul could force himself to keep swallowing the insults, keep letting himself 'lose' the confrontations he orchestrated, he had a good tool. He'd help Sean Gage whether the man wanted the help or not.

But every insult he pretended to ignore chaffed just a little more than the one before it had. And now? If the asshole didn't even show up, and didn't have the courtesy to call? Paul checked his watch. Only a few minutes late. With any other patient, it wouldn't be a big deal; Paul would extend the same benefit of the doubt in Gage's direction.

It was a bit harder to maintain his charitable attitude when Gage rolled in a few minutes later, scowl on his face, no hint of an apology anywhere in his demeanor. He was only in his early twenties, with pale skin, light-brown hair and strong features that would probably be fairly attractive if he'd just wipe the sneer off his face. But that wasn't something Paul ever expected to see.

"Let's get this over with," Gage growled. "I have somewhere to be."

"Holiday concert?" Paul suggested sweetly. A little *too* sweetly—if there was anything that got Gage's back up, it was the suggestion that there could be any sort of friendliness between them.

"*Christmas* concert." Gage's gaze was a direct challenge. Damn, he was crabbier than usual today. "You're in Canada now. We have *Christmas* concerts here."

"In Canada *now*?" Paul smiled again. He had to be careful he didn't overdo it, didn't elevate Gage's aggression to the point that it couldn't be harnessed and put to use, but he was strangely confident that he could push a little further. Or maybe he was just sick of Gage's bullshit. "I was born in Canada, you know. My parents, too. All of my grandparents, and some of my great-grandparents. The rest came over in the early 1900s. How about you? When did your people arrive?"

"*My* people are the ones who founded the damn country."

"White people, you mean? But what about your *family*? Your actual relatives." Just light and chatty, having a little conversation. Not trying to make a point at all. No, nothing like that. "When did they come over?"

"Too long ago to keep track of. So let's cut the chatter and get this over with."

"Actually, I have somewhere to be, too. If you'd like to reschedule, or cut this short—"

"If I wanted to reschedule, I wouldn't fucking be here, would I?" Gage's chin jutted out and he stared up at Paul, pure aggression and command. Even before he'd lost his legs, he probably hadn't been tall, but he'd pretty clearly always been a fighter. A terrier, ready to take anyone on, regardless of the odds.

Well, good. He'd need all the toughness he could find.

"We'll start with stretching," Paul said, and started for the mats, confident Gage was wheeling along behind him. "Do you need help getting out of the chair?"

"No."

That was a sign of progress—not physical, likely, because it shouldn't be too challenging for Gage to haul himself out of his wheelchair and onto the padded bench. But the first few sessions, Gage had insisted he couldn't do it on his own. Which meant either his confidence or his resolve, or possibly both, had improved since then. Or maybe he'd just gotten even more reluctant to let Paul touch him, gloves or no gloves.

Whatever, as long as it worked.

"You're doing your exercises at home?" Paul asked as he watched Gage move.

"If you can't fucking tell whether I'm doing them or not, why am I bothering?"

"I see improvement, but this is a long-term project. The results are going to come slowly. It's *your* recovery, not mine. You're bothering with the exercises for yourself, not for me."

"Recovery?" Luckily Gage was on the bench already, because if he'd still been in his chair, he might have wheeled over to take Paul on face-to-face. "You think I'm going to *recover*? You think my fucking legs are going to grow back?"

Shit. Aggravating a patient into making an effort was one thing, but seeming to taunt him about his injury was something totally different. Totally unacceptable. "I'm sorry—I can see how that word wouldn't seem appropriate. But you know what we're focusing on—you're feeling more pain than you need to and we can fix a lot of that with exercises to help your body adjust to its new reality. And your mobility is more restricted than it needs to be, and we can work with your prosthetist to change that. So, no, a full recovery isn't realistic. But you're young, and you were reasonably fit before the accident... we can absolutely get you to a better place than where you are now."

"A Better Place." Beneath the anger, there was something too raw, too uncomfortably *honest* in Gage's expression. "That's what my mom calls Heaven. Is that what we're shooting for?"

Paul fought to get the conversation back on even ground. "That seems a bit ambitious." Yeah, keep it light. Don't engage.

But Gage apparently hadn't gotten the memo. "You think I can't make it to heaven? I don't deserve your seventy-two virgins and permanent hard-on?"

Paul sighed. "Well, that's Islam, and I'm Sikh. Totally different religions. And I'm not sure it's the most respectful aspect of Islam to focus on, either."

"You think I need to be *respectful* to Islam? How the hell are they being respectful to me?"

"Mr. Gage." Paul had called him "Sean" one time, at their first appointment, and the reaction hadn't been good. "You're not here to discuss religion, or current events, or—" Or bigotry or racism or whatever other ugliness came out of the man's mouth. "If you get started on your exercises, I can watch and make sure your form is still good. And there are a couple new movements I can show you that will help strengthen your core so your balance is at its best when you start working with your prosthetics."

"At its best." Gage spoke the words like they were a curse, but he got down to work on his exercises and didn't complain for the next ten minutes. He didn't say *a damn thing* for the next ten minutes.

"I'm not sure you're telling me when things are too much," Paul finally prompted. "There's going to be some discomfort that we can't avoid..." He caught himself. Discomfort? Really? "Pain. Some of these exercises hurt. But if they hurt too much, you should—"

"I can handle it," Gage said. His jaw was clenched so tightly he should probably have been wearing a mouth guard to protect his teeth.

"I know. But it's not just about you being mentally tough. Pain is a signal that your body thinks it's being pushed too far. Sometimes your body is wrong, but sometimes it's right. If you tell me when it's really, really hurting, we can evaluate whether—"

"I can *handle* it."

"You could make things *worse* if you push too hard."

"*Worse*?" And the painful, raw honesty was back in Gage's expression. "What the *fuck* could be worse than this? My fucking *mother* is waiting for me outside because I can't drive a fucking car myself, can barely wipe my own ass, can't do a goddamn thing for myself, my friends—fuck, the only friend who actually wants anything to do with me is a fucking fag, my brother and sisters only put up with me because they feel *sorry* for me— three little kids who acted like I was their goddamn hero for their whole lives and now they're helping me into bed, helping me into the fucking *shower*, and they've hidden all the fucking meds so I can't even *kill myself* and get it all over with…"

"And your physiotherapist isn't just brown, he's also gay."

It took a moment. Then, "Fuck. Seriously?" Gage stared at him. "You're a fag, too?"

"Truly, I have been cursed." The asshole would catch the sarcasm, Paul was sure. "But I still find ways to make life worth living, even without the blessings of being straight and white."

"You think white men have it *good*?" Gage started. Then he stopped. "Fuck. I—there's no point getting into all that with you, is there?"

"No point in trying to convince me that straight white men are an oppressed underclass? No, there really isn't." And it was far off the point, anyway. "You're still seeing your counsellor? You've mentioned the suicidal impulses to him?"

"Suicidal impulses. That's what you're calling it? A fucking impulse?"

"Does that make it sound too flippant? Too light? I can see that. And I'm sure it's horrible, from your perspective. But it's also incredibly common. I'd say at least half of the amputees I work with mention those ideas at some point in their treatment." And Paul sympathized with every one of them. But Gage didn't want sympathy, at least not from Paul. "They get over it. They're going through a big change, and it's hard, but they're tough and they get through it and eventually things get better. Not the same as they were before, but better than they are now."

"And what if things *before* were already shitty?" Gage asked, but he didn't pause long enough for Paul to think of an answer to the question. "Fuck. Yes, I'm still seeing the fucking counsellor. That means I don't need to talk about all this shit with you. What's the next fucking exercise?"

They made it through the rest of the session without any more outbursts, and when Gage was too shaky from his exertions to make it back into his wheelchair on his own, he let Paul help him. A breakthrough, or one more defeat for a man who'd already faced too many?

He watched Gage wheel himself out of the clinic, clearly letting his rage give him power despite his exhaustion, and then realized Anna was watching, too.

"He's so *angry*," she said.

"It's a hard time."

"My little sister went to school with him and his crowd, and she said they were assholes then, too."

"You were talking about him with your sister?"

Paul didn't think there'd been an accusing tone in his voice, but Anna held her hands up defensively all the same. "She brought it up. Remember, you're in a small town, now. His mom talks to someone at the grocery store, or someone sees their car parked outside, and everyone knows what he's up to. Not a lot of privacy outside these walls."

"Interesting." Paul realized how tired he was, how much he wanted to go home to his safe bed. But he tried to rally. "So does the whole town know how things went with that guy on Tuesday? 'Cause I don't think you've told *me* about him, yet."

Anna's blush suggested he'd asked the right question. She busied herself with tidying equipment and tried to sound casual as she said, "It went pretty well. It was just supposed to be coffee after work, but it turned into dinner. And then a walk to look at the Christmas lights downtown."

"And you happen to live downtown…."

"He walked me to my door and that was all!" She grinned. "Well. Not *all*. It was a pretty excellent goodnight kiss. I'm seeing him again tomorrow."

"I can't believe you hadn't told me about it." Shit. "Can't believe I forgot to ask."

She shook her head in mock exasperation. "Yeah, you're always so selfish! Thinking about your job and how to help patients when you should be chatting about my social life. Bastard."

"I'd like to think I can do both."

"Do both and still have energy left for whatever's going on with you and Bobby?"

Paul kept his gaze on the towel he was using to wipe down the mats. "What do you mean?"

"I don't know. I guess you used to tell me about fights sometimes, but you'd also tell me all kinds of really nice stuff you did together. I feel like lately, you just… don't talk about him at all. And you seem kinda… sad? No, not even that. I don't know. Resigned, maybe? Am I totally hallucinating the whole thing?"

"Hallucinating?" No, probably not. But it felt too soon to put any of it into words. Too soon to even really look at any of it himself. Too soon, and maybe too final. "I guess things aren't great. But they aren't terrible, either. Isn't that—I think that's normal, in a long-term relationship. The infatuation stage is over and we've just sort of settled down into our routines. It's not bad. Is it?"

"If you're happy, it's not bad. Are you happy?"

He didn't have an answer, so he scrubbed at an invisible spot on the mat instead.

After a few moments, Anna sighed. "I don't mean to be nosy. You know I'm just a worrier. Just because things are going smoothly doesn't mean I can't pick away and find *something* that might *someday* go wrong, *somewhere*. Don't let me project my issues onto—"

"I think I've given up," Paul blurted out. He'd never said the words before, never even let them form fully in his mind, but as he spoke them, they felt true. "That's why we don't fight anymore. I mean, it's not like he's *wrong* about stuff, exactly. And I'm not wrong, either. We just have different perspectives. What's the point fighting about things that can never be resolved?"

Anna's frown made her opinion clear. "You can *compromise*, can't you? I mean, you fought about where to live, right? Or—not a fight, but a disagreement. He works in the city, you work up here, so you suggested a *compromise*. You said you could find a place halfway between the two. But—you live in the city, Paul. He wouldn't compromise, so he won."

"Our families are in the city. And I drive in the opposite direction of traffic at rush hour; it's not that bad."

"Your families are in Brampton, and you live downtown. You have to drive right past your family and add another forty minutes before you get home. Honestly, Brampton would have been a good compromise for living between your jobs. But you commute for an hour and a half each way, in *good* traffic, and Bobby can walk to work." She stopped abruptly and held up her hands. "Sorry. It's none of my business, obviously."

"It's *Bobby's* business," Paul tried. "And that's a cultural thing. There's a network of Sikh entrepreneurs in the city, and he needs to be part of that. We need to socialize with those people in order to maintain his contacts."

Anna nodded, but with enough hesitation to signal acceptance rather than agreement. They were silent for a while before she laughed and said, "My mom almost died when I told her I was maybe dating a lawyer! Seriously. I haven't seen her this excited about a guy since I broke her heart when I told her you were gay. She's practically sending out wedding invitations."

He felt his shoulders lower and made sure he matched her light tone as he replied. "And you like him? It's not just post-kiss hormones talking?"

"Hey! Don't knock the power of hormones!"

"Never."

They kept the chatter light as they finished their tidying and then retreated to the office to start bundling up for the winter weather.

"Did you drive, today?" Paul asked. Anna's car was so unreliable that she'd largely given up trying to use it for commuting. "It's already dark out—I can drop you at home."

"No, it's fine. I'm going to do errands on the way. Unless you want to go to the drugstore with me... and I warn you, I'm going to be buying tampons."

"I'm not afraid of feminine hygiene products."

"Well, maybe you should be."

"What does that mean?"

Anna's grin was pure mischief and silliness. "I can't tell you. I would be betraying the sisterhood."

"Fine. Keep your secrets. But I can still drive you if you want. I can wait outside at the drugstore to preserve my modesty. And the secrets of the sisterhood."

Anna shook her head. "I'm fine. It's not even that cold out, and I'm not afraid of the dark. Go home to your handsome man."

"I'm going to his mom's house."

Anna gasped. "Will there be samosas? You need to bring me some! I mean, I'm sure they're better fresh, but even day-old, Bobby's mom's samosas are tastier than anything I had planned for lunch tomorrow." She batted her eyelashes at him. "Please?"

It was almost guaranteed that Bobby and Paul would be going home with tubs and tubs of leftovers. Easy enough to pull some samosas from the bounty and bring them to work, especially since Bobby didn't generally care for food that wasn't fresh-made.

And it made the evening a bit more appealing, somehow, to think of it as a samosa-retrieval mission instead of one more in a long string of nights with Bobby's extended family. While Saachi-the-spoiled was regaling everyone with minutiae of her performance, Paul could reconnoiter the buffet table. While Bobby lectured on the economy and the importance of being fiscally conservative, Paul could offer to help in the kitchen and make sure the plastic containers were ready to go.

Damn, he actually wished there was something more difficult about the mission, wished Bobby's mom *wasn't* so intent on sending her first-born son home with enough food for a large family. It was nice to have a little distraction, but it would be even better to have a larger distraction.

And if that was a sign of something? An indication that maybe there was something not quite right in Paul's relationship, or his life? Well, then, he had a whole *new* issue he needed to be distracting himself from. And stealing some freely-offered samosas probably wasn't going to be quite enough of a challenge.

Chapter Two

Sean's arms were shaking with exhaustion as he wheeled his way up the wooden ramp outside his house. His mother would have pushed his chair, he knew—she was always at her kindest and most generous when she was bringing him home from physio—but he really didn't think he could stand having her that close to him. What if she laid her hand on his shoulder, or—

Jesus, there had been that time she'd been crying as she pushed him and he wouldn't have known except one of her fucking tears dropped down and landed on his forehead. Then they'd both had to pretend it hadn't happened and it had just been one more tiny, silent tragedy to add to the fucking pile.

No, there was no way he could handle anything like that, not after dealing with the goddamn physio.

So he forced his arms to work.

She almost caught up to him at the front door because he had to pull the storm door open and then hold it while he pushed the main door, and that didn't leave him with free hands to wheel the fucking chair. But he managed it, and ignored his mother's "Sean!" as she hurried up behind him.

He didn't want to talk to her, didn't want to dig around, trying to find a single ounce of energy to care about whatever she wanted him to care about. He just wanted to get to his tiny room, the one his friend Luke had built out of what used to be the laundry room and pantry, where he could—

"Sean." A male voice, familiar but not recognizable, coming from the living room.

It was so fucking tempting to just keep going. Pretend he hadn't heard, or skip the pretending and just show that he didn't care. But his sister Stacey appeared in the kitchen doorway right in front of him, blocking his path. Times gone by he could have just shouldered past her and done what he wanted, but now?

He was trapped.

"Sean," the male voice said again, and Sean turned his head. Father David. *Father*, even though the priest was only six or seven years older than Sean and had grown up just down the street. As soon as he'd come home from priest-school and put that collar on, Sean's mom had made it crystal clear. David Walsh was a priest, now, and he would be treated with respect.

Well, fuck it. Fuck David Walsh, fuck Sean's mom, fuck it all. "I'm not in the mood," he growled, and wheeled toward the kitchen.

And he could add another 'fuck' to the list, because Stacey didn't move. "Mom asked him here," Stacey said, her voice low and pleading. "She needs you to talk to him."

"About *God*?" Sean whirled—he was getting pretty good in the chair, and his anger had given him a burst of energy. "*Fuck that.* I'm not interested in your bullshit, buddy, so go peddle it to someone else."

"No bullshit," the priest said, his voice calm and easy. "And no God, if you're not interested."

"Good. I'm not interested." He turned his head to Stacey. "Now get the fuck out of my way."

"No God," the priest said, just a little more loudly. "But we do need to talk. Things have to change."

Sean spun the chair so he was facing the front door, where his mother stood, fucking tears streaming down her face again, and he knew—he *knew*—that if he wheeled toward her, she'd step aside and let him leave.

But he had absolutely no place to go.

He was trapped.

This was his fucking life, from now on, and he'd done it to himself. It was all his fault.

"What do you want?" he said, and as soon as he heard his voice, he wished he could take it back. He didn't want to sound that weak, that childish. He wanted to be *angry*, not defeated.

But the priest was already moving, picking up the dining room chair he'd been sitting on and carrying it over closer to Sean. That was probably supposed to be a nice touch. The bastard probably thought he was being respectful, lowering himself to speak to Sean eye-to-eye. What an asshole.

"Your mother's been suffering," David said. He looked over Sean's shoulder toward Stacey. "Your sister is worried about her, and when I spoke to your mother, *I* became worried about her."

"What?"

"Not just Mom," Stacey said quickly. She moved, now, around in front of Sean, and he thought briefly about making a break for the door she'd abandoned. But if he escaped now, it would look too much like running away. That meant he had to sit there as his sister said, "Corey and Tina, too. Everyone in this house. God, Sean. You've always been an asshole, but those two worshipped you anyway. You were their big brother. Their hero. And now? You've gone so far *beyond* asshole, Sean. You're fucking *mean*, now. Cruel. You're so wrapped up in your own shit you can't see how anyone else is being affected. But they *are* being affected. They're being torn apart. It needs to *stop*."

It felt like the world was spinning. Like the words were battering into him physically, beating him to dizziness, battering his ears so there was a dull roar laid over everything. He fought to keep his face impassive. It didn't matter. He was fine. He was tough. It was just words, and words were nothing.

"I've been looking into alternative housing," David said. For a second, it looked like he was going to reach out and lay his hand on Sean's arm, but luckily he came to his senses and didn't do it. "Obviously your physical requirements make it more challenging, and there are budget limitations, but—"

"You're kicking me out?" Sean asked, and thank god, his voice didn't sound weak. He sounded angry, and he let the emotion flow through him and give him the strength he needed as he wheeled toward his mother. "You staged this fucking *ambush* because you don't have the guts to do it yourself? You want me gone?"

"No, baby," she said, her whole body shaking with sobs he refused to acknowledge. "That was just one idea—it's not the one I like. It's *not*. I want you here! But, Sean—"

The roaring in his ears was too loud for him to hear any more and his vision was starting to cloud, dark red pouring in from the edges. If he'd been standing he'd probably have fallen, but as it was, there was nowhere lower for him to go. He wanted to run, he fucking *needed* to run away, but his fucking legs were gone, he'd never run again and he was trapped, this was his life, there was no escape from any of it—

Suddenly the air was cooler and everything was a little darker, a little more peaceful. He was moving, somehow, the chair being wheeled away from the house as if he'd been lifted up by an angel, rescued from hell and taken—where?

"Keep breathing, man," he heard, and this time the voice was as familiar as his own. Luke had him. Luke had appeared out of nowhere and he was pushing the chair, getting Sean out of that mess. Lucas Cain, the only person in the whole world who'd ever come close to understanding Sean. Maybe Father David wasn't quite as full of shit as he seemed, because Lucas showing up definitely seemed like a miracle.

But there was no such thing.

"Hold on," Sean managed. "Stop."

And Luke stopped. Of course he did. He paused for a second as if waiting for a further order, then stepped around the side of the chair and crouched down. It had been infuriating when David did it, but from Lucas, it was just right.

But Sean couldn't let himself fall into that trap. "You were part of that? You knew they were going to do that?"

"What'd they do?" The question sounded genuine. "Stacey called me about an hour ago and said she thought you might want to go for a drink tonight. She asked me to come by. When I got there, I heard your mom kinda—wailing. Is she okay?"

No, she wasn't okay. Obviously. And it was all Sean's fault. "I'm fucked," he said.

Luke just nodded. "Yeah? You want to get that drink, tell me what's going on?"

God, yes, Sean absolutely wanted that. The drink part, at least, and he was sure once he had a few shots in him the talking would come more naturally. But he wasn't even able to find that one simple pleasure anymore. "I can't drink with one of the pills I'm taking. I don't even know which one, but—it's pretty gross. Like, I puke almost right away." He frowned. "Besides, I thought you gave up drinking."

"Yeah, I did." Lucas shook his head. "Ain't we a pair?"

"If us in high school could see us now, they'd probably kick our asses."

"Probably. 'Course, us in high school were idiots."

Had they been? Maybe. They'd been bolder, definitely, more reckless, refusing to back down from any challenge or any fight. They'd been tough. But where had that gotten them?

"We could track down some milk and cookies, if you want," Lucas suggested. "Or go Christmas-crazy and buy some of that eggnog crap, the kind with no rum in it."

"Jesus. Haven't I suffered enough?"

Lucas grinned and straightened up. "Want to go up the hill, then?"

The hill. Yeah. It was exactly where Sean wanted to go. He nodded, and Lucas shifted back around and started pushing again, and they proceeded in silence down the sidewalk. The footing wasn't great—icy in parts, slushy in others—and Sean thought briefly about feeling guilty. Lucas's shoes were probably soaked. His feet were probably—well. Fuck. At least the bastard *had* feet. Besides, this was Luke. He wasn't going to get too worked up about a bit of cold.

It only took about ten minutes to make their way back through the neighborhood and then along the street that dead-ended with a graffiti-covered concrete barrier. It hit Lucas just about mid-thigh, same as it used to for Sean, back when he'd had legs, and they'd spent countless nights up here when they'd been kids.

Some of it had been stuff that made Sean ache for the loss of his legs. The wild paintball games they'd had, ranging all over the neighborhood, up and down the steep hill on the far side of the barrier, wrestling in the undergrowth, enjoying their youth and their strength and their freedom. But later, when they'd gotten older, they'd come here to drink and smoke, staring out over the ravine and into the town lights down below. God, they *had* been idiots when they'd been teenagers. They should have stayed the way they were before, wild and free in their little forest.

Now?

Now he couldn't even hoist his ass up to lean against the barrier, and wouldn't be able to keep himself balanced if he got Lucas to boost him.

"You think I'd die if I wheeled myself over the edge?" he asked.

Lucas peered over at the terrain. "How many times have you fallen down that hill? Ass over teakettle half the time, too. Never more than a few bumps and bruises."

He was right. Shit.

They sat in silence for a while, and then Lucas said, "You think that's what happened the night of the accident? Think you were trying to kill yourself?"

From anyone else but Lucas, the question would have led to an explosion. Sean had yelled at his mom, his sister, the police, the doctors, his fucking therapist—he didn't fucking remember, okay! Leave him alone! How the fuck should he know what happened? And he'd said mostly the same stuff to Lucas, in the past.

But this night? In this spot? He shrugged. "I can't remember. But— yeah. Probably. I'd definitely been thinking about it."

Sean kept his gaze locked on the town lights, but his peripheral vision showed him Luke's slow nod. Not panic, not disgust, not sorrow. Just calm acceptance. It gave Sean the strength to say a little more.

"Dick move, obviously. I mean—getting drunk, getting behind the wheel. Didn't have the guts to full-on kill myself, so I just did something so stupid I *deserved* to die. But, fuck. Imagine if I'd taken someone else out. If someone was dead because I got drunk and did something stupid."

"Yeah," Lucas said, his voice still calm, but with an extra note of something in it. "Imagine how shitty *that* would be."

"Oh. Right." Because Lucas had spent three years in the pen after killing a guy in a drunken bar fight. Shit. "Uh—"

"You're an idiot," Lucas said. It felt like forgiveness.

"I'm smarter when I drink."

"You really, really aren't."

They were quiet for a little longer, until Lucas said, "You want to tell me what's going on at your place? What was your mom so upset about? And was that the *priest* there?"

"You noticed that, huh? You got a type? Did his little priest collar get you hot?"

"You got it," Lucas said easily. "That's exactly how it went. Too bad he's Catholic—the Anglicans are a bit more relaxed about all that."

"Things still good with—your guy? Your—boyfriend, or whatever?"

"His name's Mark. If you don't want to use the labels, you *could* just use his name."

No. If Sean started using his name, it would be one step closer to accepting that he was real. That Luke was—not *gay*. It wasn't really the *gay* that Sean had a problem with. But he really didn't like thinking that Luke was in love. Not with some stranger.

"My physiotherapist is gay." Strange direction for Sean to take the conversation, but Luke could handle it.

"Yeah?" Just about the same level of polite acceptance as Luke had shown when Sean admitted he'd probably tried to kill himself. "That's the kind of thing you guys talk about?"

"I guess. I mean—he was probably trying to insult me, somehow. I can't really remember the context. But he's pretty—I don't know. Some shit he just takes, and then other stuff? He's pretty feisty."

"He was trying to insult you by telling you he was gay? That's a subtle approach."

"Not insult me, I guess. Like—*goad* me. Is that a word? He was trying to get me mad, so I'd work out harder. So I wouldn't quit."

"Because he knew you wouldn't want to look weak in front of a fag."

"Well, I sound like a bit of a dick when you say it like that."

"How do you want me to say it?"

I don't know." Sean moved—he actually moved his goddamn thigh—to kick at the snow in front of his chair. But there was no lower leg, no fucking foot to move. He just kind of—twitched. Absolutely pathetic. "He's brown, too. The physio. Not Muslim, though. Sikh."

"That's what Anala was, right? That girl you liked in—seventh grade? She was only here for a year. Wasn't she Sikh?"

"Yeah," Sean said. It felt like he was confessing to something.

"She had really nice skin. She kinda glowed."

Yeah, she had glowed. And he'd liked looking at her, and she'd liked looking at him, for whatever stupid reason. But she'd moved away and she was probably off living a beautiful, perfect life somewhere, and if she ever ran into him again she'd look at him with shock and pity and he'd want to—well. He'd want to die. Nothing new, there.

"I won't let him touch me with his bare skin. I make him wear gloves."

"Your physio?"

"Yeah."

"Please tell me you've developed some weird germ-phobia or something. Fuck, Sean, don't tell me you did that because he's got brown skin."

Sean didn't answer, which was clearly answer enough.

"Fuck." For the first time all night, Lucas sounded genuinely upset. "You're not a fucking racist, Sean. You're pretty sexist, and you've got some issues about gay people, but—Sean." Lucas shifted around so he was standing in front of Sean. "Look me in the fucking face and tell me you give a good goddamn whether someone with brown skin touches you."

"Maybe I did it because he's a fag, not because he's brown."

"Maybe you did it because you're a dick. You're hurting so you want everyone else to hurt, too. Sound possible?"

Sean didn't answer, but Luke seemed perfectly happy to continue without Sean's input. "And that's probably what you mom was worked up about, too. Am I right? Not you being a dick to some physiotherapist, but you being a dick to *everybody*. I saw Corey the other day—your own brother, that kid who used to always tag around after us and who'd do any damn thing you told him to—and he said he was saving up to move out. He's in fucking *high school*, Sean. Why does he want to move out of the house?"

"Well, he won't fucking have to. Mom's throwing me out."

"Good."

"What?" Surprising how much Luke's response hurt. The one person Sean had thought he could count on.

But Lucas wasn't acting like he'd just betrayed his best friend. He was staring Sean down, daring him to disagree.

"I said it's good. You should have moved out years ago. She should have *kicked your ass out* years ago. And you don't want her feeling sorry for you, right? You don't want her treating you like you're fragile just 'cause your legs got chopped off? If you're being a dick at home—and I absolutely believe you are—then she *should* kick you out. Good for her."

"What the fuck am I supposed to do? Where am I supposed to go? I've got no fucking *legs*, Lucas!"

"Boo-hoo, you big pussy."

"What? Fuck you, asshole. My *legs are gone*."

"I guess they cut a bit too high and took your balls, too?"

Sean had no more words. There were *sounds* in his throat, straining to get out—incoherent screams of shock and outrage, roars of anger—but he bit them back. He was... Lucas was... this whole fucking situation was...

"She say when she wanted you out?" Lucas asked, and the son-of-a-bitch was back to being calmly pleasant.

Sean couldn't answer.

Lucas didn't seem to care. "You can stay at my place for a while if you want. Mark's down at some conference in Boston—since he stopped being a priest he's gotten all involved in the political side of being an Anglican. Says he's got more power as a lay member than he ever had when he was an employee. Anyway, he's not back until Tuesday. The spare room's yours until then, if you want it. The whole house is one floor, and there's a ramp."

"I can't stay there when your boyfriend's home?"

"You start saying his fucking name and stop wrinkling your face up like that whenever you refer to him, and we can talk about it. But you're not going to live there forever, buddy. We're not looking for a permanent roommate. I'm saying a few days to give everyone at home a chance to cool down and give you time to find a better plan."

"A better plan," Sean echoed dully. A plan. It seemed absolutely impossible. Pointless to even try. But Lucas wasn't known for being overly optimistic, and he seemed to think it was a workable next step. "For what?"

"For the rest of your life, eventually. But for now—for talking to your mom, hopefully in a way that doesn't leave her sobbing and you looking like you want to murder a priest. And then probably for finding a place to live. Figuring out how to be as independent as possible." Lucas kicked the wheel of Sean's chair, not hard, but enough to make a point. "You need to get your balls back, son. First step probably involves getting weaned off your mommy."

Chapter Three

The food was delicious, of course. Bobby's mom was a great cook and other people had brought dishes, both western and Sikh, and someone had ordered pizza *and* Chinese. It was a feast.

And for some reason, Paul's parents and his sister Jas were there as well. It wasn't as if the families didn't know each other—their fathers had been doing business together for years. They'd been frequent guests in each other's homes, even before Paul and Bobby had gotten together. But wasn't this evening a celebration of spoiled Saachi's snowman song? Maybe Paul's parents were so desperate to get out of the house that they'd accept an invitation to an event like that, but what the hell was Jas doing?

He'd asked her that, soon after he'd arrived, but she'd just rolled her eyes and said, "Mom made it *very* clear that I was expected to attend. No idea why."

"And she wouldn't say?"

"She'd made her expectations clear. Why would she lower herself with an explanation?"

Right. It was typical, so Paul hadn't even bothered to press for more information. Command performances at family events were a weekly event, although usually the "family" involved was more directly connected. Paul couldn't complain about being dragged into Bobby's extended family, not when Bobby was generally gracious about spending time with Paul's grandparents, aunts, uncles, cousins....

No, Paul couldn't complain. But he couldn't find a way to really enjoy himself, either. He'd eaten, made the requisite small talk, and then started tugging his ear whenever Bobby glanced in his direction. It was the well-established signal for *let's get out of here*, but Bobby either wasn't seeing the gesture or he was totally ignoring it. Annoying, either way. Paul would give him ten more minutes and then make his way across the room for a more direct, more verbal suggestion that it was time to go.

Except before the ten minutes was up, Bobby's mom started circulating with a tray of champagne flutes, and as conversation died down, Bobby stood up.

"Thank you all for being here this evening," he said. His face and his voice were young, but the words could have come out of his father's mouth. His grandfather's, even. "And thanks to Saachi for the wonderful performance earlier."

Saachi, face flushed with excitement, made a grand curtsey and looked as if she was ready to make a speech of her own. But Bobby didn't give her the chance.

"It's wonderful to have so many generations together this evening," he continued. "It's one more reminder of how important family is. We are the core unit of strength and mutual support, and it is only when we are secure, here, that we are able to spread our generosity out to help others."

Paul wasn't sure about the accuracy of that, but he supposed it sounded good. Still, why the hell was Bobby making a speech about it? About anything?

Paul glanced around the room at the assembled faces and his gaze stopped on his mother's. She wasn't looking at Bobby. She was staring at Paul with a beaming smile that made him want to smile back.

Until he realized what was going on.

But—no. It couldn't be. Bobby wouldn't do that. Would he?

Paul stared at Bobby and got a beatific smile in return. "I'm thrilled you could all be here tonight, as family, as Paul and I take the next step in *our* family. I know we're not exactly traditional in some ways, but in others? In others we value the way things have always been done."

No, no, no. Paul actually shook his head a little, but if Bobby noticed it, he showed no sign. Instead, he was walking closer, and, oh, no, no, no, he was pulling a little jewelry box out of his jacket pocket. No. No.

Paul stood, stunned, as Bobby fell to one knee before him. "Sukhpal Singh Gill," he said, and he reached for Paul's left hand. No, no, no. "Our parents have met and given their blessings to this union. They're eager for us to formalize our bond so we can start raising children together and create another generation of strength and happiness. And I'm eager, too."

His voice lowered a little, but only enough to give the *illusion* of intimacy. Paul was sure the words still carried to every corner of the hushed living room. "I love you, Paul, and I want us to spend the rest of our lives together. Will you marry me?"

Bobby let go of Paul's hand long enough to get the jewelry case open and Paul caught a glimpse of a white gold band studded all around with diamonds. Bobby's nimble fingers extracted the band and then he set the case aside, reached for Paul's hand—

Paul's fingers curled into a fist before he even thought about it, and once he realized how he was reacting, he kept his hands tight. Not a threat, just a defense. There was no way a ring was going to get on his finger without—without *something*. Without him having time to figure out what the hell was going on.

"Paul," Bobby prompted with a sweet smile. As if he thought Paul was being clumsy, or was so overwhelmed with joy that he didn't understand the mechanics of what was supposed to be happening. "Ring."

"We need to talk about this," Paul whispered.

"Wow!" Jas said from somewhere nearby. Her voice was loud, maybe a little strained, but not shaky. "I think the guys deserve a bit of time to themselves, right? And while they're enjoying each other's company, we have all this champagne! May I make a toast?" She didn't wait for confirmation. "To family! To the love and support we've all enjoyed from those gathered here this evening."

She raised her glass, and the other guests followed her lead, some quickly, some more slowly, all of them keeping at least half their attention on Paul and Bobby.

"This is for you," Bobby, said, and Paul honestly wasn't sure if he was talking about the ring or the proposal or something else entirely.

"Can we go home and sort this out?" Paul whispered.

"I would also like to propose a toast," a new voice said, and Paul turned his head to see his mother stepping forward. She didn't even glance in his direction, only raised her glass toward Bobby's mother. "To our wonderful friends, who have hosted us this evening and on so many other occasions. Why, I was just telling some new acquaintances about that wonderful property you booked last year in Costa Rica, with the beautiful scenery and the absolutely exceptional service from the staff. You never fail to amaze us all with your gracious hospitality. So, please, everyone: to our hosts!"

Bobby looked about as dazed as Paul felt, and it was Jas who tugged on their hands and guided them toward the dining room.

"Escape while you can," she hissed.

"Escape?" Bobby managed. "We should—we should be celebrating?"

"Celebrating?" The numbness was wearing off. "What the hell, Bobby?"

"Outside," Jas ordered. "Get your coats on, go outside, and talk it through without a multi-family audience."

That made sense, and Paul's jacket was right on top of the pile anyway, since he'd been a late arrival. He grabbed it, then turned to Bobby. "Were you wearing your black one? Or the camel?"

But apparently Bobby wasn't interested in finding his coat. "Our families are waiting, Paul. They're all here to celebrate our engagement. We need to go back in there and have a toast."

"Can we please have this conversation outside?"

"This isn't the time. Whatever you're worried about, we can sort it out later. Right now, we need to join our families and celebrate—"

"Bobby! Stop. We're not getting engaged tonight. I'm sorry, but—what the hell were you thinking? We've never talked about marriage. I mean, not in terms of *us*. You really thought—"

"Guys," Jas said. "Seriously. If you *want* to have this conversation in front of an audience, stay right where you are and keep going. Alternatively…."

"What I *want*," Bobby said, his voice low and angry, "Is for us to go back in and accept congratulations from our families. I *want* Paul to stop making a goddamn scene."

"Bobby," Jas said, her voice calm and sweet but still firm. "You're the one who planned a public engagement without consulting him first. And you're the one who's refusing to go outside and discuss things in private. So if anyone's making a scene, here, it's not Paul."

"Okay," Paul said. He appreciated Jas's support, but the families witnessing a brawl between Bobby and Jas really wasn't that much better than them seeing one between Bobby and Paul. "Bobby, I'm going outside. I'd appreciate it if you'd find your coat and come with me."

And he pulled the French door open and stepped out onto the terrace, pulling his jacket on as he went. He closed the door firmly behind him and felt his shoulders relax. He couldn't stay out there forever—didn't *want* to stay out there forever, didn't want to leave his family behind, not for good. But wasn't it nice to take a few deep breaths in peace?

Except—Bobby had just proposed to him. Proposed. Marriage. That had just happened.

And the *way* it had happened was a mess, but what about the actual idea? Married. To Bobby. Was that something Paul wanted?

He heard the door open behind him, then close, and a familiar bulk came to stand beside him. They stared out into the darkened yard together, and it would have felt companionable if Paul hadn't known what had just happened. And what was likely about to happen.

But when Bobby finally spoke, he sounded calm. "I don't understand. I thought you wanted this."

Paul fought to keep his own voice just as level. "What part did you think I wanted? The proposal? You talking to my parents—your *parents* talking to my parents—before anyone thought to mention it to me? Or the marriage in general? What did you think I wanted?"

"I—all of it."

"Wait. You honestly thought I'd want your parents to talk to my parents before you even mentioned marriage to me?"

"You like tradition."

"Do I?"

"You wear your grandfather's Kara." Bobby reached over and ran his fingers over the iron bracelet on Paul's wrist.

"Yeah. I do. And—what else?"

"How do you mean?"

"Short hair, clean shaven, no turban, no Kirpan, no Kangha, I'm wearing boxer-briefs, not Kacchera—"

"That's not what I meant. We're not religious, obviously. But—it's your *grandfather's*. You value that."

"Are you honestly gearing up to tell me that because I wear a piece of jewelry handed down from my grandfather, that means I—wanted a marriage that you negotiated between our families? You thought I wanted to have the starring role in this little play, even though I never auditioned for the damn thing? You didn't think I should be consulted about any of it?"

"Paul. You weren't kidnapped and forced to marry me! This is a *proposal*. We arranged the *proposal*, not the marriage. Of course you'll be part of the actual marriage. That goes without saying."

The actual marriage. As if it was a foregone conclusion.

The whole thing was just exhausting. And it didn't have to be. If Paul would just relax and let himself be swept away by the current—by Bobby's plans, by their families' plans—he'd be taken care of. He'd have a safe, easy life, buffered from any unpleasantness, if he just stopped being so damn difficult.

Maybe that's what he needed to do. What he damn well *should* do. Sure, this wasn't the proposal of his dreams, but Bobby had tried, hadn't he? He'd had the conversations, arranged the party, gotten the ring—he'd made an effort.

"Why didn't you talk to me, first?" Paul asked.

Bobby frowned. "That would have ruined the surprise."

Of course it would have. "But—do we actually want to get married? What's that about? Why would we do that?"

"We've been dating for almost four years, living together for two. Marriage is the logical next step."

"Logical," Paul echoed. "But—you said you did this for me. The proposal? Is that what you meant? That's not about logic, that's about you trying to make me happy. Trying to do what you think I want."

Bobby's nod made it clear that he was relieved Paul was finally cluing in. "Yes. I'm doing what you want."

"You missed a word."

"What word?"

"I said 'what you think I want' and you changed it to 'what you want'. You left out the 'you think' part."

"Are we arguing semantics, now?"

"No. We're—*I'm*—trying to figure out why you think I wanted to get married."

"You've been restless, lately. And you were so happy at Ross and Michael's wedding."

"I was *drunk* at Ross and Michael's wedding. But... yeah, okay, I was happy, too. But I was happy for *them*. That doesn't mean I wanted to get married myself."

Bobby seemed genuinely shocked. "Are you saying you don't want to get married? Ever?"

"I honestly—I haven't thought about it."

"Well *I've* thought about it. And it makes sense. This is the right next step for us."

It all had to be a joke, didn't it? They'd stare at each other a little longer and then one of them would break and smirk and they'd begin to laugh? But—there wasn't even a hint of humor in Bobby's expression. Paul shook his head. "You still think—you think this is going to happen. Tonight. You think we're going to talk for a little bit and then I'll stop being stubborn and we'll go in there and laugh it all off. Your mom will open another couple bottles of Champagne and we'll just go on with the celebration."

"Yes," Bobby said. He caught Paul's hand. "That's exactly what we'll do. That's a good plan."

"I wasn't making a plan! I was saying—no." Such a short, simple word. But of course Paul couldn't leave it at that. "We're not getting engaged tonight. We need to talk this over and figure out what we both want. If we get married, it should be—it should be for something more important that just being logical!"

"Our families are inside." Bobby seemed genuinely unable to understand what was happening. "They're waiting to celebrate with us."

Yes, their families were inside. They were waiting. They'd be really disappointed if Bobby and Paul didn't come in and celebrate with them, and Paul loved them. If he didn't go inside with a ring on his finger, he'd be disappointing people he loved.

"Where's your ring?" he asked.

"What? I—well, I can't buy a ring for *myself*. We can pick out wedding rings together."

"Only I wear an engagement ring. You don't wear one?"

"I don't really care for jewelry. But you wear—"

"I wear my grandfather's Kara. That's it."

"You're really angry." Like it was a revelation. Like Bobby couldn't possibly imagine what Paul had to be angry about. But that was the whole problem, wasn't it? Bobby *couldn't* imagine. He didn't know Paul well enough to figure it out.

Paul shifted, and the slight jingle as he moved felt like divine intervention. He slapped at his pocket and felt the reassuring weight of his car keys. "I'm going to slip out the back," he announced. "If you want a ride home, you can come with me. We can sort all this out some other time."

"We can't just abandon them, Paul. We can't run away from this!"

"Okay. Fine. *We* won't. You go back inside and make your apologies—I'm sure you'll do a good job of making it clear that I'm just a flighty, emotional airhead and you'll get me calmed down in time—and I'll drive myself home. You can take a cab if no one will drop you off."

"What? No. I'm sorry, Paul, but you're being completely irrational. I can't support this behavior."

"I'm not actually asking you to support it." How liberating to say those words. "I'm just—going. I'm going to walk out and drive away. You can come with me or not. Your call."

"I will not—" Bobby began, but he stopped talking when Paul started moving. "Paul. No. This is not how this should go. You are really going to regret this, and I'm not going to have a hell of a lot of sympathy for you. You're being selfish. Pointlessly stubborn. You need to—"

Paul shut the garden gate behind him. It wasn't a solid wall: if Bobby had still been talking, Paul would have heard him, so the silence meant Bobby had finally shut up.

Paul stood there, just around the corner of the house, and imagined the scene. Bobby would be standing on the terrace, staring at the closed garden gate. What would he do next? The pathway had been shoveled and sanded, so Paul couldn't rely on the crunching of snow underfoot to tell him if Bobby was approaching. If Bobby was following, for once in his damn life.

If Bobby came after him, it wouldn't mean much, but it would mean *something*. It would be a tiny compromise, a recognition that Bobby didn't always, always, *always* get to have his way. It would give them something to build on. Maybe they'd go to a counsellor and figure out better ways to communicate. Bobby's assumption that he was in charge wasn't all his fault, after all—Paul had *let* him develop that expectation. If Paul always let Bobby win, why wouldn't Bobby expect to keep winning?

Yeah. If Bobby came through the gate, he and Paul could talk it all through. They could find a way to patch things up and move forward.

If Bobby came through the gate, it meant he was willing to try.

Paul heard a soft click come from around the corner. Movement of some sort. Was Bobby—

Oh. It had been the sound of the French door closing. Because Bobby had gone back inside.

Bobby wasn't coming after Paul. He wasn't following, wasn't making that tiny compromise.

Paul had no idea what that meant for their relationship. And he had no idea what it meant that his reaction to the uncertainty was a hell of a lot closer to relief than to disappointment.

Chapter Four

If Luke hadn't been there, Sean really didn't think he'd have made it through the rest of that night. He'd wanted to go straight over to Luke's place, but Luke thought it was important to go home and deal with the family.

Luke, of course, could go fuck himself, but words had been exchanged, Sean's manhood had been *repeatedly* called into question—and, seriously, if Luke asked one more question about where Sean's balls were, the bastard was going to get an up-close and personal view of the family jewels while Sean farted on his face—and somehow they were back at the house.

"Let your mom see you, you fucking pussy," Luke scolded. "Let her know her precious baby is okay."

"This is why phones were invented." Sean reached down and caught hold of his wheels, stopping the chair's forward motion. "Seriously. It's just going to be another fucking scene. Nobody needs that."

"It's only a scene if you make it a scene. And it's past time you stopped making scenes, so—git 'er done. Go in there, say everyone needs some cooling off time and you're going to stay at my place. Get your shit, let her fuss a little bit about her baby going on his first sleepover—"

"You're fucking obnoxious, you know that?"

"I'll shut up once you man up."

"You seriously think you're going to just bug me into going in there?"

"Yeah. I think I am."

And, of course, he was right. "You're coming with me. And if the priest is still there you have to get rid of him. Tell him you're fucking an Anglican and you're worried you're getting dragged away from the one true faith."

"I think once he knows the Anglican is a *guy*, he's probably going to focus more on that, sin-wise."

"Good. Tell him all about that. Give him fucking details. I'll give you five dollars if you talk about lube."

"You'd better hang on to as much money as you can. You're going to need it for rent."

"That's a bit of a downer. Thanks a lot."

"Just get moving. It's cold out here."

"You drove, right? We're not wheeling all the way over to your place when we're done."

"I drove. The wheelchair folds up?"

"Yeah."

Strange that Lucas didn't know that, except... not strange at all, since Sean had been so damn careful to keep Luke away from the mechanical realities of the new world. And none of that was really going to work once Sean was staying at Luke's place.

"You said you had a ramp at your place, right?"

"Yeah. I built it right after the one I built here. I had this crazy idea that you might want to come visit me sometime."

But of course Sean hadn't. He hadn't wanted to go anywhere or do anything. He still didn't *want* to, he guessed, but he didn't seem to have much damn choice.

He forced his arms to wheel his way up the ramp to the front door, and then he took a deep breath and pulled the door open.

"Hello?" he said, and heard a bustle of movement from the kitchen.

"Sean?" His mother appeared in the kitchen doorway, stared at him for half a second, then shifted her attention to somewhere behind him. Sean turned just fast enough to see Lucas with his hands spread flat, making a 'simmer down' gesture.

Kind of humiliating to think that Luke was handling people's behavior to make things easier for Sean, but at the same time, useful.

"You're back." His mom was clearly making an attempt to follow Luke's directions and keep it calm. "I was just making tea. Would you two like some?"

Sean had never wanted a cup of tea in his damn life, and his mom knew that. He'd never seen Luke drink it, either, but for some reason the bastard said, "Sure, that'd be great," and bent over to take his boots off.

"Oh, don't bother with that," Sean's mom said quickly. "With everything that gets tracked in on—"

She caught herself and cast an almost guilty look in Sean's direction.

"On Sean's wheels?" Luke supplied. "Huh. I hadn't thought of that. Damn, are you going to make a mess at my place, too?"

"Sean's going to your place?" Guilt-inducing to see his mother perk up at that. She'd been rescued from the burden of living with Sean.

"For a few days," Lucas said. Then he thumped Sean's arm a little too hard to be comfortable. "Right?"

"I guess," Sean managed.

"I'm putting in new floors," Luke said. "Just laminate, but it looks pretty good, the parts I've finished. Sean'll help me finish up, and since I'll be working him all hours, there's no point in him coming and going."

"Wait, what?" Luke was just kidding, hopefully... except he didn't usually lie. He'd joke, he'd bluff, but making up a whole home improvement project? That wasn't really his style. "I'm just going to get in the way."

"Why?"

"I've got no fucking legs, Lucas!"

Luke scowled at him. "So? You can't reach the *floor*? Is that what you're trying to say? The *floor* is too high for you to reach without legs?"

"Maybe he was planning to kick the flooring into place," Sean's mom said. His *mother* was part of this, now.

"Was that it?" Luke asked. "It's just the 'click' kind of flooring. Really doesn't take a lot of force."

"Yeah, you're both hilarious."

"And you're not as useless as you think, you lazy bastard." Luke turned his attention to Sean's mom. "Mark's out of town for a few days and things are pretty slow at work, so I was going to just blitz the floor. But if Sean's helping me with that, I can help him find a place. Is that the plan?"

Was that the plan? Sean's mom pinched her lips together. "He can stay here if he..."

"If he stops being a total dick?" Lucas supplied. Thanks, buddy. "That means it's not like it's a really urgent thing. The two of us can sort stuff out, give you a call, figure out the next step?"

"Yes," she said. She sounded close to tears again, but probably this time they were a sign of relief. Gratitude that someone else was going to deal with her problem son for a while.

"You good with that?" Luke asked Sean.

"Do I have a fucking choice?"

"Obviously," Luke said.

"Really?"

"Yeah. You can stay here, it sounds like, if you can manage to stop making everyone's lives miserable. You can come to my place and help me out and give everyone some space. You can wheel your way out into the night and look pathetic until someone calls the cops and they come take you to a shelter or something. You can figure out your own fourth option if you want, 'cause it was just your legs that got damaged, not your brain." Lucas crouched down so his face was inches from Sean's. "Basically? You can man up or you can pussy out. Your call. What's it going to be?"

Sean held his gaze for as long as he could, then shook his head and looked at the ceiling. "This isn't a fucking movie, asshole."

Lucas gave him a gentle cuff to the back of his head. "Watch your language; your mom doesn't want to hear all that." A brief moment of peace, and then, "So? You gonna go put some stuff together while me and your mom have some tea?"

Simple question, but of course it meant much more. You gonna take the chance you're being offered? You gonna start pulling yourself together? You gonna let Luke help?

Maybe not anybody else. But Luke?

Sean let his head flop forward. A nod, of sorts. He was agreeing, but that didn't mean he was going to be gracious about it.

Luke settled in at the kitchen table and Sean wheeled back to his bedroom and stuffed some clothes into a backpack. By the time he returned, his mom and Luke were huddled together over a sheet of paper with an array of pill bottles spread out in front of them.

"I'm not sure he really needs these ones," his mom was saying. "But once a day isn't a big deal."

"What would happen if he took all of them at once?" Luke asked. He was looking at Sean as he asked the question. "Like… is there enough medicine here to kill him? Do permanent damage to him?"

Sean's mom looked upset by the question. Of course she was—they didn't talk about that sort of thing, at least not anywhere Sean could hear them.

"The painkillers, maybe," she finally said. "I'm not sure."

"So if I hold onto the painkillers, he can take care of the rest of them himself? I mean—he's no dumber than he was before he got hurt, right?"

"He…" Sean's mom was clearly struggling with that question. "No. He's—but—"

Lucas nodded. "Yeah, I know. He was *really* dumb before he got hurt, so he's still really dumb now. I get that. But you've got the schedule all written out here, and you said most of the pills are kind of optional. It's not like he's going to reject an organ or something if he misses one. So probably he should be handling that stuff himself, right?"

"I…."

Lucas waited, and finally Sean's mom nodded. She turned to look at Sean. "You can manage your own medications?"

"I don't know," he said, rolling his chair the rest of the way into the room. "I'm pretty dumb."

Lucas nodded sadly. "We know."

That attitude was going to get pretty old if Sean had to deal with it twenty-four hours a day. Which was probably all part of the bastard's plan. "You've got this all worked out, don't you? The rescue, the conversation, this whole being-an-annoying-pain-in-the-ass thing. You're like a puppet master, manipulating me into doing what you want."

Lucas actually laughed. "Yeah, sure. That's me. I'm a damn mastermind." He stood up, then, and said, "You got all your stuff? Ready to go?"

Was Sean ready? He didn't think he'd ever spent more than one night in a row away from this house. That was a sad state of affairs for a twenty-three year old, but he was pretty sure it was accurate. There'd never been money for summer camps or extended class trips, and he'd had plenty of hookups but never been with someone he'd wanted to spend more than an occasional night with. This house was the only home he'd ever known, and it felt strange to be leaving it, even with the open-door policy his mom seemed to be adopting.

What would happen if he just said no? If he rolled his chair back into his room, locked the door, and refused to budge?

The bathroom would be a problem, and he'd probably get hungry pretty fast, but more than that... damn it. He'd already lost a hell of a lot. He needed to hang on to whatever shreds of dignity he could still find.

So he nodded at Luke and said, "Yeah. Okay. Let's go."

And as he wheeled himself out the front door, it didn't feel as awful as he'd thought it might. There was a sense of loss, maybe, but part of what he was leaving behind was weight, and he was lighter without it. His mom was watching him, of course; he wasn't stupid enough to think she'd suddenly lose interest just because he wasn't under her roof. But he wasn't her problem anymore.

And he wasn't Luke's problem, either. Luke would help him out, because he was a friend. There had been times when Sean had doubted that, and absolutely times he'd stretched the relationship far beyond what *should* have been its breaking point, but in the end, Luke was there for him. But just to help, not to control.

Sean was in control, now. He was still a problem, sure, but he was his own problem. And maybe there was some freedom in that. Some dignity.

"Move it, Cain!" he called over his shoulder to Luke, who was still making small talk with Sean's mom. "Let's get on with it."

Chapter Five

"Three days." Paul stabbed at his bean salad with more force than necessary. "Three solid days of him just freezing me out. I have no idea where we're going!"

Anna set her sandwich down and took a sip of water before she responded. They were in the shared office space at work, but no one else was around. "What were you expecting, exactly? Or, no, that's not fair, because you didn't really have time to *expect* anything to do with all this. But, looking back, what do you think he might have done differently?"

"Not proposed to me in front of a whole crowd without ever having even mentioned it to me in the first place?"

"Yeah, okay, but *after* that. What should he have done differently since then?"

"Talked to me, maybe? I mean, he should have talked to me *before* the damn proposal and then we wouldn't be in this mess, but—" Paul sighed heavily. "He's just behaving the same way he always has, I guess. I mean, he's *angrier* about it, now, but the level of communication really isn't that different."

"So what are you thinking?" Anna sounded like she was being careful to keep sounding neutral. "Do you... I mean...."

He knew what she meant. Was the relationship over? Was there any way to come back from something like this? And, of course, the secret, hidden question he wasn't letting himself spend too much time on.... Did he even *want* the relationship to come back?

"I'm just trying to get through the days," he said. "No decisions, just survival." He checked his watch. "Speaking of which, it's about time for our next patient."

Anna made a face. "Not who you need to be dealing with today."

"There's never really a *good* time for angry racists, is there?"

He didn't bother waiting for Anna's answer. He tidied his lunch, washed his hands, and pulled the latex gloves out from the box under the counter, and headed out to the main room to wait for Sean Gage.

Who was already there.

Feeling suddenly defensive, Paul checked his watch, but Gage held his hands up quickly. "I'm early," he said. "Got a ride from a new person. He's got a stick up his ass about getting places on time."

That was more pleasant, and more voluntary information, than Paul had expected. What the hell was Gage up to?

The confusion only increased when Paul started putting the latex gloves on and Gage said, "You don't have to wear those. Sorry. I was just being a dick."

It was unsettling. A trap, probably, but with what possible goal in mind? And, honestly, Paul didn't think he cared. This son-of-a-bitch thought he could say ugly, racist things for session after session and then wave it all away with one casual apology? No. Maybe Paul couldn't stand up for himself at home, but he could damn well do it here.

"I prefer to wear them," he said. He managed to maintain enough professionalism to keep himself from spelling out the rest of it. He didn't *say* he wanted to wear the gloves because he didn't like the idea of touching a racist piece of shit with his bare hands. No, he didn't say it, but he could tell by the expression on Gage's face that the message got across all the same. Good.

Well, good for about two seconds, the little flair of vindictive pleasure melting at least some of the chill left over from three days of icy glaring at home. But Gage just *took it*. The selfish bastard didn't fight back, didn't drag up some ugly slur, didn't even seem to be building any of his exercise-supporting anger. He just nodded as if indicating that he'd received the message, and then said, "We starting on the mats again?"

"Yes," Paul said, and they both kept their interaction professional and focused on immediate concerns until the end of the session. At the end, though, as Gage was resting in the cool-down area, Paul braced himself and said, "I got an e-mail from the prosthetist. She says you missed your appointment last week. And it was the third time you've not shown up. She said she's taking you off her client list."

"Yeah?" Not aggressive, exactly, but certainly not conciliatory. Not a promise to do better.

And Paul wasn't Gage's keeper, or even his social worker. It wasn't Paul's job to make sure the man made it to his appointments. But he wasn't totally uninvolved, either. "Our work this far has been based on the ultimate goal of getting you into prosthetics and walking. I still think that's an achievable goal. But, obviously, getting fitted for the prosthetics is a pretty important part in the process. If you're not going to do that? Honestly, we should probably get you working with your occupational therapist more—training you in ways to get used to living in the chair."

"More OT means less PT?" Gage asked quietly.

"We'd probably be done, at least for a while. You could come back if you or your OT found you needed strengthening in certain areas, or if you started experiencing negative effects. But if we're just working on general recovery and strength? You're recovered enough and strong enough for a wheelchair, already, if that's as far as you want to go."

There was a pause in the conversation as Gage heaved himself into his chair—an act he was managing with more skill and control every time—and then he leaned back and looked up at the ceiling. "I don't know. I sure would miss our time together. I think we've got a really special bond, you know?"

And then it arrived. The jolt of tension-relieving laughter Paul had been craving the other night when he'd been fighting with Bobby came *now*, here, with Sean fucking Gage. It made no sense, but it felt good, letting the quick huff of breath escape, letting his shoulders shake once and then relax. "Yeah. I understand. That'd be quite a loss for you."

"Quite a loss for both of us." Gage lifted his head as if it weighed a hundred pounds, then looked toward the front door of the facility. "I'm trying to rely on my mom less, for driving me around. But that means I'm hitting up a friend for rides. I'm not sure when I can get down to the city for the fitting."

"You haven't started working with hand controls for your car? Even if you get the prosthetics, you're not going to be able to use them for driving." Paul knew Gage's OT, Jenna, and she was usually pretty proactive. Maybe Gage just hadn't been cooperating with her. They should probably have another case conference and get this stuff sorted out.

But Gage shook his head. "I haven't got a car. Mine got wrecked in the accident. And I can't really install hand controls on someone *else's* car, you know?"

Fair enough. "To confirm—the prosthetics are still a goal for you? That's still what we're working toward, and we just need to figure out how to get past a few obstacles?"

"We?"

Huh. Yeah. How had that slipped in there? "You," Paul clarified. "*We're* working toward the goal in terms of physical preparedness, but *you* are the one who has to sort out the obstacles."

"Yeah. I—" Gage stopped. For a moment it seemed like he might be done, but then he shook his head and turned to look at Paul, dead on, for the first time since they'd met. "Can I? When I first got hurt, I saw a bunch of stuff on the internet about how fake legs don't really work if you don't have knees. And then I read some other stuff that said they can. I don't—I don't want to do this if there's no chance of it working."

Not out of laziness. Paul knew that, somehow. He knew Gage didn't want to try and fail not because of the wasted effort but because it would be just one more loss of hope, one more disappointment, one more setback for someone who'd already taken more than he was really able to handle.

Paul shrugged. "I won't lie to you. It's a lot more difficult. Having two artificial joints to deal with instead of just one? And on both legs? Those are problems. But it can be done. You're young, you're reasonably fit—and we can definitely get you fitter—and you have no health issues other than the amputation. The only factors working against you are attitude and your support system. If you can get the attitude under control? There are people who can help you get the supports in place."

"My mom's priest?"

The words were spoken with enough vitriol that Paul was pretty sure the priest wasn't going to be the answer. For a brief, ridiculous moment he thought about mentioning his own willingness to help, but he managed to choke that back. He *wasn't* willing to help, not beyond what was required by his job. He had his own issues, and if he was going to pick a patient worthy of special compassion, it would absolutely not be Sean Gage. "There are social workers who help with stuff like this. And is your mom completely out of the program? She seemed like she was pretty involved, last I saw her. And this friend of yours—is he willing to be part of it?"

"He's already doing more than he should have to. And my mom—she needs a break."

"Sean." Oh, shit. Paul's brain was sending him all kinds of stupid messages. One session of reasonably civil behavior did not mean this client was a friend. "I mean, Mr. Gage. Look—this is going to be a long-term thing. *Everyone's* going to need a break now and then. Your mom might need a break right now, but that doesn't mean she's out for good."

"She should be, though. She shouldn't have to deal with all this."

Paul wasn't sure how to respond to that—wasn't sure how the hell he'd gotten himself so deep into this conversation in the first place—so he was a bit relieved when Gage shook his head and said, "Shit. You shouldn't have to deal with it either. Sorry. No idea why I'm being this chatty."

"It's fine. This is your recovery, but I'm part of your team. It's no problem if you want to discuss strategy with me."

"My team. I was never much good at team sports."

"Well, this is your chance to learn a new skill, I guess." Paul glanced toward the waiting area and saw his next patient, a sixty-year-old woman with back issues, waiting. Sitting two chairs down from her was a man about Gage's age, wearing jeans and work boots and a leather jacket and hoodie combo.

"That's your friend?" Paul asked. "The guy who might drive you down to the prosthetist? Do you want to figure out a few times with him now, and I can see if they're willing to give you another appointment?"

"No," Gage said after a moment. "If I ask, he'll just agree to it, even if it's a total nuisance for him."

"What's your alternate plan? Your mom?"

"I don't know."

Paul wanted to walk over to the stranger, introduce himself, explain the situation, and get some dates and times. He wanted to push this forward and damn well make it happen. There was no good reason to delay, not that he could see, and the friend was obviously willing to help out.

But Gage wasn't going to get stronger if people kept diving in and making decisions for him, and if he was going to walk again, he'd need all the strength he could find. So Paul said, "Let me know when you've got something figured out. Or you can contact the prosthetist directly if you'd prefer—you have their number?"

"Yeah, somewhere." Gage took a deep breath, then nodded. "Okay. Yeah. I'll figure something out."

He rolled a few feet toward the door before half-turning back and saying. "Sorry. I kind of apologized earlier, but—I should make it clearer. I should do it right." Another deep breath, then, "Sorry for being—I mean, I'm a dick. I'm going to keep being a dick. But I crossed lines, and it wasn't stuff I actually believe; I was just—being even more of a dick than usual. I'm sorry."

Wow. Paul kind of wished he'd had his phone out to record the moment. "Thanks for saying so. You're going through a tough time—I understand that it doesn't always bring out the best in people."

Gage frowned as if he wasn't satisfied with that, but he didn't seem to be able to put his concern into words and Paul certainly couldn't imagine how to help him. He just stood there as Gage nodded goodbye, turned, and wheeled toward his friend.

"Why's he still wearing gloves?" Paul heard the friend demand, but then the two of them were outside and the door snicked shut behind them.

Paul was left behind, and in the peculiar state of *feeling* left behind. Wondering what the other two were talking about, and wishing he was part of the conversation.

Paul was lonely.

Strange to realize it, but almost certainly true. All his friends, other than those at the clinic, were Bobby's friends. With the recent freezeout, Paul hadn't had Bobby *or* any friends to talk to. Not guy friends.

So there was nothing weird about a temporary sense of loss, seeing two guys who got along with each other. Nothing special about Sean Gage, that was for sure.

It was nice to help people, sure. That was why Paul had chosen the job he had. And Gage's apology had seemed sincere, but that didn't make him a good guy. By his own admission, he was a dick. His apology had raised him from the absolute pit of being aggressively racist to the still-pretty-sad level of being sullen and self-pitying. He wasn't someone to admire. Not someone to want to spend time with.

"Did he just say he was sorry?" Anna hissed at him as he started across the room to his next patient.

"Yeah," Paul said. "Think he meant it?"

"Wait and see what he's like next time."

That was a good strategy. Wait for next time, and don't bother thinking about it before then.

Because Paul had bigger issues to worry about. Why bother himself with trying to sort out whether a patient had improved his attitude when he really needed to be trying to figure out whether he had a relationship left?

"Shelly," he said with a smile, and his patient carefully eased herself to her feet. "How are you today?"

"I've been better."

"Well. Let's see what we can do to help you out."

Let's keep our attention on our jobs. Because everything else is too complicated to deal with.

Chapter Six

In his dreams, Sean still had his legs. He moved easily through a world that had been designed with his body in mind, and nobody stared at him or worried about him or pitied him. Sometimes in his dreams he could fly, too, or swim underwater without needing to breathe, but when he woke up it was the miracle of walking that he clung to, fighting to believe in it for as long as he could before reality took over.

It was always a bitter surprise for him, every damn morning, to swing his legs over the side of the bed and realize that it was easy to do it because his feet weren't caught in the blankets. They never would be again.

"What did they do with my legs, do you think?" he asked on Tuesday morning as he sat at Luke's kitchen table and buttered toast. The two of them were going to look at one more place together right after breakfast, and then—then it really wasn't clear. Luke's boyfriend was coming back that afternoon, which meant Sean was supposed to be gone. But maybe not, if Sean promised to not be a dick to the boyfriend? That part had been a bit confused, and he probably needed to get it sorted out, just so he knew what his choices were. But he had something else on his mind right then. "Did they just throw them out?"

"I don't know." Lucas didn't seem too interested, either. "Get the butter right to the edges, asshole. I just about cut my mouth open on the crusts yesterday."

"I'm not your toast-bitch." It was a measured response. Practically mild, really. If Sean had been at home, he would have swept the plate onto the floor and rolled over it while his mother cried. But who was he kidding? If he'd been at home, he never would have been asked to butter toast in the first place.

Strange, then, that Sean wasn't exactly eager to remove himself from Luke's place and return to his mother's. Strange that the thought of being treated like a king didn't appeal. But he supposed there wasn't that much difference between being treated like a king and treated like a baby, so maybe he was right to think it was time for a change.

Unfortunately, none of the apartments they'd looked at were available for at least two weeks, and, really, none of them had felt all that home-y. They'd been designed for the elderly, more than for someone his age, and even if they were technically accessible, they hadn't felt right. Or maybe it was just that Sean had never lived alone, and he really wasn't sure he wanted to start now.

"They probably burned them," Luke said, and initially Sean thought he was talking about the eggs.

Then he caught on. "My legs?"

"I think that's what they do with medical waste. And—I mean, you didn't have a burial for them or anything, right? They didn't give them back to you. They probably got them burned."

Sean didn't like thinking about that. He'd never been a great athlete, but his legs had been strong enough, and they'd been part of him, and thinking of them burning, being charred away to ash—"This conversation is no way to start the fucking day."

"You're the one who asked the question. And—I don't know, what would be better? If they were buried? With worms and everything?"

"It'd be better if they were attached to my fucking body!"

Luke didn't respond to that, just carried the pan of eggs over from the stove and scooped half of them onto Sean's plate. He took two slices of toast off Sean's carefully buttered pile and then sat down.

"You ready to be polite to Mark?" Lucas asked.

Of course he knew to ask. Because Luke had gotten too damn big for his britches at some point over the last few years, too smart and wise and full of foresight or understanding or some other annoying quality. He knew what Sean was worrying about, and dove straight in to talking about it. Asshole.

"I don't really know him."

"That's kind of the point. Seriously, Sean, most people, if they don't know someone? Being polite to them is the default. They aren't rude until people give them a reason to be."

Sean took a bite of eggs instead of replying.

Luke didn't seem to need his input. "How did we somehow grow up thinking the opposite? That we only had to be polite to people we *knew*?"

"You're not polite to me, asshole, and you know me. You're totally rude."

"Yeah," Luke said. He sounded outraged by the realization. "Where the hell did *that* layer come from? Rude to strangers, rude to friends, polite to—who the fuck are we polite to?"

"People we respect. People who've *earned* it."

"Like who?"

That was a tough one. Sean filled his mouth with food to give himself a moment to think. "My mom?"

"*I'm* polite to your mom. You're not. Seriously, Sean, is there *anyone* you're not a complete dick to?"

Sean thought about it. "Mrs. Slater?"

"In seventh grade?"

"She was nice. And smart."

"That's the best you can do? One person, a decade ago?"

No, he could do better than that. Couldn't he? "My physio."

"You made him wear gloves! You acted like a total racist prick. No, he absolutely does *not* count."

"I apologized! We had a civilized conversation. I was polite." At least, he *thought* he had been. Hadn't he? "Mistakes were made, early on, but I turned that right around. We're good, now."

"And if I asked him, he'd agree? He'd say you were a polite, respectful young man?"

"Well, he wouldn't use those words. He's not my grandma. But he'd say...." God, what *would* he say? "He'd say I'm a racist asshole, probably."

"So... we're back to just Mrs. Slater?"

"Maybe."

"You think that's a good situation?"

"Why the fuck are we talking about me all the time? You started this off with 'we', but it turned into 'you' pretty fucking fast, didn't it?"

Lucas leaned back in his chair and held a hand up in front of him. "People who think I'm not an asshole:" he announced, and started ticking fingers off as he continued. "Dr. Clark, my therapist in prison. Father Terry. Darren, my parole officer. Alex. Elise. Mark. Your brother and two sisters. And, of course, yo momma." He smiled peacefully. "So... yeah. I think it's more 'you' than 'we'. Asshole."

"You're a smug son of a bitch, you know that?"

"You might think so, but I just gave you a pretty long list of people who think I'm a polite, respectful young man."

"Well," a new voice said from the hallway, "I was on that list, and I think you're pretty damn smug."

It felt almost indecent, watching the expression on Luke's face change. He'd been fine, before. Happy, or at least content. But he heard the voice— the boyfriend, fucking obviously—and it was like a normal lightbulb suddenly turning into a spotlight. Luke stayed in his chair, didn't even lean forward or put his fork down, but his entire focus had shifted. He was like a hunting dog pointing at game. Then there was movement behind Sean as someone came into the room and Lucas smiled and Sean felt it deep in his chest.

Luke used to smile at Sean that way, and Sean hadn't known what it meant. Hadn't known what to do with it. Hadn't known what a fucking gift it had been.

Now, the blessing was for someone else, and Sean wanted to—damn it. He wanted to *stand up* and punch the son-of-a-bitch in the face. Knee him in the gut. Throw him out the door and down the steps.

"You're back early," Lucas was saying.

"I drove all night."

"Good." Lucas finally stood, but he still didn't rush. "I told you Sean had been staying here, helping with the floor."

"The floor?"

"Did you not even notice it? Look down. It's good, right?"

"I don't want to look at the floor. I want to look at you."

"Okay!" Sean said. He guessed breakfast was over. "I'm gonna go—get cleaned up, or something. I don't know." He should probably leave the house—the guest room wasn't right next to the master bedroom, thank god, but he had the feeling this reunion was going to be extended in duration and probably spreading over a fair bit of real estate. Yeah, he needed to get the hell out. "I can call my mom and see if she can take me to the apartment this morning." What else? "I can wait for her outside." And possibly down the block.

"What?" Luke seemed to be dragging himself out of the haze of sappiness. "No, Sean, it's fine. You guys haven't really met, right? Not for real? Sean, this is Mark. Mark, Sean."

"It's nice to meet you," Mark said, stepping around and holding his hand out to be shaken.

They'd met before, of course. Not by name, maybe, but—well. It seemed like Mark and Luke wanted to ignore it, and Sean sure didn't have any reason to bring up the past. So he shook Mark's hand without saying anything.

Mark's smile in return seemed genuine. It honestly didn't seem like he was sending a 'get out of my house so I can get dirty with my man' message, but that was obviously just because he had good manners. The kind Luke thought Sean should be working on. But if someone ever looked at Sean the way Luke looked at Mark, then being polite would be pretty much the last thing on Sean's mind. That meant Mark was probably just faking it.

Except he still seemed sincere when he said, "I was happy to hear you were staying here. Lucas has really wanted you to come over. He did a great job on the ramp, didn't he?"

"Yeah." Yeah, he had. The ramp was sturdy and secure and it had been sitting there unused for months because Sean had been too wrapped up in his own crap to drop by and say hello to his oldest friend. One more piece of evidence to prove what an asshole Sean was. As if anyone in the universe actually needed more proof of the point. "Yeah, it's been great staying here. But you guys want to catch up. I can give my mom a call—"

"Sean." Luke's voice wasn't loud, but it had a tone that made it hard to ignore. It was the 'shut up and stop being an idiot' voice.

So Sean shut up. He couldn't do much about the 'being an idiot' part.

"He's been gone four days. That's all. He wasn't away at war or something. And we talked on the phone, and texted. There's not that much catching up to do."

"Yeah, but—" What was the polite way to mention welcome-back-sex? "Fuck. You've got me worrying about how to be polite!"

"Really?" Luke asked. "Dropping the f-bomb in front of an ex-priest is what you do when you're trying to be polite?"

"Really?" Mark said. He looked amused. "You think *you're* going to guilt him about that?"

"Shut up." Lucas grinned. "You're wrecking my bluff."

"Wait." Sean rolled back a few feet so he could look at both of them together. And as soon as he'd started moving, they shifted, all casual and easy, so they were both perching on the edge of the table, facing him. Just a little leaning, a little sitting, just happen to be right next to each other… just happen to have their thighs pressed together, their shoulders tight, their hands brushing.

Sean didn't need to see that. "I'm out of ways to say it, and I don't want to think about details of how you'll do it, but I really assume you two want to head for bed. Nothing I need to be here for. So I'm going to bail."

"Actually, I'm here and gone," Mark said. "Terry's waiting for me in the car; we've got a meeting at the church in twenty minutes. I just came in to say hi and pick up some papers."

Luke frowned, then shrugged and turned his attention to Sean. "As much as you don't want to hear us messing around, *double that* and you'll get how much I don't want to mess around with a damn priest waiting in the car outside."

"I thought priests were your thing." Sean wished he could take the words back even before he'd finished saying them—what the hell kind of conversation was he having, here in front of a virtual stranger?—but neither Luke nor Mark seemed too worried.

"Just one priest," Luke said, and there was the smile again, the one that should have seemed sappy but somehow didn't.

"Walk me to the door," Mark suggested.

"I'll get my stuff ready," Sean said. He didn't care if the other two had some plan to find a bit of privacy, or if they had enough self-control that they didn't need it, or anything else about *them*. Because he suddenly, desperately needed some privacy for himself.

So he jerked his chair forward and wheeled out of the room, not sure if the other two were still talking or not. He made it to the small guest room, got the door shut behind himself, then sagged forward, catching his head in his hands.

They were so in love. They had so much. Lucas Cain, Sean's best friend, Sean's—whatever the hell he had been—was in love with someone else. Maybe Sean had known it in theory, before, but seeing it with his own eyes?

It was just one more thing Sean had lost.

No. It was one more thing Sean had thrown away, one more thing he'd destroyed with his recklessness, his thoughtlessness, his stupidity. A year ago, Sean had been walking around on his own two legs and looking forward to Lucas getting out of prison and back where he belonged. If Sean had been someone different, if he'd been able to pull his head out of his ass and stand up to ignorance and fear, he could have been with Luke now. Their friendship had always had that layer of whatever the hell it had been—it wouldn't have been hard to shift it into something more. But Sean had been a dick instead. He'd listened to idiots, cared more about what they thought than about what he felt, and now he had no one to blame but himself for the emptiness in his life.

And there wasn't a damn thing he could do to change things. His legs were gone. His chance to be something more with Lucas was gone. Everything was fucking *gone*.

He wanted to scream, to roar, to smash every goddamn thing in the house, including his own traitorous body. All the good feelings of the past few days seemed to have been driven out of him, leaving behind only anger and bitterness and despair.

He didn't want to go look at an apartment. He didn't want to move on with his life or learn to use fucking prosthetic legs that were never going to be more than an embarrassment. He wanted—he wanted—

It didn't fucking matter what he wanted, because he couldn't have it.

"Sean." Luke's voice, strangely cautious, from the other side of the closed bedroom door. Had Sean made some noise? Had he betrayed himself somehow? Why the hell did Luke sound like he was being careful? "You ready to go?"

Sean needed to pull himself together. He needed to get his shit packed up, get the hell out of the house, and save what was left of his pride. Before all that, he needed to fucking *speak*, because Luke was knocking, now, and his voice was a little louder. "Sean. You good?"

He meant to laugh. The absurdity of the question, the sincerity in Luke's voice—it was funny, and Sean should laugh at it. But when he opened his mouth and a sound came out, it wasn't a laugh. It wasn't even close.

So he needed to close his mouth and stop making the strange, frightening, sobbing wail, but somehow he couldn't. He gasped for breath and it actually made a *worse* noise, and then he exhaled and the sobbing was back. He doubled over, trying to choke the sound back, but that didn't work, and then there was a warm, strong grip on his shoulder, a face pressing next to his, and Luke murmuring "Ah, Sean. Fuck, Sean, I'm sorry. We'll make it okay, Sean. We'll figure it out."

Lies, of course, and the kindness behind them made it all worse. Lucas Cain, the man who'd found his freedom by refusing to tell anything but the truth about himself, was back to lying, and it was all because of Sean. Sean was dragging Luke down, just like he'd dragged down his family.

"It can't be okay," Sean managed, although he wasn't sure Luke would be able to understand the words, not when Sean was sob-howling them into his own lap.

"We'll figure it out," Luke repeated. "We'll make it better."

Lies. And Sean should have had the strength to say so, to wheel himself the hell out of the house and straight out into traffic or off a bridge. Instead, he stayed there and cried, sobs wracking his body, tears and snot soaking his pants.

His life was over. He had no hope for a future. He'd wasted every good thing he'd ever had. Luke might say things would get better, but Luke was wrong. And Sean couldn't lie to himself about it any longer.

Chapter Seven

The condo was dark when Paul pushed the door open. Nothing unusual in that—Bobby had always worked long hours, and in the last few days of deep freeze he'd taken that to a new extreme. But when Paul tapped the control plate for the lights and nothing happened, *that* was a little strange.

"Siri," he said. "Turn the lights on."

Still nothing. He'd just ridden the elevator up from the parking garage, and the communal hallway behind him was bright. The building clearly still had power. Some sort of blackout localized just to one unit? Was that possible?

His confusion shifted to alarm when he heard the rustle of fabric from somewhere in the darkness in front of him. He had his weight shifted and was about to jump backward when there was a flare of light, just enough to illuminate Bobby's face as he held the lighter to a candle wick.

"Welcome home," Bobby said, then lit another candle, and another. "I missed you."

Paul stared, trying to adjust himself to the new situation, as Bobby circled the room, lighting one candle after another.

"Wow," Paul finally said. He shrugged his messenger bag off his shoulder and tossed his mitts and hat onto the foyer table. He unzipped his coat and stepped further into the condo, then caught himself. Boots off. Tradition demanded it, and so did Bobby. Interesting how Bobby clung most fiercely to the traditions that served his own interests, but was more than willing to be flexible on others.

Shit. Not good to be walking into whatever this was with a bad attitude. So Paul took a few deep breaths as he shrugged out of his coat and tugged off his boots, then put them away tidily in the closet. He retrieved his gloves and hat and put them away as well, and when he was done, Bobby was *still* lighting candles.

"You went to a lot of trouble," Paul said as he stepped down the two stairs that led to the sunken living room. But that was too neutral. "This is beautiful."

"Thank you." Bobby kept lighting wicks, but he nodded his head toward the sofa table and said, "Will you pour the wine?"

That sounded like a great idea. Paul opened the bottle of red while Bobby found a whole new bank of candles awaiting his lighter. Paul tried not to wonder about the building's fire detection system and whether there was about to be an issue. He tried not to wonder about much, really—this was Bobby's show, and there was no point trying to jump ahead of where Bobby wanted things to be.

"Dinner's in the oven," Bobby said, finally setting the lighter down and accepting the glass of wine Paul offered him. "Roast chicken. Your favorite. It's been in there for over an hour, so it should be almost ready."

Was roast chicken Paul's favorite? He didn't think he'd have said so, but, again, Bobby was making an effort and Paul should stop being bitchy about the details. Except—"I don't smell anything. Have you checked on it? Sometimes that oven is—"

"The chicken's fine," Bobby said. He held up his glass. "To us. Let's remember our past, celebrate our present, and look forward to our future."

And there was definitely something wrong with Paul, because he had to bite back an argument to *that*, even. He forced himself to raise his glass and sip and smile and behave like the happy recipient of a romantic gesture. "This is really nice. I'm glad—you know. I'm sorry you were angry about—"

Bobby held up his hand. "We can remember the past without rehashing it, I think?"

Well. Yeah. Sure, they could. "Maybe focus on celebrating the present, then?" Paul said. "How was your day? Did you ever hear back from—"

"Let's not talk about business," Bobby said.

Yeah, fine. Paul fixed a neutral smile on his face. Bobby clearly had a script for the evening, and Paul was tired of trying to guess what it might be. He was also pretty damn sure that if there was chicken roasting in the kitchen, they'd be smelling it by now. Whatever. At least he'd be saved from the trouble of having to pretend to be enthusiastic about it.

"Let's talk about the future," Bobby continued. He lifted the wine glass from Paul's hand, which was bullshit right off the top because Paul knew he was going to need as much alcohol as possible for whatever was coming next. But Bobby charged on, carefully setting the glasses on the sofa table before turning his attention back to Paul.

And then, god help them all, he fell to one knee.

"Bobby—" Paul started, but Bobby held up his hands again.

Fine. Let it happen.

"Sukhpal Singh Gill," Bobby said. "We've been together for a long time and we're a good team. We complement each other, and we can build a good life together. It's time for us to take the next step in our relationship. Paul—will you marry me?"

And the bastard had the jewelry box out again.

It really was far too much. "Bobby," Paul said. But now that Bobby wasn't interrupting him, he found himself unsure of what to say. "We need to actually *talk*," he managed. "We still haven't done that. Please—" *Please stop proposing, you jackass—* "Please come and sit down. Let's have some dinner—" *which means we're ordering in, because there's no way there's chicken roasting in this condo right now—* "and talk this all through."

"What is there to talk through?"

"Seriously? I mean—why do you want to get married?" It was a bit awkward to be having this conversation while Bobby was kneeling on the floor, but it wasn't like Paul could *make* the man stand up. "What is missing from our lives now that would be added if we got married?"

"Continuity," Bobby said. "Security. The—you've been restless. *You* want a change! And we could have kids. There will be some extra challenges to that anyway—it only makes sense for us to eliminate those we can. We may be two men, but at least we can be two *married* men. The kids will find that comforting."

"You want us to get married for the sake of children we don't have? And, honestly, Bobby, I'm not sure I *want* kids. I mean, maybe someday, but right now? We're both pretty busy, and the benefit of not having a woman involved is that there's no biological clock, right? We don't have to rush into anything."

"Paul. A woman is going to have to be *involved*. We're talking babies, not puppies."

"Okay, but we don't know who the woman is. It could be anyone. Are you thinking adoption? Or surrogate?"

"Surrogate, I think."

"And which of us would donate the sperm?"

"Well—we could have more than one kid, I guess. But you just said you aren't actually sure you *want* kids, and I'm absolutely sure *I* do, so it would make sense for me to be the biological father, wouldn't it?"

"And you'd take the paternity leave and make sure the baby was taken care of until it's old enough for daycare?"

"Me? But—I mean, we'd really struggle to make ends meet if we were relying just on *your* income. If one of us needs to take time off, it makes sense for it to be the one who makes less."

Of course it did. Paul sighed. "Could you at least stand up while we talk about this?"

"Why don't you just take the ring and we can work out the details later?"

"Because I don't think I want to marry you!"

Bobby's eyes widened. He seemed honestly surprised, or maybe even shocked. "What do you mean?"

"You don't listen to me!"

Bobby finally stood up, and as soon as he did Paul wished he'd crouch back down again. This had been easier when they weren't standing face-to-face. "How do I not listen?" Bobby asked.

"Are you kidding me? I mean—"

"I listen to you all the time! I listen to you talk about your work, and your family, and the books you read and what your friends are doing. I listen to all of that."

Was that true? Maybe, yeah. So what was Paul actually trying to say? "You don't listen to things that are important. You don't *respect* me. You don't care about my opinions, not unless it's something you can't be bothered to have an opinion about yourself. You don't care about my feelings, not unless they're exactly the same as yours. As soon as I feel something different, you just bulldoze over me. I feel like—"

Bobby raised his hands.

"Put your fucking hands down. I'm not finished! I feel like you've bought into that bullshit idea that there has to be a dominant person and a submissive person in a relationship—and maybe I bought into it to. You think I'm the woman—not a *real* woman, but some stupid stereotype from the fifties that probably wasn't even true back then, like you're the one in charge and I'm the helper. But fuck that, Bobby! I can help you, yeah, but you should be helping me, too!"

Paul stopped for breath, and this time Bobby didn't try to say anything. Which was too bad, because shouting down another interruption would have at least given Paul something to say, something more constructive than just looping back to the start and saying all the same stuff over again.

"So, no," he managed. "I don't want to marry you. Not now, not when we're not—I mean, I think you're right. I *have* been kind of restless and dissatisfied with the relationship. But the solution isn't *getting married*." He reached for his glass and lifted it for a gulp, his hand shaking enough that he had to pay attention, but not enough that he sloshed red wine onto the hardwood.

"If getting married isn't the solution, what is?" Bobby asked. His voice was carefully neutral.

Paul shook his head. The anger was gone, and he felt cold without it. "I don't know. I guess it depends how much you're—*we're*—willing to change. How much work we want to put into things."

"I'm not sure why work is necessary. From my perspective, things have been going pretty well."

Oh, good. The anger was back. "Maybe you should try seeing things from *my* perspective, then! Because I've just *told* you things aren't going well for me. I've just said all the words. If you still can't hear them, then— I don't know. I guess maybe you really *can't*. And that means *we* can't. We can't make things better if you can't even hear what the problems are."

"This is ridiculous." Bobby lifted his own glass of wine, then set it down without drinking. "No. I've had enough. Your mother said you just needed some time, so I gave you time, and now you're—"

"My *mother* said? You—you talk to my mother, and listen to her advice, but you can't actually listen to *me*? Well, sorry, Bobby, but my mom's a woman and she's pretty happy with my dad as far as I can see, so I don't think she's really available to marry you. Which means her opinions on this aren't the ones that matter."

"Do you blame me for trying to get advice from someone who's able to discuss the issue in a calm and rational way?"

"I think we're done." The words felt so final. *Too* final, and a big part of Paul wanted to retract them as soon as they were out of his mouth, but another part—a part that was apparently a tiny bit bigger, or at least a tiny bit stronger—told him to let them stand.

"Done," Bobby echoed. "What does that mean?"

It was a chance to back out, and Paul almost took it. He took a deep breath, and it was the absence of smell that actually gave him courage. He wasn't going to spend the rest of his life pretending that chicken was roasting when it wasn't. "I think we should break up."

"You want to break up because I asked you to marry me? What kind of sense does that make?"

"I want to break up because—because you still have no idea what I'm upset about. Because instead of listening to me when I try to explain, you're trying to tell me I'm wrong to *be* upset." He took a gulp of his wine. "And because I don't think we're going to be able to make it better."

"You want to pull the plug, just like that?" Bobby shook his head. "No. After all this time together, after the commitments we've already made, you owe me more than that. You owe *us* more than that."

Another chug of wine emptied the glass. Paul hesitated for a moment— he needed to keep a clear head, maybe even needed to stay sober enough to drive—but then gave in to temptation and filled his glass again. "What are you suggesting?"

"You just need a break." Calm, affectionate Bobby was back. The one who thought Paul was an idiot to be taken care of. "A vacation, maybe? What's the next spot on your to-visit list? Or a repeat visit to an old favorite—that place on Santorini?"

Paul didn't want to ask whether Bobby was suggesting a solo trip or whether he was thinking of a romantic couple's vacation. He didn't want to be having this conversation at all. "I've got work. This isn't a good time to be away."

"Your work is—"

"It's important to me. It's non-negotiable." Really, all of this should be non-negotiable. But Bobby wasn't completely wrong. They'd been together a long time, and they'd made commitments to each other. Paul said, "I can go stay with Jas for a bit. Give us both a chance to think things over. We could talk again next week, maybe?"

"This all seems unnecessary."

"I guess that depends how you define necessity." And Paul didn't have a lot to add to that. "I'm going to go call Jas and get packed."

"Maybe you should be the one to stay here," Bobby said. "I could get a hotel room for a few nights."

It might have been sweet, if Paul hadn't known Bobby as well as he did. But Bobby was crafty. If Bobby was the one to leave, then Bobby would be the one to decide when to return. He'd already shortened Paul's suggested week down to a few nights, and of course he might need to come back to pick up his razor, or a suit he hadn't thought he'd want, and once he was there, wouldn't it be silly for him to leave again? Wasn't this whole thing silly, really?

No way.

"I'd like to spend some time with Jas anyway. And she's got space." Space, and lots of wine.

Bobby didn't seem impressed, but that wasn't something Paul was going to let himself worry about. He headed for the bedroom, phone to his ear, wine in hand, and by the time the glass was empty his suitcases were full and he had Jas's promise to have dinner and more wine waiting for him. He'd packed more clothes than he needed for a week, but he had everything he *really* cared about. If things went wrong and he couldn't come back? He'd be okay with that.

He'd be okay if the whole building burned down, as long as nobody got hurt.

"You're really doing this?" Bobby asked as Paul left the bedroom and headed for the front door. Bobby was sitting in the leather wing-back chair they'd bought on a trip to Quebec City, and he had a glass of scotch in his hand. "You haven't come to your senses yet?"

"It's been ten minutes. You really think I can't hold a thought in my silly little head for that long?"

"I honestly no longer have *any idea* what you can or cannot hold in your head."

"Excellent. Thank you. That's a great parting phrase for me to keep in mind while I'm thinking everything over."

"You're playing games. You're trying to make me into a villain."

"I'm not. I'm just—I'm not trying to make you into a hero anymore, either."

"And that's what you think you want? What you *deserve*? A hero to gallop in on a white horse?"

"No, not really." Paul let the idea sit in his head for a moment, then smiled. "Really, I just want someone who doesn't think I'm a damsel in distress. Someone who wouldn't care, wouldn't keep score, about whether he's rescuing me or I'm rescuing him. Someone who can just let us rescue each other."

"Quite a metaphor," Bobby snarled.

"Yeah. I kind of like it. I think I'm going to keep working on it." And with that, Paul turned his back on Bobby, and their apartment, and their lives together, and he headed for the elevator that would take him to the snowy streets below.

Chapter Eight

"I'm okay," Sean growled. "Fuck off and leave me alone."

Luke slapped him upside the head. Not hard, really, but who the fuck cared how hard it was?

"Keep your fucking hands off me!"

"Watch your mouth around your mother, asshole."

"How about she fucks off and leaves me alone, and *you* fuck off and leave me alone, and then I can fucking swear as much as I fucking want?"

But of course they wouldn't do that. After the embarrassment of his little breakdown in front of Luke, they'd both gone into full mother-hen mode, clucking around him and fussing all the goddamn time. Of course, Luke's fussing had more obscenities and insults, but once you saw through that, the sentiment was the same. They were worried about Sean, they weren't leaving him alone, and he didn't have a damn thing to say about any of it.

Luke had dropped Sean off at his mom's after they'd seen that last apartment, but he'd come back in the evening after work and picked him up again and taken him back to the fucking love shack, where Mark had been totally welcoming and gracious and Sean had growled his way past that bullshit and into the relative peace of the guest room. That had bought him one night, but the next morning by the time he woke up his mom was already in the kitchen, drawing up what really looked like a schedule for who was going to be babysitting Sean at any given time. Fucking Mark was even in on it. Mark, who Sean barely knew, and who was a friend-stealing bastard. The whole thing was a disaster.

And now, Sean was getting slapped upside the head for trying to resist. "I'm an adult. You guys don't actually have any power over me. My *legs* got wrecked, not my fucking brain. I can make my own decisions."

"That's a good point," Mark said. Fucking Mark. Why was he even part of this conversation? Sean squinted at him, waiting for the trap to be sprung. "He *is* an adult. He *should* be able to make his own decisions."

Sean hadn't heard any indications of welcome-back sex the night before, but he assumed it had just happened quietly. It sure didn't look like anyone was going to have to worry about muffling noises tonight, not based on the daggers Luke was shooting in Mark's direction. "Yeah, he *should* be able to, but he's an idiot, and we're worried about—you know."

"Suicide?" Mark asked calmly. He turned his attention back to Sean. "You've talked about that, right? Mentioned it? Is it something you've actually considered? Like, have you made a plan or anything?"

It felt like an invasion of privacy. Sure, Sean's therapist had asked almost the same questions in just about the same way, but that hadn't been with Sean's mom and Lucas Cain listening. Still, his mom had cleaned his diapers as a baby and helped him on and off the toilet when he'd first come home without legs, and Lucas had always been more aware of what was happening in his brain than Sean himself was, so maybe it was time to just give up on the illusion of privacy for good. "They took my pills away. No guns in the house. What *could* I plan?"

"I can think of things you could have done," Mark said. "I don't think I'll share my ideas, and I admit they aren't quite as easy as pills or guns, but you're a smart guy. You could think of them yourself if you wanted to."

"Rolling in front of a truck," Sean said.

Mark nodded. "That would probably do it. Have you made any plans to do that? I don't mean just having the idea flash through your brain, I mean actually planning how to get to somewhere with traffic and all the rest of it. Have you planned anything?"

"What the fuck are you doing? Are you trying to call my bluff or something? Are you saying I'm too much of a pussy to actually go through with it?"

"No. Sorry. I'm—I'm trying to determine how serious the risk of suicide actually is. I'm not a priest anymore and I've never been a therapist, but I've had quite a bit of experience with people going through tough times, and I've had quite a bit of training—and done a lot of reading—on what to look for in terms of guarding against suicide. But I'm not your therapist. I've overstepped."

It still felt like a trap. Sean was stuck there in the kitchen with three people who all fought in different ways. His mom smothered him in love and guilt; Lucas came at him with truth and insults and affection; and Mark? What the hell was Mark's approach? Was he trying to *respect* Sean into submission?

"His therapist was the one who told us to take his pills away," Sean's mom interjected. "He said he didn't think there was grounds for hospitalizing Sean, but we should still take precautions."

"Did he mention round-the-clock supervision?" Mark asked. "Not that I think it's a bad idea, at least short term, but was that actually part of his recommendation?"

"No," Sean's mom said. She sounded reluctant, like she wished the doctor had given her stronger orders. That way she could have been *more* of a fucking martyr and had even *more* of Sean's guilt to use as ammunition.

"I never made a plan," Sean said. His voice sounded a bit too loud. Or maybe it was just that everyone else was suddenly silent. "I want—I want my fucking legs back. I want my life back. And it's fucking hard to know that's never going to happen. But I don't want to die. Not—not right now."

"But sometimes you do?" Mark suggested mildly. "Not often, and not for long, but little bits?"

Sean wasn't sure he wanted to be precise about exactly how often the *little bits* happened, so he just shrugged a sort of neutral agreement. His mother was crying again, of course. But Luke's hand found Sean's shoulder and squeezed, and that was all right. Luke was a lot easier to take when he was keeping his damn mouth shut.

"I think the goal, then," Mark continued, "Is to make sure you don't do something irreversible during any of those little bits of time. Does that make sense? Overall, you want to be alive. And everyone in this room wants you to get what you want. We're happy to spend time with you so we're around to help out. In case one of those bad moments happens at some time when you might actually do something about it."

"It's a mortal sin," Sean's mother said through her tears. "You'd go straight to hell!"

Well, *that* wasn't one of Sean's biggest concerns. "So I should stop arguing about the schedule?" he asked.

"Yeah," Lucas agreed. "And you should smarten up about other stuff, too."

"Like what?"

"Like your mom says the people making your fake legs called—they're pissed that you missed your appointment. And like you said—you're not a fucking kid, and you don't have brain damage. There's no reason you couldn't remember that, and no reason you couldn't tell one of us you needed a ride. *And* you need fucking wheels so you can drive yourself places. You've been collecting disability and living for free, so you've got some money. Let's go get some piece of shit, fix it up, put the hand controls in it and get you back on the road. If you want us to treat you like an adult, fucking act like one. Let's get shit done."

"You've got your own job to worry about. Your own life."

"Boo hoo, you big pussy. Since when does one of us not have time to work on someone's car?"

One of us. The group had been larger, before. Before Lucas went away and came back different. Before the cracks started to show in the friendships that had once seemed rock solid. Tinker and Mikey and Luke and Sean, hanging out with Scotty at his dad's garage—how many hours had they spent there? But Luke had been the only one to stick around once things went bad for Sean.

"Just you and me?" he asked.

"I've actually been wanting to learn more about cars," Mark put in. "I can't always rely on Luke to fix mine for me. It feels like a slight to my manhood. I'm not sure I'd be much use, but I could be another set of hands."

"Are you sure he should be driving again?" Sean's mom asked. She was talking to Lucas, not directly to Sean. "That's what got him in this mess in the first place."

"We're both pretty crappy at anything beyond the basics with cars," Luke reassured her. "It's gonna take us a hell of a long time to put hand controls in. It's not like he's going to be out on the roads anytime soon."

"Speak for yourself," Sean growled at him.

"We're gonna have to build you a ramp just to let you see the fucking engine," Luke said. "Oh, no, wait! You can roll around on the dolly underneath, do all that work. I'll go high, you'll go low. It'll work."

Sean didn't really have the strength to argue about it. But then Luke tossed a bundle of papers onto the table beside Sean's head and added, "And we should do one of these. There aren't enough guys for two real sledge hockey teams in town, so guys with working legs play, too. There's a beginners session on Thursday—you can check with your physio guy when you see him tomorrow and make sure it's okay, but I can't see why it wouldn't be. So we can start playing hockey, see how it goes."

"Hockey." He and Lucas and the others had always made fun of the assholes who came to the bar after their hockey games. A collection of small-town has-beens and never-weres, chasing after a frozen chunk of rubber and trying to impress chicks and each other. Such a fucking stereotype. And now Luke thought Sean was going to start playing? Now, with no legs?

"There's basketball, too," Luke said. "But it looks like those guys have special chairs—that'd be expensive. The hockey guys supply the sledge, and we can dig up some helmets and pads somewhere without much trouble. Or there's rugby, but it looks fucking brutal, and I swear the chairs for it were designed by the same guys who made the cars for Mad Max. You're probably going to suck just as bad at wheelchair sports as you did at regular sports, so there's no point spending a lot of money on special equipment."

"There's no point to any of it," Sean objected.

"Fuck off." Luke's retort wasn't exactly sophisticated, but it seemed sincere. "You know things suck now, but you won't do anything to make things better? You'd rather just sit around and be a fucking slug for the rest of your life?"

"Sports are bullshit! We've always said sports are bullshit!"

"We've always been idiots. Maybe it's time we changed a little, huh? I mean, stop pretending everything was good *before* the accident. It wasn't losing your legs that screwed up your life; you were screwed up even before. So acting like we had everything figured out back then and using what we used to think as an argument for how we should think now? That's stupid. You know it."

Luke waited for a response Sean didn't have, then snorted. "Hell, maybe sports *will* still be bullshit. I don't know. But getting your new legs isn't bullshit, and you're afraid to try doing that, too. So this isn't about you being too *good* for my ideas. It's about you being too *scared*."

"Fuck you," Sean said, but his heart wasn't in it.

"What's the first obstacle?" Mark asked. His voice was gentle; he made it feel like he was on Sean's side. Manipulative fucker.

"No legs," Sean said. Automatic. Easy. That could be his answer to every question.

Except Mark nodded as if he thought Sean had said something useful. "Okay. Good. So our first step should be to get you some legs." He turned to Sean's mom. "Did the prosthetist leave contact information? And do we know how long the visit will take? I'm supposed to go down to the city next Monday—I expect that'll be too soon for them to make an appointment, but if not, I'd be happy to drop you off and pick you up."

Drop off and pick up. He wouldn't stay there like Sean's mom would, making anxious noises and crying all over the place. "I don't think they're going to drop everything to fit me into their schedule. I think, actually... they may have kind of kicked me off their list."

"Who told you that?" Sean's mom demanded. She sounded like she was ready to go to war for her baby, at least if *go to war* was interpreted as shrieking at someone.

"My physiotherapist."

"The hot one?" Lucas asked.

Sean and Mark both turned to look at him. He just shrugged. "He's nice to look at. That's all I'm saying."

"Don't look at my physiotherapist." Sean felt like he should say more. Maybe a good scolding about valuing and protecting what Luke and Mark had together?

But then Mark said, "Maybe I should drive you to your next physio appointment," and Luke nodded and said, "We could both go. He's worth the trip," and Sean decided he probably didn't want to get involved in that dynamic.

"You can give him a call," Mark suggested. "Ask him to speak to the prosthetist. I'm sure they're used to some uncertainty from their clients."

"I'll call them myself," Sean said. He wasn't sure why, but he didn't want the physiotherapist involved in this. Didn't want there to be one more person dragged into cleaning up his mistakes.

"Also," Luke said, "Elise says she's looking for part-time help at the shelter. Since I started working only full-time instead of being there every waking minute, she says she's getting a backlog of jobs. A lot of them need legs, but some don't. You could scrub feed buckets, right? Measure food? Take inventory? You can count to ten? Maybe twenty? Oh, shit, with no toes twenty might be too high. We could get you an abacus or something."

"You're not funny, you know. And, seriously… how many jobs can there be that don't take legs?"

"I spend at least an hour a day scrubbing buckets. She's *obsessed* with keeping things clean, because a lot of the animals are sick. She won't let you measure the medicine until she trusts you, but there's lots of food to slice up—wild animals eat some weird shit—and you could do that, too. Probably other stuff, once you're out there and we start looking around."

It was happening too quickly. Fake legs, sports, a fucking *job*… had Sean actually agreed to any of this? What had happened to him making his own decisions? Hadn't that been Luke's shtick in the first place? Hadn't *he* been the one to first point out that it was Sean's legs, not his brain that had been damaged?

"Jesus," Sean muttered. Then he took a deep breath. Fine. He couldn't do all this. It was all absolutely going to go to hell. But it was pretty damn clear that he wasn't going to get a drop of peace until he at least tried a few things. "I'll call the physio, see what he can set up. And—fuck, I don't know, I guess I can try hockey. But the job?"

Luke snorted. "You were a lazy bastard even before you got hurt. But it's part time. You can drive out with me in the morning, act like a sucky princess for a couple hours, and I can drive you back in at lunchtime. Deal?"

No. No fucking deal. No way. Except for some reason Sean shrugged and said, "One day. Just to see. And I don't want to deal with any of your goddamn animals. They're dangerous."

"They're injured," Luke said. "But—yeah. They can still be dangerous. Just because they're hurt, it doesn't mean their natures are changed."

And then he gave Sean a wise smile, like he thought he was being profound or something. "Fuck off," Sean grumbled. But he didn't make any other complaints.

Chapter Nine

Life was easier, living with Jas. Her townhouse was in the north end of Brampton, so Paul's commute time was cut in half, but there was more to it than that. If Paul made it home earlier than his sister and cooked dinner, or even ordered in, his actions were greeted with genuine appreciation. When Jas ate what he'd cooked, he didn't feel as if he was being tested, as if she were the judge on some reality show who'd tell him whether he'd met the standard. And when she made it home before him, she'd start dinner and be happy to share the chores when he arrived, or else keep cooking while he poured them both a glass of wine, then perched at the breakfast bar and chatted.

"I'm going to get a cat," she'd told him on the first night he'd arrived, after they'd gone through all the details of the break up and were well into their second bottle of wine. "And honestly, that's about it. I'm happy to have you here and you'll be good company, but I don't really need another human in the house. A cat will be enough."

"You'd better not let mom and dad hear you talking like that."

She laughed. "Oh, if you're breaking up with Golden Bobby instead of marrying him? They're not going to be worrying about *my* commitment issues, not any time soon. You've bought me a year of freedom from nagging, maybe more."

Paul had been tempted to keep the news from his parents for a little longer, just to give himself a bit more of the freedom Jas was looking forward to, but his mother called him only hours after he'd left the condo. "We're very worried about you," she said in a tone that didn't suggest *worry* so much as *frustration*. "You and Bobby are good together. We just don't understand what you're looking for."

He'd had enough wine to be honest, which he'd probably regret. "I'm looking for someone I love and respect, who loves and respects me."

"You think Bobby doesn't love you?"

"I notice you left out *respect*. And, honestly, I'm not sure even the *love* part is accurate. I'm not sure he knows me well enough to love me for who I am, rather than what I represent."

She made a disgusted noise. "Sometimes in life, you need to compromise."

"And sometimes you need to stand your ground. Choosing the person I want to spend the rest of my life with? That's not a good time for compromise, Mom. It isn't."

The conversation continued for a while, but nothing new was said. Jas refilled his glass with a sympathetic grimace, so that was something. He wasn't alone. And he had wine.

There were similar calls each night as the week wore on. His father came on the phone once to warn Paul that the family wouldn't be subsidizing his lifestyle to compensate for the security he wasn't getting from Bobby, but mostly it was his mother. He knew her concern was coming from a place of love. Sure, there would have been benefits from sealing an alliance with another prominent local family, but his mother would never put status ahead of her children. She wanted him to marry Bobby because she was convinced it was what was best. And maybe that explained why she and Bobby seemed to get along so well: they were both so convinced they knew Paul better than he knew himself.

And maybe they were right. He'd trusted his mother's guidance in almost every big decision he'd ever made, and everything had worked out well. So why was he rebelling now?

Was he just being weak and shallow? Was he forgetting all the advice people were always giving about how you have to *work* at a relationship?

Had he ever really worked at his relationship with Bobby? He'd bitched about it, sure, but worked at it? Had he?

Maybe he was just a quitter.

Maybe he was doing all this really badly.

He could keep his doubts under control when he was talking to Jas and she was reassuring him that he was fine, being single was great anyway, they could *both* get cats and live happily ever after, and there were lots of fish in the sea. And Anna at work had just about thrown him a party when she heard the news. But when he wasn't getting encouragement from them?

It was harder. The doubts snuck in. And work wasn't always enough to keep him distracted, at least most of the time.

There were exceptions, though. When he walked into the waiting room to find his next patient and found Sean Gage sitting there, practically vibrating with some strange energy, there was no temptation to give in to angsty concerns about romantic mistakes. No, Paul needed to keep all his focus right there in the room.

"Mr. Gage?"

"Sean. I'm sorry about before—I really am. You should call me Sean."

No polite way to refuse, and maybe it was time for Paul to let go of that grudge anyway. "Okay, Sean. You ready to go?"

"Yeah. And—I called the fake leg place—they were really nice. I'm going down on Monday. I've got a ride set up. So—I don't know, I just thought you should know that. So you can make sure I'm ready?"

It was an entirely different person than the man Paul had met before. Not the aggressive racist, not even the withdrawn penitent of the previous appointment. Gage—Sean—seemed tentative, now, but also strangely energized.

Not unusual for people to go through mood swings as they worked through their recovery, of course. Paul just wasn't sure he should relax with this new personality, not when he might get a visit from one of the old ones at any moment.

So he nodded cautiously and said, "You're in pretty good shape for it now. When you get your stubbies, we can work with them and really fine-tune your balance."

"My what?"

Oh, shit. Of course Sean had been told about the process of learning to walk in prosthetics—Paul was pretty sure he'd talked about it himself. But clearly Sean hadn't been listening. "Let's get started—we can talk while we exercise."

Sean followed him into the backroom, but before he was even out of his chair he was asking, "What the fuck are stubbies?"

"They're short legs—basically just the sleeve that goes around your stump and a little square to act as your foot. You get used to being upright in them and your stump gets used to carrying your weight, before you add in the extra complications of joints and height. If you fall while you're wearing stubbies—*when* you fall while wearing them—you're close to the ground."

"Are you serious? How tall am I going to be?"

"Eventually, you'll be the full height you were before, if you want to be. But with the stubbies? Stand on your stumps and add a couple inches."

"I'll look like a fucking idiot."

Paul didn't respond to that, just directed Sean to begin his exercise and made a few comments about his form. After a few minutes, Sean said, "Is there any reason I shouldn't be around animals? Like, they might—be dangerous, or something? Give me a disease?"

"A disease? What kind of animals?"

"Wild animals. A wild animal rescue. It probably isn't safe for me to work somewhere like that, right?"

"Uh—disease shouldn't be any more of a risk for you than for anyone else. Your immune system hasn't been compromised. As long as they take normal precautions I assume you'd be okay. Mobility might be an issue... would you be working with the animals themselves?"

"No," Sean said. He didn't sound too impressed with Paul's answer. "How about sledge hockey? That wouldn't be safe, would it? I mean—I might get hurt or something?"

"At the community center tonight? Are you playing? I have quite a few patients in that game—I usually play myself, to get the numbers they need. It's great exercise for your upper body. You should definitely do it."

"Fuck," Sean mumbled. But there was none of the anger Paul was used to. There was even a hint of humor, possibly, the suggestion that... was Sean Gage laughing at himself? Was that possible?

Paul didn't have the courage to test his theory so he kept the focus on exercise for the rest of the session. At the end, though, as he was walking Sean to the front, Sean said, "That was a pretty tough workout. It probably wouldn't be safe—"

And Paul interrupted him with, "It's totally safe for you to play sledge hockey tonight. I'll see you there."

Sean's friend was in the waiting area and stood up when he heard Paul's words. "You play? Sean's been trying to get out of it, but I think it's going to be fun."

"You're coming early to get the orientation?" Paul asked. "You need to learn how to adjust the equipment properly, and they usually get you on the ice for at least a *bit* of a lesson before they throw you to the wolves."

"The wolves?" the friend echoed with a raised eyebrow.

"Maybe a bit of an exaggeration, but the regular players are pretty intense. They'll make allowances for new guys, but they're usually a bit tougher on the players with working legs. You get to stand up and walk away after the game, but *during* the game? They're going to make you pay for it."

The friend looked a little taken aback, but Sean, contrarian as usual, said, "It's okay, Lukey, you can handle it. I'll protect you from the big bad wheelchair athletes."

"You'd better," the friend said, and then he extended his hand toward Paul. "I'm Luke. I don't really think I can trust Sean on the protection thing—I dug up some helmets and pads for us, but maybe I need something more?"

"You'll probably need a hot bath afterward, maybe some Epsom salts. That's about all I can suggest."

"I guess I'll have to tough it out," Luke said.

He looked like he might be okay with continuing to chat, and Paul was pretty sure he could find some time—was *this* the friend Sean had said was gay?—but then Sean rolled forward, butting the side of his chair into Luke's legs. "Let's go. Mark's probably waiting for you at home, right? He'll be wondering where you are."

"He knows where we are," Luke said, but he nodded a goodbye to Paul anyway and started for the door.

As the two headed outside, Sean said, "Don't flirt with my physio."

Paul checked to be sure the waiting room was empty before taking a few big steps to the door and holding it open with his foot so he could hear, "I wasn't flirting," and then from Sean, "You were one second away from giggling and doing a fucking hair flip. I'm telling Mark."

The friend's laugh made it clear there weren't serious concerns on the Mark front, and Paul let the door swing shut.

Flirting. Right. That was a thing. Had no one tried to flirt with him the entire time he'd been with Bobby? Or had he just shut it down before it had a chance to get started?

More importantly, did he want to let it get started now?

Not with the friend of a patient, obviously, especially when the friend clearly had someone waiting for him at home. But with someone else? Maybe?

Not dating. Not nearly ready for that. Not sex, not even something totally casual.

But... flirting?

Was it time to start flirting again?

Well, that wasn't a decision he needed to make right then. It wasn't like he was going to be doing a lot of flirting at the community center that night—not if he kept away from Sean's hot friend—and his plan for the weekend involved finding a way to pick up his remaining possessions from the condo without having a big confrontation with Bobby, so there wasn't likely to be a lot of light socialization there.

Eventually, though? Sooner or later, he was going to have to give it all some thought.

He was looking forward to it.

PART TWO

Chapter Ten

Sean's world got better. Slowly, and not smoothly, but overall? Better.

Mark drove him to the city and Sean had a bit of a tantrum when saw the fucking 'stubbies' the assholes thought he was going to wear once everything was fitted, but he pulled himself together. It sounded like the lab or whatever they called it was going to be shut down for the holidays soon, so he'd have an extra couple weeks to get used to the idea before he had to deal with any of it.

And sledge hockey was fucking amazing. He'd never liked sports, before, but he'd always enjoyed getting in fights, and sledge hockey had a lot of the same elements. At least it did when *he* played it. Technically the game was supposed to allow body contact but not checking, but Sean didn't really understand what that meant, so he just went out and threw his body around and accepted the penalties when they came to him. After the first night, the organizers got smart and put Sean and Luke on opposing teams every game, so Sean could focus his aggression on someone who wasn't going to cry about it. Luke had more body weight than Sean, since his damn legs were still attached, but Sean was light and fast and totally willing to play dirty. Poor Lukey didn't know what hit him most of the time.

Christmas itself was spent at Sean's old house, with Luke along for the ride, since Mark was with his mother and she wouldn't admit that Luke even existed. And Luke had some friend, Alex, home from school and *also* not looking to spend time with family, so he tagged along. It was a weird day. Some crying from Sean's mom, of fucking course, but not too much drama other than that.

Sean was sober for his first New Year's Eve since he'd been about twelve, and he woke up on New Year's Day feeling—okay, really. A new year. He was ready for that.

He rolled out to the kitchen and thought about doing a big spread. It wasn't easy to cook from the chair—the counters and the stovetop were about chest-height for him now, so he could see what he was doing but his arms got tired. Still, he could manage it. Eggs, bacon, maybe even pancakes. He'd cut up some fruit since Mark seemed to care about shit like that. He'd be a good house guest. Roommate. Whatever the hell he was, he'd be the best one he could be.

Except—who the hell knew when the bastards were going to wake up? Their New Year's kiss had been a lot more intense than the quick pecks they usually limited themselves to when Sean was in the room, so probably they'd gotten up to—well, he wasn't going to think about what the hell they'd gotten up to later. There were some things his imagination didn't need to see. The point was, they'd probably been up later than him. Was Sean supposed to be some sort of miracle worker, able to keep food hot and fresh for an entire morning of waiting?

No. Hell, no.

Besides, wasn't the rule that you were supposed to start the year off the way you wanted it to continue? No way did Sean want his year to continue with him being a fucking maid.

So he poured himself a bowl of cereal, added the milk, and took his festive feast back to his bedroom where he got dressed in between shoveling food into his mouth. Classy as shit, that's what he was.

When the cereal was gone and he'd layered on enough clothes to look like a wheelchair-bound Michelin Man, he headed out the door.

The air was cold, but it hadn't snowed in days and the walkway and sidewalk were bare and dry. Good wheelin' weather. He didn't have a destination in mind but he worked up a light sweat, going nowhere at a pretty good clip. It wasn't too surprising when he found himself at the concrete barrier at the top of the hill, looking out over the town like he'd done so many times before.

He didn't think he'd ever been in the spot alone, though.

It was kind of nice.

But fucking cold, especially sitting still in sweaty clothes, so after a minute or two he turned the chair around and started for home.

There was a pile of trash right near the barrier—assholes were always dumping shit up here instead of paying to get it hauled away—and one of the plastic bags rustled a little. There wasn't any wind, so Sean braced himself to not be startled when whatever animal was digging through the trash jumped out at him. He didn't think the bag was big enough to hold a raccoon, and when he saw it move again he guessed there was a squirrel involved. Annoying tree rats, but Lucas had made a pet of one—Lucas could make a pet of any fucking animal he saw—and that connection was enough to have Sean wondering whether this was the same squirrel, whether it was just hanging out in the bag or whether it was trapped, whether he'd get his hand bit if he tried to help it and whether he'd have to go to the fucking doctor if he got a squirrel bite—

And then he heard the noises. Fucking—shit. That didn't sound like a squirrel. He rolled closer, bent over, and gingerly lifted the bag. The sound cut off abruptly, then started again, louder than before. Squeakier than he was used to, but with a tone he could recognize. The fucking bag was meowing.

He fumbled with the bundle and ended up pulling his mitts off to poke a hole in the plastic with his bare fingers. A tiny nose found the hole and the meowing got louder and clearer. Shit. What kind of asshole would—

But that was a question for another time. For now, he poked the hole a little wider, letting fresh air in, and then set the bag on his lap. Better to tuck it inside his jacket? Better to make sure the animals had air, or warmth? He had no fucking idea and didn't want to be responsible for that kind of decision. He just needed to get the little bastards home, and if Lucas had thought he was going to start his year with a relaxing morning in bed, Lucas was in for a fucking surprise.

⽗

It was a new year, and Paul was determined to start it right. No more taking refuge in Jas's guest room—she was still being lovely about it, of course—she might be just as far removed from the religious aspects of Sikhism as Paul was, but they'd both absorbed the culture of hospitality and generosity. She would never make a guest feel unwelcome, but the corollary of that was that guests needed to be careful not to take advantage, and Paul knew he was walking a fine line in that regard.

More than that, though? He needed to find his own place because that was the first step in starting a new life. He needed to make it clear, to himself and everyone else, that he was moving on. Staying at Jas's made the breakup feel temporary, and it wasn't.

The holidays had been the test of that.

It wasn't as if Christmas itself had any religious significance to his family. His parents usually put up a tree—well, had decorators put up a tree, in the front room with the two-story-high window that faced the street, so everyone driving by and peering past the gate could see the warm glow of the tree's lights through the glass—and there were usually some gifts underneath it. The family celebrated Christmas like it celebrated Labor Day or Diwali or Thanksgiving—the original meaning of each holiday was distant or lost altogether, but it was a good excuse for friends and family to get together and eat more than they should.

But this year, before the breakup, Paul's family had made their plans to spend the Christmas vacation in South Africa with Bobby's family, and his parents had made it clear they saw no reason to change those arrangements just because Paul was being silly.

"I don't have to go," Jas had told him. "It's going to be a pain anyway. Thirty-five hours each way, Paul. *Thirty-five hours.* And then only staying for a week? It's insane. And if you aren't there, it's not going to be any fun, either. I should stay here."

"No. You were excited for this trip. You're going to see lions, remember? And you love flying Emirates. Your own little suite… you can message the flight attendants by computer, so you don't even have to speak to anyone for the whole flight."

"I do love the little suite…"

"Yeah you do. The flight's the best part for a pod-loving misanthrope like yourself. So—go. Enjoy. I'll be fine here."

Brave words to cover the strange tightness in his gut, the worry that his family's frustration with him was turning into an actual estrangement, and the realization that without his family, without the network of friends he'd built with Bobby, he was largely alone.

He'd disappointed his family before—when he'd come out, when he'd insisted on going to school for physiotherapy instead of business, and then when he'd been stubborn enough to embark on a career in his chosen field instead of joining the family company—but he'd never felt as alone as he currently did. His parents might not have agreed with him, but they'd always supported him, in their own ways. Financially, of course, but emotionally as well. When he'd come out, he'd gotten the feeling he was just formally announcing something his parents had already known or at least strongly suspected, and while they hadn't approved of his career choices, they'd listened to his arguments and they'd eventually added a line to their verbal family resume, something about "Paul's dedication to helping others".

But dumping Bobby? Was it the final straw, just the latest in a long string of disappointments that had finally pushed them too far? Or were they unable to understand his decision because he was unable to actually give an explanation beyond "it just didn't feel right"?

His father had called, just before leaving the country, to make it clear that a son who didn't support the family business, at least via strategic marriage if not through actual labor, shouldn't expect any share of the family fortune. Paul didn't think he was actually being disowned, and was almost completely confident that if his parents left everything to Jas she'd share it with him anyway, but he was definitely going to be living on his own income.

Which was *fine.* He made good money by most standards; it wasn't his fault his family had grown used to more. Possibly it was his fault that *he'd* grown used to more, to the downtown condo and fine dining and luxury vacations. Yeah, he'd be careless with that. But no more.

It was a new year, he was a new man, and he was going to find a new home, one that was within his own budget. Which meant getting the hell out of the city. An opportunity to cut his commuting time, as well. A good thing. Not a banishment. Not an estrangement. Just a practical decision. It was fine. Just fine.

So he'd moved the last of his belongings out of the old apartment while Bobby was conveniently out of the country, then woken up bright and early on New Year's Day, driven to work, and started a tour of the town, trying to sort out neighborhoods and possible places to call home.

He was cruising down one residential street, deciding that it was a bit rattier than he was really comfortable with, when he saw someone in a wheelchair barreling down the sidewalk. At first he thought it was for exercise and was about to be impressed with the level of dedication, but as he drew closer he felt like there was too much desperation in the movement. It wasn't a controlled workout—this person was nearly frantic.

He pulled far enough ahead to get a look at the person's face, then pulled the rest of the way over and rolled down his window. "Sean? You okay?"

Sean didn't even slow down, just changed course, heading for Paul's passenger door. Paul hit the button to unlock it, but Sean gestured impatiently at the window.

"I don't know how cold they are, but probably pretty bad," he gasped as it rolled down, and then he was passing a plastic bag through the window into Paul's hands. He was clearly fighting for breath, but managed, "Take them three blocks down—little blue house on the left. 250, I think. Old silver pickup in the driveway. That's Luke's house. He can help."

"What?" Paul peeked inside the bag. "Kittens?"

"Yeah. Go on."

"Do you want a ride?"

"It'll take too long, with the chair." He shook his head, still fighting for breath. "I'll meet you there."

Paul wasn't sure he shared the sense of urgency, but he really knew nothing about kittens, or why these ones were in a plastic bag, or how the hell Sean Gage had come into contact with them. So it was probably best to just do as he was told and figure it out later.

He followed directions, pulled into the driveway, and glanced back down the street to see Sean as little more than a blob in the distance, moving forward not nearly as quickly as he'd been earlier. He'd exhausted himself, trying to get the kittens to Luke, so Paul needed to follow through with his part and finish the job.

He lifted the kitten bag gingerly, with his fingertips at first and then nestled against his chest, and climbed out of the car. The front door opened before he arrived.

"You here about Sean?" Lucas asked. There was tension in his voice that Paul hadn't heard before.

Not that he knew the man from anything but twice-weekly sledge hockey games and occasional small talk at the clinic, but it didn't take a detective to sense the worry.

"He's just down the street," Paul said quickly. "On his way here. He asked me to drive ahead and give you these."

Luke ignored the bag and stepped forward, crouching down to see under the branches of a nearby tree, and squinted in the direction Paul had gestured. "He's okay? We woke up and he wasn't here."

"He's fine. Worried about the kittens, though."

"Kittens?" And finally Luke took the bag, glanced inside, and swore. "Mark!" he called. "Sean's on his way back. Get me some towels, okay?"

A tall, slightly bookish man stepped into view, phone to his ear. "He's on his way here," he said into the phone. "Sorry to bother you." Then he hung up and said, "Towels?"

Luke had already set the bag down and floor and now he extricated a tiny bundle of fur and lifted it in Mark's direction. "Towels. They're wet. We need to get them dry and warm, and we'll have to call Elise and figure out what to feed them."

Paul felt totally out of place, standing there in the doorway, but then Luke looked up at him and said, "Can you check on Sean? Make sure he makes it back okay? We were—we didn't know where he was."

There were layers, there, that Paul didn't want to dig into. The worry coming from a sense of responsibility, or maybe even guilt? The reasons Sean might have given these two, who seemed otherwise reasonable, to freak out because a grown man had been temporarily out of their sight?

None of it was Paul's business. He'd played ambulance driver for the kittens, and now he'd assume temporary watchman's duties until Sean was back home. It was all just a strange diversion, a slight detour from which he would soon return. Nothing he needed to spend much time thinking about.

Still.

He walked toward Sean, and when they met at the corner he held his hands out and said, "Want me to push?"

"The kittens are inside?" Sean demanded. He was clearly exhausted, but not giving up.

"Luke has them. Mark's with him."

"Okay," Sean said, and Paul stepped behind the chair and helped Sean the rest of the way home.

Chapter Eleven

There had been a moment—a tiny, stupid, embarrassing moment—when Sean had thought about suggesting that he and Paul be roommates. Not because they were friends or anything, but just because sometimes strangers shared an apartment, didn't they? As they'd helped Lucas with the kittens, they'd chatted, Paul had explained why he'd been driving around, Luke had glanced in Sean's direction as if asking a wordless question, and Sean had actually considered it.

Thankfully, he'd kept his mouth shut, and Luke hadn't pushed.

Because why the hell would Paul want to live with someone like Sean? There was absolutely no reason for it. Which meant he'd either have said no, which would have been awkward, or he would have said yes because he was just that much of a fucking martyr, and how much worse would that have been?

So, disaster avoided. And the kittens—five of them, tiny and blind and needy as hell—kept Sean busy enough so he didn't have time to kick himself much over his temporary stupidity. Elise bustled in from the farm with formula and expertise within an hour of the kittens' arrival, while Paul was still at the house. Paul had two kittens tucked inside his sweatshirt to keep them warm, and when they scratched him he gasped and squirmed in a way that really shouldn't have given Sean the kind of thoughts it did.

Because Paul was impossible.

Paul was impossible, Luke was impossible, and fuck it, Sean was straight. Just because he wasn't getting laid it didn't suddenly make him gay. Just because he was having inappropriate thoughts, the kind of thoughts he'd had about Luke for more than a decade—that didn't mean anything. He didn't have any fucking legs, anyway, so it didn't really matter what his fucking *preferences* were. It was all theoretical.

So maybe it didn't hurt to let his mind wander, a little.

Seemed kind of hard to keep it from happening, anyway. As Elise held out a weathered hand and Paul tried to free a kitten from wherever it had lodged itself, his shirt rode up and there was a flash of warm brown skin. Paler than his face, but still darker than Sean had ever been even when he'd been working in the sun all day. It looked soft, sensitive, touchable—

"Sean!" Elise barked. "Kitten."

Oh. Right. He reached inside his own shirt and found the little ball of fur. It was warmer than it had been, at least, but it still felt impossibly fragile and his instincts said to keep it under cover, keep it next to his skin where it was safe. Instead, he pulled it out for Elise's inspection. She was gentle with it, at least, which was good, because Sean didn't think anyone would be too pleased if he punched an old lady in the face and then curled up around his kitten and refused to let anyone touch it.

"We can't feed them until they're warm," Elise said as she inspected the tiny animal. "And we can't warm them up too fast. And we can't wait too long before they get fed."

"That's a pretty fine balance," Paul said. He was replacing the first kitten inside his shirt and fishing around for the other one and god, Sean wanted to reach out and touch, to just lay his hand on Paul's strong stomach muscles…

Okay, that wasn't something a totally *straight* straight guy would want. It wasn't the first time Sean had felt a similar urge, not after all those years of sharing a bedroom with fucking Lucas Cain, but it was still a bit disturbing.

"Once they're warm we'll just have to be sure we *keep* them warm," Elise was saying. "And we can keep the first feeding small, just in case." She stretched out and returned Sean's kitten and he got it back inside his shirt where it belonged.

"After that," Elise continued, "It's just a lot of work. They need to be fed every two or three hours, and they need to be cleaned after every meal to stimulate defecation."

"To—" Sean squinted. Had she just said what it seemed like she'd said?

"To make them shit," Luke confirmed, his arms carefully cradling the bundle inside his own shirt. "The mom cat would lick them. We don't have to go *that* far, but we've got to kind of simulate it."

"Simulate?" This time it was Paul with the dubious expression on his face.

"Washcloths work," Elise said. "Warm water, gentle strokes with a soft but rough surface."

Okay, there was no way Sean should be getting turned on by a description of ways to make kittens shit on command. But… warm, gentle strokes? Damn.

One of the side effects of the pills he took for phantom pain was supposed to be problems with erections, but apparently his dick wasn't aware of that.

And, hey, maybe he wasn't gay, maybe he just had a fetish for geriatric women obsessed with animal rescue. Would that be better or worse?

"I think yours is the warmest," Elise told Sean, and he tried to call his mind back to the conversation. "Let's try her on a little formula."

"Her?"

"It's hard to be sure with kittens, but calicos are generally female."

"Calicos?"

"This coat pattern. The colored splotches."

"Oh."

"That's a problem?"

"No. Just—she probably doesn't want to be named Hulk, then, huh?"

"You named her?" Lucas sounded amused, by also possibly—worried?

"Maybe."

"Careful. They—animals die. Even when we do everything we can, they don't always make it. And naming them makes them... you know. Pets, or whatever."

"They're kittens," Sean said with as much patience as he could find. "You think they're not going to be pets? Just not giving them a name is enough to make people not care?"

"You're a softie," Elise said. She sounded surprised. "All this time you've been scrubbing buckets, I could have had you working with the smaller animals."

"Not if he gets too attached," Luke said. He was back in mother hen mode. "It's hard when they don't make it. He doesn't need—"

"I don't need someone else telling me what I can or can't handle? You're right, Luke, thanks for saying so."

The bravado might have been a bit more satisfying if Sean hadn't already been internally cringing at the idea of caring about animals and watching them die, but the principle of keeping Lucas in line overrode that hesitation.

Elise didn't make any promises, though, just turned around and pulled a little syringe out of her bag, then filled it with warm formula. Sean managed to keep his mind on business as she ran through the process of feeding, wiping, cleaning up, and then returning the kitten to the warmth of Sean's skin.

"I brought a heating pad," she told them as she reached for Mark's kitten. "Line a box with towels, plug in the heating pad, and whenever they're not in your hands, they should be in the box. And feeding every two or three hours means all through the night as well. You can handle that?"

"For how long?" Mark asked.

Was there a period of time that would be too much? If Elise suddenly turned into a cackling old witch and said, "For the rest of your lives" in a creaky fairy tale voice, would Sean be able to pull that damn kitten out of his shirt and say "Oh, that's too much, better just let her die"?

Luckily, he didn't have to test himself, because Elise said, "For a week at least. After that, maybe every four or five hours for a week. Every six or eight hours the next week. Once they're about four weeks old they should at least be able to eliminate on their own, and we can start weaning them after that."

"That's not too bad," Sean said, and it earned him a sigh from Mark, a raised eyebrow from Luke, and a smile from Paul.

"I don't live here, obviously," Paul said. "But if you guys are stuck and don't mind a stranger invading, I'm happy to help. I can come by before work, or at lunch time, or after work."

"You're not a stranger," Luke said. "And I expect we'll need lots of help."

Elise seemed to think it was going too smoothly, so she added, "You'll also need to find homes for them—assuming they all survive, you probably don't want five adult cats living here. They can be expensive, if nothing else. If you find new owners early enough, you can get them to pay for all the vet care you'll need."

My sister's been wanting a cat," Paul said. "She might be thinking of some fancy Persian or something, but I bet once she sees these guys she changes her mind."

Well, Sean wasn't about to start handing kittens out to just anyone who thought she might want one, but he could save that fight for another time. And it wasn't like he could keep all of them. Maybe he couldn't keep any of them. He was homeless, once Mark and Luke got tired of him, and didn't have enough money to pay to get hand controls installed on a car he hadn't even bought yet, and he thought he was in a place to take responsibility for another life? He had to be losing his mind.

"Like this," Elise was saying, and he called his attention back to the tiny kitten stretching up to latch onto the syringe opening. "It's dangerous to underfeed them, obviously, but we don't want to overfeed, either—you're not helping them if they end up getting sick. I'll give you a chart for how much they should get, and you need to measure carefully. No more, and hopefully no less. If they won't take enough at one go, you'll have to look at feeding them more often."

More often. It was going to be something damn close to a full time job, looking after all five of them, and Sean had never claimed to be a hard worker. He'd never thought of himself as a real animal lover, either. Strange, then, how excited he was about this. How much he wanted to be part of it, to help the innocent creatures survive. They just—they deserved a chance. They deserved to get stronger and learn to play and hunt and be *cats*. He couldn't make any guarantees, couldn't be sure he or anyone else could actually save them. But he could give them a chance.

"What do we do if we can't make them shit?" he asked. It wasn't a question he'd ever really thought he'd be asking anyone. But if it was what the kittens needed? He'd damn well make sure it happened.

Chapter Twelve

"It's not a palace," Paul said. Complete understatement, of course. His new apartment was a big step down from the place he'd shared with Bobby. A big step down from his sister's place, certainly from his parents' house. It was probably on par with the places he'd had when he was in school. But it had been *fun*, then, pretending to rough it a little while still going home to luxury whenever he felt like it. "But it's clean. Seems safe."

"You were living in Toronto before?" Sean asked.

The two of them were sitting on the floor of the living room at Lucas and Mark's house, each with a kitten on their laps. Paul had carefully kept himself from pointing out that if Sean shifted his weight just a little, and moved his left leg to the side, it would align his spine better and prevent—well. He hadn't pointed it out. He wasn't there as a physiotherapist.

So he needed to pay attention to the conversation. "Yeah, right downtown."

"And you're moving—here."

"Closer to work."

"But you've been working there for a couple years, right? The commute was okay for that long?"

"Well—" How much did he want to share? Surprisingly, quite a bit. If he wasn't there as a physio, then, strange as it seemed, maybe he was there as a friend. He could use a friend. "I was living with a guy. We broke up. We'd been living down there because it was close to his work, so...."

Sean nodded. "Bad breakup?"

"You're really *not* homophobic. Really not racist. Me mentioning my ex, who is a man, doesn't freak you out."

"You've met Mark and Luke. You know they're not just really close friends, right?" Sean shifted his kitten so it was flatter on his lap and gently patted its back. Trying for a tiny kitten burp. "So—"

He stopped, and frowned. Then he looked at Paul and there was a clear moment of indecision before he shrugged. "Actually, yeah. I've been a bit—uncomfortable with it. I'm getting better. Living here is helping. But—I don't know. It's not what I was—"

Another frown, then, "Fuck. If I say it's not what I was raised to expect, it kind of sounds like I'm blaming my mom, right? And it's not her fault. At all. She's Catholic, but she never had a real problem with it, I don't think. Never talked about it if she did."

It didn't feel like this was a casual kitten-feeding chat any more.

"If you're not used to something, you might not be comfortable right away," Paul tried. "Doesn't mean you're a bad person, not if you try to get over it."

There wasn't even a hint of hesitation before Sean said, "Oh, I'm a bad person. For lots of reasons, not just this."

This was more than Paul knew how to handle. Should he ask whether Sean was still seeing his therapist? Make a gentle suggestion that he—no, wait. Paul wasn't being a physio, here, wasn't being a professional. He was being a friend, or something like it. Had he completely forgotten how to talk to people in that capacity?

He shook his head a reached out to gently tweak the tail of the kitten Sean was feeding. "Yeah, you're a super-villain, clearly. You're helping these little guys out of the evil of your heart."

The reply took a bit longer this time. "Maybe I've got a plan for them. I only have five, not a hundred and one, so if I'm going to make a coat they need to be big. I need to fatten them up before I skin them."

"It's gonna be a pretty weird looking coat." One pure black kitten, two orange-and-white, and two with multi-colored splotches Elise had said were called calico. "It's not just the sizes you need to worry about."

"I might need to find more kittens."

"I hear black cats are the ones least likely to be adopted. People are superstitious about them, still. So if you wanted to go pure black, you could probably find lots of potential in the shelters."

"You know I'm not actually making a kitten-fur coat, right?" Sean shook his head. "Man. You were getting right into it."

"I'm a problem-solver. It's my nature."

"That's why you picked the job you did?" Sean, clearly not satisfied with the results of his previous method, lifted his kitten to his shoulder for burping.

"I guess so, yeah. I mean—I like helping people, and I like—yeah, I like the problem-solving aspect. No two cases are the same, so there's always fine-tuning to do, better ways to figure out for each patient."

Paul lifted his own kitten to his shoulder. He wasn't entirely sure Elise wasn't just making them do stupid things with kittens for her own amusement—he didn't know her well, but she seemed like the sort who might. Regardless, she'd said to burp the kittens and Sean was damn well following through on everything she'd said. So Paul would, too, even if he felt like an idiot.

"I know I've already apologized," Sean said. "For the—not just the gloves. For generally being a dick."

"Yeah. You've already apologized. And I understand. It's a difficult adjustment. You're hardly the first patient who's sent a bit of frustration in my direction. It's okay."

"It's—" Sean shook his head. "Fuck, sorry. You're here to feed kittens, not listen to my bullshit."

"I don't mind listening."

"'Cause you're a problem solver? You already got your thinking cap on, coming up with possible solutions?"

Well, yeah, he kind of was. Maybe Sean just needed to hear more positive talk about himself, maybe he needed to keep working with kittens and then maybe kids or others who could let him feel good about helping without putting too many emotional demands on him, maybe—maybe Paul needed to get a grip. "I'm still thinking about the coat, to be honest. I'm seeing some challenges because of different fur lengths and textures. There's more than just color to consider."

"Nobody's making a kitten-fur coat," Sean said firmly. Then he lifted the tiny furball from his shoulder and held it to his face. "You're okay, little guy. I won't let him hurt you."

They were quiet for a while, then, as Sean dabbed gently at the kitten's nether-regions with a warm washcloth and Paul pretended he wasn't watching the operation with weird fascination. It would be his turn, soon, assuming he didn't chicken out and pass his charge over to Sean for treatment, and if there was a way to make the process less disgusting, he wanted to know about it.

"So you're okay with the breakup?" Sean asked without raising his head. "You don't seem real upset."

"Oh. Uh—no, I think I'm okay with it. It was time. We'd—I was going to say we'd grown apart, but I'm not sure that's true. I'm not sure we were ever all that close, really. It felt like I was just waiting for some sort of breakthrough, some moment when it would all suddenly click into place and our relationship would deepen and become more meaningful. But that moment never came, and it turned out I was the only one who even really thought it was needed. So… yes. I'm okay with the breakup."

"You might change your mind about living up here, though. If you're single. Luke says most gay guys with any sense move out of small towns as soon as they have the chance. They might move back once they're coupled up, but there's not a whole lot of action up here, for single people. At least, that's what Luke says."

"I don't think I'll worry about that too much right away, anyhow. I was with Bobby for years. Seems like I should take a break for a while, at least."

"Not just going for the rebound? I thought you were supposed to do a lot of random hookups after you broke up with someone."

"You *thought*. You've never been through it yourself?"

"Nah. Not much for relationships. I've got the random-hookup stage pretty well covered, though." He shrugged. "Or I did, at least. You know. Before."

Another conflict. As a physiotherapist, Paul could offer encouragement about the likelihood of an active sex life even post-amputation. He might pass some of the more technical aspects off to the Occupational Therapist, but he could give general information, at least. He was a medical professional. But that wasn't his role at the moment. "You can again," he said. Surely that much was allowed.

But Sean had turned away, busying himself with replacing his fed, cleaned, and now sleepy kitten in the box and pulling out the next. He stayed turned for a little longer than was probably necessary for the job, and when his face appeared again his expression seemed too carefully neutral. "Luke says not to name them," he said, "but that's bullshit. I think this one is Cyborg."

He was holding the smallest of the kittens, a delicate calico with a patch of black over one eye. Paul said, "That one's female, right? Elise said that color means they're girls."

"Yeah—that's why Cyborg. Like the MMA fighter?"

"Oh. I don't follow MMA."

"Oh. Weird. But, yeah, the real Cyborg is tough, so… that's what I think we should call this one."

"Because she seems like an especially tough kitten to you?"

"For inspiration." Sean positioned the tiny animal carefully on his thigh. "Because she needs to *get* tough, even if she isn't naturally that way."

Because the world was a hard place for little kittens. Maybe it had been a hard place for little boys, too, back when Sean had been growing up, and maybe sometimes it had been tricky for him to draw a precise line between "tough" and "rough", and then between "rough" and "mean".

Paul had meant it, when he'd said Sean didn't need to apologize any more for his earlier aggression. There hadn't been any point, and it was over, and they should just move on. But right then, watching the man carefully arranging a tiny animal on his lap? Right then, there was more than forgiveness in Paul's heart. There was understanding. Sean Gage's life had been hard enough even when he'd had legs, and losing them had probably felt like a final challenge he just wasn't strong enough to face.

But he'd been wrong about that. He was stronger than he'd given himself credit for, even if he hadn't realized it yet.

And Paul could help him realize that. As a physiotherapist, sure, but also as a human being. A kitten-care-colleague. A friend? Maybe. Strange as it seemed, yes. Maybe as a friend.

Chapter Thirteen

The stubbies were too fucking much. The fake-leg doctor said Sean was supposed to wear them all the time, but the doctor was fucking nuts if she thought that was going to happen. It was—Jesus Fucking Christ, it was like they were trying to make him into a joke.

"At least you'll be upright," Luke said. He'd been the one to drive Sean to the fitting, and was the one driving him home, now; he seemed to think that meant Sean should give a good goddamn about his fucking opinion. "And they're temporary. Get a feel for it, get your balance back, and they'll stretch you up to longer legs. Give you knees and ankles and shit."

"They can just do that now."

"You'd fall over. You're not used to being upright. The doctor said it's even worse, for you, because you waited around for so long before coming down and getting started. Your body isn't used to being vertical anymore. You're like an astronaut or something, coming back to Earth after too long on the space station."

"The doctor said I'm like an astronaut?"

"Well, no. I added that part. But it makes sense."

It made sense because Luke and Mark were in the middle of some weird space exploration kick, watching documentaries all the time and generally being unbelievably nerdy and annoying. If it weren't for the kittens, Sean absolutely would have moved out of the house by now, just to get away from the space talk. "There's no way I'm wearing those fucking things in public."

"You barely go out in public anyway, so I don't think it's that big of a deal. Wear them around the house, wear them to physio—"

"I'm *not* wearing them to fucking physio!" It came out louder than Sean had expected.

Luke didn't answer right away, and when he did his voice was more careful than usual. "It's his job, Sean. To help you get used to them. To strengthen the right muscles so you can move on to the next step. He can't do his job if you won't let him help."

"I'm not wearing them to physio." More controlled this time, at least.

"Will you wear them around the house, when Paul's over?"

"I'm not going to wear them at all."

"Yeah, you are. With me and Mark. You'll wear them when it's just us. Us and the cats."

The bastard thought Sean was going to soften up if they started talking about kittens. So predictable. But Sean could resist. "I'm on the ground most of the time with the cats. It's not like I'm carrying them places."

"But you could, if you wore the stubbies."

"I can in the chair. It's better in the chair, really. Built-in lap."

"Are you saying you want to stay in the chair forever? You're giving up on learning to walk?"

No. Of course he wasn't. He just—he just—there had to be some other way to make it happen. Didn't there?

"Have you thought about getting a different physiotherapist?" Luke asked. He was keeping his eyes on the road and made the question sound totally casual and friendly, which was how Sean could tell it was a trap.

"Why would I?"

"I don't know. Just—because Paul's hanging out at our place more. I mean, I know, it started because of the kittens, but they're two weeks old, now. They don't need to get fed nearly as often. He still comes over a lot, and he hangs out after feeding time is done. So—I don't know. I don't hang out with him nearly as much as you do, but even so, if I needed a physio for something kind of—kind of personal, or whatever?—I wouldn't want it to be him. It's easier if you have a clear line, sometimes, right? If you can pretend that doctors or whatever aren't real people. They're just health-care robots, and it's not embarrassing if you show a bit of weakness to a robot, is it? But Paul isn't a robot anymore, so—"

"Robots, now. First astronauts, now robots. Jesus Christ, Luke, what's happening to you?"

"Whatever. The point is, you could get a different physio, if you wanted. If that'd make things easier."

"There's only one clinic in town, and the fake-leg guys say I'm supposed to be going three times a week. You want to drive me down to the city three times a week just so I can see a different physio?"

"I could."

He could. And he *would*, and then Sean would have one more martyr in his life, one more person to feel guilty about. As if it wasn't bad enough already.

"I need to get the hand controls in the damn car," he said. They'd found a not-that-old Accord for a price he could afford, but had run into problems getting anyone to sell them hand controls they could put in themselves. The bastards were all so worried about liability they wanted to be in charge of every detail of the installation, and it was going to end up costing more to adapt the car than it had to buy it in the first place. Still, it was worth doing. Sean needed to be able to get around on his own.

"Yeah, okay," Luke agreed. "And it'll probably take some time to make the switch between physios. You can start looking for someone new, if you want, and I can drive you for a while, and then once the car's fixed and you know how to use it—and once the weather's better, 'cause you were a shitty winter driver even when you had legs—then you can start driving yourself."

That easy? "By the time that's all taken care of, the kittens will be grown and Paul won't be coming over anymore anyhow."

"You think that's the only reason he's coming over? And you think as soon as the kittens are gone you'll go back to not minding if you look weak around him?"

Weak really wasn't the word Sean would have chosen, but he wouldn't have chosen to have any part of this conversation, really, so maybe he needed to stop thinking that his choices made any damn difference. He slammed his head back into the seat cushion. "I don't fucking know!"

And he didn't want to think about it. Everything was okay, just as it was, and it had been too damn long since he'd felt that way. He didn't want to make any changes, didn't want to disrupt the incredibly fragile balance he seemed to have found. He didn't want to wear stubbies, didn't want to change physios… didn't want the kittens to grow up so Paul would stop having a reason to come over….

So, again, he was stuck wanting things that were impossible.

"I talked to the landlord at the second apartment—the one that's ready for the start of February."

Luke took a moment to catch up to the topic change, then nodded. "And?"

"He said a cat's okay. I have to pay an extra damage deposit, but other than that it's fine."

"Just one cat? Not five?"

It's a one-bedroom. I think five would be pushing it."

"You think they each need a bedroom of their own?"

"I think it's a small place. Maybe too small for even one. Maybe I should be looking for other homes for all of them. Better places, with more room." More stable owners, one who could afford to buy more treats and toys and whatever else cats want.

"Mark and I already said we could keep one or two. I'm pretty sure Paul's going to take one, and his sister's coming over tonight to meet them—she'll probably take one. So why don't you take the last one and we don't even have to bother looking for other people?"

Yeah, maybe. And maybe if the other people chose theirs first, then the one left over would already be kind of a loser cat, the kind nobody else wanted, and that would make it okay for Sean to keep it? He wouldn't be ripping some kitten out of a perfect world to go live in his shit-hole, he'd be helping make sure it didn't go somewhere even worse. Except....

"Wait. Did you say Paul's *sister* is coming over? Tonight?"

"Yeah. Oh, yeah, he called when you were talking to the doctor. I forgot to tell you."

"Tonight."

"It's Paul's sister, not the queen."

"Yeah, but—" What, exactly? Why was Sean worried about some strange woman coming by someone else's house where he just happened to be staying? He didn't even have to meet her, did he? No, he didn't. It would be kind of pathetic to hide in his room, and it was still too damn cold for him to just go for a walk—a wheel, whatever—but he could... go visit his mom! He could have dinner over there, do some more work on making his brother and sisters like him again. Although possibly he'd have a better chance of that if he stayed away from them.

The pickup slowed and Sean pulled himself out of his thoughts enough to see they were turning into the gas station, which sent him off on a whole new path of gloom. He could offer to pay, and Luke would probably take enough for half a tank or something, but back in the day he'd have gotten out of the car and stood around while Luke pumped the gas. Maybe he'd have gone into the store for some snacks and to say hi to whoever was working, because this was a local gas station and the odds were pretty good he'd know whoever was behind the counter.

But now, it would be a five-minute struggle to get the damn wheelchair out of the backseat, get himself transferred over into it, then have to go through the whole stupid process again to get back in—he wasn't going anywhere. No more casual trips out of the car for him. But if he had legs? If he learned how to use them properly?

"Shit," Luke said under his breath.

Sean looked up. Oh. Tinker and Mikey at the pump right in front of them, filling up Tinker's old pickup.

"Be cool," Sean said, but he glanced over and saw that his words had been completely unnecessary. Luke had his calm, smirking face on, the one that made it clear to anyone and everyone that he wasn't worried about them and they'd probably be wise to worry about him. It was classic Lucas Cain. Or at least it had been.

Sean needed to find his own game face, and he should probably do it pretty fast, because Tinker and Mikey had clearly noticed them.

It wasn't going to get physical. Not in broad daylight, in a gas station that probably had security cameras.

But, no. It wasn't either of those things that would keep Tinker and Mikey under control.

It was Sean's legs. His lack of legs. He wasn't man enough for them to bother fighting.

Luke rolled each of the windows down about an inch, then shut the pickup off and, instead of pocketing the keys, handed them to Sean. "Hang onto these, okay?"

Because Luke was making sure he was safe. Sean could hear what was going on through the partly opened windows and if things went bad he could lock the cab doors knowing the only keys were inside with him. He could leave Luke out there to deal with whatever came at him, while Sean was tucked away, watching it all. It was fucking gallant, was what it was. Luke was a big fucking hero, taking care of the little woman. Fuck!

Luke had the door open, now, and climbed out all casual and relaxed. "Hey," he said to the other two, and then he ignored them completely, slotting his credit card into the machine and hitting the code to pay.

Sean tried to remember just how bad things were between Luke and the others. How had it all been left? There had been threats on both sides—Luke's a fair bit more credible than the others—but it had all more or less faded away, hadn't it? They'd all been living in the same town together for months without anything flaring up.

Of course, they probably hadn't seen much of each other. They weren't really running in the same crowd, not since Luke had stopped drinking and got his life straightened out. And Tinker and Mikey had both come by to see Sean exactly one time since the accident, so it wasn't like he'd been the glue holding them all together.

They'd come by to see him, once, and now he was sitting in the passenger seat of a pickup driven by someone they hated.

But they couldn't take it out on Sean. Not because of the locked doors, but because of his legs. That meant they were pissed off, and there was only one available target.

Sean twisted around. Luke had the gas pumping and was leaning against the bed of the truck with such relaxation that for a second Sean doubted his own understanding of the situation. Was he just being stupid? Then he remembered that Luke had left the keys behind. He'd done that for a reason.

Shit.

Tinker pulled the nozzle out of his gas tank and hung it back up, but Mikey didn't take his eyes off Luke. Luke's body was still relaxed, still calm—yeah, easy for *him*, he wasn't the one stuck in the goddamn car while all this happened.

"You're driving him around?" Mikey said. His voice was loud enough that Sean had no trouble hearing it through the window opening. "Like a fucking—like a trophy? You proud of yourself, you fucking pervert?"

"What?" Luke asked.

"You think the whole fucking town doesn't already know? You and that fucking child molester couldn't keep your hands off him, could you? He gets in some trouble and it didn't take you much fucking time at all to swoop in and drag him off to your fucking pervert paradise."

"Seriously?" Luke sounded like he was trying not to laugh. "That's—that's what you're going with? You want to fight that bad? I don't know, man. It's pretty weak."

"You think I'm fucking *joking*?" Mikey said. He was by the driver's window, now, his whole body so tense it was practically vibrating. And Tinker was right behind him.

It didn't make sense. There was no reason for them to be this angry, no reason for them to pull this shit in broad daylight, in public... but Mikey and Tinker had never been known for their brains, and rage came to them as naturally as breathing came to regular people. Strange to think Sean had been like them, once.

Fuck it, maybe he still *was* like them, because he'd be damned if he'd sit there and just watch this happen. He wanted to help Luke, sure, but he wanted to fight, too. He wanted to feel his fist connect with someone's face and didn't much care if he got hurt in return. He wanted the rush, wanted to feel like he was still at least some part of the man he'd used to be.

Lucas moved slowly, still calm, while Sean kicked himself into high gear. Lucas carefully pulled the nozzle out of his truck and replaced it on the gas tank; Sean dragged himself across the center console of the car, jammed the keys into the ignition, and turned them enough to get the electricity flowing. Lucas turned to face Mikey, who was still ranting about Luke being a pervert, corrupting Sean; Sean hit the button to roll the window down.

Mikey took the first swing, but obviously Luke had known it was coming and had his arm up to block. He stepped backward, too, making Mikey stumble forward, but that meant Luke was moving out into the open, which was no good. In the narrow space between the pickup and the gas pumps, only one guy at a time could get to Luke, and he could handle that. But as he moved backward, into the open lot—

Mikey surged forward and Tinker charged along behind him. Sean didn't think, he just moved. Hands on the sides of the window, rocketing himself forward, all the hard-won muscles of his upper body finally getting their chance. There was nothing graceful about it, but he managed to catch Tinker around the waist, then slide down a bit to his knees. Sean locked his arms around Tinker's legs, felt the big man lose his balance and stumble forward, and the two of them fell to the ground together.

Mikey and Lucas were off fighting their own battle, but Sean couldn't care about that. He didn't care about *anything* beyond getting a better grip on Tinker, pulling himself up, anticipating Tinker's roll and being right there, ready, with a fist to the asshole's jaw.

Tinker had been bigger than Sean even before the accident, but stuck there between the truck and the pumps, there wasn't much room for size to matter. Sean had enough weight keep Tinker off his feet, at least, and enough strength to keep the hits coming. Tinker got an arm free and tried for a big swing but ended up with his hand somehow tangled in the undercarriage of Luke's truck. That gave Sean a chance for a few more punches but he was having the same trouble getting any real power with so little space.

Then Tinker go his hand free and caught hold of Sean's shirt, slammed him sideways into the panel of Luke's back passenger door, and then slammed him again, hard enough to jar his teeth and make his head spin.

It was perfect.

The scuffle continued, both of them throwing weak punches, Sean struggling to find leverage without his lower legs, Tinker fighting to keep his longer limbs from tangling. At some point he hooked a foot around the gas hose and the spout jerked loose and fell on his head, which was fucking beautiful, and there was some blood from some source or another or maybe several, and swearing and insults and roars and every goddamn thing Sean had been missing for far too long.

He was somehow back on top of Tinker, pulling his arm back for another blow, when he heard the siren. Police, and not too far away. He froze, Tinker froze, and then Luke's voice yelled, "Get back in the fucking car, Sean!"

Too late for that, wasn't it?

And kind of tricky, actually, because the doors were still locked and Sean wasn't tall enough, without lower legs, to reach in through the window to unlock them.

"We done?" he snarled at Tinker, and cops or not, he'd have been pretty happy if the answer had been *no*.

But fucking Tinker had apparently chosen the exact wrong time to grow some common sense, because he just grunted, "Get off me," and there were no more punches.

Sean rolled to the side, Tinker struggled to his feet, and then the flashing lights pulled into the parking lot. There was some more yelling, of course, from the cops and from the excited gas station attendant who'd obviously called them. Sean leaned back against the gas pump and tried to catch his breath, and he watched tiredly as first Tinker, then Mikey, then Luke's were slammed against the side of Luke's truck as their hands were cuffed behind their backs.

Luke had his face turned in Sean's direction as it happened, and through the blood, Sean saw his favorite version of Lucas Cain. He looked alive, looked proud and wild, and as their eyes met Sean knew—he *knew*—that Luke saw exactly the same thing in Sean's face. They were born and bred to be warriors, and they might know that they couldn't live that way anymore—might accept that it was dangerous, antisocial, unwise—but their brains couldn't deny what they felt in their souls. When they fought, they were able to forget the rules that kept them bound so much of the time, and they could be truly free.

"On your feet," someone ordered from behind Sean, and he turned to meet the gaze of an angry constable.

"I'd love to," Sean said. "But—there's a problem."

He looked over at Luke, who looked back at him, and they both laughed.

Yeah, there was a problem. There were a million of the damn things. But Sean was a fighter. He'd fight. He might not win, but that wasn't even the point. The thrill was in the battle. And he had good friends ready to fight by his side.

Chapter Fourteen

There was a weird vibe in the little house that night. Jas seemed oblivious to it, but she was pretty good at faking her way through awkward social interactions, so her ignorance wouldn't be confirmed until Paul had her alone for questioning. In the meantime, he had to try to puzzle it through on his own.

The problem was clearly related to the bruises evident on both Sean and Luke's faces. Paul had asked about the injuries as soon as Luke had opened the door, but Luke had just shrugged and turned his attention toward Jas. When Paul had seen Sean's face, his immediate concern had been that the two had fought each other.

But that made no sense. Sure, neither was shy about hitting the other on the back of the head or giving an arm-punch, but they always seemed to get along pretty well, in their own way. More significantly, there was no trace of anger between them.

Between them and Mark, on the other hand?

Well, still not anger, exactly. But Mark seemed frustrated, maybe even disappointed, while Luke was clearly feeling guilty. Sean, on the other hand, was absolutely unrepentant. Despite the cut over his eye, the fat lip, and the bruise on his cheekbone, he'd given Paul a huge smile of greeting and then been absolutely charming, maybe even gallant, with Jas.

All that was strange, but fine. The part that was—damn it, the part that was bothering Paul, for whatever reason, was how Sean was treating Luke, and how Luke was responding, when Mark wasn't paying attention. The furtive grins, the sense that they were somehow—co-conspirators?

Paul's imagination wouldn't rest. Had Luke—had he cheated on Mark? With Sean? And then Mark found out and beat them both up...

Obviously not. It wasn't just the violence that would have been unbelievable, but also the cheating. Mark and Luke were a loving, solid couple. Luke was a decent guy. And Sean, of course, was straight.

So there was absolutely no reason for Paul to be feeling the strange tightness in his gut that he could only identify as jealousy.

He wasn't *jealous* that Sean had a best friend, wasn't jealous that the two of them had a secret that seemed to involve facial lacerations. The whole thing was absurd.

"I want them *all*," Jas cooed from her spot on the floor beside him. Sean was helping her feed one of the calico kittens, the one with the longer hair who always bit the plastic nipple when she was done eating. "They can all come home with me. I'll quit my job and be a full-time cat lady. That's legit, right?"

Sean nodded. "It's been working pretty well for me. I mean, technically my boss seems to think I'm just taking a leave, but I'm planning to find some more kittens once these ones are too old to need nursing. I figure I can be a cat-daddy for the rest of my life."

"Your job is *at* an animal shelter," Lucas said. His smile was affectionate and made something tighten and turn over in Paul's stomach. "Quitting a job at an animal shelter because you want to spend more time looking after animals doesn't make a lot of sense."

"I'm a cat specialist. A deer that got hit by a car is nothing to me. I only care about cats."

"Deer probably aren't as cuddly," Jas said, running her hand lovingly over the kitten on her lap.

"They don't have razors strapped to their toes, though," Luke said. "That's a good feature of deer."

Mark wasn't part of any of this, Paul noticed. He was still in the room, and he wasn't some brooding, glowering presence or anything, but he wasn't joining in the silliness the way he normally would.

Awkward, but more than that—worrisome. Was it just Paul's self-confessed instinct for problem-solving acting up? Did he want to understand the situation better so he could find a way to solve it?

Maybe, but not as some remote academic exercise. He wanted to solve the problem because he cared about these people. He genuinely *liked* them, all three of them, and wanted them to be happy and at peace with each other.

And, damn it, he was being selfish, too. The little house felt more like home than his apartment did, and had more warmth and companionship than he'd felt while living with Bobby... sad, but true.

That meant whatever the hell was going on to make Mark unhappy had just better stop. Paul wanted his haven back.

"Are you guys going to keep a couple of them?" he asked Mark, trying to sound casual and upbeat.

Mark shot a glance in Luke's direction. They hadn't had a fight about *kittens*, had they?

Not likely, because the look Luke sent in return seemed pretty calm. "We'd like to," he said.

"I don't know." There was a mischievous gleam in Sean's eye, and Paul wanted to shush him. If things were already tense, the room probably didn't need Sean's brand of trouble right then. But Sean apparently didn't receive Paul's psychic message, and he certainly couldn't be counted on to listen to his own common sense. "These are some pretty nice kittens—I don't think I can let just *anybody* adopt them. They need a stable home, sure, but they need to be able to have fun sometimes, too. Sometimes they're going to blow off a bit of steam, and that's okay. That's just cats being cats. Not a big—"

"Sean." Luke stared Sean down. "Stop."

There was a moment when it all seemed balanced and undecided, but then Sean shook his head, let out a sigh of mock disgust, and turned his attention back to Jas. "You'd be okay with a cat being a cat? You can't go cutting her toes off if she scratches your furniture a bit, right?"

"I'll get her a scratching post." Jas bent over and buried her face in the fur of the kitten's tummy. She stayed like that for a moment, then sat back up. "A scratching post for every room. And she can wreck my furniture if she wants to—I can always get a new couch!"

"How about the shedding?" Sean waved a vague hand toward Jas's body. "You look pretty put together. You probably wear nice clothes all the time, right? You going to be okay with cat hair all over everything?"

"There's a woman at the office who has cats—like, *lots of them*—she's my new hero—and she has lint rollers stashed all over her office. She gets her assistant to give her a good roll-down first thing each day, and then she touches up as needed. I could do that."

"Do you *have* an assistant?" Sean asked.

"Sure. I'm not confident she really wants to give me a daily roll-down, but we can negotiate."

"What do you do?" Sean sounded as if he wasn't really sure he believed Jas about the assistant-having.

"Family business," Jas said.

"She makes it sound kind of mysterious, doesn't she?" Paul grinned at his sister. "She started off managing a gas station. Six years in university, fancy MBA in hand, and she was pumping gas."

"I very rarely actually pumped the gas myself." She shrugged. "It was a self-serve station."

"You need six years of university to run a gas station?"

"Our father's a big fan of starting at the bottom." Paul wasn't sure why he was getting into all this, but it was easier than whatever was going on with Mark and Luke. "But she only did it for, what, three or four months?"

"Four months," Jas confirmed. "Four *boring* months. Then I got a few more stations to manage, some real estate, a dry-cleaning plant—none of it was very exciting, but at least there was more variety."

Sean was frowning. "That's—that's your family business? You own gas stations and real estate and a dry-cleaning plant?"

"We sold the dry-cleaning plant last year," Jas said. "We're always buying and selling things. We're not in any one business, you know? We're just *in business*. Whatever opportunities we find."

"But not you." Sean had turned his attention to Paul. "You don't do any of that?"

"He's the black sheep of the family," Jas said. "Not even a full-on doctor. Not that a doctor would have been *great*, but it would have been better than a physiotherapist."

"Seriously?" Sean looked—oh. How strange. Paul thought he'd gotten over this, thought he'd come to accept that his parents' prejudices were their problem, not his. But if that was the case, why did Sean's clear outrage mean so much? Why did it feel like a validation, a confirmation, a benediction? "He helps so many people, every single day, and that's not good enough?"

"It's good enough for me," Jas said. And Paul knew she meant it. "I'm proud of him. But—you know how families are. They always have their own ambitions for their kids."

Sean and Luke exchanged a look that made it clear *all* families didn't follow that model, but Jas had her face buried in the kitten's belly again and wasn't paying attention.

They all returned to their cat tasks for a while, burping and wiping and snuggling, until Luke said, "Mark—you want to go get dinner with me?"

Mark looked surprised by the idea. Paul and Bobby had eaten out more often than in, but that didn't seem to be the pattern in this house. Possibly because Luke and Mark actually enjoyed spending time with each other and didn't need to find distractions and outside entertainment, but also probably because, as Paul was noticing now that he was on a limited budget, going to restaurants was expensive. Regardless of the reasons, the suggestion was out of the ordinary, and Luke clearly wasn't sure what reaction he was going to get.

"Okay," Mark said. "But—I don't mean to sound paranoid, but is that safe? Is there going to be more trouble?"

Ah. Trouble. Some hint about the bruising and the tension...

"They're probably still locked up," Sean said. He seemed pretty pleased about that. "What kind of losers start a fight when they're carrying meth?"

"Meth?" Jas sat up fast, the kitten forgotten for at least the moment. "What?"

"Not us." Sean sounded more amused than insulted. "Some other guys. Old—used to be friends. But nothing to do with us, now." He lifted the kitten off his own lap and waved its forepaw in Jas's direction. "Hugs, not drugs," he said in a squeaky voice, his head ducked down behind the cat's.

"Even if they're out, they won't be a problem," Luke told Mark. "Not when I'm with you. You're my protection."

That—seemed unlikely. Mark was taller than Luke, which made him taller than Sean had probably been, but there was nothing about him that suggested he was a fighter, none of the compact toughness so evident in the other two. But if Paul spoke up to ask for clarification, the others might return to their secrecy, so he busied his eyes with his kitten while his ears stayed alert for more news.

"You're sure?" Mark asked.

"Let's go," Luke said. The words were soft. A suggestion, not an order. An apology, an explanation, a promise? The secret language of successful couples—not one Paul had ever mastered.

Mark, though, had clearly received the message. "You can watch the kids?" he asked Sean.

"We're gonna raid the fridge the second you're gone." He lifted the kitten up to eye level to speak to it. "Have you tried ice cream, yet? It's probably time you learned about ice cream. And Cheetos. And—"

"They'll be fine," Paul said. Bold of him, obviously—he didn't live here, and the cats weren't his responsibility. But Sean's smile was relaxed and easy. Paul hadn't overstepped.

There was a bit of activity as Mark and Luke got ready for their unplanned night out, and somewhere in the middle of it Jas's phone rang. She wandered into the kitchen for the call and came back with her nose wrinkled.

"I have to go," she told Paul. "That stupid deal for the building by the GO Train—dad's flipping out." She turned to Sean. "If I am honored with the care of one of the babies—or, you know, all of them, if you want—I will have a strategy in place for times like these. A cat sitter or... well, probably a cat sitter, I guess. But my fuzz ball won't be left alone all the time, I promise."

"I think cats are usually okay alone," Sean said. "I mean, not forever. But for a while."

"But if I'm away at work all day, then I should spend time with my precious at night—oh! I could have an elaborate play structure that is only accessible when I leave at an unexpected time. Then me being away would turn into a *treat*, really." She frowned. "Not that I want to set up a system where my cat looks forward to me going away...."

"You can fine tune the details," Sean said. He lifted his cat to cover his face and used the squeaky voice again. "We'll be fine! We'll just find something expensive and shred it to pieces."

"Oh, good solution!" She gentled booped the kitten on the nose with her forefinger. "You have my permission to shred at will."

"At *her* house," Mark said firmly as he and Luke headed for the door. "You can shred at her house. Not here."

"You don't have to drive her?" Sean asked Paul.

"No. We came separately. But—I can go if you want. Give you some peace and quiet."

"I don't like peace all that much." Sean leaned back and hooked his elbows on the seat of the couch behind him. His shirt rode up a little, but Paul was good at not noticing things like that. Most of the time. "Besides—someone has to cook dinner for me. I've got no feet, man. No knees, even. And I suffered from a physical trauma today. I can't possibly make my own food."

"Don't listen to him," Luke said from the doorway. "He was supposed to cook tonight. It'll probably be spaghetti—it's always fucking spaghetti—but it's pretty good, as long as he doesn't go too crazy with the spiciness."

"Too spicy?" Paul exchanged a look with Jas, who shook her head in mock amazement. "Don't think it'll be a problem." He turned his attention back to Sean. "Bring it on, white boy."

Chapter Fifteen

It was frustrating, making dinner with someone who knew *exactly* what Sean's body was capable of. Even with Luke, he could usually shirk off some tasks by saying the angle was wrong or it fucking hurt, damn it, and wasn't that enough?!? But Paul, the problem-solver, wouldn't just accept any of that and move on.

"Lock the wheels of your chair and angle yourself up in it," he suggested. "You've got to get used to being vertical again anyway—might as well start now." And in response to a later complaint, "You should be able to do that okay. Where's it hurting, exactly? Does it feel skeletal or muscular?" When Sean admitted that possibly *hurting* wasn't exactly the right word, Paul just snorted. "Keep stirring, then. And bring your left shoulder forward a little so you're not twisted around."

"Am I gonna get a bill for this?" Sean asked.

"I'm a PT... I start billing you for OT work and I'm in trouble."

"I have no idea what the hell the difference is between any of you. Except you're the one who causes me the most pain."

"Given the low pain threshold you've just demonstrated, I'm not going to worry about that accusation too much." Paul made his voice whiny and annoying. "I can't stir the sauce—it hurts my back."

"Is that supposed to be me? That voice, just then—that was your imitation of me?"

"Maybe."

"Careful, buddy. I've fought people for less."

Paul looked up from the bread he was slicing. "Is that what happened today? Someone made fun of you so you had a fight?"

"Nobody made fun of me." No the bastards wouldn't be that direct. They'd picked on Luke instead, because Sean was beneath their notice. At least, he had been. "But, yeah, a fight. A couple guys we used to know started something with Luke. If I hadn't jumped in it would have been two-on-one."

And he would have hated himself forever. As it was, though? "Luke's all conflicted about it—makes sense, I guess. I mean—do you know the history with him and Mark? Mark's brother?"

Paul shook his head.

"Lukey used to be—we both did, I guess, but I carried on longer than he did—we used to be pretty rough. Drinking, fights, the rest of it. It was—" What had it been? A way of life. A way of *understanding*, really. "You ever been in a fight? A real one?"

"Uh—not really, I guess. Pushing and shoving, play fights that went too far when I was a kid. Never anything serious."

"They're awesome. I mean—like, maybe literally awesome? Like, they're—impressive, kind of. Powerful. Even if the guys fighting aren't strong, even if they don't know what they're doing, a fight is just—I don't know. Pure? In a good fight, a fair fight, it's just you and the other guy. It doesn't matter who has more money or who's better at school or has a good job or a hot car or anything else. It's just—it's like a bubble, and inside the bubble it's just who's toughest, who can take the pain and keep going."

"Who can take the pain? So I'm guessing you lost a lot of fights?"

Paul's voice was light and he was smiling, but Sean still had the urge to do something wild in response. There was a knife on the counter next to him: he could pick it up and slice his forearm and watch the blood drip on the floor and ask Paul who was tough, now.

There was a time when he would have done it. He'd done wilder things, stupider things, far too many times.

But either he was finally growing up, or at least he was finally listening to a body that had taken far too much abuse and wasn't willing to suffer more just so Sean could make a point. He made himself smile and returned to stirring his sauce.

"I've seen you working out," Paul said into the silence. "I've seen you push yourself. I know you can handle pain. I was just joking."

Huh. Apparently no slicing had been necessary. Good work stopping yourself, Sean—that would have been messy to clean up.

"What's the deal with Mark's brother?" Paul asked.

"Oh. He's dead. He and Luke got in a fight. In a bar—Lukey was drunk, and the brother started it. But—yeah. The brother died. So Mark doesn't really see fighting the way we—the way I—always did. You know."

"Shit. That's—wait."

Sean nodded. "Yeah. Mark's living with the guy who killed his brother. It's fucking messy."

"They seem fine. Good together. I mean, they seem totally in love."

"You'd have to be pretty crazy about someone to get past something like that, wouldn't you?"

"Shit," Paul said again. Then, "So this fight today. You enjoyed it. And maybe Luke did too? But Mark sees it as—"

"He knows Luke wasn't looking for trouble. Luke doesn't drink at all anymore, and he's got a really good grip on himself. The guys today were gunning for him—the cops saw that on the security video, and that's why we're both free, without worrying about charges or Luke's probation being busted or anything." Sean pulled out a spoonful of sauce and waited for it to cool a little. "But, yeah. It's probably a pretty tough reminder for Mark. About his brother, but also—he's in love with a guy who loves to fight, and I don't think he really understands that. Like—like if Luke was a junkie, and he kicked the habit, and then somebody tricked him and got him high somehow. You can't blame him for getting high, but you probably also have to worry about it a bit. Does it feel so good he's going to go back to his old ways? Something like that."

"You sound really understanding. But earlier it seemed like you were bugging Mark about it, like you didn't think it was a big deal."

Huh. Good point. "Sometimes people pussyfooting around doesn't help, you know? I mean, if it's such a big deal, I'm not likely going to make it much bigger by being a bit annoying." Sean tasted the sauce, then reached for the jar of dried oregano. "Also—I'm a dick. Any time you're trying to figure out what I'm doing or why I'm doing it, don't forget the 'Sean's a dick' part."

"I'll be honest—you're making it harder to remember."

Damn. The words, and the tone. Sean wanted—but it didn't fucking matter what he wanted, because he wasn't going to get it. He pushed the thought, the emotion, the emptiness, as far from his mind as he could. "You're really okay with spicy food? I don't want to make racist assumptions just 'cause you're brown."

"You can assume I'm okay with spicy food. I also don't wear sunscreen and I look *fantastic* in white. *Unbelievable* in orange. Like—stunning."

Sean could believe it, but he wouldn't let himself make the images in his mind. "I think those last few might be tied in a bit closer to your skin color than the food thing is."

"It's all part of being me." Paul nodded his chin at the bread. "You want this whole thing garlic-and-cheesed up, or just enough for two of us?"

"Oh, I was thinking that loaf was just for me. I guess you could have a crust or two, but—I like my garlic bread. I think you should do it all."

"Careful. Learning to walk will be a lot harder if you're carrying extra weight."

Nope. Sean wasn't going to think about that, not right then. "Don't get between me and my garlic bread, man. It's cruel."

Paul didn't say anything in agreement, but he did start slapping the garlic butter on the bread, so that was okay. They worked in silence a little longer until Paul said, "What did Luke mean, earlier, about Mark being his protection?"

Sean smiled, remembering. "Well, two things. First one's kinda boring. Just—Mark's respectable. If he gets jumped, the cops are going to care, people are going to be outraged or whatever. So people won't likely mess with him because they know how much trouble it would cause. But the second thing?"

He turned the heat down on the sauce and up on the pot of water. "Luke set it up. Mark used to be a priest—not a real one, just Anglican or something—and he worked in a half-way house for ex-cons. He did a good job, I guess, 'cause a lot of the guys really respected him. And Luke got a bunch of those guys together and they made it clear to—to the guys who used to be our friends. Mark's under their protection. Anyone who messes with Mark is messing with them, and, trust me, these are *not* guys you'd want to mess with."

"They protect Mark, but not Luke?"

"They don't owe Luke a favor. And... you know. It's fine for Mark, 'cause this isn't his world. But Lukey wouldn't really want to be under someone else's protection. You know? He'd want to take care of himself." Just like Sean wanted.

At least, Sean wanted it when it came to things like fighting. Other stuff, though? "If you could hurry up with the bread, you could set the table. I don't know if you noticed, but I don't have any feet. Not even any knees. I can't be expected to—"

The slice of bread was cold and greasy when it hit Sean's face. Slapped right over his eye and stuck there for a second before sliding down and flopping onto his lap.

"Did you just throw a slice of untoasted garlic bread at me?"

"I guess my hand slipped. I was trying to wade through all the bullshit you were spewing and I kind of lost my balance somehow."

"Right." Sean unlocked his wheels and rolled over to the sink so he could mop the butter off his face. And while he was there—he turned on the faucet, then reached for the spray attachment. There was a mature way to handle this. A way to show Paul the respectful system to handle disputes in the kitchen, or at least a way to keep the remaining garlic bread dry.

Sean hit the handle on the spray anyway.

His aim was good and the streams of water hit Paul right on the neck. A few drops probably made it down to the bread, but most of it splashed up to his face, or soaked into his shirt, making the fabric cling to the round, solid muscles beneath it. Shit. Not something Sean had needed to see.

He had the sudden urge to back away. To let the sprayer drop, hold up his hands in surrender, to fucking cower and wince and make this confrontation go away. Not because he was afraid of Paul, not in the slightest. But the expression on the man's face, the surprise changing to something more intense, something challenging and somehow intimate— Sean couldn't handle that expression. Violence would have been fine but this? He wasn't ready for this.

He wouldn't back down, though, so he just shrugged and said, "I guess my hand slipped. Must have been greasy from the butter I was wiping off my face."

Some of the tension left the room, at least until Paul smiled, a casual expression that shouldn't have felt nearly as dangerous as it did. "Watch your back, Gage. That's all I'm saying."

And that made dinner a more interesting event that it might otherwise have been. Both of them wary, refusing to turn their backs on each other. Paul's expression as he shook hot sauce onto his pasta, gaze locked on Sean's the whole time. Cautious hands reaching across the table to take food, eyes always on the other, waiting for the next attack.

It was absolutely ridiculous, but Sean couldn't remember the last time he'd felt so alive, so completely focused on what was going on right there in the room. No time for worrying about the past or the future, not when Paul might seize any possible opportunity. No energy for being self-conscious, not when Sean needed to keep searching for his own chances.

The whole thing was stupid, but intense.

Which was a pretty good summary of how Sean had always lived his life.

And look where that had gotten him. Jobless, legless, futureless.

Fuck.

Was he ever going to learn?

"Truce," he said as Paul cautiously reached for the last piece of garlic bread. "We're even now, right? And we have to feed the kittens soon— they won't like it if things are all tense."

"We need to stay together for the children?"

Nope, not a thought path Sean was going to follow. "We need to not physically attack each other for the children."

"Can I trust you on this?"

Sean wanted to say no. He wanted to say he was wily and unforgiving and would never give up, not until he'd achieved total victory. Instead, he nodded. "Yeah. I'm done. I promise."

Chapter Sixteen

The paperwork had come in that morning, and Paul still felt the strange sense of betrayal as he drove to sledge hockey that evening. Paul had fed kittens with Sean practically every night that week, had dinner with him two nights ago—and he'd never said a word about getting a new physiotherapist. So when Anna had called his attention to the request for a transfer of records, it had been a shock.

No, that was too strong. He had to be professional about this. It was just a surprise. He was curious about the reasons. That was all.

The most professional approach, of course, would have been to call Sean and ask him about it. But Paul had fumed all day, instead, and now he was going to play hockey with the bastard with the questions still unanswered. That wasn't good.

When he arrived at the rink and saw Luke lifting Sean's chair out of the back of his pickup, he didn't just go inside and start getting ready for the game the way he should have. Instead, he walked—stormed?—across the parking lot and stood by the hood of the truck waiting for Sean to settle himself in the chair. Then, "You're switching physios? To a place in *Brampton*? If you're trying to get away from brown people, you're going the wrong damn direction."

The expression on Sean's face made it clear that while some of Paul's accusation may have been completely imaginary, there was *something* strange going on. Because Sean looked totally guilty. He cast his eyes in Luke's direction as if hoping for rescue, but Luke just shook his head in disgust.

"I didn't know they were going to be so fast," Sean said lamely. "I was planning to tell you. At some point."

"Tell me what? Why are you changing clinics?"

"It's not a big deal," Sean said.

"Okay. Fine. What's the small deal behind you changing clinics?"

"I just—they have specialists down there. You know, guys who work with fake legs all day long. You're more of a generalist, right? You said you like the variety. And I get that. But… it's kind of a delicate thing, so I just figured it would make sense to go with the people with the most possible experience."

It wasn't a terrible reason. It stung a bit, sure, that Sean thought he'd be in better hands elsewhere, but there *were* specialists in the city, and they probably *did* have a better grasp of the nuances, so—so why did Sean still look shifty and guilty?

"What's the real reason?" Paul asked.

Luke made a frustrated, guttural noise. "Sean, I'm either going to tell him myself or I'm going to go in and leave you here to make up stupid shit without me having to listen to it. Which do you want?"

Sean threw his hands up in the air. "It's my fucking body! I can take it to whatever physio I want!"

But Luke wasn't having it. "You want me to tell, or you want me to go?"

Sean snarled at him, then turned to Paul and spoke quickly, looking at something somewhere in the middle of Paul's chest. "I don't want you to see me like that. Struggling. We're friends now, kind of—I mean, I know it's just the hockey and the kittens, but—whatever. And I'm going to be a fucking mess when I'm learning all this and I'll probably go back to being a mean little bitch about stuff, and I just—it'd be easier to do all that with a stranger. You know?"

Oh. Paul didn't *know*, exactly, but it certainly made sense. "Why didn't you want to tell me that?"

"I don't know," Sean said, in a voice that was aggressive enough to make it clear he absolutely *did* know.

"Because of—because of the *friends* part?" Paul guessed. It was a shot in the dark, but it seemed to fit. Sean clearly hadn't felt too secure about using the label. "I mean, I think of you as a friend. For sure. Not just for hockey and kittens—you're a good guy, when you're not being a self-pitying pain in the ass."

Luke nodded. "I should write those words down—we can put them on his gravestone when he dies, seventy years from now—I bet they'll still be true."

"Shut up," Sean said. He was staring at the ground, now, clearly embarrassed. "So—whatever. That's why. Sorry I didn't tell you before."

"No problem. I mean—it's no problem if you want to keep working with me, either. It's a pain to be driving down to Brampton all the time, and I'm pretty used to seeing people go through painful transitions. I don't think it would affect our friendship."

"You don't know how much of an asshole I'm planning to be about all this. You threw bread at me because I wouldn't set the fucking table—there's no way you could handle me at full strength."

"He threw bread at you?" Luke asked. "At my house?"

"It was really childish," Sean confirmed. "Totally inappropriate behavior."

"Good work," Luke told Paul. Then he started walking, leaving Sean to wheel his way through the parking-lot slush on his own.

"How about a push?" Sean asked Paul. He was wearing his what's-going-to-happen expression, which Paul should not have found nearly so—

So *attractive*? Was that what he was feeling? Attraction?

A crush on a straight guy? That was a recipe for pain, absolutely.

"Push yourself," he growled, and he stalked after Luke.

"My hands are getting cold!" Sean bellowed after them, but Paul could tell from the sound that he was moving.

Paul jogged a few steps to catch up with Luke and spoke in a quiet voice. "He's got this figured out? How to get down to the city all the time?"

"I know you're talking about me!" Sean bellowed from somewhere behind them.

"Yeah, he IS a pain in the ass," Luke said in an overly loud voice. Then he dropped the volume and said, "His mom's going to help. We've got a hand-controlled car on the way, but they're taking their time. Mark goes down at least once a week, and hopefully they can get their schedules matched up." He raised his voice again and said, "If Sean stops being a total dick, his sisters and his brother can help drive him." More quietly again, "I think we're okay."

"Let me know if you need help. My schedule's not too flexible, but I can make things work if I know ahead of time. And I've got family down there; I could go visit them or whatever while I'm waiting."

"Thanks." Luke pulled the arena door open and stepped behind it to wait for Sean to wheel through. There was a door that opened automatically, but Sean never seemed happy using tools designed to make his life easier. Nice that Luke remembered that.

And strange that Paul knew about it.

Was he actually attracted to Sean Gage?

He turned and watched the man wheel toward them. The strength in his upper body, the determination on his face—fuck. Paul could absolutely imagine how Sean would be in bed. Feral. Primitive. Selfish, in the way that meant Paul could be selfish too and they could both just use each other without being self-conscious or feeling guilty. Sean would want control— Sean *always* wanted control—and once he had it he'd probably want to play with it, toy with Paul—

Yeah. Not cool to spring a hard-on at a public arena, so Paul needed to get his thoughts back on track.

And he absolutely needed to stop thinking about Sean that way. They were friends. Sean was straight. No point making things weird, or being miserable from wanting something impossible.

Paul probably needed to get laid. That was all. He might not know anyone suitable in the area, but he had a damn car. If Sean could drive all the way down to the city to get physio, then Paul could certainly drive down to get fucked.

He'd take a night off from kitten duty, he'd go find some angry white boy with something to prove, and he'd get it all out of his system. A rebound guy. That was all that was needed.

"You ready to get slammed?" Sean asked as he wheeled through the door.

"What?"

"On the ice. I'm gonna ask them to put *both* of you fuckers on the other team, and then I'm coming for you. I'm taking you both down."

"It's sledge hockey," Lucas said, clearly unconcerned. "We're already down."

"Not as far down as you're gonna be," Sean promised.

It wasn't sexual. Even Paul's desperate subconscious struggled to find any innuendo in it. But his cheeks warmed, regardless. Great. The color might not show against his skin, but the implication was clear nevertheless.

He was going to be a total weirdo until he got this out of his system. So. The solution was clear. And Paul was nothing if not a problem-solver.

Chapter Seventeen

The new physiotherapist was stocky, greying, and his accent and attitude combined to make Sean pretty damn sure he was ex-KGB. So... perfect, really.

"You must wear them always," the Soviet bear grunted at him, tapping the little plastic squares that were suction-cupped onto Sean's stumps. "Everywhere."

"Bed?" Sean asked.

"No. Take them off at night."

"When I'm having a bath?"

"No, not in bath."

"When I'm playing sledge hockey?"

"No. Not then."

"So—it sounds more like *sometimes*. I must wear them *sometimes*. Some places. Does that seem like what you were trying to say?"

"If you don't take this seriously, you will not succeed."

"Oh, I'm dead serious. I'm going to do exactly what you say. I'm going to follow your instructions *precisely*. That's why I need to be sure you actually mean what you say. You know?"

The bear glowered at him, and Sean smiled back. This fucker was going to make Sean hurt, and it seemed only fair that he get at least a little aggravation in return.

"We start with standing up," the bear said. "Not on mat—it's too puffy. Too hard to stand on. Get on ground, over there."

"Won't the ground be kind of hard to *sit* on? It feels like six of one, half dozen of the other, really."

"You are already good at sitting. You are not good at standing. So you move to the place that is easier for the part you aren't good at."

Well, that made too much sense for Sean to argue with. He scooted over onto the linoleum floor and went through the exercises. It was strange to be vertical again, even the kind of vertical that involved a lot of hand-waving and grabbing at the beefy shoulders of ex-spies in order to stay upright.

"I'm lower than I am in my chair! This is bullshit."

"Is for learning. And for some jobs—if you move something heavy, even after you are good with your full legs, you should use stubbies. If you go down a hill. If you drink too much. Stubbies."

"Wait. These are the officially recommended legs to use when getting shitfaced?"

"Yes." There was no hint of humor in the man's reply. "Now, again. Sit down. Then use bar to stand up."

By the end of it all, Sean's glutes were bruised and trembling, his hamstrings throbbing, and his pride in even worse shape. But the physio nodded in approval and said, "Good. Good start. You do exercises at home tomorrow. Come back next day and we do more."

"I don't think I'm going to be able to *move* tomorrow."

"Hot bath. And—you have someone? Someone to massage for you?"

Well, that would probably be taking the roommate experience a little too far, especially since Sean wasn't actually paying rent.

"Girlfriend?" The physio prompted. "Wife?"

Sean couldn't say why he did it, but somehow the word came out of his mouth anyway. "Boyfriend."

"Oh. Okay. Good. Stronger hands."

Well, Sean had been hoping for a bit more of a reaction, there. "But he's away. In Alberta, working on the tar sands." What the hell was he doing? Why was he saying all this? "He gets paid really well out there. Just construction, but they're flying in workers from all over."

"Still?" The physio frowned. "I thought that was over."

Fuck, was it over? The Alberta oil boom—had it ended while Sean had been paying attention to something else? "They cut back," he decided. "Kept only the best guys. You know. He's pretty good at his job."

"So no one to massage your muscles."

Right, that was how this whole insane exchange had started. "Well—there's someone else. Maybe. I mean—my boyfriend's pretty far away. You know how it is." Great. Now he was cheating on his imaginary gay lover? What the fuck was he doing?

The Russian shook his head in disapproval. "That's not a good idea. You need trust. A solid relationship is important when you're doing something difficult. Learning to walk is difficult. You should be true to your boyfriend."

"Well, I'm pretty sure he's cheating on me." Sean needed to stop, but instead he seemed to be shifting into high gear. "I mean, he was good right after the accident, but he had a job offer here, one that would have paid almost as much as in Alberta, and he took that job. So that says something, right? He's running away. If he wanted to be here, he could be here. So—yeah. I'm not sure the relationship is all that solid, really."

Apparently this was a little too much melodrama for a proper Soviet conversation, because the big man just shrugged. "If you can get a massage, it will help. If you can't, take a hot bath. Is not as good, but is something."

And that was the end of Sean's imaginary romance. He salvaged a little from the conversation by asking for clarification about whether he should or should not be wearing the stubbies in the hot bath, but that really wasn't much comfort.

Maybe the lack of reaction from the physio was what made Sean still antsy as he worked his way into the passenger seat of his mother's car and waited for her to load the wheelchair and return to her driver's seat.

"How was that?" she asked as they pulled out into traffic.

"Fine, I guess. I hurt all over, but... whatever."

"Well, you have to suffer for progress."

And that was what did it, really. Not the antsy-ness, but the idea that Sean hadn't already suffered enough to earn at least a little damn progress without more pain. "I told him I'm gay."

His mother didn't say anything right away, but he could see her grip tighten on the steering wheel. They'd driven two more blocks, in heavy city traffic, before she said, "Are you? I mean... you told him you're gay. Are you telling me, too? Is this real, or all just—just one of your games?"

She could handle it, if it were true. If he said it was real, she'd be upset—she wanted grandkids, she was worried about his eternal soul already and wouldn't want one more black mark on his record, and she had friends who really wouldn't be too understanding. But she'd be able to get through it. She wouldn't let him down.

Still, he shook his head. "I was just playing. I mean—I like chicks! You know that—you've been nagging me about not getting someone pregnant since I was fourteen. You told me that whole story about how some sins are worse than others, and condoms are better than abortion—remember?"

"You could be 'bisexual' or something." She spoke the word as if she'd never heard it, only seen it written down. "Honestly, Sean, you and Luke—you were always so close. When it turned out he was—gay, or whatever they're calling it—it made me wonder." She took a deep breath. "You're my baby boy. You make me crazy and I want to hit you most of the time, but I love you from here to the moon. You know that. If you're—anything. It doesn't matter. I love you, no matter what."

He'd already anticipated the response, and still, hearing the words was enough to make his throat tighten. He needed to smarten up. "It's not like it matters. I mean, my race is run anyway, right?"

"No!" she sounded fierce, like she was ready to fight anyone, including him, who disagreed with her. "There are lots of people with your disability who go on to have families and rich, wonderful lives. You're going to be walking again, soon! If you're wearing long pants, people might not even know about your legs."

"You think I'm going to go on to have a family with someone without ever taking my pants off? You've got four kids, Mom—I shouldn't have to explain this stuff to you."

"You can find someone who doesn't care. Someone who can see the wonderful person you are, legs or no legs."

"Wonderful person?" And that was what it came down to, really. Maybe there were people out there who were so great they could still attract partners without legs. Their bodies might be wrecked, but they had good brains or hearts or something. Sean, though? What the hell did he have?

"I was just fucking with him," he said firmly. "None of it matters, so I was just playing around. Next appointment I'll tell him something else—maybe I'll tell him I've got eight kids, each with a different mother. Or my legs got cut off after a bear attack. I don't know. I'll think of something new."

"Why don't you try telling people the truth?" she asked, and it sounded like maybe she wasn't just talking about the physiotherapist. Not just about bear attacks.

"Can't reveal my weaknesses to the enemy," he told her. "Once they know you, they know how to get you."

"Nobody's trying to get you."

Well, that was pretty fucking true, wasn't it? Nobody was trying to get him, or get with him, or have any fucking thing to do with him. He was retired from the human race. He wasn't gay or straight or bi or any other damn thing. He was nothing.

"I was just being a dick," he mumbled, and he slumped down in his seat and stared out the window for the rest of the long drive home.

Chapter Eighteen

Anonymous sex would have been easier. Better in every way. But Paul had told himself he was too old, too settled, too mature for that sort of thing. He wasn't some horny club kid. He hadn't broken up with Bobby because he wasn't ready for a serious romantic relationship; he'd broken up with Bobby because *that* relationship hadn't been the right one.

So—dating. Sure, he'd gone online for the initial connection, but he'd made it clear he was looking for someone to build something with. Someone with similar values and similar goals for the future. Someone Paul's family would approve of.

Yeah. They'd thought Paul was crazy for giving up Bobby, but wait until they met the new guy, who would be better than Bobby in every way, *and* who would want to build true intimacy and love.

"It was really *authentic*," New Guy Candidate Number One said as the server cleared away the remains of their appetizers. "Spending time with the people in their own homes like that? It's the only way to really get to know a country. It turned a simple vacation into an experience of growth and learning."

Paul nodded. He couldn't even remember what country the guy had been visiting when he'd had his wonderful experience. Somewhere in South America. "Is it really all that authentic, though?" he asked. Shit, he should have kept his mouth shut.

But the Candidate smiled: an invitation to share. "How do you mean?"

"Well—I mean, if a stranger from another country came to stay in my house, I feel like—well, to start with, I wouldn't allow it. Would you?" He waited for agreement but got only a curious head tilt, like a German Shepard trying to figure out where the tennis ball had gone.

"People would only really do it if they needed the money, I expect," he continued. Stupid. Time to change the subject. Why was he trying to diminish this guy's experience? But he kept at it. "But I assume the agency who finds the hosts screens them to make sure the homes will be pleasant enough to suit the tastes of tourists? That means you're already in a really limited subgroup of people—those with reasonably nice homes but who still need money. So say I was in that category of people." Say he'd broken up with Bobby and wanted to stay in the luxury condo. He'd have had a nice home, but need money to maintain it.

"I'd try to put on a good show, right? I mean, Sikh hospitality aside, I'd want to make sure the guests didn't complain to the agency. Maybe I'd be hoping for a good tip. I'd avoid having any domestic arguments, and I'd emphasize the positive side of things and find the fun places for my guests to visit and all the rest."

"There actually *was* a domestic argument while we were there," the Candidate said. He sounded quite pleased, and it wasn't clear whether he'd enjoyed the argument itself or just the opportunity to use it as evidence now. "Quite intense. Quiet, but fiery."

"Wonder what it would have been like if you *hadn't* been there."

The Candidate smiled, giving the impression that he had a wonderful retort but was too generous to use it, then said, "How about you? What's the best trip you've been on lately?"

Santorini, absolutely. Daily massages, infinity pools and endless cocktails. Candlelit dinners on their private balcony followed by slow, easy sex on crisp white sheets. The last time things had actually felt real with Bobby. And out of respect for whatever they'd had, Paul wasn't going to share details of that trip. "I visited family in The Philippines in August. That's their rainy season, which isn't great for tourism, but it's my favorite time to visit. Less crowded."

"You have family there?" the Candidate asked, and they talked about Paul's far-flung relatives through most of the main course.

It felt like a job interview. No, not quite, because at least a job interview would be based on Paul's own qualities and abilities. This was the more subtle but just as judgmental process of establishing contacts and classes. It made Paul feel like a character in an Austen novel being judged for *connexions* or lack thereof.

In his case, he was able to give answers he knew would be at least adequate if not impressive. Who was the family in the Philippines? Mother's brother. An engineer, which was questionable, but he owned a firm that did business all over the world, so that was just fine! Where else did Paul have family? Pakistan, India, the US, the UK, Malaysia… each branch was discussed and dissected. On the surface it was all just a pleasant get-to-know-you conversation, but Paul knew what it was really all about.

What would he be able to contribute to the financial side of a future partnership? The Candidate specialized in trading textiles, and was always looking for new sources, new opportunities. He'd never been to Malaysia but was certainly interested in knowing more about it. What did Paul's family do, there? Who did they know? What was their status?

It was a business thing, not a Sikh thing. Paul had looked for Sikhs when he was online, but he'd also looked for successful entrepreneurs, men who were go-getters and would impress his parents. He'd gone out of his damn way to find a guy like the Candidate, so he had no right to be petulant just because the conversation was predictable.

No right to be petulant about any of it.

So. This was what he'd signed up for. Time to make the best of it.

And maybe time to turn the tables a little. "You said your sister and her family are in Paris? How long have they lived there?"

And what do they do there, and who do they know? How do they fit into the puzzle, and can they provide any missing pieces that might prove useful?

That was the game. Paul liked the perks of it all—he liked vacations in Minorca, liked having dinner in fine restaurants, liked knowing that his family was proud of him and felt he was contributing to their success. And it wasn't like the Candidate was offensive. Not at all. He had all of Bobby's good qualities, with the added bonus of being attentive and interested. He seemed to be listening to what Paul said, or was at least better at pretending he was.

It was a pleasant evening, with the promise of more pleasantness to come. When they'd finished eating and walked out to the parking lot together, the Candidate said something about wishing Paul didn't have such a long drive home, and it was nice to have that little bit of recognition. Sure, they'd still met in the city rather than somewhere closer to Paul's place, but the city had the good restaurants, and it wasn't like Paul actually minded driving. Just hearing someone *acknowledge* the distance was enough.

Yeah. It was all enough. Paul shouldn't be greedy.

And he absolutely shouldn't have checked the time and then told the hands-free system on his car to make a phone call.

"Hey," Sean answered. "You feeling guilty for missing the feeding? The kittens say you're dead to them now, in case you were wondering."

"The kittens can practically eat on their own, now. At some point you're going to have to wean them, you know. You can't keep them kittens forever."

"Did you seriously just call me up to lecture me about cats you can't even be bothered to come visit?"

"Something like that."

"How was your dinner? Your friend good?"

Well. Yeah, that was how Paul had described it when he'd said he couldn't make it to the house that evening. He was having in the city with a friend. He hadn't said 'date'.

Why the hell hadn't he? Because—because it was none of Sean's business, sure, but that didn't feel like the real reason.

"It was fine. My friend's fine."

"But you missed us. Right?"

Yes. God help him, it *was* right. He'd missed them all—Luke, Mark, the kittens—but it was Sean he'd called. Well, the kittens didn't have phones, obviously, but—yeah. It was Sean he'd missed most.

Abrasive, absurd, seeking out confrontation as if it were the only way two people could communicate. Touchy, grumpy, and profane. That was the Sean that Paul had been missing. What the hell was wrong with him?

"I'm afraid the kittens will say their first words and I won't be there to hear them."

"Oh, you're already too late, man—they were talking up a storm tonight. Mostly swear words, and all directed at you. I'm serious—they were pissed you bailed on them. You'd better wear armor the next time you come over, 'cause they've got their claws sharpened for you."

"Yeah, okay." Paul wanted to push. He wanted to tease and say that maybe it wasn't the kittens who'd missed him; maybe it had been Sean. He could make it sound like a joke... it would *be* a joke, obviously. But he couldn't take the chance.

Instead he said, "How'd physio go? You sore?"

"The new guy's even more of a sadist than you are. I hurt all over."

"Excellent. What exercises did he show you?"

And they talked about physio and kittens and Luke's pet squirrel who was building a nest in the eaves of the garden shed and their respective high school PE teachers and any other stupid thing that came to mind, until somehow Paul was pulling into his parking space at home, more than an hour away from the restaurant.

"I have to go in, and my phone has a habit of hanging up when I turn the car off," Paul warned.

"My battery's about dead anyway. You coming over tomorrow after work, or have you abandoned the kittens altogether?"

"I can't miss two days in a row. I'll be there."

"Stay for dinner, if you want. It's my turn to cook. I'm thinking I'll make the same sauce as usual, but put it on rotini instead of spaghetti. That's good variety, right?"

"I can cook, if you want."

"That's even better."

"When I say I'll cook, I mean I'll be the head chef and you'll be doing all the work. You understand that, right?"

"Look, buddy, I have no feet. No *knees*, even."

"I'll bring the kind of food that doesn't use anyone's feet in the preparation process. I don't think I'll have much trouble finding a recipe."

"Hey, can you cook Indian food? I like Indian food."

"Most of my family recipes are vegetarian. You ready for that?"

"Couldn't you just add some chicken or something? Make it good?"

"I think that might be a bit disrespectful to my vegetarian ancestors."

"It might be a bit disrespectful to my carnivorous ancestors to pretend a meal is good without any meat in it. But, you know, we can compromise. I don't give a shit if the Indian food is an actual family recipe. You can look something up on the internet for all I care."

"That's generous of you."

Paul didn't want to go inside. He wanted to stay in the car and talk to Sean about more stupid stuff, or even better, to drive over to Sean's place and talk to him in person.

But Sean said, "Okay, my phone's about to die. I'll see you tomorrow," and Paul didn't argue. He just ended the call, then sat in the car for another few minutes, cursing his own stupidity, before he finally gave up on it all and went inside to bed.

Chapter Nineteen

The kittens were eating solid food with enthusiasm, and Sean wasn't impressed. They could at least show a little gratitude, couldn't they? He'd nursed them around the clock for almost a month and then they just moved on without a backward look?

"They still love you," Paul said. There might have been the hint of a laugh in his voice, but it was subtle enough to be ignored. "They don't need you for food anymore and they still come running as soon as you walk into the room, so—that's *better*, really. They see you as a cuddle-buddy and playmate, not a provider of essential nutrients."

"I don't *walk* in," Sean corrected.

"Figure of speech. But if you want to stay grumpy, fine. Focus on that, instead of on the fuzzy black demon on the sofa, about to pounce on your head."

Ah, Panther, always ready for a scrap and totally unable to judge the odds. Taking on a human, head-first? Yup, that was Panther's style. Sean had to respect him. Envy him.

"You brought ingredients?" Sean asked, nodding toward the cloth grocery bags Paul had left by the front door. "This is starting to seem like more work than I was planning on."

"Mark and Luke aren't even home yet, and they usually want to unwind before dinner, right? So there's no rush. We can hang out with the cats for a bit."

"You're just trying to keep me still until Panther completes his attack, right?"

"He's so close. His little butt is wiggling... Oh, he's recalculating. Okay, he's good again, butt-wiggle engaged...."

Sean didn't really want to sit still and wait for tiny kitten claws, sharp no matter how often he trimmed them, to latch onto his skull. But he couldn't bring himself to move away, not when staying as he was gave him the excuse to keep staring at Paul. Just because he was waiting for an update on the cat-attack, and Paul was his only source of information.

Not because Sean liked watching Paul, just for himself. For the way Paul's dark eyes lit up as he glanced from the kitten to Sean's head and back again, for the way his mouth twitched into a grin, exposing impossibly white, straight teeth. Oh, fuck, for the way he licked his lips in unconscious anticipation, the way he leaned forward, toward Sean, as if—

"Jesus!" Sean hissed as the kitten's claws met his scalp. All four feet, claws digging in frantically, and then some tugs that suggested the little bastard was biting at Sean's hair, pulling and—oh, shit, bracing himself with his back feet so he could use all his body weight for tugging. "Shit, shit, ouch…."

Paul was laughing, but he was moving, too, kneeling next to Sean on the floor and gently pushing Panther down into Sean's head so his claws would release.

"He's fierce," Paul said, and Sean tried to ignore the proximity. If he turned his head, his mouth would be against Paul's chest, just one thin shirt between Sean's lips and all that warm skin.

"Okay." Paul shifted and the weight of the kitten was gone. "He gets a time out?"

"Yeah," Sean agreed. He hated to do it, but, on the plus side, it wasn't actually him taking the kitten to the bathroom and locking him inside. If Panther hated Paul for breaking his spirit, well, that was Paul's problem.

When Paul returned, he was carrying cotton balls and a tube of ointment. "He drew blood in a few places."

"No shit. Little fucker was going *hard*."

The other kittens had gathered around now that their more aggressive companion had been neutralized, and Paul had to walk with a peculiar shuffle to make sure he didn't step on any of them. Sean had already given up on using his chair when the kittens were in play mode—too easy to roll over an innocent tail or foot. Now, he thought, "Would this be a good time to wear stubbies?"

"Around kittens? Yeah, I'd think so. I mean—it's more weight on a smaller area, so if you *did* catch one of them, you might do some serious damage. But it'd be easier to avoid them, I think? With you closer to the ground?"

Well. It wasn't like Sean was going to wear the damn things around Paul anyway. He wasn't sure why it was less embarrassing to drag himself around the house legless than it was to wear the stubbies, but it damn well was. "Probably hands and ass is safest, though. If I sit on one of them, it's no big deal."

"I'd be a bit concerned about the safety of my bits, if I were you. Seems like there might be a bit of temptation to take a swing at something hanging around right close to the ground…."

Sean's hands instinctively cupped his crotch. "Great. One more thing to worry about."

Paul was back on his knees, now, his belly pressed against Sean's shoulder so Sean could feel the rumble of his laughter as well as hear it. "You could do your own first aid down there, at least."

A cautious dab, then the coolness of the ointment, and Sean let his eyes drift closed. It was strange, how good it felt to be taken care of like this, after all the anger and resentment he'd developed for *other* people who'd taken care of him. Help him with serious medical conditions in order to save his life? *Fuck off.* Slap some ointment on a few scratches that probably would have been just fine on their own? *Oh, thank you, that feels good.*

"You still sore?" Paul asked, and his voice was quieter than usual. He was closer, so he must have been deliberately lowering the volume. Considerate, but it made things feel a bit more intimate than Sean could really handle.

Also, there had been a question asked. Was Sean sore? "My head?"

"No, your body. From the physio."

"Oh. Yeah." Paul had learned to knock and then just enter the little house—probably if Luke and Mark ever wanted real privacy, they'd lock the front door, but that wasn't Sean's problem to worry about. So Sean had been on the floor the whole time Paul had been there. "I can barely move without crying like a little baby."

"The moving's important, though. It'll help you loosen up."

"My new physio said a hot bath would help. I had one last night. Not exactly a magic cure."

"Massage is better. And movement."

"Massages are expensive." And there was no way Sean was allowing yet *another* stranger to stare at his ruined body. "And moving hurts. I'll take a couple Advils before bed."

He thought about his weird boyfriend lie. Should he tell Paul? No. There had been no reason for the lie, and it would just make him look weird and pathetic if he shared it now. Of course, he'd just had a kitten surgically removed from his scalp, so possibly it was a bit late to be worrying about either "weird" or "pathetic"—

"I can help, if you want," Paul offered, and Sean's brain skidded, then stalled.

"Where does it hurt most?" Paul continued, apparently oblivious.

Well, it was Sean's *ass* that hurt most, but there was no way he was going to say so.

"I'm just being a baby," he managed.

"No, it's legit. I know how much work it is—and your body's really not used to it, right? I mean, your upper body's in great shape, and we worked your legs a *bit*, but nothing like what you're looking at now, right? And how about your stumps?"

Well, there was no fucking way they were going to talk about that, either, but Paul seemed oblivious.

"A bit of soreness is to be expected, but if there's any extra redness, or if the skin starts to get irritated, you need to let us know." Paul stopped, mercifully, and when he started again a few seconds later, his voice was different. "Not 'us'. Not me. You need to let your prosthetist know, or your doctor, or even your physio. Someone involved in your case."

Jesus. Was Paul—was he *hurt*? Insulted that Sean wasn't working with him? No, they'd cleared all that up. It was fine. They just needed to stop talking about this, stop talking about a fucking *massage*, as if the images associated with that idea weren't going to keep Sean tossing and turning all night, and get back to normal.

"I'm fine," he said. "But getting hungry. What's for dinner? And you know how I love to help with cooking—what can I do?"

"You can chop," Paul said. It sounded like he was surrendering. "You can sit at the table in your chair so you're only moving your arms, and you can chop. You'll be holding a knife the whole time, if that's comforting to you."

"It better be a *sharp* knife," Sean grumbled. He'd hoped it would make Paul smile, but he only got a raised eyebrow before Paul went back to looking like he'd just lost a game he'd wanted to win. Which was stupid. Especially since Sean was somehow feeling the same way.

Chapter Twenty

Candidate Two was allergic to cats. Paul hadn't fully dismissed Candidate One, yet—a convenient business trip out of the country meant there was no need to deal with him, one way or another, for at least a week—but it had seemed efficient to keep things moving, so he'd set up a coffee date with Candidate Two.

"Could you get shots or something?" Paul asked. "I mean, if you needed to. If there was some situation in which you had to be around cats?"

"I—" The Candidate shrugged. "I've never had reason to look into it, and I can't imagine I ever will. I mean—why wouldn't I just continue to avoid cats?"

That took care of that.

It was efficient, too, because they'd met in Brampton on Saturday afternoon, so Paul wasn't all that far from home, and he still made it over to Sean's in good time for dinner. Which Luke was cooking, which meant it would probably be pretty tasty. The afternoon couldn't have gone better, really.

Mark and Luke had clearly gotten past the strain in their relationship after the fight and were canoodling in the kitchen while Sean and Paul hung out in the living room. The kittens were napping, snuggled up all around the humans and each other in jumbled balls of warm fur, and it was snowing just hard enough outside to make everything that much cozier in the house.

It was perfect.

Or it would have been if Paul had just been a couple inches closer to Sean, close enough for their shoulders to be brushing. That was all he needed. Not some big sex scene or proclamation of undying devotion. Just—a tiny, tiny bit of contact. That would have been great.

Paul sighed and let his head flop back against the sofa. A crush on a *regular* straight boy would have been bad enough, but a crush on *Sean Gage*, prickliest straight boy in town? It was ridiculous.

"You okay?" Sean asked. Then, "Bored?"

"Bored? No, not really. Why, are you?"

"We should be, shouldn't we?" Sean made it sound like a genuine question. "We're just—sitting here. Watching kittens sleep. Talking a little, maybe. But—we aren't even watching TV. Should we be watching TV?"

"TV might wake up the kittens."

"Then we could play with them."

"But they might be cranky. You can barely handle Panther when he's in a *good* mood."

Ah, yes, that hit home, just like Paul had known it would.

"I can *handle* Panther just fine. He's a kitten. I weighed them this morning—he's the second-smallest of the litter! I could pick him up with one finger."

"He'd claw the crap out of that finger, though, wouldn't he?"

"Because he's a fighter. They all are. That's why they're still alive."

"But does he *always* have to fight? I mean—he likes you. Loves you, probably, if cats can feel love. You're his buddy, for sure." Paul hadn't meant for this to be some big metaphor, but now that he was part way in, he kind of liked it. "He likes you, but he fights with you anyway. He attacks you, teeth and claws, at least once a day. He'll curl up on your shoulder and have a nice snooze, then wake up and latch on. Why's he do that, Sean? What's up with that little cat?"

Sean snorted, then leaned over and scooped a sleeping Panther off Paul's legs. He held the kitten up to his face and said, "What's up with you, little cat? Why are you such an asshole?" Then he moved the kitten to his ear, holding him as if he were an old-fashioned telephone. Panther was clearly still mostly asleep, his body drooping along Sean's wrist, but apparently he was conscious enough to give Sean the answer he was looking for.

"Oh." Sean nodded, and carefully replaced the kitten on Paul's legs. "I get it."

And then he said nothing more.

Paul waited. If he were mature and wise, he would just let the whole silliness go. Bobby would have expected him to let it go. Candidate One would have expected the same, unless Paul could somehow sell him on the idea that discussing inane topics with rednecks was an authentic cultural experience. Candidate Two? He'd be too busy sneezing to have any opinions. But in the abstract, Paul was sure there'd be a general air of disapproval.

He made it about ten seconds before giving up. "What did Panther say?"

"Hmmm?"

The bastard was going to drag it out. Of course he was. "When you asked Panther a question, just now? And then listened to his answer? What did he say?"

"Oh," Sean said, totally nonchalant. "He said he's just being himself. Just catting the only way he knows how to cat. He says if people don't like it, they can fuck off. Or he'll fight them. He doesn't care which."

Paul looked down at the black furball snuggling back to sleep on his lap. "Really. That's what he said."

"I don't know why you asked if you weren't ready to believe the answer."

"I guess I thought maybe it'd be something more about—I don't know, feeling vulnerable? Needing to protect himself? Something like that?"

"Not according to Panther, no."

"So that's all there is to it." Paul wasn't sure if he was disappointed or, strangely, relieved. "Panther's going to randomly attack people, sometimes. That's just the kind of cat he is. Nothing to be done about it."

"Panther says if you can't handle him at his worst, you don't deserve him at his best."

"Does Panther spend a lot of time reading crap on Facebook?"

"He's stuck at home. Doesn't have a lot to do all day."

Were they admitting they were talking about Sean, now? Had they crossed that bridge? No, not a safe assumption. If Paul said something Sean found threatening, he'd slam them back to a cat conversation with a well-timed scoffing. Best to keep it safe. Keep it feline.

"I feel like he's not actually trying to hurt us," Paul said. "When he fights. It's not about us; it's about him. Does that sound right?"

"You saw the conversation we had, right? He talked to me for, like, ten seconds. I didn't get a full psychological profile."

Yeah. Retreating to cat-land to keep himself safe. Still, Paul pushed a little. "I thought you might a little insight to offer from your own perspective. You know... as someone who... who is occasionally... mildly abrasive? Not that you attack people's heads—thank you for that—but, you know. Sometimes I do wonder whether Panther is your spirit animal."

"Maybe I'm his," Sean said, which was a bit strange, metaphysically, but didn't seem to be a complete denial of the similarities.

"We haven't talked about who's taking which kitten when they're old enough to split up." Paul shifted a little, and Panther dug a claw into his thigh. For balance, maybe, or maybe as a warning against further movement. "I'm hoping to take Panther."

"What? You just had a whole spiel about what an asshole he is."

"You're the one who used that word. I was just—wondering about his behavior. That's all. But I guess it doesn't really matter why he acts the way he does. I like him anyway. I like him *because* of it. It's nice to have that little bit of uncertainty. I can't take him for granted. I have to think about him, try to see every new thing from his perspective. He keeps me on my toes. I *like that*."

Sean was staring at him. Paul stared right back. Tempting to look away, but he resisted. This wasn't about a straight-boy-crush, not anymore. He wasn't coming on to Sean, he was just trying to—trying to make him understand. He had value. He was appreciated. He was a total pain-in-the-ass and could be a complete dick, and Paul still liked him. Yeah, not about coming on to him at all. Except—

"I told my new physio I'm gay," Sean said, and Paul blinked. Hard. Sean kept going. "I don't know why. And then I had to go to the dentist yesterday and I did the same thing. To the hygienist. She was all busy, taking the arm off the big leather chair and fussing around about how to transfer me over most easily, and I said it was too bad my boyfriend wasn't there—he could have just lifted me."

"You're—you have a *boyfriend* now?"

"He's in Alberta. That's what I told the physio. I told the hygienist he was in the navy. I'm not sure we even have a navy—do we?"

"Of course we have a navy. Arctic sovereignty, national defense—" Why the hell was Paul talking about the Canadian Navy?

But Sean seemed satisfied. "Good. I need to pay more attention to stuff like that. I think I screwed up the Alberta thing too, to be honest. I guess it's not really a big deal anymore? The tar sands?"

"Why are we talking about Canadian current events? I mean—why did you tell all these people you had a boyfriend?"

"I don't know." Sean seemed genuinely puzzled, and strangely un-defensive. "With the physio it just kind of came out. But with the hygienist? I'd planned it. Not the navy part. Not even the lifting part. But I went in there knowing I was going to find a way to mention my boyfriend."

"Is this a game you're playing? You're just—you're fucking with people in a more cerebral way than usual?"

"I don't even know what *cerebral* means. But—I don't think I'm fucking with people. Maybe the physio, a bit? But, no, not really. I was fucking with him about just how often I should be wearing the stubbies—his definition of 'all the time' needs a bit of work—but I don't think the boyfriend was part of that."

It meant something. Sean telling him this, now, meant something, too. But before Paul could figure it all out, Mark appeared in the doorway to the kitchen.

"Dinner's ready," he said. "Or it will be by the time you guys disengage from the sleepers and make your way in here."

"Okay," Sean said. Maybe his voice was a little too bright, as if he was hiding some deeper emotion, but maybe not. Maybe this whole thing had just been one more weird scene from a man who seemed congenitally unable to do anything the easy way.

"Got it," Paul confirmed, and began lifting kittens off his legs and placing them in a pile on the couch.

He couldn't help himself, though. When he lifted Panther, he stood up with the little cat still in his hand, and lifted him up to face-level. "You're a strange little guy, aren't you?" he asked.

The kitten didn't even open his eyes, but Paul went through with the whole kitten-is-a-telephone charade anyway, and when he'd held Panther to his ear for long enough, he nodded. "You are so right."

Then he set the kitten down on the couch and headed for the kitchen.

"What'd he say?" Sean called after him. When Paul didn't respond, Sean's voice got more belligerent. "Hey! What'd my cat say, asshole?"

Tempting to just let Sean stew, but instead, Paul turned in the doorway. "He said sometimes we think we're lying when really we're just trying out a new truth."

"Yeah? Did he get that off Facebook?" Sean was moving, now, pulling himself across the floor so aggressively that Paul actually felt a chill of intimidation. Then he saw the gleam in the Sean's eye, the sense of—fuck it, the sense of connection between them, and the chill didn't go away, but turned into a much more interesting variety of shivers.

"I didn't ask where he got it from," Paul said. "But it's kind of interesting, isn't it?"

Chapter Twenty-One

It was another fucking charged dinner, with way too many looks that meant more than they should and a general sense of electricity that made Sean's skin fucking crawl in the best fucking way. It was all bullshit. He knew that. He *had* to know that. But for thirty minutes of chicken casserole and raspberry pie, he pushed what he knew to the background and let himself enjoy what he felt.

Wasn't that real, too, in a way?

A totally fucked up way, obviously, but how was that any different from anything else?

And then after dinner Luke sparked up a joint. He wouldn't drink anymore, but he and Mark had apparently talked it through and decided that weed was legal, peaceful, and a totally acceptable thing for an ex-con and an ex-priest to do with their ex-legged friend and his ex-physiotherapist on a Saturday night. Ex-cellent.

Sean watched to see how Paul reacted. Legalization was still pretty new and some people seemed to be hanging on to the sense of weed being something taboo, but Paul took a drag like it was no big thing before passing the joint along. Almost disappointing—it would have been fun to corrupt a pure soul. But probably good, overall. Pure souls could be a pain in the ass.

Sean took a deep drag and held the smoke in his lungs. He'd never liked weed that much—always thought it took away an edge that he needed to keep honed—but at a time like this? With friends he trusted? He could afford to let the edge dull a little.

"I'm thinking of becoming a beautiful disaster," he said into a silence that had come up at some point after about three passes of the joint.

"How's that different from what you've been so far?" Luke asked. *Luke.* Luke could be his role model for the new campaign.

"More emphasis on the *beautiful* part," Sean explained. "The disaster is kind of—given, right? But a person can be a disaster like 'look at that fucking car wreck'—" and, yes, it was a blessing on Sean's life that he couldn't remember any details of his own personal car accident—"or there's that kind of—you know. That person who fucks everything up but is still—I don't know. Still…."

"Still strong?" Luke suggested.

"Still trying?" Mark said.

"Still you." Paul looked at him like he had a telescope right into Sean's brain. "Still pure, still fighting, still tough as hell."

"Pure?" Mark asked.

It was Luke who answered, not Paul. "Yeah. Pure Sean." He made it sound like it was a good thing.

And in his weed-addled state, Sean was almost able to accept that, especially with Paul looking at him like he was.

Mark cleared his throat. "Okay. Luke—you want to go for a walk while the servants take care of the dishes?"

"Yup," Luke said.

"Nobody's going to ask if *I* want to go for a walk?" Sean asked. He looked over at Paul. Funny, right? Not walking? Funny?

Paul shrugged noncommittally.

Well. Fine. "We have to clean up?"

"We cooked," Luke said. He was already on his feet.

"You don't usually clean up when *I* cook."

"You dump the spaghetti into the pot with the sauce and put the pot in the fridge," Luke said. "There's not a lot of cleaning up to be done. And, honestly, *learn to cook something new*."

"Part of the purity of my disaster involves spaghetti," Sean said. "It's fucking symbolic. The noodles represent my legs. Did you honestly not see that?"

"The noodles represent your *brain*," Luke retorted.

It might have turned into a scrap but Paul was there, and he said, "We can look up new recipes on the internet when we're done cleaning up," and Mark was there and he said, "It's a full moon. Lots of light for walking," and then somehow Mark and Luke were gone and it was just Paul and Sean, sitting at the table.

"If I carry everything over from the table, you can wash?" Paul said.

Because—because that's all that was going on. They were doing some dishes. That was it.

"You okay with it if I boost myself up and sit on the counter? It's kinda hard on my back, but it's better than having to wheel the fucking chair in here."

"Fine with me." Paul was already scraping plates and making a tidy stack. "As long as you don't turn the sore back into an excuse for you not doing your share of the cleanup."

Sean eased himself off the chair onto the floor. He was like a fucking creature from a horror movie, dragging himself along like—well, like a fucking creature from a horror movie. But Paul had already seen him like this. Maybe the *beautiful* part of being a beautiful disaster came from owning your own shit. Sean had no lower legs. Paul fucking knew this. Fine. Carry on.

He made it to the counter side and Paul *didn't* offer him a boost, just like Luke never would. Sean's mom, his siblings, even Mark, they all would have offered to help. But Paul and Luke just left him to do his own thing. In this case, that involved Sean dragging one of the chairs from the kitchen table over to use as a ladder up to the counter. Yeah, he was physically lacking, but he was fucking tenacious. That counted for something.

Also, a little bit stoned, which certainly helped. He dragged his chair into position, hauled himself up on it, took a deep breath, then braced his hands and heaved.

Graceful? No. But he was up on the fucking counter, so he wasn't too worried about the details.

And if Paul had noticed any of the fuss, at least he didn't comment on it, beyond, "They keep the dish soap down under the sink. You want me to reach it for you, Princess?"

There was no fucking way Sean was climbing all the way back down, so he snarled instead. "If you want soap, you should add it. Otherwise, I don't care."

"Fucking Panther," Paul mumbled, but he bent over and found the soap.

They didn't talk while the water was running, and Sean entertained himself by adding far more soap to the sink than could possibly be justified. When the suds had bubbled up so high they were starting to overflow onto the counter even though the sink was only a third full of water, he admitted, at least to himself, that it had been a fairly stupid game.

"Get me some greasy dishes over here, stat! I need something to counteract the suds."

"You're supposed to start with glassware."

"Fine. Squirt some grease into a glass and give it to me."

But Paul just handed him the water glasses from dinner.

"Shit." The suds were dripping onto the floor now, and Sean reluctantly turned off the faucet. Still not enough water to do much washing, but the pressure socks on his stumps were covered in suds.

Logical thing would be to take them off and keep them dry, but he wasn't going to do that. Sure, Paul had seen his bare leg-remnants in the past, but things were different, now.

He left the socks on and played with the bubbles a little, scooping them up in the empty glasses and pouring them back and forth. He looked up and found Paul watching him.

"Too many suds," Sean explained, just in case Paul hadn't figured it out already.

"I wonder how that happened."

"I guess we'll never know."

Paul carried the heavy roasting pan over from the oven. He'd already put away the leftover chicken and cleaned out the big chunks. "You said you needed more grease, right?"

"Yeah, but—"

Too late. Paul had the pan at about head height when he let it go and watched it fall into the pile of suds below.

Paul stepped back quickly enough to make it clear the whole thing was deliberate. The fucker had *wanted* the suds to explode, the water to splash, up and all over Sean.

Sean tried to scramble backwards, but of course he was too slow. Too slow and too clumsy and he couldn't get a good grip with his wet socks and somehow his hand slipped and then his ass and suddenly he was sliding sideways, heading for the edge of the counter, and the fall to the floor wasn't going to kill him but it was going to fucking hurt and be absolutely, brutally humiliating—

But then strong hands caught him. One on his shoulder, one on his leg, inches away from the stump as if it was totally natural for someone to touch Sean there.

"Whoa," Paul said. He was close, using his torso as a sort of barrier to keep Sean from slipping any further off the edge. "Sorry. I didn't think that through."

So close. He was so close. The heat of his body bleeding through the wet fabric of Sean's shirt, the strength of his hands holding Sean tight.

"You okay?" Paul asked. Right. Because Sean should have said something by now. Paul thought he was freaking out about almost falling.

And it would be safest to leave it that way. Best to let Paul think Sean was a coward, was worried about a three or four foot drop to linoleum. Better for him to think that than to realize—to understand—to *pity* Sean for having such a doomed hope, such a pathetic crush.

That was the common sense answer. The *only* answer. Still, though. Instead of speaking, Sean lowered his head, only a little, until somehow his forehead was resting against Paul's.

Paul's fingers tightened on Sean's shoulder, loosened on his leg. He inhaled sharply and Sean braced himself to be pushed away. Laughed at.

No, Paul wouldn't laugh. His gentle silence would be even worse.

Instead, though, Paul stayed still, and almost whispered, "Why have you been telling people you're gay?"

"I wanted to see what it would be like," Sean whispered back.

"You know, usually when people experiment with being gay, they start with the *sex* part of it all, not the *coming out* part."

"I like to do things my way."

Paul's huff of laughter sent warm air over Sean's cheek. "Yeah. I noticed."

They stayed still like that for another breath or two, and Sean wasn't sure whether he wanted to pull away and get some relief from the tension or stay like that forever, locked in the perfect torture of being so close.

Then Paul said, "Are you interested in the other part? The physical part? Experimenting with that?"

Experimenting wasn't the right word, but maybe it was the one that would make sense to Paul. And Sean absolutely wasn't in any state to come up with a better description of his own, so he just nodded.

The first part of the nod brought his chin away, his forehead toward Paul. The second part brought his chin forward. Toward Paul. And somehow Paul had tilted his own head, too, so when Sean nodded forward, his mouth didn't find the couple inches of air he expected. Instead, his lips met Paul's.

The kiss was instantly desperate and hungry. No hesitation, no fucking *exploration*, just tongues and teeth and a sense of rightness that was impossible to ignore. With every beat of his racing heart, Sean felt it. *This*. This was right. This strength, this stubble, this masculine cologne and this broad back under his hands. This, this, this.

And then Paul was pulling away. No. Not good.

"What?" Sean demanded. He kept his grip tight on Paul's shirt. What was the fucking problem?

Then he came back to himself. He was sitting on the sopping wet counter of a friend's house because he didn't have a place of his own. He'd somehow squirmed around so he was on the edge of the counter and Paul was between his thighs, but the thighs fucking *ended*. There were no calves to wrap around Paul's waist, no feet to lock together. Sean was a damaged loser, and of fucking *course* Paul wanted to get away from him.

He let go and he shoved, hard enough to slide away and bang his head on the cupboard, hard enough for Paul to take two steps backward and have to catch himself on the kitchen table when he stepped in a puddle and almost wiped out.

"Fuck," Sean said. He felt like his face was too naked. His pupils felt dilated, his lips swollen, his cheeks flushed. He must look like a horny fucking teenager. A *pathetic* horny fucking teenager who wanted something he couldn't have and was taking a fucking pity-kiss way too seriously. *Experiment?* Sure, Paul would help with that, but it didn't mean anything.

"What?" Paul asked. It was a good a question as any, probably, but Sean didn't feel like it was one he could answer.

"This place is a fucking mess," he said. "We were supposed to do the dishes, not turn the kitchen into a swamp."

"We can clean it up." Paul sounded careful, like he was talking Sean down. "Everything's fine."

"Get a fucking mop," Sean ordered. He should probably provide directions to the mop-place, but he had no idea where that kind of stuff was kept. "Or a towel."

"Sean," Paul said. He stepped forward, like he was maybe going to touch Sean, and that was absolutely out of the question. No more pity.

"They'll be back soon and I'm already a shitty guest. I don't need to add a wrecked kitchen to the list of sins."

Paul looked doubtful, but he kicked himself into gear, at least, heading for the bathroom. By the time he was back with a towel, Sean had mopped the counter almost dry—mostly by using the dish sponge to sweep everything onto the floor, but that was just a technicality—and had the stopper of the sink pulled out so he could run fresh water and try to wash away some of the suds. If he'd been magically able to wash away his humiliation, that would have been even better, but life wasn't so kind.

"Are you okay?" Paul asked. He still sounded like he thought Sean might break down if the wrong words were used. Fuck, he was probably right.

"I'm fine. Get the floor cleaned up, will you? They could be back any time."

"Sean," Paul started, but then the universe actually threw Sean a fucking break, because the front door creaked open and Mark and Luke's voices reached them.

"My god! This house is full of kittens!" Luke yelled, and then there were sounds of what was probably him pretending to be attacked by felines.

"Mop!" Sean hissed.

It was stupid. Luke and Mark wouldn't care about a bit of water on their floor. On the list of roommate sins Sean had committed, this was probably way back on the third or fourth page. But it was something to worry about, and that was nice.

Something to distract him from how totally screwed he was.

Chapter Twenty-Two

The towel was sopping wet by the time Paul was done mopping the floor, but he knew where the laundry room was and wasn't at all sorry to have a bit of time alone, without Sean snarling at him. By the time he came up from the basement, Luke was at the sink, drying the dishes Sean handed him.

"I should go," Paul said. Sean didn't argue, obviously, but even Luke, usually a gracious host, only gave him a smile that was clearly a polite agreement. Paul had overstayed his welcome, possibly about the time he'd started making out with Luke's straight friend who'd just smoked up and probably hadn't known what the hell he was doing.

At least Paul had stopped it before it had gone any further. Maybe things were still salvageable? Maybe?

Fuck, what if they weren't? What if he'd ruined everything?

"You okay to drive?" Mark asked. He still had his jacket on. "Or do you want to go for a walk first and clear your head?"

Paul didn't think it was the weed making his head spin, but he nodded anyway. Mark was being a responsible host. "Yeah, okay. I'll do that."

Somehow Paul hadn't expected Mark to stand in the front hall, waiting while Paul got dressed for the outdoors, and then accompany him. But he wasn't sorry about having the company.

They walked in silence for half a block before Mark said, "Things seemed a bit tense back there."

"Did they?"

Mark shrugged. "Not exactly unusual with Sean, but—he doesn't generally get that way with you, that I've noticed."

"Oh, we've had some moments." Not lately, maybe, but certainly at the start.

"So—was it bad that Luke and I cleared out? We thought maybe you'd want some time alone, but then we thought maybe we were totally misreading it so we came back, and—well, you'd think we'd have learned our lesson and we'd stop trying to help, but as soon as Luke saw Sean he started shooting me the get-Paul-out-of-here-so-I-can-talk-to-Sean looks, and of course I'm enough of a busy body myself that I was happy for the chance to talk to you, but you're both grown men. One of you even seems relatively mature and self-aware. If we're pushing boundaries, please let us know."

"Boundaries? I don't—I don't think so. I'm just not quite sure what you're talking about. I mean, you went for a walk because you thought Sean and I...."

"Oh." Mark sounded genuinely disappointed. "Total misread, maybe. Sorry. We thought maybe there was something between the two of you."

"Something…."

"Something romantic. Sorry. I guess Luke and I are still in that we're-in-love-so-everyone-else-should-be-too phase. Kind of obnoxious, I imagine."

"I—" Paul stopped walking and turned to face Mark head-on. "Am I the only person under the impression that Sean Gage is *straight*?"

"Oh. Uh—I'm sure you're not the only person in the world to think that, no. But of the people who had dinner at our house tonight? Yeah, I think you might be the only one."

"Are you serious?"

"I don't know if he's gay or bi or what—it's really not something he and I have ever discussed. As you can imagine."

"Well—I feel like possibly my imagination isn't quite up to this. Do you mind spelling things out for me a little more?"

Mark started walking again. "I've always been a bit—hesitant?— concerned, maybe, about Luke's relationship with Sean. Not about cheating. I trust Luke completely. But—I've come to understand Sean in terms of pre-therapy Luke, if that makes any sense. Before I knew him, Luke went through a lot of changes. Coming out, at least to himself, was part of that, but he also left behind a lot of anger. You know the pattern, I'm sure—boys are taught that the only acceptable emotion is anger, so too many of them channel every drop of fear and insecurity and sadness into that one acceptable outlet. And both Sean and Luke had a lot of fear and insecurity and sadness to get rid of. Hence, a lot of anger."

Paul nodded. Mark was right about the pattern being recognizable, although it was one he'd largely avoided following himself.

"And Sean hasn't gone through those changes," Mark continued. "Or at least, the process isn't complete. So I've always worried about his relationship with Luke. Bringing that bit of chaos into our lives is—well. For someone like me, it's frightening. But Luke and Sean seem to thrive on it. And I've had to accept that it's part of who Luke is. And of course I admire his loyalty to a friend in need."

This time, it was Mark who stopped walking. "I'm sorry. I'm not sure any of that was at all relevant to what we're supposed to be talking about. It seems I've brought my own bag of worries along tonight."

"It's fine," Paul said, but his brain was screaming *Go back to the part about Sean being gay!*

"Well, I suppose it's not completely disconnected," Mark said. He started down the street, and Paul followed. "That is—Sean and Luke have always been close. Luke says nothing has ever happened, and of course I believe him, but I think their relationship—I think possibly it added a fair serving of confusion to the anger-cocktail they had brewing. I think there was always an intensity between them, and if they'd been raised in a less homophobic environment I expect they would have acted on it."

"I can see that," Paul agreed. It felt like he was making an argument against his own self-interest, somehow.

"It would have been a complete disaster, of course." Mark shook his head. "They *were* in a homophobic environment and they were prone to anger and violence and of course they were drinking heavily and—well. It wouldn't have worked. Not then."

"And now?" Paul asked, but he wasn't sure he really wanted to hear the answer.

"Now, Luke loves me. And he has himself under control. That's more important to him than it is to me, really. And Sean? Sean sees a healthy gay relationship. He lets go of at least some of whatever homophobia he had internalized. He's no longer spending time with the idiots who reinforced his bad ideas. Of course, he's also going through a very difficult process of adjustment to his new physical reality. Honestly, I think being gay—or bi—is probably not Sean's biggest worry right now."

"He pushed me away." It felt strange to be talking about this to someone who was undeniably more connected to Sean than to Paul, but somehow Paul trusted Mark's discretion. He'd been a priest, after all. Paul wasn't clear on the details of all that, but wasn't there something about the confidentiality of a confession? And definitely something about making the confession providing relief. "We kissed, tonight. It was—I thought it was good. Really good. But then I realized he'd been smoking and maybe wasn't clear-headed, and—well. He'd said a few things about being gay, but I thought it was a newer thing. I didn't realize how long it went back."

"So you tried to be honorable." Paul could hear the smile in Mark's voice. "And you discovered that Sean Gage has a slightly different definition of that word than most people you know."

"Is that what I discovered?"

"Well, I can't say for sure. I expect only Sean can. Do you think there's any chance you could get him to talk to you about it?"

"You think Sean's going to say as much as a single word before he's damn good and ready?"

"I think the problem with Sean is that he has *windows* of readiness, and you have to hit the exact right time in order to have even a prayer of getting anything out of him."

They continued in silence for a while before Mark said, "I like you, Paul. I'm glad you've come into our lives and no matter what happens with Sean I hope you're still a friend. With that in mind, can I just say—Sean's a complete pain in the ass. He's the furthest thing from easy and a relationship with him? I don't know. Intense, I imagine, but also frustrating, heartbreaking... did I mention frustrating? If there's any chance of you being able to walk away from this—you might want to take it."

Walk away. Was that possible? Walk away from that kiss? From the strong, proud man he'd shared it with? "What if I can't walk away? What if I don't want to?"

"Then maybe we should head back. Sometimes Sean gets better when he has a bit of time to cool off, but sometimes he just digs in and gets worse. I have no idea what the situation will be this time."

Neither did Paul.

And that was part of the appeal, he realized. He *wanted* to be unsure. He wanted to feel like he was taking a chance, like things could go horribly wrong or beautifully right. *Beautifully...*

"A beautiful disaster," he said softly.

Mark clapped him on the shoulder. "Better you than me."

They walked back to the house in silence, but when they reached the front door Paul caught Mark's arm before he could reach for the knob. "What am I supposed to say?"

"No idea," Mark said. He sounded strangely cheerful about the whole situation. "I assume Luke has tried to talk him down, but it probably didn't work. So—just go with it, I guess? Or, you know, head home and get a good night's sleep and think it all over. This doesn't have to be now. Maybe it *shouldn't* be now."

Maybe it shouldn't. But Sean was in there, and he was upset, probably about something that Paul had done, and that wasn't something Paul could just walk away from. He took a deep breath, nodded to the doorknob and said, "I'm ready. I'm going in."

Mark pushed the door open for him and Paul stopped in the front hall long enough to get rid of his snowy boots but not long enough to take his jacket off. He padded back to the kitchen, braced for the worst, and found Luke peering into the fridge, apparently making a grocery list. Luke looked at Paul, then over his shoulder to Mark, then wagged his eyebrows at Paul and nodded his chin toward Sean's closed bedroom door.

Okay. Sean's safe space. Was it a good idea to harass him in there? Paul had no idea. He stepped forward anyway, took another deep breath—he was going to hyperventilate if he didn't find a better way to brace himself—and knocked on the door.

"Fuck off!" Sean bellowed.

"He thinks it's me," Luke said calmly from the kitchen.

So Sean didn't want to talk to his best friend in the whole world but he was going to want to talk to Paul? It seemed unlikely. Still, Paul knocked once more. "It's me. Paul."

An uncomfortably long wait, and then, "Fine. Come in."

Paul pushed the door open.

Sean was sitting on the bed wearing a shirt and a pair of shorts. His legs were stretched out in front of him, his stumps uncovered, pointing at Paul almost like an accusation. No attempt to cover them, which was unusual for Sean. This meant something. Sean showing him this…

"Holy fuck," Paul said. He couldn't be right. Could he? "Are you… Come on, Sean. You think I'm *that* bad at my job? You think maybe I *forgot* that you're a bilateral transfemoral amputee? Is that…"

It couldn't be that. No. But the expression on Sean's face? The jutting chin, the bravado of it all—*this is me, and you can't handle it*—and, of course, the little boy beneath it all, the one who wanted to be accepted so badly, but couldn't just ask for what he needed.…

Paul fell to his knees beside the bed, then reached out and cupped Sean's closest stump in his hands. "I'm aware of this. It's not a big deal to me. It's not a problem."

Sean didn't speak, but he didn't pull away. They were close; Paul could feel it. If he could just navigate past the last few mines, he might be safe.

He shifted cautiously on the floor and brought his other hand closer to Sean. "You know why I don't care too much about this?" he asked, and he gently squeezed what was left of Sean's thigh. "It's because I know about *this*."

And slowly, so slowly, he stretched out and laid his free hand over Sean's heart. "Because I see *you*. All of you. And you're so much more than just a couple of legs."

"I don't—" Sean said. "I can't—"

Paul waited, his hands still on Sean's body. And finally, with a suddenness that made it feel as much like surrender as victory, Sean relaxed. He actually groaned a little, as if whatever tension was leaving his body had sent vibrations over his vocal cords on its way out. And then he nodded. "Okay," he said.

Okay. That seemed positive, but it was a little vague. "What's okay?"

"I don't know. Whatever, I guess." It should have sounded like a sullen teenager, but it didn't. It sounded like Sean was actually open to— something. To whatever.

"Can I kiss you again?" Paul asked.

Sean's tongue flickered out and licked his lips. That seemed like a good sign, but Paul wanted more. He'd done the work, and now he wanted the damn words.

"You're not making a good decision, here," Sean said.

"That's what people said when I dumped Bobby, and it was the smartest thing I've ever done."

"I'm a mess."

"I'm okay with that."

"You're an idiot."

Paul smiled. Not exactly the words he'd been hoping for, but close. "So neither one of us is a prize. You willing to take a chance on an idiot like me?"

"This is a terrible idea," Sean said. But he was moving as he spoke, shifting closer to the side of the bed and bringing his hand up to the side of Paul's neck. Warm fingers against Paul's skin, still chilled from the outdoors, and then warm lips on his.

This kiss was sweeter than the last one. Gentler. Sean smiled partway through and that made Paul smile back so their lips didn't fit together properly and that was perfect. Paul's neck was at an awkward angle and he thought about climbing up onto the bed but he didn't want to freak Sean out so he stayed where he was and somehow that was perfect, too.

It was their perfectly imperfect kiss and it lasted quite a while.

They didn't break apart until Paul felt the scratching at his leg and reached down to find a furry body trying to climb up him. He kept a grip on Sean's neck but pulled his face away enough to look down and see a tricolored blur. "Cyborg," he said, and scooped her up onto the bed.

"She keeps wanting to sleep with me." Sean let the kitten climb up onto his lap.

"She's not the only one."

Sean's eyebrows rocketed up his forehead. "Did you just say that?"

"A bit much?"

"A *bit*?"

But Sean was laughing, and Paul laughed to, then groaned as he shifted his weight and his knees complained. "I should go. But—do you want to do something, sometime? Like, something besides hanging out with kittens?"

"Like what?"

Well, Paul had no actual idea. "Dinner?"

Sean wrinkled his nose. "The chair's a pain."

There were plenty of wheelchair accessible restaurants in town. But Paul didn't push. "At my place, maybe? I could cook. Hey, you could *bring* the kittens. You were saying we should start socializing them, right? They've had lots of experiences *inside* this house, but not many outside. And there are kids living on my ground floor—they seem pretty nice. I bet their mom would lend them to us for half an hour so the kittens can get some exposure."

Sean looked like he was going to argue, but he nodded instead. "Yeah, okay. When?"

"Tomorrow? After hockey? It's an early game tomorrow. I could follow you home from the rink and we could scoop the kittens and go to my place for dinner. I should get a litter box and some toys for my place anyway. And, hey, if I'm the host, I can do all the cooking. You don't even have to help."

"Well, *now* this sounds like a good idea."

"It is," Paul promised. It was a great idea. He leaned forward for a quick kiss, ended up bumping noses pretty awkwardly, and found himself smiling anyway. There was room for improvement. That was fine.

"Okay," Sean said again. "Now—go away. Me and Cyborg are going to sleep."

It was still pretty early, but Paul didn't argue. He looked back from the doorway, and smiled at Sean, and Sean smiled back. That was enough.

"So," Mark said from the sofa as Paul headed past the living room toward the front door.

"So," Luke said back. He was on the floor with kittens all over him.

"So," Paul agreed. He pulled his boots on. "We're going to take the kittens over to my place tomorrow after sledge hockey. Socialize them a little."

"Smooth," Luke said, and Paul resisted the urge to throw a glove at his smirking face.

Mark's smile was more respectful as he said, "Good for you. That's good."

Yeah. It was.

Paul said his goodbyes and stepped out onto the porch. The night air was cold and dry and he could see about a million stars. He wanted to look at them with Sean.

But there was lots of time for that. The stars weren't going anywhere, and neither was Paul. Not if he could help it.

Chapter Twenty-Three

Sean fell asleep that night feeling fairly calm about the whole thing. He woke up the next morning in a full fucking panic. Possibly the weed had helped him through the night before, and if there was ever an argument for a wake-and-bake lifestyle, that was it.

He'd—Jesus Christ, he'd kissed a—no, wait, *kissed* wasn't the right word. He'd full-on *made out* with a guy. And not some random loser. Even when Sean had been at his best, someone like Paul Gill would have been way, way, way the fuck out of his league. And with no legs?

The whole thing was a nightmare. Sean had made a fucking fool of himself, no doubt about it. He needed to—

Well, fuck.

He had no idea what he needed to do. What he *could* do, that would have even a chance of digging him out of this pathetic, ridiculous hole.

Could he leave the country? Was that an option?

Could he stay in the hole he'd dug and dig it even deeper, tunneling down into a burrow of some sort for safety? Could he just stay in bed, hidden beneath his blankets, forever?

Damn. He'd really screwed everything up. The weed must have been way the hell stronger than he'd thought.

He, Sean Gage, had kissed a boy, and he'd fucking liked it.

He was a fag.

Or bi.

Whatever. The exact word wasn't the goddamn issue. He was supposed to be *straight*, and he fucking wasn't. He might have always known it, but he hadn't always had *proof*, not like this.

Luke had corrupted him, just like Tinker and Mikey had said. Well, they'd said Luke had dragged him off to pervert paradise, which was a bit much—wherever Sean was, it definitely wasn't any kind of paradise—but they'd seen something. They'd *known*. That was why they'd attacked. Because they'd seen the weakness, and they'd realized it was spreading, and they needed to weed that shit out, purify the town before—

Okay, no. Even at his worst, Sean had never believed that shit about other people, so why was he ready to believe it about himself?

He wouldn't believe it about *Luke*. That—that actually helped. Sean was a bit more like Luke now, that was all. He liked guys. Sometimes. Maybe. Luke liked guys, and he wasn't weak. He wasn't impure and he wasn't contagious and there was nothing wrong with him, and if Sean believed all that about Luke, then he could really believe something different about himself, could he?

"Fuck," he groaned, and he flopped back onto the mattress.

From the other side of the almost-closed bedroom door—no point trying to shut it all the way, not with five kittens who would spend all night scratching and meowing if they couldn't get in or out of the room—Luke called, "You awake? If you want breakfast cooked for you, get out here now. Otherwise you're on your own."

Sean scrubbed his hands over his face. Breakfast. Right. The world didn't stop turning just because he was gay or bi or whatever.

"I know your tricks," he bellowed back. Way more volume than necessary, but it felt good. Manly. God, he was a loser. Still, he had to keep doing *something*. "You say you'll cook for me, but as soon as I get out there you'll give me a job."

"The toast ain't gonna butter itself, toast-bitch."

Toast. Sean looked down at his hands. The same hands that had been on the back of Paul's neck the night before, that had—fuck, he'd had his fingers up in Paul's hair, and it had felt so right, and he'd wanted to tighten his grip, grab hold and never let go—and now he was supposed to use them to butter some fucking toast?

A quick knock, and then the door was shoved further open and Luke appeared, shuffling his feet through the swarm of kittens dancing around him. "You freaking out? Something happen with Paul last night, and now you're being weird about it?"

"I know it's your house and everything, but can you not at least fucking *pretend* to give me some privacy?"

"Well, it's my house and everything…." But then Luke shrugged. "I've been through it too, you know. We believed a lot of stupid crap, growing up. And even if we don't *really* believe it anymore, it's still there."

Yeah. It was there. Like a pit of snakes in Sean's gut, churning and biting and—okay, not snakes, because he was pretty sure there was some scratching going on, too, and snakes couldn't do that. The one fucking good thing about snakes was that they couldn't scratch.

Lizards? Homophobic lizards in his gut? That was getting a bit weird. And it wasn't exactly helpful. He needed to stay on topic. "What do we do about it?"

"We butter the fucking toast, and keep the eggs from burning." Luke took a step back toward the kitchen. "Seriously. It works. Just—keep living. Get on with it. Give yourself some time to adjust, but don't wallow in it. Realize that you and me used to be idiots. Look at people like Mark and Paul and see how totally unworried they are about this shit. I mean—they're smarter than us, right? They went to university and everything. No point in doing a whole lot of thinking ourselves, not when we've got smart people around to do the heavy lifting. They've thought it through, and they're fine with it, so we can just trust them on that."

"Seriously? That's your advice?"

"My advice is to haul your legless ass out of bed and get to the kitchen if you want to eat. Anything past that? Worry about it when you get to it."

"I fucking got to it!" Sean yelled as Luke walked away. "Last night! I got to it, and now I'm worrying about it, and you're no damn help at all."

"I thought you wanted privacy? And, seriously, get your ass out here. Wash your hands, from the sound of things, and then butter the damn toast."

Sean shifted off the bed. He should take the time to put his stubbies on, but they were still a hassle to get set up right—maybe they always would be—and he didn't have the patience. He dragged himself to the bathroom, took a piss and washed his hands, then made it to the kitchen to find the traditional pile of dry toast waiting for him.

"It doesn't matter anyway," he told Luke as he heaved himself up onto the chair. "Paul's totally out of my league."

"Because you're not as smart? Or because of the legs?" Luke stirred at the eggs in his pan—scrambled, looked like, with cheese and ham—"Or just the personality thing? Like, he's a good guy and you're a dick. Oh, fuck, and the job. He's got a good job. You, not so much. He's better looking than you, too. You're kinda—well. Your nose is a problem, and that's just a fact. And he's got a pretty nice car. What else?"

"Fuck you."

"Oh, yeah, the swearing. That's no good. He doesn't swear nearly as much."

"What happened to him being smart, so we should just trust him? Huh? If he likes me, do you really think you're smart enough to be telling him he's wrong?"

"Wow, Sean, that's a really good point. I guess we *should* just trust him when he decides who he's going to like. You've turned me completely around on this. Thanks."

Well, fuck. "One of these times your reverse psychology bullshit isn't going to work."

"And won't that be a sad day for all of us?"

It kind of would be. Still. "There's nothing wrong with my nose!"

"Yeah, okay. If that's what you need to believe. Now—the eggs are ready. Are you done with the damn toast?"

Sean growled a little and got down to work. After they'd eaten, he strapped on his stubbies drove with Luke out to Elise's farm and scrubbed buckets and chopped animal food until noon, when Luke drove him home, and all that time he barely thought about Paul at all.

It was a bit trickier when he was home alone all afternoon, but he did his exercises and practiced walking in the back yard and swore a bit at Luke's squirrel when she saw him fall down, and then Luke was home from work because the sledge hockey game was early that day and he'd had to rearrange his schedule to make sure he could be there.

Paul had probably made changes to *his* schedule, too. Two able-bodied men messing with their routines in order to play sledge hockey when they could have just played regular hockey at a regular time. Or not played hockey at all.

They were both saints, probably, although you wouldn't be able to guess it from the way they behaved on the ice. Or from the way Paul kissed...

But Sean was trying not to think about that. He was trying, damn it.

In keeping with their negotiated agreement, Luke dropped him off at the front door—Sean refused to wear the stubbies out in the parking lot where anybody might see him—and as soon as he slid out of the truck and hit the ground, he started scanning the area for Paul. He was going to be there, and Sean was going to see him, and it would be a bit weird, but if he could see him *first*, before he was seen, at least he'd be able to build up a bit of— something. Courage?

"Shut the door," Luke ordered. And of course as soon as Sean did, Paul appeared, standing by the hood of the truck. Sean had been hidden behind the truck door like a little kid, and now Paul was there, looking down at him, *seeing him*, short and awkward and totally unprepared.

"Hey," Paul said. The warmth in his eyes was a trap. It seemed genuine, but that was impossible. Not when Paul was—and Sean was—

"Fuck," Sean said. Paul raised an eyebrow, but Sean was already turned and stumping away. It wasn't like it mattered whether he was polite or not. There was nothing he could say that would make any of this even remotely fucking tolerable, so the best thing was just to get away from it as fast as he could and then... well. He'd worry about that after he managed the getting away part.

The problem with stubbies—*one* of the problems with stubbies—was that it was impossible to actually move fast in them, and the harder you tried, the weirder you looked. Sean's escape was really only possible because Paul clearly wasn't trying to stop him.

Which was good, Sean reminded himself. It was a clean break. And if there was a part of him that felt like shit that Paul was letting go so easily? That part was stupid. What had it thought was going to happen? Paul was going to come running after him and sweep him off his non-existent feet?

No. Fairy tales were for little kids, or at least for people who still had their legs attached. Sean couldn't afford to let himself believe any of that crap.

He stubbed his way into the change room, realized that Luke was bringing the gear in from the truck so there was no changing to be done, yet, and then turned around to leave because as awkward as it was to move around in stubbies, it was even fucking worse to stand there like a kid waiting for his big brother to arrive and take care of him.

Paul was standing in the doorway, of course, and Sean-with-legs could have shouldered him out of the way and least gotten a bit of satisfaction from the movement, but if Sean-without-legs started trying shit like that— well, the first problem would be that his shoulders now were pretty close to ball-height on someone standing up, and pushing someone out of the doorway was an acceptable level of violence, but shouldering someone in the damn balls? That was a bit more than even he could justify.

It didn't matter anyway because Paul stepped out of the way before Sean even got there. Sean refused to make eye contact, or look up at all, so he didn't actually know what Paul's expression was, but it wasn't too hard to imagine. Paul was a good guy. He cared about other people. He'd be looking concerned. Pitying. Poor, legless, hopeless Sean Gage was having a tough time with something, and that was really sad, and Paul was sad and everyone was sad and the whole thing was just—

"Hey, asshole, you were supposed to wait for me at the front doors." A hockey bag full of gear landed in front of Sean. Luke had his own bag still slung over his shoulder. "You told me the stubbies are for carrying shit, so *carry shit*. I'm not your damn Sherpa."

It usually would have worked. If Sean was upset about something, having a stupid fight with Luke was a good way to burn off some frustration. But this time his nerves were too jangly; he felt like he was one wrong word away from breaking down and crying, right there in front of two teams worth of sledge hockey players. It would be a disaster. His one release, his one fun activity, and he was about to ruin it by being a sucky little bitch. He needed to get hold of himself.

But he had no idea how to do that, so he just stood there, frozen, waiting for disaster to strike.

"Hey," Luke started, and it was pretty clear he was about to produce the wrong word that would set Sean off. Aggression hadn't worked, but compassion was going to be even worse.

Then an unfamiliar voice cut through Sean's desperation. "Excuse me."

A good-looking brown guy in a suit with no tie, standing beside Luke, trying to get his attention. "I'm looking for Paul Gill. I was told he would be here. Do you know Paul Gill? Can you tell me where he is?"

And then Paul's voice from somewhere behind them. "Bobby? What are you doing here?"

Chapter Twenty-Four

It was a collision of worlds, and Paul really wished he'd had more time to brace for the impact. Or to steer better in order to avoid it entirely, but he really didn't think this was something he'd had a chance of foreseeing.

"Bobby?" he repeated. "What's going on?"

"You didn't return my call."

Well, that was true. Bobby *had* called and left a message a few days before, and Paul hadn't called him back. He'd been planning to, eventually, but....

"Is there something wrong? Something urgent? Why did you drive all the way up here? And how did you find me?"

"I went to your office. The woman there wouldn't tell me where you were, but there was a calendar on the wall behind the desk and I recognized your writing for today's date. *Off at four for hockey.*" He sounded proud of himself, like he was a detective, not a snoop.

"But why are you here at all? Why are you in town?"

"We need to talk." He said it with such gravity, such a sense of ominous portent, that Paul half-expected the next words out of his mouth to be *I'm pregnant with your baby.*

But back in the land of reality, Paul just said, "If it's not an emergency, you'll have to wait until after the game." Good. Boundaries. That was reasonable.

"I think this is more important than a game of sledge hockey, Paul. It's not like you're at the Olympics."

Bobby would keep this up until Paul gave in. It was their pattern. It was Paul's fault as much as Bobby's. Patterns didn't get set because a person tried something and got shut down; they got set because a person tried something and it worked. Paul had to take responsibility, and he didn't want to cause a scene.

One more try, though. "Can you tell me briefly what you want?"

"We were together for four years, and you can't give me the courtesy of a private conversation?"

"*After* the—" Paul started.

But Bobby shook his head in disgust. "Honestly, Paul, you expect me to freeze my ass off in some small town arena waiting around for you to be done with your silly game? Can we just get this over with?"

Right. Get it over with. Avoid the scene. Paul took a step toward Bobby, and then Sean was there, between them. Looking not at Paul—*still* not looking at Paul—but with his head tilted back at an angle that made it clear he was staring Bobby down.

"Did you not fucking hear him?" Sean asked. He sounded genuinely incredulous. "He said after the game. Did you hear him say that?"

Paul looked around. A scene. It was going to be a scene. Where the hell was Luke? He could calm Sean down when no one else could. Except—he was looking at Bobby with the same hostility Sean was showing. Luke was standing back, letting Sean handle it, but he definitely wasn't stepping in to calm things down.

"Who the hell are you?" Bobby asked.

"Sean Gage. You can call the cops and ask about me, if you want. Probably a good idea, really. You should know who you're fucking with."

"I'm not—this doesn't concern you, whoever you are. This is between myself and Paul."

"Paul told you he'd talk to you *later*. This isn't later. Fuck off until then."

"Paul—" Bobby started.

And Paul knew he should end it then. *He* could calm Sean down, if he had to. A hand on his shoulder, reassurance that it was all fine, not a big deal—Sean would stay mad, but he wouldn't interfere any more. Not if Paul asked him not to.

But, damn. Was this a scene? Sean's voice had been raised, and people were watching. It qualified. And it really wasn't that bad.

Strangely liberating to realize that. There was nothing being said that Paul was ashamed of. Nothing he needed to keep secret. So why the hell *shouldn't* there be a scene?

That said, it didn't need to be an *extended* scene.

"We've got a game, Sean," he said. "You got your gear?"

"Got it," Sean said. He didn't turn around immediately, though. Instead, he kept staring at Bobby, until Bobby half-turned and cast his eyes in Paul's direction. Pleading? Needing to be rescued? Well, too fucking bad for him.

Paul picked up his own gear bag and turned, making the movement big and obvious enough for Sean to pick up in his peripheral vision, and sure enough, Sean took the hint and dragged his own gear bag to his shoulder.

"That's your ex?" Sean asked as they headed for the change room. Paul was vaguely, comfortingly aware of Luke falling in behind them, an extra layer of insulation against Bobby's presence.

"That's Bobby. I have no idea why he's here."

"Is that going to bug you?" Sean asked. "Not knowing? Maybe I should have stayed out of it so you could have talked to him and figured it out. But he was being a dick, right? Why'd you let him get away with that?"

"If I'd wanted to talk to him, I'd have talked to him." But Paul needed to say a bit more than that. "It's easier. To—to go along. But I don't want to do that anymore. I don't want to do what's easiest. So, thanks. For backing me up."

"No problem," Sean said, and then they were inside the crowded change room, jostling for space on the bench, and conversation time was over.

They played their game, Sean on the opposite team from Paul and Luke, as usual, and taking obvious pleasure in checking them into the boards whenever possible, also as usual. He seemed to have gotten over whatever his problem had been when he'd first arrived at the rink, but it was a bit hard to be sure—not like there were a lot of opportunities for deep, meaningful conversations in the middle of a game of sledge hockey.

Even with the possible tension there, though, it was a still a lot more pleasant to think about Sean than it was to think about Bobby. What the hell was Bobby doing so far from home? What did he want?

No. Much nicer to think about Sean, and the way his pale skin had grown rosy as they'd kissed the night before. The way he'd leaned into Paul's kiss, run his fingers through Paul's hair—okay, maybe not *too* much thinking about that. Best to keep his mind on the game.

But when the game was over and they'd changed back into their regular clothes, he didn't have that distraction anymore.

"Might need to make a bit of a change in plans," he told Sean as they left the change room. "I should talk to Bobby and figure out what's going on. But I can call you when that's done? It hopefully won't take long, and I then I just have to hit the store for cat stuff and dinner food, but that won't take long either. I can be at Luke's in an hour or so, hopefully?"

"Oh." And, no, things *weren't* okay, because Sean still wasn't really making eye contact. "Don't worry about it. You've got stuff to deal with."

"What? No. I mean, if there's something major with Bobby, I'll give you a call, but otherwise—seriously, an hour or so. I can just get takeout pizza if you don't want me to take the time to buy groceries."

"Jesus, Paul!" And now Sean *did* look at him, and Paul kind of wished he wouldn't. 'It's fine. This doesn't have to happen. Take the fucking excuse, buddy."

"The excuse? You think—I'm not looking for an excuse. Bobby just showed up! I kinda have to deal with him, don't I? But it's not—"

"Paul. For fuck's sake. Look at him." He jerked his head toward the exit door where Bobby was impatiently waiting. "Look at his fucking clothes. His suit alone probably cost more than every piece of clothing I've ever bought in my entire life, all added together."

"Yeah. It probably did. What's that got to do with anything?"

"*That's* your type," Sean said firmly. "That's the kind of guy you want to be with. Not this exact one, maybe, but someone *like*—"

"Did you not fucking hear me?" Paul said. He didn't get it completely right—didn't have quite the same level of incredulous aggression Sean had produced—but it was pretty close. "I said I'd be at Luke's in an hour or so. Did you hear me say that?"

Sean raised his eyebrows. Yeah, he recognized the words, if not the tone. "Okay, but—"

"I'm Paul Gill," Paul continued. "You can call the police and ask about me, but they won't have any idea who you're talking about. Still—you shouldn't fuck with me. If I say I want something, I want it. And *I'm* the one who decides that, not you. Is that clear?"

Sean's expression was hard to read. "Yeah. Clear, but—"

"No buts. If you don't want me to come over, say so. Otherwise, I'll see you in about an hour."

"I—fuck." Sean frowned as if trying to trace how the conversation had gotten away from him, then shook his head as he abandoned the effort. "In about an hour, then. But it's no big deal if you can't—"

"Shut up," Paul said. And he turned and walked away, gear bag banging against his ass to punctuate every step.

He didn't let himself look back, no matter how much he wanted to. Get through the crap with Bobby, then get to the good stuff with Sean. That was the right order for all this.

"What's up?" he asked when he reached Bobby.

"You have a place in town, right? Can we go there and—"

"No." There was no way Paul wanted Bobby anywhere near his new apartment. "You can tell me what this is about right now, and then if it's something we need to talk about more, we can go sit in one of our cars or something." That's right. Channel his inner Sean. Paul wasn't going to get pushed around. He might even drop an F-bomb or two, just to prove his point.

Bobby squinted at him. "What's going on?"

"Bobby. That's what I've been asking you for quite a while now. What *is* going on? Why are you here?"

"You—" Bobby started, stopped, squinted again, then shrugged. "You never actually broke up with me."

"What?"

"You said you were going to stay at your sister's. For a *week*. And then you didn't go on vacation with our families—"

"And I moved all my stuff out of the apartment while you were away."

"Not all of it."

It was Paul's turn to squint. "What'd I forget?"

"Some toiletries. A couple T-shirts. Nothing major, but—enough."

"Enough? Enough for what?"

Bobby sighed. "Enough to give you an excuse to come back. Enough to make it clear you weren't really committed to leaving."

"Bobby. Come on. Some toiletries and some T-shirts? We use similar products, and we wear the same size. I probably just wasn't sure if the stuff was yours or mine, so I left it for you."

"Or you weren't quite ready to pull the plug entirely."

"No. I—I'm sorry. I guess I should have made things more clear. I'll do that now. We're broken up. We're over. I'm sorry."

"Your mother tells me you haven't been seeing anyone else."

"That's not entirely true."

Bobby smiled as if that was the answer he'd been hoping for. "You aren't seeing anyone else you think is worth introducing to your mother. Doesn't that tell you something?"

"Not what you want it to. We're done, Bobby."

Paul was half-turned, ready to walk away, when Bobby said, "Who was that guy, before? The one with no legs. Is that the sort of person you're spending time with these days?"

"The sort who don't put up with your shit? Sure. Yeah. That's the sort of person I'm spending time with."

"I'm worried about you, Paul. You're not acting like yourself."

"You don't know me well enough to have an opinion on that."

It felt good to have the last word. And it felt good to know that what he'd said was the truth: Bobby *didn't* know him, and didn't care enough to pull his head out of his ass and *get* to know him. Paul hadn't really had any doubts before seeing Bobby, but it was still nice to get some extra confirmation. Breaking up had been the absolute right decision, and the only worrisome thing was that Paul had stayed with him as long as he had.

Now if only Paul could figure out a way to make his parents come to the same realization.

But that was a worry for another day. He had a hot date with a new guy and a basketful of kittens.

Chapter Twenty-Five

Sean lost and regained and lost and regained his nerve about five times in the next hour. He showered, got dressed, got the kittens as ready as they could be without actually packing them into their carrier, and then he sat on the floor in the living room and fretted.

He was in over his head. He was going to get hurt. He had no idea what he was doing. The whole thing was a fucking mess.

But...Paul. His sweet smile, his surprising stubborn streak, the way he'd stood up to Sean...yeah. He was probably worth getting hurt.

"I'm glad I used to have legs," he told Luke, who was in the armchair by the window, reading something boring-looking.

Luke looked up from his book. "Uh... yeah. Legs are good."

"I mean—if I'd been born without them, I'd be way better at all this stuff by now. And I'd have grown up differently, right? I wouldn't—I don't know. I wouldn't be used to being taller, wouldn't be used to being able to do stuff I can't do anymore. I wouldn't *miss* my legs, is what I'm saying."

"But you're still glad you had them."

"Yeah. We had some good times, me and the legs. It's good that happened. So now I miss them, but that's okay."

"Better to have loved and lost than never loved at all?"

"What? I'm not talking about—I'm talking about *legs*, Luke. I don't think I was in love with my own legs."

"Yeah. You're talking about legs. Okay."

"I am."

"Got it."

Paul arrived about then, and visited a bit with Luke and Mark while Sean packed up the kittens and tried to act as if everything was casual and fine and he wasn't about to squirm right out of his damn skin from nervousness.

He made it out to the car on his stubbies and didn't complain when Paul loaded the kittens into the back seat instead of setting them on Sean's lap the way he'd imagined. It wasn't a long drive, and the little guys had each other for comfort, but it was still pretty fucking heartbreaking when the first plaintive meow drifted forward.

"They're fine," Paul said, but Sean reached an arm back anyway, stuck his fingers in the carrier, and was rewarded with some cold-nosed sniffs and a few experimental chomps from sharp kitten teeth.

"I need to keep an eye on them," he told Paul as they were parking the car. "They could learn bad habits at a new place, and so far they've been great about using the litter box—I need to make sure they don't get confused. I need to pay attention to them, without being distracted."

Paul gave him a long look, then nodded. "Yeah. Okay. Message received."

"What?"

But Paul was walking away, long legs confident even on the icy sidewalk, kitten carrier in one hand, keys in the other, heading for the front door of the apartment.

Sean lagged behind, staring at the terrain, taking each step only after making sure there was nothing there to cause him problems. Which was stupid, really; he'd fallen down about a million times since he started wearing the damn stubbies, and it really wasn't a big deal. Still, he didn't want to do it in front of Paul. Or behind Paul, in this case. He didn't want to do it anywhere in Paul's general area.

So he was paying attention to the ground, and that meant he only caught a blur of movement, a quick, quiet "Shit," and then Paul was in the snowbank, twisted onto his back, the kitten carrier held up in the air above him like a trophy.

"They're okay," Paul called. "The doors are still latched. They're okay."

Sean picked up the pace and made it to Paul's thighs before looking down and saying "Are *you* okay?"

"Probably. Pretty nice of someone, piling all this snow right here."

"Might have been nicer if they'd piled a bit of salt on the sidewalk instead."

Paul waved the carrier a little in Sean's direction and he took the cue, lifting the case and peering inside to see five curious, furry faces looking back at him. "Paul fell down," he explained to them. "But he saved you. You're safe. He's your hero."

"A hero, huh?" Paul was carefully stretching and bending, clearly doing some sort of physiotherapist-self-assessment.

"Something like that." Sean set the carrier down on the sidewalk. "Look. Are you—I mean—last night was just a thing that happened, right? It's not like we're engaged or something. We can both just walk—well, you can walk away, I can do my thing. Okay?"

Paul sighed. "Is that what you want?"

"What?"

"Simple question, Sean. I mean, I get it—this is new for you, you're hesitating, you're freaking out, whatever. And we can take things as slow as you want, or we can stop altogether if you want. Totally your call. But, seriously. *It needs to come from you.* Stop trying to make me do it for you, because I'm not going to. I'm getting pretty fed up with your bullshit, but other than that I'm still into this. I'm not trying to back out. If you want out, that's your call. But I'm not going to make it for you."

"You're still into it?" Sean said. "For sure?"

"Yeah. For sure."

Sean set the carrier down carefully on the sidewalk. "Okay, then." And he let himself fall. He landed beside Paul on the snowbank, which wasn't quite as fluffy as it looked, and wriggled as needed until their faces were level. "Still okay?"

Paul's smile was the only answer Sean needed. Their kiss was sweet, and real, but only lasted a couple breaths before the kittens started meowing and Paul said, "We should go inside."

"Okay. Yeah. We should."

It was all easier, after that. They went upstairs and opened the carrier and it wasn't really all that different from playing with the kittens the day before.

Well.

Okay, it was pretty different. There was more kissing, absolutely. But Sean hadn't been kidding about wanting to be sure the kittens didn't learn bad habits, and it was pretty hard to *really* get in the mood when he was constantly monitoring to be sure none of the five had forgotten where the litter box was.

That was okay, though. Good, even. Kissing, like this, was new. Kissing someone he really *liked*, someone who seemed to like him back? New. Kissing someone while they were both sober? New. Taking breaks to talk, to smile and laugh, to scold or tease a kitten, and then coming back to the kissing as if it was the most natural thing in the world for these two mouths to be spending so much of their time joined together? New. And pretty fucking nice.

When the animals finally exhausted their passion for exploration and collapsed into a ball of fuzziness on the ground between Sean and Paul's thighs, the two men petted them for a while, and then Paul stood up and shifted to Sean's other side. "Don't want to squish them," he explained, and then he kissed Sean in a way that made it clear why squishing was a potential risk.

Roving hands, all over Sean's chest, his belly, his back, his arms. A roving *mouth*, kissing down Sean's neck, up to the tender, ticklish, shiver-inducing spot by his ear. And then a slide down Sean's body that made it seem as if things were about to get *very* interesting, except Paul went a bit too far and instead of undoing Sean's fly he slid right past and ran his fingers up under the cuff of Sean's cut-off jeans to the pressure sock beneath it.

Oh. Fuck.

They had to do this? They couldn't just ignore the whole thing, couldn't just—

Sean gasped when Paul's lips found the tender skin where the sock had been. More kisses, some of them on the numb-ish scar tissue but others finding surprising little sensitivities. Sean wanted to pull away, to hide, maybe to leave altogether, but—but maybe he could do this. Maybe he could let this happen.

Paul moved over to the other leg with his mouth, but kept his free hand cupped almost protectively over the first stump. He rubbed gently, slid his fingers up under Sean's jeans to find new skin, and all the while worked the pressure sock off on the other side.

It was too much. Too intimate, too gentle, too fucking loving towards something unlovable. Paul was damaged. His legs were horrible. Ugly. Disgusting, even.

"You don't have to," he started, and Paul lifted his eyes to look up at him.

"Don't tell me what to do," he said, and then he licked a long, deliberate stripe up the end of Sean's leg.

Sean gave up. He let his head fall back on the sofa cushions and stared up at the ceiling and then he took a deep breath and let himself *feel*. Paul was okay with this. Fuck, Paul seemed to be enjoying it, and if there was some sort of fetish at work Sean would decide how he felt about that later. For the moment? He was safe. Paul wouldn't judge him, wouldn't shy away, and clearly wasn't grossed out.

"Hey," Paul said gently. He still had one hand on each of Sean's stumps, but his attention was on Sean's face, now, on....

"Fuck." Sean brushed quickly at his eyes. "Sorry."

"No, I'm sorry." Paul scooted up closer. "Shit. I pushed too far? I wanted—I wanted you to understand—"

Sean moved fast. He didn't have the words, but maybe he could make himself understood anyway. The kiss was a bit saltier than usual and there wasn't a lot of finesse, but maybe that was just Sean's style. He put as much honestly as he could in it, as much appreciation and affection and sincerity as he was feeling, and maybe it was enough, because when Paul finally eased away, he didn't seem nearly so worried anymore.

And Paul kept his face up near Sean's for a while, but he didn't shy away from running his hands over Sean's legs, either. Like it was all completely natural. Not a big deal at all.

"You have really long fingers," Paul said, lacing his own through Sean's and then spreading their hands out for comparison.

There was probably a dick-size joke in there somewhere, but Sean was too shy to try for it. Sean. Shy about a dick-size joke. The world was turned upside down.

"Like an artist," Paul continued. The words were stupid, obviously, but Sean couldn't help liking the sensations, Paul twining their fingers together, sliding in and out, like he was examining Sean from all angles. Like he was *admiring* what he saw.

"I think my fingers are probably the only part of me that's artistic," Sean managed.

"Your forehead?" Paul suggested, and now Paul's hand roamed there. "Your eyes, definitely. You look—tempestuous. Tortured by the beauty and horrors of the world."

I think you might be making some of that up."

"If *I* were an artist, I'd paint you. And you'd see how I see you, and you'd understand."

"I'd have to sit still for a long time for that, wouldn't I? To get painted? So, hate to break it to you, but it's probably not going to happen."

"Maybe I'd catch you in your sleep." Another kiss. "Do I get to see that? Get to see you sleeping?"

"When? Tonight?"

Paul's laugh was soft. "Holy smokes, I think every sphincter in your body just clenched. Don't worry—I'm not rushing you." He sat back, but kept his fingers laced with Sean's. Holding hands. Sappy, but—Sean didn't pull away.

"But have you thought about it?" Paul continued. "You're new to being with a guy. Have you thought about what you want to do? What you want done to you?"

Sure, Sean had thought about it, if picking the right porn to jerk off to counted as *thought*. But he wasn't sure he was ready for big discussion. "I guess I figured we'd play it by ear."

Paul nodded slowly. Clearly he wasn't thrilled by that approach, but he didn't seem ready to argue about it.

"I should get started on dinner," he said. "You want to watch me cook?"

Yeah, Sean did. But—it was all suddenly a bit too much for him. It had been less than twenty-four hours for all of this to change, for him to go from sneaking peeks at Paul and telling himself to stop being an idiot to now, somehow, being invited to perv on the guy in his own kitchen? Perv on the *guy*. Like that wasn't part of the intense weirdness of the situation.

"I'm going to keep an eye on the kittens," Sean said.

Paul gave him a bit of a strange look, but he didn't argue.

And the kitchen was only about fifteen feet away, with no wall between it and the living room. Sean could still hear Paul, could still see whatever parts of him weren't blocked by the breakfast bar.

"You want music on?" Paul called.

"I'm fine."

"TV?"

"Not unless you do."

"You're just going to sit there?"

"I'm watching the kittens."

"Are they doing anything interesting?"

"They're fucking fascinating. Shouldn't you be paying attention to your damn dinner?"

"You know I promise not to make you help, right? Even if you come over here, you don't have to actually cook anything."

This was better. Easier. Now that they weren't fooling around anymore, this was back to just being him and Paul, and he could handle that.

Of course, as soon as he realized that, he started remembering how good it had felt, Paul's smooth hands, his soft lips and wicked tongue....

Clearly Sean was one of those people who was always destined to be dissatisfied. As if he hadn't known that already.

He leaned his head back and spread his arms along the sofa cushion like wings, then let his eyes drift shut. He was in Paul's apartment. He'd just been making out with Paul. That was—it was—

Jesus Christ, what was he doing?

This was too fast, way too fast! He needed to—he wasn't sure. Think it through, probably. Alone. He needed to get the fuck out of there and take some fucking time. He could get into his chair by himself, get out of the apartment, and the building, but then—if he were better on his stubbies he could make it home alone. But his stumps were already sore, and his chair was at Luke's. He was stuck. No, he could call a cab. Fucking humiliating to deal with some asshole cabdriver staring at him as he climbed into the back seat, but that didn't matter. He had to go, and there was no way he was going to ask Paul to drive him, because that ride would be fucking impossible to live through, and Sean needed to—he needed to—

"In case you're wondering," Paul said from far too close, and Sean squished his eyes shut to resist the urge to look. "We're not fooling around anymore today."

Well, *that* got his eyes open. "What?"

Paul shrugged and put a plate of sliced vegetables on the table next to a bowl of what looked like humus. "I think I need some time to think it all through and figure out where I'm at. So—we're just going to eat. Play with kittens, maybe? We can watch a movie or something if you want, or I can just drive you home right after dinner. Whatever you'd prefer."

"What the fuck do you mean you *need some time to think it all through*? What the fuck do you need to think through?"

Paul's smile would make the fucking *Mona Lisa* jealous. "It's just a lot of changes. I'd like some time to adjust."

"Are you—what are you doing? Is this reverse psychology? Have you been talking to Luke?"

"I don't know what you mean." Paul took a slice of pepper and dipped it in the humus, then popped it in his mouth, all without losing that shit-eating grin.

"You think you're fucking smart?" Sean demanded.

Paul laughed, then said, "You need to watch your language in front of the kittens. Don't want them to grow up with potty-mouths."

Well, that was about enough. Sean scooped up the nearest kitten—Panther, of course, sprawled on top of his siblings like he was king of the castle—and held him up to his ear. "He says you're full of shit," Sean reported.

"It'd be a lot easier for me to live with my no-more-making-out decision if you'd stop being quite so adorable."

Adorable. Like—like a fucking kitten. Probably Sean should be offended by that, but honestly, he was too fucking confused. He set Panther, eyes still mostly closed, back down on the kitten pile. "Fine. I didn't want to fool around with you anymore anyway."

"Okay, sure," Paul said. He took another slice of pepper, engineered a big dip of humus, then started back for the kitchen.

"I didn't," Sean growled after him.

And Paul, the crafty fucker, turned around and sweetly said, "Why not?"

Shit. "Because… what you said. About a lot of changes. I mean, I have *way* more changes than you!"

"Really? Because I haven't fooled around with anyone but my boyfriend in five years."

"I haven't fooled around with a guy before. *Ever*."

"Not even Luke?"

"*Luke?* Jesus, no!"

"Really? You guys seem pretty close. And he's pretty hot. If I'd been sharing a bedroom with him, I'd have—well. I think moves would have been made."

"Jesus Christ, you're talking about *Luke*, now? Is that what this has all been about?"

Paul tilted his head and looked at Sean like he was speaking a different language. "Is it what *what* has all been about?"

Sean waved his arm at the apartment, which wasn't really too helpful, then at the kittens, who probably weren't involved at all, and then dropped his arm and settled for a scowl. "Everything. Have you just been trying to get to Luke?"

"Oh, right, you've seen through my plan." Paul was back in the kitchen now, stirring something, but there was no trouble hearing him. Unfortunately. "As soon as I saw Luke, that was it. I broke up with my long-term boyfriend, moved into a crappy apartment, made friends with a client to the point that I actually *lost* the client, spent every night with the ex-client looking after kittens, learned how to massage a kitten's damn ass to make it shit on command, cleaned up the kitten shit, hung out more with the ex-client, put up with endless crap from the ex-client, *seduced* the ex-client into making out with me, invited the ex-client to my home and cooked dinner for him... and it's all because I'm after the ex-client's friend, who happens to be in a fantastic relationship with someone else and who's *also* super loyal to the ex-client and would never, ever do anything to hurt him. That's a fantastic plan I came up with. I'm a genius."

"Luke hurts me all the time," Sean protested. It wasn't the main point, but he had to say something, didn't he? "I've got a permanent bruise on my arm from him punching me."

"I'd be happy to kiss that better for you, but—not tonight."

Right. Yeah. *That's* what they were arguing about. "Because you say so."

"That's how it works, cowboy." Paul had finished with his stirring and was putting plates and cutlery on the table. "If one person doesn't want to fool around anymore, then you don't fool around."

"And *you're* the person saying that, right now."

Paul straightened from the table and came over to the couch. "Yup. If you're really, really, *really* sweet through dinner we might negotiate a goodnight kiss, but, honestly—what are the chances of you being that sweet?"

It was bullshit, obviously. Total manipulation. And Sean didn't appreciate it, not one bit.

Still.

He didn't have quite the same panicky need to escape as he'd been feeling earlier.

"Is dinner going to be any good? If it's really tasty, I might be able to come up with a compliment about that, maybe."

"You think one compliment is getting you anywhere?" There was a definite sassiness to Paul's walk as he returned to the kitchen. Was this what Paul was like, in private, in his own home? Was he *sassy*?

Sean had no idea. But he was definitely going to stick around long enough to find out.

Chapter Twenty-Six

The weirdest thing about the next week or so was how completely un-weird it was.

Well, there were little bits of strangeness. Paul had decided to continue with his program of zero-pressure fooling around, and it was pretty interesting to watch Sean wanting more without seeming to know exactly what *more* he wanted. Frustrated groans as he waited for Paul to make the next move, tentative fumblings as he gave up on waiting and tried something on his own—interesting, hot, but, yeah, a little strange as well. In the best possible way.

Everything else, though, settled into a routine pretty easily. Paul would swing by Luke and Mark's place after work, play with the kittens for a bit, maybe visit a little if Luke and Mark were around, then he and Sean would pack up one or more kittens—they were taking turns, letting each of them get used to the idea of being on their own—and head over to Paul's place.

The apartment that had started as a serviceable place for him to sleep and store his stuff was turning into something more as he and Sean shared time there together. That was Sean's favorite chair, the one he always sat on sideways so he rested his back on one armrest, his thighs on the other. That was the rug the kittens played on, the place Sean and Paul were most likely to get horizontal—because they hadn't made it to the bedroom, yet, and Paul was resolute that he would not be the first to suggest the move. Over there was the table where they ate and laughed and gave each other the best fuck-me eyes they could manage before returning to the exquisite frustration of fooling around like high school kids.

It was all pretty normal, for a given sense of the word, but when Paul showed up at the little house on Saturday morning, Sean greeted him with slit eyes that suggested something was up.

"You good?" Paul asked, trying to be casual. He crouched to greet the mass of kittens that tumbled over each other in their eagerness to reach him.

"I got my meds adjusted yesterday," Sean replied. It sounded like an accusation, or a dare.

"Yeah? Did they make a big change?"

"Took me off some painkillers. Since I quit smoking I don't really have any phantom pain, and the other stuff isn't that bad. So I didn't need them. I've still got a bottle for if things flare up."

"That's good. Right?"

"No more side effects."

"Shit. I'm sorry. I didn't know—I mean, you said one of your pills made you feel gross when you drank. But I didn't know you were dealing with other side effects."

"Neither did I."

Paul gave up on trying to get the kittens off his toes and slid his feet out of his boots instead. Let the little monsters chew on the leather if that's what they wanted. He was free to walk over to the spot on the floor where Sean was sitting and crouch down in front of him. "I'm not sure what we're talking about. What side effects did you not know you were experiencing?"

"*Decreased sex drive*," Sean hissed.

Paul squinted at him. Was he joking? It didn't look like it... "You really didn't seem to be having problems in that area."

"I didn't think so either. But then I went off the pills."

Paul didn't mean to raise his eyebrows, but once they were already moving, it seemed appropriate to give them a bit of a waggle. And he hadn't meant to laugh, but once he started it wasn't easy to stop.

"I'm fucking *dying*," Sean said. At least he was laughing now, too. "I've jerked off four times since midnight, and I haven't even had breakfast yet."

Well, that was interesting news. Paul leaned in a little closer. "What did you think about, while you were doing it? *Who* did you think about?"

Sean shook his head and actually seemed to blush. "You fucking know who I thought about."

Very interesting. Paul wasn't sure who else was in the house, so he kept his voice low as he asked, "What were we doing?"

Sean actually squirmed, a pink flush on his freckled cheeks, and Paul wanted to remember the moment forever. "A variety of things."

"And—are there any of those things you might want to try in person? Or are you totally drained? Was four times your limit for the day?"

Sean was quick and strong, and when he caught the back of Paul's head and pulled him closer, it was as much a demand as a request. Which was just fine with Paul. Their kiss was wet and dirty, and Sean's free hand caught Paul's and dragged it to his groin, where there was clear evidence that four times was *not* the limit in any way.

"Who's home?" Paul managed to ask between kisses.

"Who cares?"

Paul made himself pull away. "We both do. Where are they?"

"Luke's at the barn. Mark's at some church breakfast or something. I don't know. Get back here."

"Let's go to my place."

Sean shook his head and pulled Paul back toward him. "Too far!"

Common sense dictated one path, but damn it, Paul had been good for too long.

Still, he had his pride, or his stubbornness, or whatever it was that demanded he continue with his program of not making any first moves. So, fine. Sean wanted to kiss? They could kiss.

If Sean wanted anything more than that he could damn well come and get it.

And he did. Maybe the medication actually *had* been affecting him, maybe he was just using the change as an excuse, but either way, the fumbling, uncertain Sean was gone.

Paul surrendered willingly. He let himself fall backward, his arms spread to the sides as Sean sprawled on top of him. More kisses, but then Sean tugged at the hem of Paul's shirt.

Well, Paul still had some shred of a brain cell functioning. "Your room," he said. He tried to sound firm, not desperate, but he wasn't sure he made it. "I'm not taking my clothes off in your friends' living room."

"They wouldn't mind," Sean grumbled, and then he grinned as Paul laughed. "Fine. My room. But—I want to fuck. That's what I was thinking about, while I was jerking off. I want to fuck you."

"What if I want it the other way around?" Paul didn't care, really—he'd always been versatile. But he wanted to know what Sean would say. And while he was at it, "Or what if I don't come, just from fucking? I don't, usually. I mean, it feels good—great, even—but if I don't come, etiquette says the other guy needs to get me off, after. Your hand at least, but really, I'd prefer your mouth."

Sean took a deep breath. "I want to do that. To—you know." Another deep breath and a bit of an eye roll as if he was anticipating that Paul was going to pressure him for more precise language. "I want to blow you. Okay? Is that what you want to hear?"

"Well, yeah. I think just about every guy wants to hear that. But is it true?"

Sean didn't answer right away, and Paul could feel the tension growing. He liked it. He liked knowing he was pushing Sean further than he wanted to go, that Sean could snap at any moment and turn aggressive. *Why* he liked knowing that? He had absolutely no idea. Still, there was something exciting about it, so Paul waited Sean out instead of coming up with some polite topic change.

Finally, Sean nodded. "Yeah. I want to do it. But—fuck. I'm not going to be any good at it, you know?"

Oh. And just as much as Paul had wanted to push Sean's boundaries moments earlier, now he wanted to comfort and protect him. But he had to be careful with that, so he snorted and said, "Dude. Have you ever in your life had a bad blow job? I mean, sure, some are better than others, but they go on a scale of, like, good-to-mind-bending, right? The lowest score possible is still just fine."

"This is so fucking weird," Sean said, and he rolled off to the side.

Fuck. So much for fucking.

"I say you'll be fine at blowjobs and that makes you not want to fool around?"

"I'm—I've never fooled around with anyone who's *gotten* a blowjob before, you know?"

They were back to that. Or still there, really. They'd never gotten past it.

"It's only been a week," Paul said, as much to himself as to Sean. Less than that, even. If Sean had been cautious for some other reason—maybe because he was getting over a bad breakup, or was just naturally conservative—Paul wouldn't be having such a hard time with it. So why was it bothering him now?

Because he thought Sean might be changing his mind. Regretting his decisions. But there'd been nothing real to suggest that, and a quick glance at the front of Sean's sweatpants showed significant evidence to the contrary.

And Sean said, "I've been thinking about it since—I don't know. Since I started thinking about any of this shit. With girls or guys. Not with you, obviously. I mean, this didn't all start with you. It's not *new*. Not the thinking about it part. It's just weird to actually be *doing* it."

"Maybe it's also a bit weird to be doing it on your best friend's living room floor?"

"Nah," Sean scoffed, but he was grinning as he said it.

"It's possible I've been a bit of a dick about it," Paul said. He waited for Sean to object—any polite person would disagree, wouldn't they?—but gave up after Sean's raised eyebrows made it clear he would like to hear more details of Paul's transgression. "I've been making you make all the moves. And that's partly been to be sure I wasn't pressuring you into something you aren't comfortable with, but I think it's also been a bit— defensive, I guess? Protective? I didn't want to try something and get shot down. Didn't want to take the chance of being rejected. So that means that the one person here who more-or-less knows what he's doing—and I stress the 'more-or-less' part, because obviously this is a team effort and there are going to be variations when I'm with a new person—hasn't been doing a lot to make it all go more smoothly."

"I like it when you make speeches," Sean said. His voice was slow and lazy, and once he knew he had Paul's attention, he slowly trailed his fingers down his chest, his belly, and then under the waistband of his cut-off sweatpants.

"Okay!" Paul sat up abruptly. "You mean it that you want to have sex? Full-on penetrative sex, today, *not* on Luke and Mark's living room floor."

"Yeah." Sean was stroking himself now, his gaze locked on Paul's face.

Paul closed his eyes and fought for control. "Let's focus on the *not here* part. Your bedroom? Do you have stuff? Condoms, at least, and preferably some lube?"

Sean snorted. "You are fucking terrible at sexy talk."

"Somebody has to be practical."

"Fine. So… no. Technically, I don't have *stuff*. How the hell was I supposed to get any of that? Maybe when my mom and I were at the drugstore yesterday to get my prescriptions filled I could have detoured to the gay sex aisle?"

"We don't have our own aisle. And, for future reference? There's a little thing called the internet, and if you learn to use it you can buy just about anything you want and get it delivered right to your door."

"I'm using up all Luke's bandwidth downloading gay porn. No space left for shopping."

"My place, then." Not that Paul didn't want to discuss porn with Luke, but he'd rather do it somewhere he could hope for some physical gratification afterward. "And don't tell me it's too far. We'd be there by now if we'd left when I first suggested it."

"Really? Because we can teleport?" But Sean was just grumbling, not really arguing. He was, in fact, moving as he spoke, sitting up and gesturing imperiously toward his chair, which was parked at the side of the couch. "Grab that, will you?"

"Not your stubbies?"

"I'm supposed to take a break. Skin's getting irritated."

"Oh. But you're okay?"

"I'll be fine if you stop talking about stupid shit and grab my fucking chair."

Paul did as he was told.

And it was nothing new. Nothing they hadn't been doing all week. Just another drive over to Paul's place.

So there was no reason for Paul to be suddenly nervous. He forced his fingers to relax their grip on the steering wheel and glanced over to find Sean in the passenger seat, frowning at the glove box as if trying to control it with his mind.

Wow. Romantic.

"Was the painkiller you stopped taking the same one that makes you sick when you drink?" Paul asked.

"Yeah."

"It's still pretty early in the day, but—you want to have a glass of wine or something when we get to my place?"

They were at a stop sign, so when Sean turned to look at Paul, Paul could look right back, and he was rewarded with the slow, sly grin that always made his knees weak.

"You trying to get me drunk?" There was a purr in Sean's voice that went straight to Paul's dick. Had he been thinking this wasn't romantic? Fine, it wasn't, but who the hell cared when Sean sounded that perfectly wicked?

"I was thinking more for myself." Paul reached over and found Sean's hand. They hadn't made a habit of this, but it felt right, just then. Not *holding* hands, exactly, not when their fingers were as mobile as they were, twining and flexing and promising more. "But it seemed rude to drink if you couldn't."

"I can," Sean said. "But I'm not sure I will. I think—" The smirk this time was more self-deprecating but just as powerful. "I think I might want to keep a clear head. I think I'm going to want to remember every detail."

Chapter Twenty-Seven

They'd been inside the apartment for about thirty seconds before Sean was regretting his bravado about alcohol. Everything was just *awkward* all of a sudden. He wished they'd brought a kitten or two—playing cat-phone wasn't exactly a mature form of communication, maybe, but it was a fuck-ton less painful than hanging out in the hallway, staring at each other.

"No drinking," Paul said. "So—bedroom?"

"You're pretty fucking smooth, aren't you?"

"Okay, it's been a while since I had a first time with a guy. And I'm not sure I've ever been completely sober for one. And, honestly, I was just fucking around with making you make the first moves all the time, but the truth is I usually *don't* make the moves. So—no. Not smooth. But you're no better."

That was true enough. But, fuck. This was stupid. "Get a glass of wine," he said.

"Just for me? You still don't want one?"

"Just for you."

"Well, if you're not—"

"I didn't ask," Sean said. This was almost certainly a bad idea, but it wasn't like anything else was working. "I *told* you to get a glass of wine."

"Okay. We need to have a little talk about the difference between *making the first move* and *being a controlling dickhead*."

"Sure. We can talk about that. After you have your glass of wine."

Paul squinted at him, and Sean kept his own gaze level and calm. He might not know anything about gay sex, but he'd been bluffing confidence since he was a toddler.

And after a long moment, Paul headed for the kitchen and pulled out a wine glass. Sean wheeled over as Paul was pouring. Red wine, which somehow seemed even more decadent at ten in the morning.

Paul turned and held the glass up in front of himself. "You're sure you don't want any?"

"No. And I don't want you to drink it, either. Not yet." Damn, he was making this up as he went—it probably didn't make much sense. He was one step away from suggesting that Paul do the hokey-pokey and turn himself around. Instead, he managed, "Take your shirt off, first."

"You want me to—"

"I feel like we can save some time if you just skip right over the double-checks on these things. I mean, you can always say no. But if you don't say no, you should probably just go ahead and do whatever it is I've told you to do."

"It's generally a good idea to talk about kinks before you indulge. And, also, I'm not sure it makes sense to jump into something like this the first time you're with someone."

Sean didn't answer. He just waited.

And, finally, with an impatient huff, Paul undid the top two buttons of his shirt, then pulled it and his white T-shirt off over his head.

"Good. Now, take a sip of wine."

"This is going to get old pretty soon."

"That'd be a lot more convincing if I couldn't see your dick trying to break out of your jeans."

It was true, and Sean couldn't say that he was exactly calm himself. He hadn't planned this, hadn't even thought it through, but... damn. There was something pretty interesting going on.

And, of course, seeing Paul with no shirt was pretty nice, too. His skin was a smooth, warm, golden-brown and it stretched over muscles tight enough to be interesting without being stupidly large. His chest had a dusting of black hair that Sean had felt before but never seen. And now—now he could look. Stare. Just how much of this could he get away with?

"Turn around," he said, and made a little spinning motion with his finger.

"Seriously?" But Paul did as he was told.

"Stop," Sean said when Paul was facing away from him. Jesus, was he really going to keep doing this?

Fuck, yeah, he was, right up until Paul refused. "Hands on the counter."

Paul did as he was told, and Sean thought his cock might burst. But he had to be cool. He was the one in control, here. So he wheeled forward, slow and calm, and locked his wheels when he was right behind Paul.

God. He wanted his legs. Just once, one fucking time in his life, to be able to stand behind a man like this, to be able to strip him naked and bend him over and just—fuck. No. Even if Sean got the artificial legs figured out, he wouldn't have that kind of balance. Fake legs wouldn't allow him to do something so athletic and easy and fucking natural. That chance was gone.

But there was still stuff he *could* do. He reached around Paul's waist from both sides and undid his fly, then snaked a hand inside the denim. They'd done this before. The angles had been different, but Sean had felt Paul's cock, at least through fabric. He knew the heat of it, the weight, the *strength*, if that was a word that made any sense. He knew what it felt like. But now he wanted more.

He eased his hand inside the waistband of Paul's underwear. He hadn't gone this far before. Hadn't actually managed skin-on-skin, not—not *this* skin. It should have felt about the same as Sean's own cock, surely, but it really, really didn't.

He hadn't realized his head was nestled in against Paul's side until he felt *and* heard the hitch is Paul's breathing. And that was what made all of this so different, so unfamiliar, and so fucking hot. There was another person involved, another man, one who wanted Sean, who gasped when Sean's fingers wrapped around his cock, one who had his arm wrapped around Sean's head, fingers laced in his hair, holding him tight as Sean explored his new world.

"Push your pants down," he managed, his voice low and strained, and maybe it was a command, maybe a request, maybe a desperate fucking plea. Whichever it was, Paul complied, and then there Sean was. A near-naked man beside him, cock straining under—was that *Sean's* hand? Sean's fingers squeezing tight, sliding from base to head and back again, slow and relentless?

Well, yeah, it fucking was, and Sean was going to have to get past it, because the part of his brain that was running this show wasn't interested in giving him a lot of time to adjust. "Turn around," he said. "So you're facing me."

Paul was slow to move. Maybe he was rebelling against the orders, maybe he was just self-conscious. Hell, maybe he was having trouble keeping his balance with his pants pooled down around his ankles. He ended up moving, though, shuffling around until his cock was right there, smooth and dark and hard, inches from Sean's face.

He could have gotten out of it. He could have given some new orders, deflected, distracted. But he didn't want to. Not only for Paul's sake, but for his own. He wanted to taste. He wanted to feel. He wanted to do this, to commit to it all. If he was going to be a cocksucker, he'd damn well suck cock.

But when he leaned forward, Paul pulled away.

"What?" Sean demanded.

"You don't have to."

"Yeah. That's right. I don't have to do shit. I'm the one in charge. I'm the one calling the shots. So—get your dick back over here. Now."

"And you say *I'm* not romantic."

"Oh, baby, please. Let me suck your big thick cock. Oh, I need it. Please, baby—"

Paul's dick came at him pretty fast, then, but it felt more like an order to shut up than a passionate gesture. Still, Sean was ready for the opportunity. He caught the shaft in his hand, took a deep breath, allowed himself a quick *Holy shit, you're really doing it* and then pressed his lips to the head of Paul's cock. A kiss, maybe, until Sean pressed forward, let his mouth open, tasted the salt, felt the weight on his tongue, and kept at it.

God, he wanted this. Needed it. He wrapped one arm around to grab Paul's ass, another around his thighs, and pulled himself closer. He knew what this felt like, knew how to make it good, and was amazed to find that those little tricks were what he wanted to do anyway. Sucking Paul's cock deep down his throat? Yeah, he wanted that, as deep as he could take it. Flicking with his tongue, sucking so hard his cheeks hollowed, moaning so the vibrations weren't just sent to Paul's cock but somehow down through Sean's body to his own—it was all perfect. He was a fucking cocksucker, and he loved it.

So why the hell was Paul pulling away? God, Sean needed to fight the instinct to sink his teeth into his prize and hold onto it like a dog playing tug-of-war—that'd make Paul rethink his no-bad-blowjobs idea pretty quick—but he held on with his arms around Paul's body and sucked harder.

"I'm gonna come," Paul gasped.

Which was the whole damn point, so Paul wasn't making a lot of sense.

"If we're going to do more," Paul managed, "I want to wait."

Okay, it was kinda hard to argue with a dick in your mouth, which meant Sean's two instincts didn't seem to be compatible right at the moment. Fuck. He released Paul's cock but kept his face close, running his stubbled cheeks over the sensitive, wet skin as he said, "Why?"

"Do you still want to fuck?"

"Yeah, but—with *my* dick. Why does it matter if you come now?"

"I want to be hard when we fuck. I want to come with you inside me."

Jesus Christ, the words were almost enough to make Sean jizz in his fucking pants. From a chick they'd have had him rolling his eyes, but from Paul? Totally different, for reasons Sean was in no mental condition to puzzle through.

"Fine," he grumbled, and he sat back in his chair.

"You were fucking awesome at that, by the way." Paul still had his fingers laced in Sean's hair, but they were smoothing, now, combing through affectionately, as if Sean were one of the kittens. "Made me doubt it was your first time."

"Well I'm probably going to be terrible at fucking, so brace yourself for that. You're going to be wishing you'd come now, 'cause it was probably your last chance."

"You want to go to the bedroom?" Paul asked. There was something in his voice…

Oh, right. Sean was supposed to be in charge. "Shoes and socks off, get right out of your jeans and underwear, and meet me in the bedroom."

"Meet you?"

Yeah, meet him, because Sean was suddenly wondering—worrying—about the details of the bedroom. The apartment was small, which meant the bedroom probably was, too. Was there room for the chair beside the bed, or was Sean going to have to climb over the foot or something? How high or low was the bed, and would he be either dragging himself up or flopping himself down? What other fucking obstacles were there going to be?

Yeah, Paul was used to dealing with people with physical challenges and he wouldn't be a dick about it. But it'd be a bit of a boner-killer, wouldn't it? And Sean really didn't need that kind of stress.

He wheeled out of the kitchen a bit faster than was dignified and made it down the hallway past the bathroom, decided against turning the bedroom lights on—there was morning sun coming in through the thin curtains, and that was more than enough—and found Paul's bed, tidily made, and blessedly at about the same height as Sean's own. He could do this transition, no problem.

He peeled the covers back enough to have a triangle of sheet exposed, launched himself over onto to clean fabric, and shoved his chair away. Fuck, he shoved it too fucking hard and it crashed into the wall. The bedroom *was* small, he'd been right about that.

"Are you wrecking my apartment?" Paul called from the kitchen.

"Come find out."

And then, just because fair was fair, he pulled his own shirt off, then shimmied out of his pants and underwear, hard cock bobbing like a cob of corn in a windstorm as he worked. He thought for a second before he pulled the blanket up to cover the bottoms of his legs. He wasn't trying to hide anything, it just—it wasn't something anyone needed to see.

"I like you in my bed," Paul said from the doorway. Had he seen the cover-up move? Sean couldn't worry about that.

"I'd like *you* in your bed." Sean needed to get his attitude back. He was confident; he was in charge. Fake it 'til you make it. "Come over here."

Sean let himself appreciate the view as Paul made his way to the other side of the bed. God, the man was beautiful. Sean wanted to touch. And he was allowed to. That was the craziest part of all this—not that Sean Gage was in bed with a man, but that *this man*, this incredible creature, was in bed with Sean fucking Gage. It made absolutely no sense, and if Sean let himself think about it too much he'd go crazy, so as soon as Paul had the covers back and was sitting down, Sean launched himself.

Across the bed, wrestling past Paul's surprise, then Paul on his back, Sean on top of him, and fuck the stumps, they were nothing Paul hadn't seen before, so Sean let himself bring his legs up so he was straddling the warm, muscular stretch of Paul's belly.

"You know this is a better position for you *getting* fucked, right?" Paul ran his hands up and down Sean's thighs, cupped the end of his stumps like they were fucking *cherished*, then bucked his hips so the tip of his cock nudged against the top of Sean's ass.

"I want to do that, too. Maybe. But not this time." Still, Sean shifted his weight a little, arched his back, let Paul's cock slide into the wedge between his ass cheeks. Paul gasped in appreciation and Sean moved a little, exploring the sensation. Fuck, yeah. He wanted this.

He rose up enough so the head of Paul's cock slid against his puckered hole. It felt good there, natural, and maybe that made more sense. Maybe Sean should just change the angle, let himself slide down, engulf and absorb—

"It'll hurt like a son-of-a-bitch if you go for no stretching, no lube on your first time." Paul, always the voice of fucking reason. "And we need to use condoms."

Sean leaned forward so their faces were inches away. His cock was dragging across the ridges of Paul's abs and that was a *very* interesting sensation, but Sean kept his attention on the conversation. "Do we really need condoms? I've been in and out of the fucking hospital for eight months—they would have mentioned if I had something, wouldn't they? And you were dating the same guy for years. Did you fool around on him?"

"No. But he might have on me." Paul shook his head. "We can go get tested if you want, but not right now."

Yeah, fair enough. "Where are they? Your condoms?"

"Bedside table."

Made sense. Sean heaved himself over and groped in the drawer, pulling out a little bottle of lube and an opened box of condoms. "Wait. You didn't use condoms with your boyfriend. That's why you might have something, if he cheated on you."

"Yeah..."

"So why do you have these?" Had he been seeing someone *since* the breakup? Someone while he and Sean had been friends?

"I went to the gay sex aisle, Sean. I could have ordered them off the internet, but I went to the store instead. Is that really what you want to be talking about?"

"But why's the box open?"

"Are you kidding? Is this—what are you doing? The box is open because I opened it. I took the plastic sealer stuff off the lube bottle, too. Because *usually* when I'm about to have sex with someone, we don't want to spend a whole lot of time fumbling around with condoms and lube and talking about it all. You like to do things differently, I guess?"

Paul didn't sound mad, exactly. Exasperated. That was the word.

"You were worried you might come too fast," Sean tried. "I wanted to help you out with that."

"You're a trooper. But I think I've got myself under control, now, if you wanted to get your ass back over here."

Well, yeah, Sean did want that, so he scooted back over and stretched out as far as he could next to Paul, wasted a couple seconds wishing he had feet he could rub down Paul's calves, then forced himself to let go of that and move on. He was here, such as he was. He needed to appreciate what he had.

And, damn, he had a lot.

They went back to their comfortable making-out routine for a bit, although it was a hell of a lot more intense when neither of them had any clothes on, and then Sean let himself explore. His lips were swollen and sensitized from kissing, and they felt every hair, every ripple of skin, and every delicious shiver as he nibbled his way down Paul's glorious chest, along the thin line of hair leading lower... and then Paul's fingers tightened in his hair, again.

"You're pretty tenacious," Paul said, and there was a gratifying ribbon of tension in his voice. "But I'm still too close."

"You said I was good at it. I want to play to my strengths." And, really, "You *also* made it sound like me asking you about the condoms was killing the mood. So—what happened there?"

"I may have exaggerated a little." He tugged on Sean's hair, pulling him upward, and Sean let himself slide along every inch of Paul's body, earning another pretty satisfying groan. "You're killing me."

"Are you kinda wishing you'd let me get you off in the kitchen? You'd be hard again by now, probably."

Paul huffed out a half-laugh. "I didn't think it through."

"Maybe it's time for you to stop thinking. Let me be in charge."

"Because of all your experience and expertise."

"I've been *thinking* about this stuff for fifteen years. I may not have a lot of experience, but I've got some ideas, for sure."

"Like what?" Half dare, half genuine question, from the sound of Paul's voice. Well, Sean could work with that.

"Like...." Sean slid around until he was on his side behind Paul. Spooning, except one of the spoons wasn't as long as it should be, didn't have—fuck! Not what he needed to be thinking about. Better to focus on the warm, smooth skin, the hard, round muscles. And even better than all that?

Sean pushed himself up on one elbow and twisted his torso around, and Paul rolled his own shoulders so they were face to face. The best part was *Paul*. Not just skin and muscles, a tight ass and a hard cock. Paul. One raised eyebrow, ready to challenge Sean at his worst, and a gentle smile, ready to accept him at his best.

None of the rest of it was new, really. Sean hadn't been with a man, before, but he'd done lots of stuff with women, and reaching around to find a cock wasn't much of a difference, not when he'd already had that cock half-way down his throat.

The new thing here? The part that made it all something Sean wanted to pay attention to, wanted to savor and to remember? Paul. A friend. Someone Sean cared about. This wasn't two random bodies rubbing against each other until they got off; it was Sean, and it was Paul. Together.

Not something Sean could ever say out loud, obviously. But maybe Paul heard it anyway, in Sean's gentle murmurs. Maybe he felt it in the kisses that turned into smiles that turned back into kisses.

Sean hoped Paul knew. Their bodies moved easily together—stretching, sliding, reaching, receiving. The way Paul's breath caught when Sean eased himself inside, the way Sean froze and made himself wait for Paul to relax. The way they worked together, Paul's back arching, Sean's body curling, then both straightening, then bending together again. It felt too perfect to just be fucking. It had to be more.

Paul closed his eyes as his breathing grew ragged, and Sean whispered, "Let me see," and Paul knew what he meant. He opened his eyes and kept his gaze locked on Sean's for as long as he could, until his orgasm washed over him and he was taken away, and by then Sean was lost, too, so maybe they couldn't see each other at the perfect moment but they were still together, somehow, entangled bodies only one way they were connected.

It was all crap, Sean reminded himself as he eased their bodies apart and collapsed back onto the mattress. It was just sex. That was all. Not something he needed to—not something he could *afford* to—get sentimental about. He'd fucked a man. He'd liked it. That was world-shaking enough, without him trying to make it all philosophical or poetical or whatever other bullshit his orgasm-brain wanted to feed him. It was just sex.

But then Paul rolled over so his body was snug against Sean's, and he nuzzled in and kissed Sean's neck in the ticklish spot below his ear, and Sean didn't pull away. He didn't even want to.

"Stop thinking," Paul said, his lips brushing Sean's skin.

And, for at least a little while, Sean did as he was told.

Chapter Twenty-Eight

"I locked the kittens in your room," Luke told Sean as he and Paul made their way into the kitchen of the little house. "I was trying to make dinner and they kept climbing up my leg."

"You put them in jail because they wanted to play with you?" Sean demanded, but there was something different in his tone, at least to Paul's ear. Less raw aggression, more—was it possible to sound *happy* when accusing a close friend of animal mistreatment? No, probably not. Paul was just projecting his own good mood.

Except Luke, who surely knew Sean's tones better than anyone, stopped chopping broccoli and turned to squint in Sean's direction. Then he took a quick glance at Paul, grinned, and went back to his task. "They didn't want to play with me; they wanted to eat the chicken. But it's in the oven now, so if you want to let them out, that's fine."

"Cyborg likes broccoli," Sean said, but he was wheeling toward his bedroom as he spoke.

"She doesn't like it enough to climb my leg and launch herself at the counter to get it." Luke looked over at Paul and said, "You guys have a good day?"

Just enough of a smirk to make it clear Luke thought he knew what they'd been doing all day. And, of course, he was right. It was like being back in school, living in a dorm where every hookup was public knowledge suitable for mass discussion.

And, really, Paul didn't mind. He'd have *liked* to talk to someone about it—hell, maybe they could have giggled and drunk hot chocolate with Bailey's and done each other's hair as they chatted. But Sean was already on his way back from his bedroom, his lap full of kittens, with Panther galloping ahead of the procession, and there wasn't much fun in gossiping about your crush when your crush was actually in the room.

Also, Paul was a grown man. Important to remember that.

So he just bent down and scooped Panther up for a quick cuddle, which the animal returned with full enthusiasm for at least five seconds before squirming to get free.

"You put the litter box right next to my pillow," Sean said, sounding aggrieved.

"You should be glad I put the box in there at all," Luke replied, scooping the broccoli into a pot. "Or you could have had something a lot nastier than litter a lot closer to your pillow than the box was. I would have done it except I didn't want the kittens to learn bad habits."

"You don't want *your* kitten to learn bad habits," Sean said. "You don't care about the rest of them."

"I care about Mark's, too."

"Do you know which ones you want to keep?" Paul asked. He resisted the urge to hide little Panther from view.

"Seq, probably?" Luke glanced at Sean as if asking for permission, which was wise—Sean was still pretty possessive about the creatures. But it made sense—Luke had been the one to name the orange kitten—Sequoia, with the argument that a namesake could be mighty without being violent—and had shown a preference for him from the start. Mark seemed to have bonded with the other orange and white cat, the one everyone was calling Tiger. So they'd have a matched pair. Romantic? Maybe.

If Paul took Panther, that left Cyborg for Sean. Was there anything matched about them? Stupid to even think it, this early in a relationship, but—they were the two smallest kittens, and the feistiest as well. They might not match on the outside as well as Seq and Tiger, but they seemed to be a pretty good team anyway.

"Why are you cooking broccoli?" Sean demanded. "You can't have Seq unless you stop trying to feed me that shit."

"I'm not trying to feed you anything." Luke added a little water to the pot. "If you don't want it, don't eat it. I don't care."

Apparently even Sean found it hard to argue with that. Instead, he turned his attention to Paul. "You staying for dinner?"

"There's plenty," Luke said before it could get awkward. "You can eat Sean's broccoli, but there's lots of everything else, too. I've just started thinking in terms of cooking for four."

"It'll be an adjustment when Sean moves out," Paul said.

But Luke raised an eyebrow in return. "Have you seen Sean's cooking? I don't see him having a lot of meals at his own place anytime soon."

Paul pushed down the urge to say he'd take care of Sean. He shouldn't say that, shouldn't even *think* it. Not only because Sean would kick his ass for suggesting he needed to be taken care of, but also because it was too damn early.

And it wasn't what Paul wanted. Sure, in his first glow of hormonal warmth he wanted to nurture and protect and serve and create a damn nest to shelter Sean from any of life's hardships. But it wasn't the relationship he wanted. He wanted equals, taking care of each other, but also letting each other try and fail and try again. Sean didn't need protection; he needed respect.

But not too much, so Paul said, "If you put parmesan on it, spaghetti has all four food groups. If he took a multivitamin or something, he could probably live on that for quite a while."

"Three meals a day?" Luke asked.

"I can make eggs." Sean wheeled toward the living room door, clearly done with the conversation. "And sandwiches. Eggs, sandwiches, spaghetti—everything's taken care of."

"I don't think I'll come for dinner too often," Paul said, and immediately wanted to kick himself. Was he assuming he was going to be *asked* to eat over? Ever?

But Sean clearly wasn't put out. "When you come for dinner, you can cook." And with that he wheeled to the living room.

Paul was about to ask whether Luke needed any help, but then his phone rang, playing the light melody he'd programmed in for his mother's calls. It wasn't a sound he'd heard often in the last couple months.

"I need to take this," he told Luke, who didn't seem too concerned one way or another.

Paul should channel that attitude. His mother was calling. No big deal. She used to call him a few times a day, to the point he'd had to tell her he wouldn't be picking up and would call her once a day on his drive home from work. If there was an emergency, his dad or Jas were supposed to get in touch. But that had all changed, and now… he had no idea.

He tapped the phone and lifted it to his ear. "Hi."

"Paul. Good. You answered. I'm in your neighborhood and thought I'd stop by for tea."

Like everything was casual. Normal. "Do you even know where my neighborhood *is*? I'm not in the city anymore."

"I know. You gave us your new address, and I used the GPS to find it."

"Wait. When you say 'in the neighborhood' do you mean you're parked outside my building?"

"Yes." No sense of awkwardness, absolutely no acknowledgement of how strange everything was. His mother was a queen, serenely floating above the petty concerns of the peasants beneath her. Peasants like her son.

"I'm not even home."

"But you're in town? It's not a large community—I imagine you can get home without making me wait too long."

He could have said it was impossible. There'd been a time, back when he'd been trying to enforce boundaries like his phone call rule, that he would have refused her as a matter of principle. She couldn't expect him to drop everything and run home just because she'd decided to take a drive.

But things had changed. This seemed like a chance at reconciliation, an opportunity to rebuild the family ties he'd cut been missing so much. So he said, "Alright, yes. I'll be there in five or ten minutes."

"Excellent." And she ended the call.

Paul stared at the phone for a moment before Luke said, "Got a stalker?"

"Kind of. My mother."

"You going to go see her?"

"Yeah. I guess I am."

"Want some broccoli for the road?"

Some of Paul's tension huffed out of him with his little laugh. "I think I'll be okay. Thanks for the offer, though."

"If you want to come back over when you're done, feel free." Luke stepped a little closer, then. Not enough to be Paul's space, just—oh. Enough to make it less likely Sean would hear from the next room. "You're always welcome here. Whatever goes on with Sean—Mark and I consider you our friend, not just his."

Luke stepped back, then frowned. "Did that sound like I was suggesting you and Sean were going to break up? That's a bit weird, right? Sorry."

Break up. Was it even possible for Paul and Sean to *break up*? Were they *going out* formally enough to make breaking up possible? It was an interesting question, and one that Paul would have liked to take some time to sort through—probably with Sean, possibly in bed—but he had another priority right then.

He thanked Luke again, said goodbye, and headed for the living room. Sean was on the floor, of course, and covered in kittens, of course. "It's no wonder they try to climb Luke—you've trained them that humans are furniture."

"My work here is done, then." Sean yawned, arms stretched above his head, and Paul wanted nothing more than to crouch beside him, run his hands along the extended muscles of his torso…but it wasn't the right time.

"I have to go," he said instead. "My mom just called. She's in town."

"Your mom?" Sean sat up straighter. "She called you? Out of the blue?"

He sounded like he understood what a big deal this was. Like he'd actually been listening to Paul when he talked about his family, and had actually understood what he'd heard. Maybe even understood a bit of what he *hadn't* heard, and figured out how Paul was feeling. Sean, after knowing Paul for only a couple months, could understand him better than Bobby ever had, after years together?

Well, maybe that wasn't fair. Bobby had understood Paul well enough to manipulate him pretty effectively. The difference was, perhaps, that Sean *cared* how Paul felt, just for Paul's sake.

"I don't know what she wants," Paul admitted. "It might be—I guess it might be awful. Maybe she's dropping off paperwork that formally disowns me from the family forever."

"She doesn't sound like the sort of person who'd do her own dirty work like that."

"No, you're right. She'd send lawyers for anything unpleasant."

"So this is good." Sean smiled. Maybe not his full strength *I see you for who you really are and I like what I see* expression, but something encouraging, at least. "You should get over there and see what she's up to."

"Yeah." Except he suddenly didn't want to go. Maybe it was easier to stay here and stay hopeful, rather than travel to the apartment and discover that his hope had been unjustified. Also, now that he was thinking about the apartment— "Did we leave the place pretty tidy?"

Sean frowned, clearly trying to remember. "Keep her out of the bedroom. That probably wouldn't be an issue anyway, right? Unless she wants a tour. Don't let her have a tour."

That wasn't a concern; Paul's mother wouldn't be interested in a place so completely lacking in style or architectural merit.

"There may be some clothes on the floor of the kitchen," Sean said.

"No, I picked that stuff up."

"You're probably okay, then."

Right. So—he just needed to go. For a short, reckless moment Paul thought about inviting Sean to come along. But it wasn't fair to inflict that kind of awkwardness on the guy, not just so Paul could have a human security blanket. He needed to man up and do this himself. "I'll call you later."

Sean nodded his understanding, then turned his attention back to the kittens as if Paul was already gone.

Well. Okay. No big emotional goodbyes, and that made sense. They'd had sex, not gotten married, and Paul was going to meet his mom, not being drafted to fight in a foreign war. He was being stupid.

It felt wrong, though. Something was off. But his mom was waiting for him; he had to go. "Don't eat all my broccoli," he said, and he left, shutting the door gently behind himself.

Chapter Twenty-Nine

Sean waited until he heard the car drive away, then displaced the kittens and dragged himself back to the kitchen, suddenly restless.

When he arrived, Luke was sitting at the table, not doing anything, just—waiting. For Sean. Which couldn't be good.

"What?"

Luke shrugged. "You and Paul. That's going well?"

"It's fine. And none of your business. Cook your broccoli."

"It doesn't really take a lot of attention to cook broccoli. And obviously I'm not going to start cooking it when Mark isn't even home yet. So—I've got time for my oldest friend. I've *made* time for you. Let's share it, mindfully."

"You're done with being a space nerd and now you're going to be some new age freakshow? Fantastic."

"I just wanted to check in. Make sure you're okay."

"Maybe Paul was right—maybe it's time I moved out." A topic change. Just what was needed.

Luke squinted. Good. Let him worry that he was being a bad host, pressuring a friend and guest, being completely ungracious and rude. Except the squint led to Luke saying, "Yeah. Maybe. You gave up the place that was free on the first because the kittens still needed you round the clock, but they're about ready to be separated now. Maybe it *is* time you moved out."

"Wait." It had just been something to say. Sean didn't want to—" Weren't we talking about something else? Me and Paul? Yeah, we're good. Wow, great, thanks, this has been a good talk."

"You've got money for the rent. Are you just being lazy and you want to stay here where you've got meals made for you? Or are you worried about it? You've never lived on your own, right? Would that be weird? Is that the problem?"

"There's no fucking problem!"

"If it's just laziness: fuck you, get out, you're a slug. But if you're worried about something, we should figure it out. You don't want to be stuck living here just because you're afraid to live somewhere else, right? You don't want to be afraid of stuff like that."

"This is a rich fantasy world you've developed, Luke, really, but don't drag me into it. I'm not afraid of getting my own apartment. That's just weird."

"We'd still check in on you. You could still come over for dinner. Or, here's an idea, you could invite us over to your place and you could cook something that isn't spaghetti and be a fucking host for a change. That might be fun."

"Nah, doesn't sound like a good time."

Luke shook his head. "You haven't been nearly as annoying as I thought you were going to be, living here. But you still need to get your own place."

"I've only been here for a couple months. You lived with me for *years*. You owe me more time."

"I lived at your mom's house. If your mom needs a place, I agree, I owe her and she can stay as long as she wants to. But you? You need to get your own place." He paused, then said, "For *you*. Do you understand what I'm saying? If you actually needed a place to stay—*when* you actually needed a place to stay—then this is that place. Absolutely. You're always welcome here, if you need to be here. But if you don't need it? Get the fuck out, Sean. Get your own place, be independent, realize you're totally capable of looking after yourself... all that shit. Your mom should have kicked your ass out years ago. Pushed you out of the nest so you could fly on your own. Whatever."

He paused, then said, "Also, you should get a haircut. And Elise has been holding your job. She says you can probably bump up to full time for the spring, 'cause it's always extra busy during baby-animal season. And while we're at it—using different pastas instead of spaghetti does *not* count as learning to cook something new. It's still the same food. What else? Are you flossing every day? It's just as important as brushing your teeth, you know. Maybe *more* important. Be true to your teeth and they won't be false to you. You could probably stand to shave a bit more often, too. Stubble is fine, but you let it go all the way to scruffy sometimes, and that's not cool. Also—"

"Okay, fuck, I get it. You're going to be super-annoying until I move out. That's the plan?"

"Probably after you move out, too. Just to reinforce the message."

"I'm really not sure you get to keep a kitten if you're kicking me out of your house."

"You'll do what's best for Seq. I'm not worried about that."

"Are you going to pick on him like you pick on me?"

"I'll offer him guidance and wisdom, just like I do for you, sure."

Sean shook his head and made his way back to the living room. He settled onto the floor and let the kittens climb up on him.

It was a lot. A lot of changes, all coming at once.

A new place to live, and a job, and losing the kittens. Whatever was going on with Paul. With being gay or bi or whatever the hell Sean was going to be. A hell of a lot of new stuff.

Sean leaned back and bellowed, much more loudly than was needed for Luke to hear, "There's nothing wrong with just cooking spaghetti! I'm not learning to cook anything else. You can't make me!"

Luke didn't bother answering, but that was fine. He'd heard. Sean had made his point. New things? Okay, fine. He could do new things. But he'd do them his way. On his terms.

"Spaghetti has all four food groups," he told the kittens, and they didn't disagree.

Chapter Thirty

Paul's mother was as perfectly put together as always. Black pants, a colorful blouse, not a hair out of place as she climbed gracefully out of her Mercedes. She always looked her best, and for the first time in his life Paul wondered why she spent so much effort on her appearance. Who was she trying to impress? Or was it more of a protective thing, a perfect veneer she wore as a barrier between the harsh world and her tender soul?

Assuming her soul actually *was* tender.

"It's good to see you," he said, and leaned down for a cheek kiss.

"And you." She said it without warmth, and the whole greeting would have been as cold and formal as an exchange between mere acquaintances, but then she lifted her hand and laid it on his cheek. She used her thumb to tilt his head so she could inspect more thoroughly. "You look well," she finally decided.

"So do you. Would you like to come inside? Or there's a restaurant on the corner, if you prefer."

"Inside, please. I should see where you're living."

Should. So she could judge how far he'd fallen? So she could fulfill some virtual checklist of things a responsible mother knows about her firstborn?

But there was no point overthinking it all, and he needed to get the surprising sense of resentment under control if he was going to have a prayer of making this reconciliation work. Assuming it actually was a reconciliation.

He led her through the glass doors and up the stairs, glad to avoid the sometimes-odorous elevator. He had to brace himself before he opened the door to the apartment itself, had to remind himself that it was a perfectly serviceable space, clean enough and big enough and damn well good enough. It was a step down from what he'd been used to, but it was his, paid for with his own earned money, and that was more than he'd ever been able to say before in his life.

Still, there was an awkward moment when they stepped inside and his mother looked around as if searching for something to say. Or possibly for the rest of the apartment.

Then she tugged her boots off, stepped into the living room, and crossed directly to the bookshelf on the far wall. Reference books, a few novels, and the rest of the space taken up with framed photographs. She lifted one of them up and turned to him with a smile on her face. "I remember this day."

He nodded. The photo was of him and Jas when they'd been quite young, each wearing a man's dress shirt backwards, like a smock, and each covered in a rainbow of various paints. "The mural," he said.

"I was so pleased with your enthusiasm. Enrolled you both in all those art classes, and blamed the teachers when you didn't demonstrate as much passion as I'd expected. I thought I had two blossoming artists to nurture…"

He wanted to ask whether that actually would have been okay. If both of her children had wanted to be artists instead of going into business, would the family have accepted their decisions? But there was no point arguing about something that had never happened, so instead he said, "I think it was the forbidden aspect that we really loved. Getting to make a mess and paint on the walls. We felt like we were getting away with being bad."

"I had the wall painted with primer to be ready for you, and there were drop cloths all over the floor…"

"Yeah. That was good, too. We got to *pretend* we were being bad, without worrying about actually getting in trouble. It was a nice compromise, I think."

"A compromise," his mother mused. "Yes. It was. And now we need another one, it seems."

"You want another mural?"

She ignored his comment. "Are you happy here? This life? Without your family close by?"

That was a lot of questions, and he wasn't sure they all had the same answers. "I've missed the family. Of course I have." But he'd found another family. A strange one, but—a family, all the same. Even if the kids were furry and had razors strapped to their toes.

"We've missed you, as well. And Bobby has missed you."

"Please tell me you didn't drive all the way up here about *Bobby*. Mom, that's over. It's done."

She went back to her inspection of the photos on the shelf for a moment, then said, "Yes. And he's moving on. His mother says he's started meeting new people—prospective partners. She's been helping him with that. Networking, I suppose you could say. Nothing has clicked yet, but he hasn't been at it long. It's just a matter of time."

"I'll be sincerely happy for him when he meets the right person."

Her snort was not entirely ladylike, but she compensated with an absolutely exquisite flick of her wrist, dismissing his silliness in the most graceful way possible. "The point is: it's time for you to move on, as well. Time for you to start looking for someone new. A suitable young man. And I'd like to help you with that."

"I don't—I—I've already met a few people, actually."

"Yes. Jasminder mentioned that."

"She did?" His stomach tightened. Everything with Sean was too new, too fragile—it couldn't handle the delicate brutality of his mother's attentions.

"I don't dismiss the value of the internet entirely, but I think it would be foolish to ignore your other options."

He stared at her. It was an abrupt topic change, and didn't seem relevant to—anything. Then he realized—Jas hadn't told their mother about Sean. Jas didn't even *know* about Sean, not really. She'd just mentioned the Candidates. Nothing important.

Still, Paul needed to handle this all carefully. He *had* missed his mother. Being with her brought that all home. Her high expectations, her elegance, the traps she laid, the way ever conversation had to be negotiated rather than just blundered through—it reminded him of Sean, in a way. Not the elegance part, or the expectations, but the need to pay attention, to be prepared.

So Paul needed to stop thinking about Sean and keep his mind on the current conversation. "What are you suggesting?"

"Your father and I would like you to come to dinner tomorrow evening. Nothing grand—just a gathering of friends and family."

"Friends and family?"

She smiled. "Do you remember Nate Martin?"

"Nate Martin? He's—wait. When you talk about suitable men, what do you mean, exactly?"

Another wave of her hand, this one a little less elegant, a little more impatient. "Of course it would be lovely if we could find a Sikh man for you, but, honestly, it's not the most important element, is it?"

"What are the elements that *are* important?"

She lifted a perfectly manicured hand and started ticking off points on her fingers. "Financially successful. Emotionally stable. Family oriented. *Local.* Darling, if we were willing to go world-wide with this, of course we'd have many more options, but we want you close, if at all possible." With that resolved, she returned to her finger-ticking. "Similar values. That's where being Sikh would be helpful, but, really, none of us are terribly observant, are we? Our values are largely secular. So, what else? What haven't I covered?"

Funny. Stubborn. Brave. Gentle. "Handsome? Virile? Muscular?"

"Well, I suppose I can't speak to certain elements of his virility, but Nate Martin is certainly an attractive man. Don't you think?"

Of course he was. Attractive was an understatement, really. Nate, three years older than Paul, had grown up next door to the Gills, and Paul had spent many teenage days trying to catch glimpses of his neighbor lounging by the pool, or jogging along the street. Followed by many teenage nights lying in bed, replaying images in his mind, imagining a different world, one where golden, muscular Nate might actually notice skinny, geeky Paul....

"Why is he coming to dinner? Does he know you're trying to set him up?"

"He's just back from Sydney—he was living there for quite a while. His mother says he even picked up some of the accent. He's lost touch with many of his friends from when he was younger, so he's looking for a new social circle. I mentioned that you were in a similar situation, and his mother and I decided it would make sense for the two of you to meet. That's all. Not a set up. Not necessarily."

Just a meeting. A chance to renew an acquaintance, maybe make a new friend. And, more importantly, a return to Paul's family. After an entire life in which he'd rarely gone more than a week without visiting, he'd spent months away. Not because he'd travelled somewhere distant, not because he was too busy, but because he hadn't been invited. Hadn't been welcome.

And now, he could go home.

"Wednesday." he said. "Yes. I'll be there. Thank you for thinking of me."

His mother inclined her head in acknowledgement of his gratitude, then cast her gaze around the room. "This is fine. For a temporary space. It's not terrible at all. But we can do better, can't we?" She crossed the room and linked her arm through his. "Are there any shops worth visiting in this town? I've had my eye on a lovely divan at Wasserman's—it's wonderful, but too modern for my decor. But if we used it as inspiration? As an anchor piece for the rest of your space? I think we could do something really special. Small doesn't have to mean plain, after all. Doesn't have to mean cheap."

And just like that, he was back in the fold. Swept up in the current of his mother's plans and enthusiasms.

She had wonderful taste, and he'd always admired her designs. Always appreciated that she shared her efforts and took care of him. And, of course, she'd be more than happy to pay for the negligible expenses that came from furnishing a tiny apartment. Everything was so much *easier* if he just let himself be washed along.

He said, "I haven't actually done much shopping up here. But there are a few places downtown you might find interesting. Do you have time to go visit them now?"

"I want to be back in the city by dinner. But that gives us several hours." She beamed up at him. "Let's go shopping."

Chapter Thirty-One

Paul didn't come back to the house that night, and that was just fine with Sean. It wasn't like they had to spend every second together. It wasn't like they were a couple. They were just friends. No big deal.

Paul hadn't even needed to text, really. He *had* texted, saying he was spending the afternoon with his mom, but that hadn't been necessary.

Sean had his own shit to deal with, after all. He didn't need to waste any energy caring about how things were going with someone else's family, not when he was calling his future landlord and dealing with damage deposits and rent payments and all that other crap he'd never had to deal with before.

So it was all just fine, and if he woke up kind of grumpy the next morning, maybe that was because he had no fucking legs and his best friend was kicking him out of the house, not because he'd been hoping for some time with Paul the night before.

"The place is empty," he admitted to Mark over the breakfast table. Luke had already left for work, and Mark was easier to talk to, anyway. He was sneaky, twisting conversations around so they made whatever point he wanted made, but that was better than Lucas coming at Sean head-on.

"That means you could move in whenever you were ready?" Mark took a casual, non-threatening, non-judgemental bite of toast.

"That's what he said."

"And he's okay with a cat?"

"I had to pay an extra damage deposit."

"That's pretty standard."

"I guess."

"Do you have a day in mind? You said the place is furnished, but you'll need linens—sheets and towels and whatnot—and maybe kitchen stuff? Just how furnished is it?"

"Just the big stuff. Bed and a couch and a table. That kind of thing."

"Your mom might like to help you with the extras. I think she's been a bit anxious with you out of the house. Might be nice to let her be part of this."

Like Sean would be doing his mom a favor. Yeah, Mark was smooth.

Still, Sean wasn't in any position to be proud, so he nodded and said, "I'll give her a call."

Mark leaned back in his chair. "This is really happening? You're moving out? It feels strange. I guess I've gotten used to having you around—no, I've *enjoyed* having you around. You and Paul and the kittens—you've all been great."

Well, Sean wasn't going to think about Paul right then. "Don't tell Luke, but I think you guys can keep a couple of the kittens, if you want. So *that* won't be a big change."

"Two kittens aren't the same as five kittens and two friends, but— they'll soften the blow, sure. And thank you for trusting us with them." Another bite of toast, and then, "Have you spoken to your therapist about this? About living on your own?"

"Uh—I guess so, yeah. I mean, that's been the plan all along."

"But you haven't discussed moving out right now. Like, you haven't checked in to be sure this is the right time to make this change?"

"Luke just kicked me out yesterday. I don't have an appointment with the therapist until next week."

"You could give him a call, if you wanted. We both know Luke didn't really kick you out, not in those exact terms. If you need to stay, you can stay. And if it'd be easier for you to have that message come from your therapist instead of saying it yourself? We can set it up so it happens that way."

"Wait. Do you think Luke is wrong? I shouldn't be living on my own yet?"

"No, I think he's right. But it's not what he or I think that really matters. If *you* don't think you're ready, give your therapist a call, express your doubts, and have him tell me and Luke that it's best for you to stay with us for longer time. You're absolutely welcome, if you need to be here."

It was a way out. Maybe Sean couldn't absolutely *stop* all these changes, but he could slow them down, at least. He could go back to work at Elise's, maybe part time to start, and figure out what was happening with Paul—not that anything was happening there, it was just a weird thing they'd been doing and it was probably already over, really—and then go back to his safe little room next to Luke's warm kitchen, not to a cold, strange apartment all by himself. He could take baby steps instead of a giant leap. It made sense.

So it was a bit strange to hear himself say, "No. I'm ready. Thanks, though. I appreciate the thought."

"Well, we're always here if you change your mind," Mark promised. Then he stood up and went off to work, and Sean called his mom about helping get the apartment set up and everything just rolled along like a wheelchair going down hill.

By that night, the apartment was set up, mostly with second-hand stuff his mom had pulled out of her own cupboards or collected from her friends, and he could have spent the night there, if he'd wanted. But Cyborg was still at the house, and even if he went and got her and brought her back, she wouldn't settle down well, not if he just plopped her down in a whole new place without her siblings, so she'd keep him up all night, and it just made sense to spend one more night in the little room at Luke's. He wasn't hiding, he was just being smart.

He asked his mom to drive him back to Luke's place, and as soon as he saw Paul's car in the driveway he knew he'd made the right decision. Paul was there, and there could be one more night of all of them together before things changed.

"Thanks for everything," he said, and his mom smiled in a way that let him know she'd be crying before she'd got the car backed out of the driveway, but somehow it didn't seem as tragic as her tears normally did. She was an emotional person. No big deal.

He grinned at her and headed inside. The other three were in the kitchen, working on dinner, and he took his outside clothes off then leaned into the kitchen doorway. "Wow. Kinda crowded in here. I'll just wait in the living—"

"Get in here," Luke ordered, at the same time as Paul said, "There's plenty of room," and Mark added, "We wouldn't want you to be lonely."

Luke looked at the other two, then back at Sean. "Don't be a lazy ass. Get to work."

"That's it," Sean said. "That's the final straw. I've had enough of your bossiness and emotional abuse. I'm moving out."

"Yeah," Luke said with a fond smile. "You are. Congratulations."

Chapter Thirty-Two

It was stupid for Paul to be nervous, but also stupid to pretend he wasn't.

Part of the problem was the time crunch. He'd had to work until past five, then rush home to shower and change, then battle rush hour traffic to get into the city—there hadn't been a lot of time for quiet contemplation, or even to take a deep breath.

He'd wanted to call Sean on the drive down, just as a distraction, but Sean was busy settling into his new apartment. His new life. The night before, at Mark and Luke's place, had felt like a goodbye party—to the house, obviously, but also to that whole stage of Sean's life. The dependent stage, while his recovery had been as much emotional as physical. Now he was stable, ready to be on his own. It was good, of course, but every graduation has a touch of melancholy under the surface. And Sean hearing Paul's whining wasn't going to help him work through any of that.

So Paul didn't call. He just drove, and got more and more tense the closer he was to the house.

Brampton was hardly a prestigious part of the city, but it had pockets of wealth, and Paul felt the difference as he turned onto the tree-lined, winding streets of his parents' neighborhood. He'd taken it for granted most of his life, but now? The houses were set back behind tall hedges and wrought-iron fences, clearly designed for privacy, but also making the whole place feel cold, somehow. Empty. Even as a short-term visitor to Luke and Mark's house, Paul knew their neighbors on both sides *and* across the street well enough to wave hello and have a pretty good idea of what was going on with whom.

Here? If a party was large enough for the valets to have to use the street for parking, the neighbors would know something was up, but otherwise? The place was a neighborhood in name only.

Which was fine. Nice, even. Frustrating when he'd been a kid trying to spy on Nate Martin, but in general it was good to have some privacy, to have a property that was close enough to the city to be convenient but far enough away to allow a couple acres of space for each house. It was a nice neighborhood, a wonderful place to live.

So why did it feel so strange?

He didn't have long to think about that before he arrived at the curving driveway of the family home. There were only a few cars parked out front, which meant his mother had been telling the truth about it being a small gathering, at least.

He was still nervous, though. Why?

Why the hell did he still care? He knew who he was, didn't he? If things went poorly with his family, wasn't that their problem as much as his? He'd done fine without them. And Nate Martin? That wasn't a thing, was it? Not—

What if it was? What if he got in there and Nate Martin was as gorgeous and charming and fascinating as he'd always been, and what if he was interested in Paul? What would that mean?

He and Sean were—what? Nothing declared. Nothing really contemplated, really. They were friends, they got along well, they—

The front door opened, and Paul's mother stepped out, arms wrapped around herself to ward off at least some of the cold. "Come inside!" she called. "Everyone wants to see you."

She'd been watching for him. Waiting. And she'd been worried enough to come out and urge him in. She was just as nervous about this as he was, although of course she'd be better at hiding her discomfort.

He jogged up the broad front steps and she extended both hands toward him. "It's good to see you here," she said. She turned to walk beside him, linking their arms, then spoke more quietly. "Your father is grumpy. Things aren't going well with a project—nothing dramatic, but he's in a mood. Jasminder is handling him. But don't be surprised if he's snippier than usual."

Oh, excellent.

"I'll take your coat," his mother said as soon as the door was shut behind them.

"I can hang it up." He wasn't a guest, really, was he? Had his mother ever treated him like one before?

She stood quietly while he took care of himself, then linked their arms again and guided him toward the back of the house. The casual great room, not the formal living room. A good sign.

There were a dozen or so others gathered on the oversized leather couches and clustered around the bar, all people Paul recognized. His own family, including a cousin from Mumbai who was serving a sort of internship with Paul's father; the Dillons, who lived down the street; and, of course, the Martins.

"You all remember Paul," his mother announced as they entered. "And I'm sure he remembers all of you."

Waves of greetings, but it was only Nate Martin who detached himself from the crowd at the bar and crossed the room. Nate Martin, tall and blond and broad-shouldered and smiling, dark sports coat over dark shirt above dark pants, all well-tailored to his perfect body. And then a smile that brightened the entire room. Damn.

"It's been too long," Nate said, extending his hand. "You were just a kid when I last saw you."

Well, that wasn't true, really, but maybe Paul had been a kid when Nate had last *noticed* him. If he'd ever noticed him at all.

But now? The handshake was warm and it came with eye contact that was almost too much for a family gathering, too close to flirtatious. Flattering, but dangerous, and also mystifying. There was no way a man who looked like Nate Martin needed to come on strong, especially not with someone as utterly unremarkable as Paul.

"It has been a while," Paul said. "I hear you've been in Australia?"

"For almost five years. I should have planned my return a bit more carefully—I'd forgotten how cold it gets here in February! I've always come back to visit during the summertime, so I'm not acclimated at all."

"Sorry," Paul said, and immediately felt like an idiot.

Nate smiled. "I'll forgive you this time. But in the future, please arrange better weather for me. Or figure out a way for me to have better common sense. In the meantime, though, I'm warming myself with your father's excellent Scotch." He tipped the last of the amber liquid from his glass into his mouth. "Join me for the next round?"

Hell, yes. Paul turned to excuse himself to his mother, but she was already gone, drifted away to her other guests. And Paul's father seemed to be ignoring him, which was just as well, if he was in a grumpy mood. Jas was in the group by the bar, and gave Paul a smile with just the tiniest eyebrow waggle as he approached. She clearly remembered Paul's childhood crush, but with any luck she'd keep her mouth shut and not embarrass him.

"More scotch?" She was already reaching for the bottle. "Paul, you going to help yourself, or can I keep playing bartender?"

"If you're in charge, I'm going to ask for something really complicated. What was that drink we had in Glasgow?"

"*The Commonwealth.*" She grinned at Paul, then turned her attention to Nate. "We were over there during the Commonwealth Games, and there was an ingredient from each participating country."

"Was it any good?"

"It was okay," she said. "But probably not quite worth the effort." She turned back to Paul. "So, no. I will not be making you one of those. You can have a Scotch, a beer, a glass of wine, or you can mix something up for yourself."

"You're still taking lessons on the 'gracious hostess' front, I guess?"

She snorted. "You're no more a guest than I am. Just because you've been *persona non grata* lately doesn't mean I have to play hostess when you *do* show up."

"*Persona non grata?*" Nate raised an eyebrow. "Everything okay?"

"Besides my sister being a terrible hostess *and* having a big mouth? Everything's fine."

Paul ducked behind the bar to pull a beer out of the cooler, but he was still close enough that Nate could have pressed him for details if he'd wanted to. Instead, he sipped the Scotch Jas poured for him, then leaned on the bar and watched quietly as Paul twisted the lid off his bottle and lifted it for a drink.

"I missed my family," Nate said quietly. "When I was away. I still saw them a couple times a year, but it wasn't like living in the same town. There was a hole in my life, definitely. But—" He took a sip, then smiled. "There was an element of freedom to it, as well. I felt like there was a chance to re-invent myself, at least a little, without people who loved the *old* me trying to keep me from making any changes."

"And what changes did you make?"

Nate smiled. Damn, he had a nice smile. "Nothing major, actually. I think I just appreciated the possibility." He took another sip of his Scotch. "Seems like you've been able to make your own decisions even living close to everyone, though. Good for you."

"Oh, I don't know about that."

"Our moms talk, you know. I've heard about the family not appreciating your career choice. Which is crazy, by the way, but—I know how families can be. And I heard something about a recent breakup?" He sipped again, a little too casually. Yeah, he'd heard something, all right.

"Apparently my parents have a better idea than I do about who I love and should spend the rest of my life with."

"Pretty arrogant of you to think you could make that kind of decision on your own, really."

"Arrogant, immature, irresponsible—you name it."

"Same thing I was talking about, really, isn't it? Our families love us, sure. But they only know one version of us, and they think that's all we are. All we can ever be." Nate looked down at his glass, then around the room, and he snorted. "Apparently the version of *me* that comes out when I'm around my family is the whining, self-pitying one. Oh, boo-hoo, my family loves me and supports me and wants what's best for me, but they don't do it in the exact way I want them to."

It was nice how Nate had used "us" when he was saying kind things, and shifted to "me" when he'd gotten critical. Not a big deal, but—nice. Relaxing. Comfortable.

Paul glanced around the room and saw his father, over in the big armchair by the fireplace, and his father saw him looking, and nodded back. No real warmth to it, but courtesy, and approval. A benediction. Paul was back in the fold.

He'd stood up for himself, made his point, and now? No more Bobby. No more arrogance and control and impatience. Paul could have his family back, his *life* back, as long as he made a few small compromises.

Spending time with someone as good looking and pleasant as Nate Martin? Was that the only price Paul was expected to pay?

He'd created a problem and his parents had found a solution, just like they always did. They'd made it possible for Paul to return. And there was no logical reason for him to walk away from any of it.

Chapter Thirty-Three

Work sucked, of course. Using energy for someone else's goals, doing everything to someone else's schedule—it was all bullshit. But if Sean *had* to work somewhere? Elise's barn was probably the best option, especially since she'd decided to trust him with some of the animals.

Holding a squirrel still while a cranky old lady checked the dressing on a fuzzy little broken leg wasn't something Sean had dreamed about doing when he was a kid, but it was kind of satisfying. But he couldn't quite figure out why.

"We don't exactly have a squirrel shortage," he said as he cradled the tiny body. "They're not endangered or anything, are they? Why are we spending this much time on one tree-rat?"

Elise sighed. "We don't have a human shortage, either. We're not endangered or anything. But it's still worthwhile to help each other out when we can, isn't it?"

"You help people out when you can?"

"No. I help *animals* out when I can. People can go to hell."

Yeah, she was crusty, but he knew she was a softie underneath, even with humans. She'd given him a job, hadn't she? Sure, he was turning out to be not-terrible at it, but she'd had no reason to think that when she'd first met him, and she'd given him a chance anyway. Sean's mom would have said Elise was on the side of the angels. That seemed vague enough to be worth shooting for... not fully committing to being an angel yourself, but at least helping them out when you could.

Like Paul did. Like Mark. Like Luke, maybe, although Luke definitely still had a bit of devil in him. Could Sean be like that?

"Pay attention," Elise ordered. "Move your finger—I need to see if he's still got mobility."

Sean did as he was told, and when the treatment was over he stubbied his way to the wire cage and eased the squirrel inside. Always a bit of a trick, setting the animal down gently, but still getting his arm out the door fast enough to prevent an escape—he made it.

When he turned, he found Elise still standing by the counter. Usually she'd have bustled off and started about four other jobs by now, but this time she was just watching him. Waiting.

Was he about to get fired? Probably, although he had no idea what he'd done wrong.

"Lucas is taking a course at the community college this spring," she said. "The classes are during work hours, so he'll still get paid. And I'm paying the tuition as well. He'll have to study on his own time."

So, not being fired, unless Elise was taking a hell of a weird path to do it. And, yeah, Sean knew about the course. He'd been planning to stop by Goodwill when he had a chance to pick up a backpack—My Little Pony or Paw Patrol or whatever was the most embarrassing—so he could set it up with a juice box and some goldfish crackers for little Lukey's first day at school.

"It's only a single course, so far. Not that much time or commitment." Elise seemed to think it was important for Sean to hear all this, so he stayed still, but didn't engage. Then she said, "I think you should take it, too. It's just basic science—some biology, some chemistry, even a little bit of physics—but it's a good foundation."

"A foundation?"

"For future learning. Veterinary technician, certified wildlife rehabilitator—there are a variety of directions you could consider."

Directions Sean could consider. It was—what was it? Crazy, obviously. Sean hated school, and school hated Sean. It made no sense to even think about going to college, not when he'd barely scraped through high school. And crazy to think about directions. About real jobs—a vet tech? a wildlife rehabilitator? Those were jobs for—for people with—well, with legs, to start, but also with brains, and responsibilities, and futures. Not Sean.

"I can't really afford it," he said.

"I'd pay. Not for your study time. But tuition, and any time missed from work. You and Luke could probably share the textbook?"

Jesus. He *still* couldn't afford it. Couldn't afford to let himself hope, couldn't afford another goddamn failure, another disappointment. Except—

What if he could? What if there was room in his life for a bit of uncertainty? He'd already made changes. He was—well, he had no idea what he was with Paul, but he was *something.* He'd taken a chance and the world hadn't fallen apart. He'd fucked up with the accident, but he was walking again—on fucking stubbies, but they were just temporary. He hadn't failed, there, even though he'd screwed around and wasn't exactly a perfect patient. He had his own apartment, and his car was supposed to be ready for him to learn to drive pretty soon, and—

And if he had an actual plan, a fucking *direction* he was moving in, wouldn't that mean something? With Paul? Would it somehow make that feel less temporary, less doomed to failure? A physiotherapist and a marginally employed cripple wasn't a good match, but a physio and a vet tech? A physio and a wildlife rehabilitator? That almost made sense. They'd both be helping their patients recover from injuries and get back to their lives. A wildlife rehabilitator who could stand up and walk on full-height legs. It was all still a long shot, maybe, but it was a hell of a lot closer than the way things were if Sean did nothing.

"Can I think about it?" he asked.

Elise raised her eyebrows. "When I first suggested it to Lucas, he said 'no', flat out. Didn't want to even discuss it. Are you going to be more reasonable about this than Lucas, Sean? That would be impressive."

"Well, Lukey's pretty irrational, really. He doesn't think things through, you know? I think you'll find that I'm smarter than him in most ways, once you get to know us."

She almost smiled at that, then said, "Fine, you can think it through. But don't take too long—the course starts next week, and I'll need to contact the instructor to get him to pull some strings to let you in. String-pulling sometimes takes a while."

"Wait. Why would you have to do that?"

"You haven't gone through the usual process for being accepted to college. This is a real course, not an evening pottery class or something. It's not a big problem—the instructor is an old friend, and if he's somehow not able to make things work I can always go higher up the ladder. It's helpful to have lived as long as I have, all in the same town. I know everybody, and their mothers and grandmothers too. It won't be an issue. But I don't like to be rushed."

"When do need to know by?"

"Tomorrow morning?"

A night to think about it. To talk about it. With Luke, maybe, but mostly with Paul. He'd called earlier and suggested they meet at the house after work, pick up Panther, then go to Paul's place for the night. Sean had said he couldn't leave Cyborg alone in the new apartment, but Paul had said she was always welcome at his place, too. So, a bit more cat-transporting than was convenient, but otherwise a good plan.

And Sean could mention the course to Paul. See how he reacted. See whether he saw the increased potential, see whether that might mean anything. Was there a chance at a future for them, or was Sean just daydreaming? Yeah, he needed the night to figure that out.

Luke called to him, then, from somewhere outside the barn, and Elise looked at her watch. "Oh. Time for you to go. Luke will have finished the feeding, and I'm done in here until the evening rounds."

It always felt weird, leaving a little old lady behind with all the duties of taking care of the animals, but Sean knew Luke had offered to work a split shift so he'd be there for the morning *and* evening routines and she'd apparently been seriously insulted. She could take care of the animals herself, thank you very much, and no young whipper-snappers should suggest otherwise.

Sean stubbied his way out of the barn, through the drift of late-season snow on the path, and down to the car. He was careful because of the ice, but Luke only gave the horn one impatient honk, so Sean was clearly making okay time.

"She wants me to take the same course as you," Sean said as Luke eased along the snowy driveway.

"Yeah? You gonna do it?"

"I hated school. You hated school. Why the hell would either one of us go back to school?"

"We've been through this. You and me used to be dumbasses. It doesn't make sense to think about shit we used to not like and think we still won't like it."

"Now that we're smartasses?"

"Something like that."

"Do you think you're going to like taking a basic science course?"

"No, I'll probably hate it. But that's just too bad for me. Because I want to do something more, and something more means I need more school, so...."

"You think you can handle the competition? You won't turn into a big baby when I get better marks than you do?"

Luke snorted. "I'm really not worried about that."

No. He wouldn't be. Still, maybe Sean could edge past him on a quiz or something. He could sneak-study, maybe at a time he knew Luke was distracted by other stuff, and then pounce on test day. That'd be worth doing.

There was an unfamiliar car parked in front of the house when they got home. No big deal—street parking was free, and any neighbor might have taken the space. But Luke said, "Shit. Are we late, or is she early?"

"What? Who?"

"Jas. Paul's sister. I guess I didn't mention that. She called earlier—wanted to come over and see if she could convince you to give her a kitten."

"Oh."

"You can't keep them all, buddy. And she seems like she'd be a good owner—lots of money, and I know that's not the only thing that matters, but it doesn't hurt. You know she's not going to be scrounging up pennies for the vet bills or whatever."

Sure, he knew that. And she was Paul's sister, not some total stranger. She'd seemed nice enough. Still. His kittens should all stay at the house together forever. Was that too much to ask?

Well, considering he'd already taken Cyborg home and Paul was planning to take Panther that night, maybe it was a bit late for *all* the kittens to stay. Still.

"She lives in the city. We never socialized them to city life."

"She's got a townhouse—she's not a street person. And she was talking about building a catio on one of her balconies. You know those things, where they screen in an outside space so the cat can get fresh air? I'm thinking I can build one here, too, up against the side of the house with the basement window to let them in and out."

Great. So everyone else's cats were going to be living in outdoor luxury while poor Cyborg was stuck inside. Because she got stuck with Sean, and he was a broke loser.

Unless vet techs or wildlife rehabilitators made okay money? He needed to look into that.

"Sean." Damn it. Luke's tone of voice that always made Sean pay attention, even when he didn't want to. "She'll take good care of your baby. Unless she says something totally mental when we go in there, you're going to give her the kitten. Right?"

Sean sighed. "Yeah. I guess."

"Okay, then." Luke swung his door open and started for the house, and Sean followed him, more slowly and carefully.

Jas was already inside, as was Mark—apparently he'd come home early that day—and she had the fifth kitten, the calico they hadn't named because they'd all known she was going to have a different owner some day, on her lap. The kitten was playing with an unfamiliar toy, some sort of feathered-mouse-thing, that Jas must have brought with her.

When Jas heard them come in and looked up, her expression was so sweet, so hopeful and gentle and tentative, that Sean knew resistance was futile.

"You came to pick up your rat?" he said. "We haven't started their vaccinations yet—you need to do that soon. And we can send some of the food she's been eating along with you. You aren't supposed to change their diet too suddenly, so you need to mix in a new food gradually. And she really likes that fishing pole toy. You can take that. Make sure your vet knows she might go outside—that might affect the vaccinations." What else? What else? He didn't want to stop talking because then he might start thinking, and that was no good. "She bites sometimes. They all do—they're just being kittens, but you need to discourage it. Don't hit her—don't ever hit her. But if you get a can of coins and shake it hard, she really doesn't like the noise. So that can be her punishment if she's bad."

"Seriously?" Jas interjected. Her tentatively hopeful face had morphed into something much more animated. "You're going to let me have her? I know kittens aren't hard to find, but I really love *this* kitten! She's so—" She gazed down at the little animal with enough adoration to make Sean relax at least a little about the whole situation. "She's just perfect. Paul warned me that you were going to be really conscientious about this, and I think that's absolutely justified. I brought some paperwork—it's apparently sort of difficult to actually *hire* a vet when you don't have a pet yet, but I printed out reviews for every vet in Brampton and I've narrowed it down to a few, but if you disagree with those choices I can give any of them another look. And I've talked to a contractor about building a catio on my balcony and a bunch of elevated pathways through the townhouse— have you seen those on the internet? Like long bookshelves with no books, so the cat can run around overhead. And some hiding spots. And nice places to nap, of course."

She lifted the kitten for a quick snuggle, then let her return to the toy. Damn. This was going to be a lucky cat.

"What are you going to name her?" he asked, and he pulled off his jacket and gloves.

Mark and Luke went into the kitchen to start fussing over dinner—it was amazing how long it took to come up with a meal when you were trying to be creative and original all the time—and Sean stayed in the doorway of the living room. He felt suddenly self-conscious. How was he supposed to have a conversation with this woman—polished and rich and beautiful and a fucking cat-lover on top of it all? The cat thing *should* have made it easier, he supposed, but he'd already agreed that she could *have* the fucking cat, so it wasn't like he had any kind of power over her anymore. And he'd already given her all the cat-knowledge he had. Why had Luke abandoned him?

"Where's Paul?" he demanded. Too fierce, probably. Well, judging by her surprised eyebrows, too fierce, *definitely*. He tried to soften his tone. "He's supposed to be here after work, right?"

"That's what he told me," she agreed. Then she shrugged. "I guess his plans might have changed. But he probably would have called Luke or Mark, right? He wouldn't leave Panther here without arranging it with them first."

He might have called Luke or Mark. Not Sean. Because—because as far as Paul's sister knew, there was absolutely no reason for him to be making any calls to Sean. "Why would his plans have changed?" he asked. Stupid question, but he wasn't sure what else to say.

She held back for only a moment before grinning. "Maybe he met somebody. Maybe he's got a date."

Was this—what was it? Why was she smiling? Because she was teasing Sean? No. Because she had no idea Sean would care about Paul's dating life one way or another. And because—"Has he met someone? Someone he might have a date with?"

There was nothing vindictive in her expression, no hint that she had an ulterior motive or was anything other than a loving sister happy that her brother might have found happiness. "Nothing serious. Just—I don't know. We had a family gathering last night, and it was a bit of a set-up. A neighbor Paul had a crush on when he was younger—he thinks nobody knows, but my god, he was *so* obvious. Anyway, our moms set it up, and they seemed to get along."

Last night. Paul had called Sean on his way home. He'd said it went well. He'd seemed excited. Sean—stupid, clueless Sean—had thought Paul was happy because he was making up with his family. "The guy's single? He's interested?"

And maybe there was something in Sean's voice that gave her a clue, but didn't tell her exactly what the problem was, because Jas's response was a bit more guarded. "Oh, I don't know. I'm just gossiping, really. Sorry. I'm kitten-giddy. I've found my fuzzy little love so I want everyone else to be just as happy. Paul's probably just working late."

Working late. Sure, that was probably it. But Paul hadn't mentioned this guy when he'd called Sean the night before, and that had to mean something, didn't it? He was either keeping it from Sean deliberately, or, even fucking worse, he didn't think it was anything Sean had a reason to know about. Why would someone like Paul bother to mention a possible romance to some guy he'd been slumming with for a while? Why would any of it be any of Sean's business? Who was he to think he had a right to know?

"You take good care of the kitten, okay?" he said. He grabbed his jacket and gloves and headed for the door.

"You're leaving?" she said. She sounded alarmed.

Of course she did. The fucking gimp needed to be babysat, and she wasn't sure who had the duty right then.

He forced his cockiest smile as he turned to say, "Got a cat of my own at home. I need to go check on her."

"You're—" She stopped. She didn't know. Was the gimp allowed out on his own? Did he have some sort of car, some form of independence? What were the rules, here? What was the moral responsibility for someone like her, towards someone like him?

"I'm fine," he said, and then he was out the door, pulling on his jacket and gloves as he moved.

He wiped out on the way down the ramp—of course he fucking did—and this time he landed hard, his hip bashing against the low wooden curb that would have kept his wheelchair from slipping too far. Sharp pain that turned into a throbbing ache, and he almost wished it was worse. Wished it hurt more, for longer, so he could pay attention to it instead of to every other goddamn thing.

But he was just hurt, not injured, and after a second of lying on his side, cursing at the stars and the snow and everything that wasn't kittens, he rolled onto his back, grabbed the nearest post, and rocked to his—not his feet. Never his feet, never again. He rocked up so he was as close as he could get to pretending he was a real human adult, and he started moving again.

His phone chirped when he was at the end of the driveway. A text. He thought about ignoring it, but what if it was Paul? What if this was all—something. He couldn't even think of what it might be, but he'd never had that much of an imagination, so he pulled the phone out of his pocket and saw the message from Luke.

Where the fuck r u going?

Home. And then his pride made him add, *Cyborg needs me.*

You're walking?

Obviously.

Can u actually walk that far?

Yeah, good question. He definitely never had before, not since the accident, and he'd already spent most of the day on his stubbies at work. But there was no way he was going back to that house. He texted, *Guess we'll find out.*

You're a pain in the ass. Call if u need a pick up.

And that was that. Luke had done his duty, and now he'd give Sean his space. Just like Sean wanted. He'd slink—well, stump—back to his den and lick his wounds in private.

No. Wait. No fucking wounds. He hadn't been that stupid. He hadn't let himself care about Paul, so he wasn't hurt that Paul was moving on. Not hurt. Annoyed? Maybe he could be annoyed.

But—at what? He and Paul hadn't had a thing, so Paul starting a thing with someone else wasn't anything to be annoyed about.

Shit.

Aw, fuck it, he wasn't hurt, he wasn't annoyed: he was just tired of it all. He didn't want to play anymore. He was taking his toys and going home, except for the part where he didn't have any toys.

And the part where home was so fucking far away. Jesus Christ, he'd only gone a couple blocks and his stumps were already screaming. His glutes were almost as bad. But if he stopped, he'd never get going again. He couldn't call Luke for help, not when there was a chance Paul might be at the house and hear about it. His mom?

He could call his mom. She'd come, or send one of his siblings to come pick him up. And they'd be careful not to upset him and they'd say how great it was that he was trying, but maybe next time he should try just a little bit less.

He could call a fucking cab. An anonymous stranger. That sounded just about perfect. Except it would be just one more failure. One more thing he couldn't fucking do.

No. No chance. He'd come two blocks. There were only another six or seven to go. He could do it. He damn well would do it. This one tiny, stupid thing… he'd make it happen, and the pain in his legs would be a good distraction to keep him from thinking about anything else.

Chapter Thirty-Four

Sean wasn't at the house. Strange how deflated Paul felt when he realized that, but it was good to see Jas happy, playing with her kitten, trying out names, and being silly and relaxed in a way she didn't often manage anywhere but in her own home.

"She's all mine," she crowed for about the fifth time. She was lying on her back on the floor, swarmed by all the kittens, but really only paying attention to her own little calico. "She's coming home with me."

"And Sean didn't seem too upset to be letting her go? I was braced for him to have a problem with it."

"He was a bit strange," she admitted. "Gave me a bunch of instructions, which was great, but he did it kind of like—I don't know. Like they were challenges, somehow. Challenges he thought I was going to fail."

Yeah, that sounded like Sean, at least if he was in one of his more defensive moods. "He didn't stick around, though? I thought he'd want to monitor your interactions for a while, make sure you weren't going to betray the trust he'd put in you."

"No. He left pretty quickly." She sat up and leaned a little closer to where he was sitting, her voice pitched low enough so Mark and Luke couldn't hear her from the kitchen. "Maybe too quickly? Luke seemed concerned."

"Luke didn't drive him?"

"No, he went on his own."

"He took his chair? The sidewalks aren't exactly clear yet. It's still snowing."

"I think he was walking. I mean, he walked when he went out the door—does he keep his wheelchair outside?"

"Luke," Paul called, standing up and stepping toward the kitchen. "Was Sean *walking* when he left here? On his stubbies?"

Luke appeared in the doorway and nodded. "Yeah. I texted and he said he'd call if he needed help."

Oh. That was okay, then. As long as—"Do you think he meant it? Will he really call, or is he too stubborn?"

Luke shrugged. "Could go either way. But—he's not going to die or anything, right? He'll be on pretty busy streets the whole way. If he gets in trouble and doesn't want to call, he can ask someone else for help."

"He might injure himself."

"Slip on some ice and break his ankle? Oh, no, that's probably not going to happen. Twist his knee? No, I guess not...."

"So you're not worried at all?"

Luke snorted. "Of course I am. I spend half my life worrying about the son-of-a-bitch, and the other half worrying I'm worrying too much. But— he's a grown man, right? He makes his own decisions. Some of them are probably going to be stupid, but there's not a whole lot I can do about that."

No. There wasn't. And Luke was right—Sean was a grown man *and* Sean was sometimes going to make stupid decisions. "He makes it really hard to care about him sometimes, doesn't he?"

"You were warned," Luke said with a smile. Then, "You guys want to stay for dinner? Vegetable lasagna—possibly a bit heavy on the mushrooms."

"I think I should take my little angel home and let her have some time to get used to the place before bedtime," Jas said. "But thank you. For your hospitality, of course, but also for helping to take care of the kittens. I'm really, really, grateful."

"I should get home to Panther, too," Paul said. "He's used to the place, but I think he still misses all the action over here. He needs some playtime." And Paul needed to get in touch with Sean, because they'd had plans, damn it. Plans Paul had really, really been looking forward to. He deserved playtime at least as much as Panther, didn't he?

"Wow," Luke said. "Just me and Mark and just two cats. For a whole night. That's going to be weird."

"The new normal," Paul suggested.

Mark came out to say goodbye, and Paul and Jas headed down the ramp toward their respective cars. When they reached Jas's, Paul helped her load the kitten's carrier into the back seat and make sure it was secure. Then she stopped by the driver's door. "I may have screwed up," she said. "Possibly. Through no real fault of my own."

"Really? I look forward to hearing about it."

"Well. It may not actually be anything, but—you said something, inside, about Sean making it hard for you to care about him. Was that—did you mean care about him as a friend? Or as more than that?"

Yeah, he'd suspected she'd pick up on that phrasing. He'd wanted her to, really. He didn't like the idea of keeping any of this secret. "As more than a friend," he said.

"Shit."

"Not quite the reaction I was hoping for."

She spoke quickly. "I told him about Nate. Not a lot—there isn't a lot to tell, not from my perspective. But I told him you'd been set up with someone last night, someone you used to have a crush on. I told him the two of you seemed to get along well. And he left, abruptly, right after I told him. So—shit. I screwed up, right?"

"Oh. Shit."

"In my defense, you never told me you were involved with Sean. I didn't even know he was gay. So, yes, I should have kept my mouth shut about your private life, but I thought it was *innocent* gossip, not bad gossip." She paused. "Also, possibly I should stop worrying about *my* part in all this and worry more about how you and Sean are doing. Since you're the ones actually affected by my screw up. Sorry."

She wasn't wrong. "You didn't know. It's not your fault."

"Yeah." She wrinkled her nose, then said, "If this is none of my business, tell me so, but—what's going on with that? If you're serious about this guy—about Sean—then why the hell *don't* I know? You've always talked to me about guys in the past. I heard all about your candidates when you were trying internet dating. Why didn't you tell me about you and Sean?"

He didn't really have an answer, and when she saw that, she shrugged. "I'm sure there are lots of possible reasons. But, listen, Paul. If the reason is that you're not sure where things are going with Sean, or that it's just a casual thing you're not that into? Then think about what you're doing. Because Nate seems like a good guy, and he seems pretty interested, and you two got along well. And Mom and Dad like him. They like the two of you together. Nate is your pain-free chance back into the family good books. I know you've missed the money, but you've missed the family, too. Don't try to tell me you haven't. And, really—you're not a cheater, Paul, and you knew this thing with Nate was meant to be a set-up. If you were in a serious relationship with Sean, you wouldn't have gone to meet Nate, would you?"

Damn. It was a lot of truth, all at once. A lot to think about. He'd been operating on instinct for too long and hadn't actually sat down and thought things through. He'd been acting like Sean, really, playing his life by ear. He needed to take some time and get things back on track.

Except… "He left right after you told him about Nate? Did it seem as if he was leaving *because* you'd told him about Nate?"

A wince. "At the time, I just thought he was being weird. But knowing what I now know? Yeah. I think he left because I told him about Nate."

And now he was out there in the cold, trying to walk farther than made any sense for someone so new to wearing prosthetics. Sean was hurt. Angry. Alone. And it was Paul's fault.

"I need to go find him. Make sure he's okay."

Jas nodded. "Of course. Again, I'm sorry. But also—think about it. Think about Nate. You guys could be good together. And, selfishly—I'd really like it if everything got back to normal. I miss having someone to kick under the table at family dinners."

Paul missed that, too. He missed the ease of it all, the familiarity, and the security of knowing his parents were there to back him up. And Nate was lovely. Surely not a sacrifice to be with someone like him?

Yes, he needed to think it all through. But first he needed to make sure Sean was safe. He said his goodbyes to Jas and waggled his fingers through the window at the kitten and started off in his own car, following the route he assumed Sean would be taking.

It didn't take long to find him. The town wasn't that big, and Sean's full-sized torso and short, short legs made him a distinctive silhouette against the white snow. Full-sized torso, short legs, and head bent so far forward it looked like he was climbing Everest. Every muscle in his body was clearly in play, every drop of strength he could find, anywhere, was being dedicated to the cause of forward motion, no matter how slow.

Paul pulled the car over before he reached the struggling figure, and he just watched. There was less than a block to Sean's apartment, and he needed to make it on his own. He'd already put so much into this journey, and he didn't need Paul swooping in to rescue him when he was so close to his goal.

So close. And still, Paul had to force himself to stay in the car, because the more he watched, the clearer it was how Sean was struggling. He had to be exhausted, in agony, but he was still pushing. He wouldn't give up, wouldn't lie down in the snow and call a cab or a friend or a damn ambulance, which was probably the best choice at this point. No. Sean's stubbornness had clearly been activated, and it was in control of him now.

That was when Paul realized it. Sitting there, watching Sean struggle through the snow, he knew. It didn't matter that Nate was easier to get along with, or more family-appropriate, or wealthier. It didn't matter how much sense Nate made, not when watching Sean pulled this string of emotions out of Paul. Admiration and frustration, pride and tenderness and exasperation. And through all that? Love. He wasn't sure when it had happened, but somewhere along the line Paul had fallen in love with the stubborn son-of-a-bitch out there wading through the snow.

And that was the end of thinking about Nate. It might be the end of thinking in general, because how the hell was Paul ever going to come up with a *rational* argument for being with someone so completely unsuitable. It wasn't about being rational, not anymore. It was just about *being*. With Sean.

So Paul waited until Sean was at the front door of his building, then climbed out of the car and jogged across the street. He arrived just as Sean was fumbling for his keys.

"Sean," Paul said. The name felt perfect on his lips. Sean. Yeah.

Sean turned slowly, as if even the slightest movement was an effort for him. He saw Paul, *must* have seen Paul's smile. Still, he said, "Go to hell."

And then he pulled the door open, stepped inside, and began inching toward the elevator without even looking back.

Chapter Thirty-Five

It was done. It was over. Sure, there was an empty pit in Sean's chest, but he'd had that feeling before and he knew exactly how to handle it. Lots of alcohol, a fight, then some more alcohol.

Well. The fight might be harder to come by than it used to be. Not too many people would want to take on a guy with no legs. Maybe Sean needed to find some sort of underground amputee fight club. Hell, if he couldn't find one, maybe he'd *start* one, but that seemed pretty ambitious for right then.

And he had no fucking booze in the apartment.

And he was too fucking tired to move. He never wanted to move again.

Wait. He almost laughed. Not because it was funny, but because he was an idiot and an asshole, and laughing at idiots was what assholes did.

He didn't ever *have* to move again. Everything *was* done. It was all over. He'd had a little extra burst of life, maybe, one last gasp of breath. But he'd been stupid to think there was anything permanent about it.

He was dead. He'd died in the accident, or maybe even before that. Maybe the first time he'd betrayed Lucas had been the end of him.

It didn't matter if he couldn't put a precise date on things. What mattered was that he'd finally stopped fooling himself. He'd been dead for a long time and he was just stinking the place up. It was time to finish the damn job.

He had enough pills. Pills could be tricky, he knew. Hard to swallow enough to kill you without puking them up. Maybe he needed to do a bit of research. He'd screwed up killing himself once; he wouldn't let that happen again.

He didn't have a computer, so he'd have to use his phone. That was fine. It was in his pocket. He pulled his mitts off, unzipped his coat, pulled the phone out of the inside flap, and braced himself for pain as he took one tiny step toward the second-hand couch in his living room. He could take the stubbies off, there, and he could ignore whatever the hell was going on with his stumps, whatever the source of the pain was, because soon he wouldn't have to worry about that ever again.

Another tentative step and his prosthetic caught on something. He was falling again, just as he'd done so many damn times on the walk home. But this time there was an angry yowling sound, and when he landed on the hard floor something landed on top of him, in the middle of his back.

A hiss, and then two light but sharp blows to the back of his head. "Cyborg," he said. "Fuck. I'm sorry. I didn't mean to step on you. I wasn't attacking."

He rolled carefully onto his side, and felt the cat move with him so she was still perched, now on his ribs. Another shift and he was lying on his back, with Cyborg on his chest. She stared down at him, green eyes challenging him to hurt her again and just see what happened.

"I'm sorry," he said. He moved his hands slowly toward her. "Are you hurt? You came to say hi to me. You were happy to see me and I ignored you, and then I fucking *stepped* on you. I'm an asshole. I'm sorry."

She let him touch her, let him run his hands over her tiny body, searching for an injury. After a few moments, she relaxed and lay down on his chest, her purrs vibrating through his body.

Little Cyborg. She trusted him. She wasn't an easy cat—a *normal* cat would have run away after being stepped on, not launched a counter-attack, and most people wanted normal in their pets, he was pretty sure. What would happen to Cyborg if he wasn't around?

How would his mom feel? She'd almost stopped crying, lately. Was he really going to set her off again?

And Luke. Mark. Elise, even, and the animals at the shelter.

His old life was over. There was no way around that. And he'd been stupid, stretching too far, thinking he could be happy, could be in fucking love. But even if he couldn't be happy, maybe he could be useful. If he stopped trying for impossible shit—if he stopped thinking a guy like Paul could ever actually be interested in him, if he put all Elise's crap about taking courses right out of his mind and just settled down into being a good little drone—maybe he could be okay.

He could start drinking again. Even if there were no fights, being drunk was a good way to forget stuff, a good way to dull the pain of dreams that could never come true and shouldn't ever have been thought up in the first place. Yeah. More drinking. That was key.

"I fucking hurt, Cyborg," he said, and she kneaded his chest with her paws.

"That doesn't actually help." He carefully eased himself up onto his elbows, and she shifted a little to accommodate the new angle of her throne. "I'm a loser, and my stumps are fucked up, and it's my own fault."

She didn't agree or disagree. That was probably a good thing.

"Paul's gone. We're not going to see him any—" The catch in his voice caught him by surprise. He'd known he was emotional, but crying? Was he going to start fucking crying, now, when he'd been dry-eyed earlier?

No. He pushed himself all the way up to a sitting position, ignoring the dirty looks from the cat, then laid his palms flat on the floor and scooted himself backward toward the couch. He was too busy for crying. He had to get his prosthetics off, figure out how much damage he'd done, maybe have a hot bath with some of those Epsom salts the Russian bear had told him to buy. He needed to eat dinner. Go to bed. Be a responsible citizen.

Instead, he scooted to the couch, carefully deposited the kitten on the cushion, and stayed on the floor. Taking off the prosthetics was going to fucking hurt, and it wasn't like he was dying to see just what was going on under there. He'd just rest a while, first. He'd give himself a chance to gain some strength.

He let his head flop back onto the couch cushion and Cyborg curled around him, then started licking his hair.

"I don't actually like that," he told her. She showed no sign of stopping.

He sat there and let it happen. He was too tired to fight. And maybe fighting wasn't the best way to handle every single situation, anyway. Maybe sometimes it was okay to just endure.

Chapter Thirty-Six

"What should I do?" Paul asked. He was back on the couch at Luke and Mark's, so clearly their plans for a quiet evening, just the two of them, had gone to hell. And Paul felt bad about that. He did. But Sean was a priority. Fixing thing with Sean was a priority. "He's safe. I saw him go inside the building and head for the elevator. He's not freezing on the streets or anything."

"But he's mad at you," Mark said. Paul had already explained the whole situation, leaving out the part where he'd realized he was in love, so Mark wasn't exactly covering new ground with the *mad at you* part. But he got a bit more innovative when he added, "Good for him."

And Lucas nodded in agreement. "You fucked up. You hurt him. He's got every damn right to be mad."

"It wasn't like I cheated on him," Paul protested. He was right—wasn't he? "Not even a kiss. And Sean and I never discussed being exclusive."

"So if Sean lied to you about having a date with an old crush, you'd be just fine with that?"

"It was a family dinner, not a date. And I didn't lie, exactly. I mean—I just didn't tell him."

"A sin of omission," Mark said. He shrugged. "Still a sin."

"Well, I'm not Christian, so I'm not too worried about the sin aspect of things."

"It's my understanding that there's a similar concept in Sikhism."

"We're getting off track," Luke interjected. "This isn't about God or something. It's about Sean. You didn't tell him something you knew he'd have wanted to know about. You did something you knew he wouldn't have liked. So why the hell are you surprised that he's mad at you?"

"I'm—I'm actually more surprised that you guys seem to be mad at me. I thought—I don't know. I thought you'd understand that I was just trying not to hurt him."

Luke raised an eyebrow. That was all, but it was enough. Bastard had good eyebrows. "Fine," Paul said. "I was trying to do the easy thing instead of the right thing. I should have told him. Or maybe not gone at all. Or gone with a clearer understanding with my parents that I wasn't looking for a setup. But I honestly—I wasn't sure that I *wasn't* looking for a setup. I mean—at the time. I know it now. I know I want to be with Sean."

"But Sean isn't sure he wants to be with you," Luke said. He sounded— approving?

"It's just a misunderstanding," Paul tried. It sounded pretty weak, even to his own ears.

"Okay, then." Luke smiled blandly. "Problem solved."

Paul was getting a better idea of what Sean was talking about when he called Luke smug. And also a better idea of why Sean kept coming back to Luke for more advice, despite the smugness. "Yeah, fine, it's not *solved*. He's—he wasn't mad the way he usually is. He just walked away. Like he was done."

A moment's silence, and then Luke stood abruptly. "I'm going over there."

Mark frowned at him. "You're worried? You think…."

"He'd better not be that stupid. But I don't ever want to count on Sean not being stupid."

They were talking about—no. But, yeah, of course it was something they should be worried about. Hell, Sean had talked about suicide *to Paul*, and it hadn't been that long ago. How had he let himself forget that? "Can I come with you?"

"No." There was no room for negotiation in Luke's tone and he was too busy tugging on boots and jacket to even turn and look at Paul. "This is separate. Him putting up with your shit? That's between you and him, and it's none of my business. I don't want to get distracted with that right now. Not until I'm sure he's okay."

"Call when you get there," Mark instructed.

"Yeah." And with that, Luke was out the door. Paul turned and watched out the window as the other man jogged to his car.

Once the car was out of the driveway, Paul turned back around. "I screwed up. Should I—do you want me to go?"

Mark frowned. "Of course not. Paul—you're our friend. Sean's our friend, too, of course. We're not impressed with your decisions right now, but we're not impressed with Sean a lot of the time, either. And it's not like Luke and I don't screw up fairly often ourselves. No one is expecting perfection, here. You're our friend regardless." He paused, then smiled. "Honestly, if we were able to put up with Sean, *in our house for several months*, I think you can see that we're not the sort to easily drop people."

"Thank you. I—I don't think it was about Nate, really. I mean, sure, it's fun to think about someone you used to have a crush on. Think about reconnecting or whatever. But if I'd been thinking about the dinner just in those terms I think I would have—maybe I wouldn't have told Sean. I like to think I would have. But I would have at least *thought* about it in terms of Sean. As it was, though, I just barely considered him, because what I was really thinking about was getting back into my family's home. Getting back into my family, period. *That* was the part that was really important to me. Seeing Nate was just a fun bonus."

Mark nodded slowly. "So—you've chosen Sean over Nate. That decision is made, and if you can convince Sean to forgive you, you're ready to go. But maybe there's a larger decision you haven't made, yet." He smiled. "I'm being a bit mysterious. Sorry. But I'm wondering—how would Sean do with your family? They seem to have some fairly precise standards for the sort of man they want you involved with, and I suspect Sean won't match up too well. Is that going to be a problem?"

Of course it was going to be a problem. Paul tried to imagine one of his mother's carefully orchestrated dinners, and then tried to insert Sean into one of the seats at the table. He just wouldn't fit, and it didn't have a damn thing to do with his legs.

Sean wouldn't be comfortable with the scene, and uncomfortable Sean tended to be aggressive, abrasive, profane—nothing that would work in the Gill social circle. And Paul's parents wouldn't approve of Sean, even before he started acting up. He was working class, if he was even working. He wasn't well-educated, well-connected, well-cultivated. He was a weed, tenacious and wild, and no matter how beautiful he might be he had no place in the manicured gardens of the Gills' lives. Shit.

It wasn't new information, really—it wasn't like Paul hadn't known what his parents were like, or hadn't known what Sean was like. But he hadn't really thought it through before. Now that he was—

"It wouldn't work at all," he admitted. "It'll be a huge problem."

Neither one said anything for a while. Then Mark shrugged. "I'm head-over-heels in love with a man my mother refuses to meet, discuss, or acknowledge in any way. I don't blame her for her rejection, but—obviously it makes it more difficult to have a traditional relationship with her. Or with him. Sometimes I feel like a child of divorced parents, with a carefully negotiated schedule of holidays I'll spend in one home or the other. It's a challenge. But it's not the end of the world."

"But your mother still sees you. She still welcomes you in her home."

"Your parents would go that far, you think? They'd reject you completely?"

Paul shrugged. "I don't know. I hope not, but—they wouldn't call it that, of course. They'd be much more subtle. They know my partner wouldn't be comfortable with them, and of course they could never wish to come between me and my partner, so as much as they'd love to have me visit, of course it wouldn't be appropriate. Something like that."

Mark nodded. "Tricky."

"Also, your mother has a pretty compelling reason for feeling the way she does about Lucas. I mean—he's a great guy and I love him. But I don't think I can really be critical of her for not wanting to spend time with him."

Another nod. "What would your parents' reasons be for not liking Sean? That he's white?"

"No. I kind of thought they'd want me with a Sikh guy, but Nate's white. I mean, if it was just race, it'd be so easy to tell them off, right? But I don't think this has anything to do with race, or culture. I mean, family is really important to lots of Sikhs, but it's really important to lots of non-Sikhs too, right? So, really, this is classism, I think. I mean—not money, exactly. They wouldn't love it if I brought *you* home, for example—you don't have any valuable business contacts, or any money of your own—but I think they'd accept you eventually. You're educated, you're polite and presentable…."

"Well, I'm flattered. But taken." Mark grinned.

"I said *example,* cowboy. Settle down."

Mark tipped an imaginary hat in Paul's direction. Then he said, "I haven't told Lucas about this, but—my mom wrote me out of her will. Said she wanted me to have her money but couldn't stand the thought of 'that man' benefiting in any way. Said she didn't want him living in a house her money had bought, or eating food or going on a vacation or anything else paid for by her bequest. It's—logical. And I don't care about the money. But I was surprised by how hurt I was when she told me."

"We can think of ourselves as being adults, sure. But they're always going to be our parents, right? We're always going to care, even if we don't want to."

"Well, this is a fun conversation." Mark pushed to his feet, took a few steps toward the kitchen, then turned and took a few steps back. His phone rang while he was still standing, and he pulled it out of his pocket and lifted it to his ear. "Everything okay?"

Paul sat frozen, trying to hear anything from the other end of the conversation. After a moment, Mark said, "Maybe you should talk to Paul about that? Oh. Well, that's a bit stupid. But—can *I* talk to Paul, and tell you what he says?"

Apparently he got permission, because he pulled the phone a little away from his mouth and said, "Sean's stumps are a bit of a mess. He overdid it on the walking."

Because you hurt him. Because you drove him to it. But also, *because he's a stubborn bastard with no common sense.* The same strength that Paul had admired when he'd seen Sean fighting his way down the street? It was that strength that had caused the current problem. "What does it mean to be a mess? Are they just bruised, or are there sores? Has the skin split?"

Good, yeah. Think about the practical side of things. The physical problems that are easy, or at least easier, to address. Put the emotions away for now.

Paul stood up, as if being closer to the phone would help the communication flow more clearly. "He'll have ways to treat most of that at home, but he might need a trip to the emergency room for some things. He won't talk to me? Doesn't want Luke to talk to me? Okay. Just have Luke tell you what he sees."

It wasn't an efficient way of handling things. But Luke was with Sean, and he'd make sure nothing *too* stupid happened. So Paul wasn't going to waste energy bitching about a little inefficiency. He was just going to make things work, any way he could.

Chapter Thirty-Seven

Sean woke up sore the next morning. His whole body ached, bruised and overworked and unhappy with the way he'd treated it. His stumps? He'd been able to persuade Luke that a visit to the ER wasn't necessary, but there was definitely a trip to the doctor in his near future. The swelling had gone down overnight, but it wasn't gone, and there were some sores that—well. That weren't good.

So, an excuse to not wear the fucking stubbies, and, of course, as soon as he couldn't wear them he immediately missed them. Luke had made him call Elise and say he couldn't come in to work for one day, maybe more, so it wasn't like he actually *needed* to be upright. He could wheel himself to the doctor as easily as he could stub there. But—well. Maybe he was just a whiny bitch, only happy when he had something to be unhappy about.

Or maybe being unhappy about not wearing stubbies was just easier than any of the other reasons he had for being unhappy.

No legs, no future, and, of course, no—fuck it, no, he wasn't thinking about that.

He dragged Cyborg's warm, soft body from the crook of his neck and left her nestled up to the pillow, then dragged himself into the bathroom for a piss and to run water for a bath. He'd never liked baths, and had moved back to showers as soon as he was allowed after the accident, but sometimes it felt good to soak. Except as soon as he eased into the hot water and his muscles relaxed, his self-control seemed to disappear right along with the physical tension. On dry land he could tell himself what he was allowed to think about, but in the watery world of the tub, his mind went where it wanted.

Straight to Paul. His smile, and how it made Sean's whole body relax. The gentle strength of his touch. The honesty, the affection, the hope....

Yeah. The fucking *hope*. That had been the problem. Sean had known better but he'd still let himself get caught up in that. He'd let himself believe that Paul saw no obstacles, had no hesitations about any of it. But of course Paul hadn't hesitated, because none of it had been a big deal to him. Sean was just some loser he'd been slumming with for a while, waiting for the next *real* man to come into his life.

His phone rang somewhere in the other room. An actual call, not just a text or something. But there was absolutely no one in the world he wanted to talk to, so he ignored it. Without full-length legs, it was easy to let himself slide down in the tub so his ears were underwater.

It was nice, lying there like that. Peaceful. As long as he stayed in the water, he could feel like he was in another world. He hadn't screwed up and let himself care about a guy who didn't care back; he wasn't that pathetic. He wasn't *anything*, not if he stayed in the tub. He was just floating, warm and safe, insulated from the world. Yeah, baths were pretty awesome.

The phone was ringing again, out there in dry-land, but he waved his hands a bit, frothing the water, and that was enough sloshing against his ear drums to drown out anything else.

No slippery sidewalks, no pitying looks, no counters that were too high or gas pedals that were too far. No heartbreaks, no frustrations, no loss. No Paul.

The shower curtain twitched. Sean hadn't bothered pulling it across the tub, so this wasn't some Psycho situation, with a murderer lurking on the other side of a flimsy barrier. The curtain twitched again, more violently this time, and a little white paw appeared, claws dug into the fabric. Another twitch, another paw, and then Cyborg's entire head was in view.

"You coming for a swim?" Sean asked, letting his ears rise above the waterline.

The kitten ignored him, at least until she was finished her climbing and had managed a safe transfer onto the side of the tub.

"You don't like water," he reminded her. "We've tried this before."

She lifted a paw and licked off some imaginary dirt, and he pooled a bit of bath water in his palm and offered it for her inspection.

The fucking phone rang. Again.

"I'm asleep," he told the cat. "Or—no, fuck it, I'm in the fucking bath. That's a legit reason to not take calls. Right?"

Cyborg lay down on her belly and stretched a paw out to bat at the water in the tub. That was clearly going to end in disaster—she'd slip, fall in the water, panic, claw for anything she could climb, which would be *Sean*, and he'd end up shredded. It was cute, though, watching her try to balance.

But, damn it, he was doing it again! Letting himself give in to something and ignoring the pain it was absolutely going to cause him in the not-to-distant future. The cat was destined to fall, just like the guy had been destined to leave. Sean needed to smarten up and stop signing up for this crap.

"Get down," he said, and he scooped the kitten up in one hand, leaned over the edge of the tub, and dropped her somewhere near the floor.

The shower curtain started twitching almost immediately. Shit.

He flipped the lever to lift the plug and let his warm comfort drain away. Maybe next time he'd have enough sense to lock the kitten out of the bathroom.

In the meantime, he dried off, got dressed, and wheeled to the kitchen for breakfast. On the way, he found his phone on the couch and looked at the call history. Four missed calls, all from Paul. Best to ignore those. Also a text from Luke, demanding a check-in.

I'm sore but fine, Sean typed. *Leave me alone.*

A moment later, the response. *Fine.*

And that was all. Luke wasn't going to ask any more questions? Wasn't going to invite Sean over for dinner or something? He was going to leave Sean alone, just because Sean had told him to? What the hell was going on?

"They're all assholes," he told the kitten, who had abandoned her attempts to conquer the tub as soon as he'd climbed out. She flopped on her side and he leaned down to rub her belly.

The kitten was on his team. That counted for something. Apparently it was about all he had going for him.

*

"He's a stubborn son-of-a-bitch," Paul raved. Yeah, he was raving. Pacing around Luke's living room like a lunatic, going so far as arm-waving at a few points. He was frustrated, damn it.

"I've been calling him all day! How am I supposed to apologize if he won't talk to me? How the hell can I start making things better if we're not even communicating?"

"Have you ever been dumped before?" Luke asked. He sounded genuinely curious, like Paul was part of a sociological survey Luke was conducting.

"Dumped?"

"Yeah. I mean—after a certain point, it stops being a fight, right? You're not really fighting with Sean—you got dumped. So, really, you're not supposed to apologize. You're not supposed to start making things better. You're supposed to wallow for a bit, and then move on. That's how dumping works, as I understand it."

Dumped. Like it was over. Permanently. A horrible emptiness started to open in Paul's chest, but he pushed it closed again. "He never actually said that. He told me to go to hell, but that's just conversation for Sean. He says that kind of stuff five times a day. It doesn't mean anything."

"How many times have you called him today?"

"Six or seven."

"And he hasn't answered any of those calls. That—it doesn't sound good, really. Do you think?"

Of course it didn't sound good. It sounded completely unworkable, which was why Luke needed to get Sean to stop being such a pain in the ass. Or if Luke wouldn't do it... "Should I go over there? To the apartment? Security in that building is shit. I could get past the front door no problem, and then—"

"I think the point where you start thinking about how to bypass security is the point at which you need to ask whether you're turning into a stalker."

"What if he's sick? What if he's hurt, or suicidal?"

Luke picked up his phone, tapped at the screen, then lowered it. A moment later it pinged, he read the screen, then turned it so Paul could see.

At the top: *Evening check-in. u sick, hurt, or suicidal?*

And below it the response: *No. Fuck off.*

Luke waited for Paul to finish reading, then turned the screen around and tapped some more. Another pause, and then a ping of response. Luke looked at the screen and sighed. "You may not want to read this one."

But of course Paul did, so he gestured, and Luke turned the screen.

If u dumped Paul, u should man up and actually tell him.

The response said *He's not stupid. He can fucking figure it out.*

So. That simple. That final.

It felt impossibly wrong, and it was making Paul feel a twinge of sympathy for Bobby, which was completely unwelcome. "I need another chance," he said. "I need to change his mind."

"Change his mind. Sean. Change Sean's mind." Luke raised an eyebrow. "Sure, no problem."

Paul remembered the night before, Sean forcing himself to keep walking, keep fighting his way home. Not because there was no alternative, but because he'd decided he was going to finish the trip and he would damn well do it, no matter how much it hurt. The same stubbornness Paul had admired the night before was his enemy, now.

"There has to be a way," he repeated. "If I can just—I don't know. I don't know. But—" He stopped. He was in the room with the world's foremost expert on Sean Gage, so why was he talking instead of listening? "Do you think I could be good for Sean? I mean—if I could change his mind, would that make him happy?"

"Bulldozing over his decisions isn't going to—"

"Not bulldozing. Just—convincing him not to be stubborn. If I could legitimately persuade him to change his mind, would I be able to make his life better? Was he happy, before, when he and I were together? Could the two of us be happy together again, if he let it happen?"

"That's a lot of *ifs*. But, yeah. Sure. You were good for him. You made him happy. I'd like to see you guys together again."

Paul let out a breath, and released at least a tiny bit of the tension he hadn't realized he'd been holding. "Okay, then," he said. "I need your help. Just to get my foot in the door. Please. You're the only person who has any chance of making this happen."

Luke frowned. "Do you have an actual plan?"

"A plan? No, not really. But—I think him and me being in the same room has to be the first step, don't you?"

Chapter Thirty-Eight

The third text from Luke came about ten minutes after the first two.

I'm coming over.

Sean texted back: *You're not fucking invited.*

You lived in my house for three months, and u think I need an invitation to drop by your place?

Fucking Luke. Sean texted: *It's my place. I decide who comes here.*

So when I get there, don't let me in.

And that was all. Luke had called Sean's bluff, for about the fifty millionth time in their lives.

One day, Luke was going to have a pretty big surprise; one day, he'd pull crap like this and Sean wouldn't let himself be manipulated. But he was sad and sore and lonely and low, and having Luke come over would actually probably be helpful. It wouldn't cheer him up, but it would aggravate him enough give him a little energy, at least.

Ten minutes later when the buzzer sounded from downstairs, Sean hit the button to unlock the door. And a minute after that, he wheeled over to the apartment door and pulled it open. Luke was just stepping off the elevator, but he wasn't alone.

"Seq!" Sean crowed. He lifted his hands up to greet the kitten, but Luke had the animal on a leash and tucked inside his jacket and didn't seem inclined to release him until they were inside the apartment. Luke's practical nature was getting in the way of Sean's big reunion moment.

"I thought it would be good to keep him and Cyborg hanging out on the regular so they don't forget each other," Luke explained. He dumped the kitten on Sean's lap and pulled his own jacket off. "How're you doing? How're your legs?"

"They're short. And sore. But I'll survive."

Cyborg came galloping in from the other room and Sean got Seq's leash off just in time for the two to be able to wrestle without getting totally tangled up.

Sean wheeled backward, away from the siblings. "I'd offer you a beer, but—"

Luke just grunted, then dropped onto the nearest couch. "Paul came by tonight. Said he's been trying to call you."

Yeah. Of course Paul had done that. And of course Luke had decided to get involved. "That's done. It was stupid, and now it's over. How's that coyote at the barn? Is its leg looking any better?"

"No. It's not looking good."

Shit. Sean wished he hadn't asked. Of course not all of the animals at the rescue made it, and it wasn't like the coyote was a special pet of his or anything. He'd just been trying to distract from the Paul issue. But the suffering and death of an animal wasn't exactly the sort of distraction he'd been hoping for. "How about Rascal?" he tried. The raccoon was a pet, and in perfect health except for her malformed feet—she'd be safe.

Safe, but not too distracting, because Luke said, "She's fine," and that was the end of that.

They sat there in silence for a minute or two, watching the kittens play, and then Luke said, "We don't know how to be hurt."

Sean gave himself a moment to absorb the words, then said, "What the fuck are you talking about?"

"You and me. Other guys, too, I think. We don't have those eat-ice-cream-and-cry rituals like chicks have. When we get hurt, we just turn it into anger, just like we do with fear and sadness and every other negative emotion."

"Are you doing therapy again?"

"No. But I talk to Mark, and I read stuff. And when I read something that feels true, I think about it. Are you telling me I'm wrong? What do you do to deal with it when someone hurts you?"

Sean didn't answer. He knew what he *used* to do—he used to beat the shit out of the person, or whoever else he could get his hands on. But that answer would obviously feed into Luke's theory. And now, now that he wasn't in any shape to fight anyone? "I don't fucking know. I just try to make sure it doesn't happen, I guess."

Luke slapped his hands together, like he was celebrating a great shot on net. "Fuck, I thought it was going to take a lot longer to get there. But, yeah, I think you're totally right. You—and me, too, but I'm trying to get better about it—we just try to avoid getting hurt, emotionally. I mean, that makes sense. Everyone tries to avoid it. But sometimes it's going to happen, right? If we're living our lives, taking the chances we need to take, sometimes things aren't going to work out, and it's going to suck. But when we don't know how to deal with that, we're maybe not going to take as many chances as we should."

"I think we've had this conversation before. And I think it usually ends with you calling me a pussy."

"I was trying to do it more compassionately this time. Trying to be more empathic or whatever. Kinder and gentler."

"You suck at that."

"That's hurtful. You have hurt me. And instead of responding with anger, I will allow myself to feel the true emotions, even though they are painful."

"Shut the fuck up. And tell your cat to stop biting Cyborg."

"She's biting back. It's mutual battle. Nobody's crying." Luke shrugged. "Kinda ironic that the *cats* aren't being pussies...."

"Fuck off."

"Paul fucked up," Luke said. Kinda a quick topic change, but Sean appreciated the general sentiment, so he didn't object. Except Luke couldn't leave a good thing alone. "Thing is, we *all* fuck up. You, my friend, fuck up a *lot*. So you expecting someone else to be perfect? That's not a great look on you."

"Seriously, fuck off."

"If you give him another chance, you'll get hurt," Luke said.

Sean's head was spinning. "What the fuck? Are you doing reverse psychology again, or have you just completely lost track of what you're talking about?"

"I'm just saying... that's what you're scared of. You'll get hurt. Guaranteed. And that's scary. I get it."

"If it's guaranteed to end bad, why the fuck should I start it? Again."

"I didn't say it would end bad. I said you'll get hurt. That's not the same thing."

"It's not?"

"Mark's got something going on with his mom. I'm not sure what, but he came back from the last visit with her and he was—weird. I don't know how, exactly, just not right. And he's not telling me what the problem is, and I feel like I tell him every fucking thing I ever even *think* about feeling, so him not telling me this feels like he doesn't trust me or something. And then I think of all the totally good reasons he has to not trust me, and I understand but I also feel bad, and the whole thing fucking hurts. Not a sharp pain, just a bit of an ache. You know?"

No. Sean did *not* know. Obviously Luke was trying to make a point, but he was also talking about something real, something with Mark and Luke that sounded borderline serious. It was another one of Luke's fucking traps, but it was one that seemed to be baited with a tiny piece of Luke's heart, and that felt unfair and brave at the same damn time.

"You're an asshole," he said. Solid opening. "Mark loves you. He's probably trying to protect you, or something."

"Yup. Hurts anyway. But I'll survive. *We'll* survive. It's not the end of anything, it's just a little boo-boo."

"You think this thing with Paul was just a fucking boo-boo?"

"No. I think it was bigger than that, and I don't know; maybe it's a sign that he's not worth taking a chance on. But you not even talking to him? That's how I know this isn't some rational decision you came to after you weighed all the pros and cons. Not talking to him makes it pretty damn clear this is because you're hurt, and you're scared of getting hurt worse. Or hurt again. Whatever."

"I can't just be mad?"

"When in your whole damn life have you been *just* mad and not wanted to yell at the person you're mad at? Or beat the shit out of the person you're mad at? When you're mad, you want to fight. This running and away and hiding thing? This isn't about being *mad*."

"You're a pain in the ass."

"But you get past the pain because you love me."

It was a strange thing to say. Breaking out the *love* business. That just wasn't a word they used. And, sure, Luke was just making a point, and he was being a bit of a smart ass, or at least it was close enough that they could both pretend that's what he was doing, and they could ignore the word and just go back to their usual way of getting along.

But for some reason, instead of doing the smart thing, Sean nodded. "Yeah," he said. "I do."

Luke looked startled. Then he grinned. "See? That wasn't so hard, was it? Peeling back that crusty shell and giving me a look at the soft skin beneath? It felt pretty good, didn't it?"

"I think I'm going to throw up."

"Nah." Luke leaned forward. "Actually, I think you're on a roll. You've got this whole honesty thing really working for you. You're probably ready for the next step, right?"

"The next step?"

"Paul. He's downstairs." Luke lifted his hands defensively. "Outside. I didn't even let him in the building. I mean, someone else probably has, by now—it's kinda cold out. But, technically, I didn't do it. Anyway—why don't you let him come up? You can yell at him. I can stick around, if you want, or I can leave. I can wait downstairs, I guess, but I'm not standing around outside. Gotta draw the line there, champ."

Paul was downstairs. Whatever else Luke was babbling about had washed over Sean like meaningless drizzle. Paul. Downstairs. Waiting. Wanting to come up, to talk, to— to what?

Jesus. Sean's stomach was clenched, butterflies that were more like fucking pterodactyls, flapping and clawing and churning everything up. He didn't want to see Paul. It was over. It was over. It had to be over, because he couldn't—

"You're stronger than you think," Luke said. His voice was gentler than Sean could remember ever having heard it. "You're scared, and that's totally legit, but you're strong enough to not let being scared get in the way of what you want to do."

What Sean wanted to do. Was that even something he thought about? What he fucking *wanted*? He wanted his damn legs back. He wanted to take back about three quarters of the mean shit he'd ever said or done, and for the remaining quarter he wanted to go harder and further than he actually had. He wanted his family to be happy. He wanted Luke to keep loving him. He wanted the kittens to be safe. He wanted... he wanted...

"Tell him to come up," he whispered. He needed to get his voice under control before Paul arrived. Needed to be able to talk like a normal human adult.

"Tell him yourself," Luke said, nodding his head toward Sean's phone.

"Can you not even—" Sean snapped, and then he ran out of words. Was he about to suggest that Luke wasn't helping him enough? After every damn thing Luke had done for him?

"It's your choice," Luke said quietly. "You're the one inviting him. Not me."

Like there was a whole separate set of rules Luke had dragged up from somewhere and was now following. Emotional Etiquette or some such shit.

"Fuck," Sean growled. But he reached for his phone.

Chapter Thirty-Nine

If you're still downstairs, you can come up.

That was all. Not exactly a gracious invitation, but Paul was just grateful for what he was getting. Luke had clearly worked his magic with Sean, but now it was up to Paul. If this was going to go any further, if there was any damn chance of it working out, it would be because of what Paul did. What he said.

And he still didn't have a plan. An apology, obviously, but that wasn't enough. The more he thought about it, the more the whole issue felt like an excuse. Not that he hadn't screwed up, and not that he didn't need to make amends, but... Sean's reaction was about more than Paul seeing an old crush and not being totally truthful.

Maybe that was the first thing he needed to try to sort out.

Assuming he had any control over the direction the conversation took, which was far from certain. Maybe Sean was just calling him upstairs so the dumping could be made official. Maybe Paul was going to get a good yelling-at and then be sent out into the snow.

Luke was waiting in the apartment doorway, and he shrugged noncommittally in response to Paul's questioning look. "I'm supposed to stay in the apartment but keep my mouth shut," he said. "That's all I know."

Possibly Sean just wanted an audience for whatever insults he was about to throw in Paul's direction. Excellent.

But Paul took a deep breath and stepped inside anyway. This was his chance, and he wouldn't run away from it.

Sean was in his chair in the living room, a pillow clamped over his thighs as if he was back to thinking he needed to hide his stumps, his scars. He was back to that because Paul had pushed him back, and that meant that all the rest of this didn't matter. If Sean wanted to yell, Paul would damn well take it, and he'd just hope the yelling did at least a little good for Sean.

It felt presumptuous to take off his coat, so he just stepped out of his boots and then padded into the apartment dressed for the outdoors, except for his feet. Sean was staring at the window on the opposite wall and didn't even glance in Paul's direction.

So. This was going to be Paul's show after all, at least to begin with. He perched gingerly on the arm of the sofa, leaned forward and said, "I'm sorry. I messed up. I didn't give you—or this relationship—the respect it deserved."

And then he was more or less done. There wasn't much else to say, was there?

For a few painful breaths, the room stayed frozen. Then Sean shrugged. "Maybe you gave it exactly the respect it deserved. It's not a big deal. We were just messing around, right? No big thing."

It would have been easier to believe him if his voice hadn't been quite so expressionless.

"It was a big thing to me. I didn't realize how big until last night. Until this morning, when you wouldn't take my calls. Sean, I—yeah. I thought we were just messing around. Friends with benefits or something. But now I know it's more. For me, at least. I want to be with you. I hate the idea of not seeing you. This is real, for me."

Sean snorted. "That sucks for you. But it's not my problem."

"You're happy with the way things are? You don't want to see me again? This is all just fine with you?" Paul leaned further forward. "So look me in the eye and tell me that. Let me see your face while you say the words. Give me that much closure, at least."

At first it seemed like Sean wasn't going to comply, but then he shifted his weight, met Paul's gaze, and the bottom dropped out of Paul's heart.

Sean was hurting. He was afraid, he was sad, he was hopeless, he was lost. Angry too, maybe, but Paul didn't see much of that. Sean found the courage to show Paul his pain, and Paul was the first one to look away.

He stood up. God, part of him wanted to run. He hadn't caused all this—he knew that. He'd just added the final drops of water to a balloon that was already close to bursting. But he *had* added those drops. If he could manage to get through this with Sean, was he supposed to spend the rest of his life making sure he never, ever added any more?

No. But he could damn well do what he could to help Sean squeeze a bit of the pain out in manageable amounts. And he could help Sean get stronger, and build more capacity for any pain that *did* sneak past Paul's best intentions. He wanted to do that. He wanted to be the kind of man who was strong enough to help someone else be strong, too.

He had his phone out before he thought it through, and found the number and hit dial before he lost his courage. The phone rang twice, and then a familiar voice answered.

"Mom," he said. "Hi. Sorry if this isn't a good time, but I'm with someone, and I really want him to hear me say this to you. Okay?"

"Say what?" She sounded amused. That wasn't going to last.

"I need to apologize to you. I let you set that meeting up with Nate, and I shouldn't have. I was wasting your time, and I guess I was operating under false pretenses. Trying to get back into the family by not being completely truthful."

"What do you mean?" Yeah, the amusement was gone, now.

"I've already met someone. Someone really incredible. He's not what you want for me, but he's what *I* want for me. He hasn't got a high-powered job or a rich family or anything, but he's brave and strong and funny and when I'm with him, I'm a better person. I'm more *me*." Strange how true that was, and how long it had taken him to recognize it. "He's the one I want to be with. It was wrong of me to waste your time, and Nate's time, because I'm not on the market. At all. Sorry."

He knew Sean was looking at him, was listening and hopefully really hearing all this, but he needed to keep himself together, so he didn't look back. He stared at the same window Sean had been staring at earlier, and he waited for his mother's response.

Which was, when it came, exactly as poised and concise as he would have expected. "I'm not prepared to discuss this with you right now. Your father and I will call you later. Tomorrow, possibly."

The phone clicked in his ear. He shook his head. "Being with the family—doing what the family wants me to do—that would be easier. I know that. I'd be taken care of. But I don't need to be taken care of. I don't *want* to be taken care of. And I don't need easy. I can do hard."

He made himself turn, now, the phone still at his ear, but his attention all on Sean. "I think we can do it, together. If we can figure this out, we can take chances together, and when one of us is struggling the other one can help out. But I need you to help me out. I need you to fight for us, because it's *not* going to be easy. Will you do that?"

Sean squinted, then whispered, "You want your mom to hear all this?"

"Oh. No." Paul tossed the phone onto the armchair. "She hung up on me halfway through. She heard the first part, though."

"Your mom hung up on you? Is she mad?"

"Furious. But that's not what I'm worrying about right now."

"You're—"

A gentle throat clearing from the doorway interrupted him. Sean didn't even turn. "Go away, Luke."

"Thank you, Jesus," Luke said, and then the apartment door opened, shut, and it was just Paul and Sean.

The two of them stared at each other, and then Paul shifted off the sofa, knelt so quickly it was almost like falling, and forced himself *not* to reach out and touch Sean. Not yet. Maybe not ever, but definitely not yet.

"I'm sorry I screwed up," he said.

Sean shrugged. "You'll do it again."

"What? No, I won't! I didn't realize what we had, but now I do, and—"

Sean raised a hand. "You'll screw up again. In a different way. And I'll screw up. Possibly in the same way over and over again—I'm not all that creative. And what it comes down to is just—is it worth it? You know? Is there going to be enough good to outweigh the bad?"

"I—I don't know if I can answer that. I mean, I *think* there will be. I want there to be. I'll work hard so there is. But I can't guarantee anything."

Sean nodded. He slid his hips forward and let his shoulders slide down the chair so he could flop back and look at the ceiling. "Yeah. No guarantees."

"That's just life, Sean. That's—there's nothing I can do about that."

Sean didn't respond right away. When he did, his voice was a bit lighter than it had been. "You really said all that to your mom? The first part of the call—she heard all that?"

"Yeah."

"And she didn't like it."

"Not at all."

"I know I haven't met her or anything, but—I don't think I like your mom very much."

"I think that's totally mutual." Paul shifted his weight enough to bring him a little closer to Sean. "And that's okay. I mean, in a perfect world, you'd all love each other. But the world isn't perfect, and I can deal with that. It's probably about time I grew up and stopped relying on my family for so much, anyway."

"You can still count on Jas, can't you? She seems solid."

"Yeah, she's great. And I can count on her. Absolutely."

"So you're okay. You've still got some family."

"Not as much as you do."

"Most days, I'd be happy to lend mine to anyone who's willing to take them off my hands."

"Okay. Sounds like we could make a deal. I'll borrow them from you, but you should probably introduce us, first."

Sean exhaled. Not quite a snort, but close. "You really think we're at a meet-the-family stage?"

"I'll be happy as a clam if we're at *any* stage. If there's a *we* at all." He waited, didn't get the response he'd hoped for, and decided he could stand to prod a little. "Is there? Is there a *we*? You gonna give this another chance?"

"Fuck." Sean leaned back even further in his chair, staring even harder at the ceiling. "You could do so much better, man. That Nate guy—he'd be so much better. Wouldn't he?"

"No." Simple, and true. "Because he's not what I'm looking for. I don't care about money or contacts or status. I just want someone's heart, and you've got the biggest heart I know. It's wrapped up in protective barbed wire, obviously, but you've let me get close enough that I can see it. And now that I have, I can't go back to someone with less. I want you."

And that was all Paul had, really. He'd given this his best shot. He'd been as honest as he could, as persuasive as he could, and if that wasn't enough? It wasn't enough. There was nothing to do but wait.

And wait.

Finally, Sean shifted his hips back, his shoulders forward. He looked at Paul, held his gaze, and said, "I don't know if you've noticed, but I've got no feet. No knees, even."

And somehow, everything was okay. Because if that was the final barrier Sean could throw up? Paul could bust through that one no problem. "Yeah. I've noticed. I'm not too worried about it."

"I can't cook."

"I love spaghetti."

"I'm an asshole."

"Yeah, you are. I'm okay with that."

"I'm getting weepy in my old age." And Sean punctuated that with an impatient swipe of his hand across his cheeks.

"I'm okay with that, too," Paul said, and he edged closer. This was okay, wasn't it? He wasn't pushing too far, too fast? He stayed alert for any resistance, but none came, and then his face was right in front of Sean's, and Sean's eyes, still crying a little, were locked on his. "You'll give us a chance?"

He didn't get an answer right away, so he leaned in and kissed one cheek, tasted the salt, then switched and kissed the other side. He couldn't be expected to walk away now, could he? Not after all this?

But he couldn't move forward, either, not without some measure of encouragement. He just sat there, frozen, for half a lifetime, until finally Sean exhaled, closed his eyes, and nodded.

The joy burbled up in Paul's chest but he pushed it down. Cautious, cautious… "You're saying you'll give us a chance? I don't mean to be demanding, but it's been a pretty stressful twenty-four hours and it'd be really excellent to hear something, like actual words, coming out of your mouth—"

But then Sean's hand was on Paul's neck, tugging him forward, and it turned out that words probably weren't the best use for mouths after all, not when there were kisses like this to be had. Deep and strong and true, the extra salt a reminder that there'd always be pain, the softness a promise that they'd find a way through it together.

"Luke's definitely gone, right?" Paul asked when they came up for air.

"He better be."

"Then is there any chance we could take this somewhere more horizontal?"

He could feel Sean's smile against his own lips. "You read my mind."

"Yeah?"

"Bedroom's over there. You lead the way to clear out any piled-up kittens on the floor."

"Damn. That's romantic."

"Hell, yeah," Sean agreed. "That's what you've got to look forward to."

"Sounds good," Paul said. And he meant it.

Epilogue

"I can't believe it's over," Luke said. He sounded dazed. "After all that work, it's just—done."

"Thank god," Sean said. "I never want to write another exam in my life. Now shut up. I've got to concentrate." The hand controls on the car weren't tricky, exactly, but they were *new,* and Luke knew that. So he kept his mouth shut while Sean got the car parked in front of the house, and *then* he knew enough to stay quiet while Sean maneuvered his legs out and used the roof of the car to help pull himself upright. He still needed the crutches Luke extracted from the back seat, but he was at full height, finally. And he wasn't using that stupid old-man walker they'd tried to give him at the fake-legs place. Crutches were better.

Everything was better. Almost a year since the accident, and he'd gone through some serious low points, but things really seemed to be going smoothly, now. That meant it was probably time for the next disaster to hit, but he wasn't going to think like that. Not right then.

He followed Luke up toward the house, concentrating on his foot work, and almost wiped out when he heard someone yell, "Hey! We're back here!"

Mark, calling from the gate to the back yard, looking strangely flushed. Was he actually doing some gardening? That was usually Luke's job, but Luke had been busy with the course; maybe Mark was picking up the slack?

The two of them obediently trudged to the back yard, and that was when the "we" in Mark's statement came clear. Because there were a lot of people back there.

"Surprise!" they yelled, kinda at the same time.

"What?" Sean asked. He left *the fuck* off the end because Elise was one of the people in the yard, and she didn't appreciate that kind of language.

"You're done the course!" Sean's mom said. She was crying, of course. "You passed."

They'd just written the exam and it wouldn't be marked yet, but, yeah, they'd gone in with high enough grades that there was no way they could have failed. There was nothing new, really. Nothing that seemed like a reason for this kind of gathering.

It wasn't a big crowd, really. Sean's family, Elise, Luke's friend Alex— who'd just finished his first year of university and must have passed a hell of a lot more courses than Sean and Luke had, but who seemed to think this party was still somehow worth coming to anyway—Luke's probation officer, that priest friend of Mark's, Jas, and, of course, Mark and Paul, standing together by the food on the picnic table, looking....

Looking proud. Sean had no idea what all the fuss was about, but, damn, he liked seeing that expression on Paul's face.

"We—" Luke started. He turned to look at Sean. "I mean—yeah. We passed. But—"

"Let us celebrate," Elise said, coming forward. "Personally, I think the biggest test was just having the courage to take the course in the first place, but it's also good that you worked hard and did well."

"Thank you," Sean managed. "For setting it up."

For half-a-second, she looked as if she might smile, but then she shrugged. "I need you two educated if you're going to be of use to me. It's all part of my plan."

"Thanks for having a plan, then."

"You're welcome. Now... celebrate!"

A year ago, the idea of a party that wasn't fueled by drugs and alcohol would have made no sense to Sean. Now, though? He kinda wanted to hide—too many people paying too much attention to him, when the attention was this positive? It felt unnatural—but he also wanted to let himself feel it. All of it, for real, without a chemical buffer.

He worked his way through the crowd, got enough hugs to have him almost falling over about, and finally made it to the table where Paul was waiting.

"It's not that big of a deal," he said quickly. How many years had Paul spent in school, after all?

"It's emblematic," Paul told him.

"It's what?"

"Symbolic? It's a celebration of *all* your achievements. And Luke's, too. Both of you have turned your lives around. You've worked hard. Everyone's really proud of you."

"So when I screw up, I'll be letting everyone down."

"Shhh. Be negative later. Right now, just enjoy."

It didn't feel natural, but for Paul, Sean would give it a try. Just enjoy. Just shift the crutches to his other side so he could have an excuse to lean on Paul, to line their bodies up together and snug an arm around to tuck inside the waistband of his jeans. Just look at all the people there to have a good time and say nice things about him. About *him*, Sean Gage. Unbelievable.

"I'm glad you snore," he said quietly, his mouth close to Paul's ear.

"You are? Because you hit me in the head with a pillow last night. Three times. That's a weird way to show you're happy about something."

"It's how I know this all isn't too perfect to be real. That one tiny little thing. Well, no, that one fucking annoying thing that keeps me awake the night before a goddamn exam. *That* thing. Not tiny at all. But, anyway—if it weren't for that, I'd have to think I was dreaming."

"So you're gonna be happy to hear about another thing, too? Because Panther is back to stealing socks, and I have no idea where he's stashing them this time." Paul nodded down to his feet. "I had to wear sandals whether I wanted to or not."

"Huh. Socks. No, not something I need to worry about. Sucks for you, of course, but... not a problem for me."

"You've got no feet—no knees, even—and you have to use my snoring as the one bad thing in your life?"

"Shhh," Sean said. "Be negative later. Right now, just enjoy."

And so they did.

About the Author

Kate Sherwood, Cate Cameron, Catherine Dale... and probably a few new names, eventually. They're all one person.

One person who's lucky enough to get to live a bunch of extra lives through all the characters in her books, and who's trying desperately to keep all the lives organized into some sort of categories... so each name writes a different type of story.

But really, beneath the genre categories? All the stories will have some kind of humour, even in the darkest times. They'll all show characters who are far from perfect, but who are trying to be better.

Basic bio stuff? Kate/Cate/Catherine lives in Cottage Country, the water-filled world north of Toronto, Canada, the land where summers are sunny and crowded with visitors and winters are snowy and isolated. She loves it there. Not that she doesn't sometimes miss the city, especially when her internet is acting up or she wants something delivered!

She works full-time at a non-writing job but would love to shift into a more writing-centred life. There's a five-year plan. It might work....

Writing as Kate Sherwood (m/m)

All That Glitters – contemporary romance
Long *Shadows, Embers, Darkness, Home Fires* – four book contemporary action
Feral, Lap Dog, Twice Shy, Pure Bred – four book NA contemporary romance
Sacrati – fantasy/alt history
In Too Deep – NA contemporary romance
Chasing the Dragon – angst and adventure!
Mark of Cain, The Long Way Home – contemporary romance
The Fall, Riding Tall – two book contemporary romance
The Shift – contemporary fantasy novella – monster hunters!
Room to Grow – contemporary romance novella
The Pawn, The Knight – two book futuristic romance with plenty of angst
Poor Little Rich Boy – contemporary romance
More than Chemistry – light contemporary novella
Beneath the Surface – contemporary romance
Dark Horse, Out of the Darkness, Of Dark and Bright – three book contemporary romance with extras
Shying Away – NA romance
Lost Treasure – contemporary romance

Writing as Cate Cameron (m/f, YA)

The Billionaire's Forever Family – contemporary romance
Center Ice, Playing Defense, Winging It, Breakaway – contemporary YA hockey romance
Just a Summer Fling, Hometown Hero – contemporary small town romance
Shining Armor – contemporary romance (originally published under "Kate Sherwood")

Writing as Catherine Dale (YA, contemporary fantasy, general fiction—everything but romance!)

Dark Houses – Speculative YA

www.ingramcontent.com/pod-product-compliance
Lightning Source LLC
Chambersburg PA
CBHW031730170626
46808CB00005B/1947